Praise for M. C. Beaton and Agatha Raisin

"M. C. Beaton has a foolproof plot for the village mystery."
—*The New York Times Book Review*

"[Beaton's] imperfect heroine is an absolute gem." —*Publishers Weekly*

"Anyone interested in a few hours' worth of intelligent, amusing reading will want to make the acquaintance of Mrs. Agatha Raisin."
—*The Cleveland Plain Dealer*

"Beaton's Agatha Raisin series just about defines the British cozy."
—*Booklist*

"Beaton, author of the Hamish Macbeth series, has created the best English sleuth since Miss Marple. Write home about this one."
—*Tulsa World*

"In *Agatha* Beaton has blended perfectly the classic ingredients of a village with secrets and stock characters. The irascible but endearing personality of Agatha Raisin is like a heady dash of curry. May we have another serving, please?" —*Detroit Free Press*

"It is always fun to read an Agatha Raisin mystery."
—*Midwest Book Review*

"If you've never read an Agatha Raisin novel, it's time to start. . . . All of them are cunningly plotted, beautifully written, and more fun than you can imagine." —*The Globe and Mail*

"Beaton has thus launched a new series featuring an eccentric sleuth with human foibles galore, combined with an indomitable spirit, who will long persevere and endear herself to the village (and the reader)."
—*San Antonio Express-News*

"A strong narrative drive comes from Agatha's changing personality, as awkward and perilous situations shape her into a softer, more admirable person." —*Chicago Sun-Times*

Gift ¹⁰/₀₉ 14.95

This is a work of fiction. All of the characters, organizations, and events portrayed in this novel are either products of the author's imagination or are used fictitiously.

INTRODUCING AGATHA RAISIN: AGATHA RAISIN AND THE QUICHE OF DEATH © 1992 by M. C. Beaton and AGATHA RAISIN AND THE VICIOUS VET © 1993 by M. C. Beaton. Printed in the United States of America. For information, address St. Martin's Press, 175 Fifth Avenue, New York, N.Y. 10010.

www.minotaurbooks.com

Library of Congress Cataloging-in-Publication Data

Beaton, M. C.
    Introducing Agatha Raisin : The quiche of death ; The vicious vet / M. C. Beaton.—1st St. Martin's Minotaur pbk. ed.
        p. cm.
    ISBN-13: 978-0-312-54453-9
    ISBN-10: 0-312-54453-7
    1. Raisin, Agatha (Fictitious character)—Fiction. 2. Women private investigators—England—Cotswold Hills—Fiction. 3. Cotswold Hills (England)—Fiction. I. Beaton, M. C. Agatha Raisin and the quiche of death. II. Beaton, M. C. Agatha Raisin and the vicious vet. III. Title.

PR6052.E196 I58 2008
823'.914—dc22

2008024760

First St. Martin's Minotaur Paperback Edition: October 2008

10 9 8 7 6 5 4 3 2 1

INTRODUCING
AGATHA RAISIN

The Quiche of Death

†

The Vicious Vet

M. C. BEATON

St. Martin's Minotaur ⚭ New York

For Patrick Heininger and his wife, Caroline, and son,
Benjamin of Bourton-on-theWater, with love.

THE

QUICHE OF DEATH

ONE

†

MRS. Agatha Raisin sat behind her newly cleared desk in her office in South Molton Street in London's Mayfair. From the outer office came the hum of voices and the clink of glasses as the staff prepared to say farewell to her.

For Agatha was taking early retirement. She had built up the public-relations firm over long hard years of work. She had come a long way from her working-class background in Birmingham. She had survived an unfortunate marriage and had come out of it, divorced and battered in spirit, but determined to succeed in life. All her business efforts were to one end, the realization of a dream—a cottage in the Cotswolds.

The Cotswolds in the Midlands are surely one of the few man-made beauties in the world: quaint villages of golden stone houses, pretty gardens, winding green lanes and ancient churches. Agatha had been taken to the Cotswolds as a child for one brief magical holiday. Her parents had hated it and had said that they should have gone to Butlin's Holiday Camp as usual, but to Agatha the Cotswolds represented everything she wanted in life: beauty, tranquillity and security. So even as a child, she had become determined that one day she would live in one of those pretty cottages in a quiet peaceful village, far from the noise and smells of the city.

During all her time in London, she had, until just recently, never gone back to the Cotswolds, preferring to keep the dream intact. Now she had purchased that dream cottage in the village of Carsely. It was a pity, thought Agatha, that the village was called plain Carsely and not Chipping Campden or Aston Magna or Lower Slaughter or one of those intriguing Cotswold names, but the cottage was perfect and the village not on the tourist route, which meant freedom from craft shops, tea-rooms and daily bus parties.

Agatha was aged fifty-three, with plain brown hair and a plain square face and a stocky figure. Her accent was as Mayfair as could be except in moments of distress or excitement, when the old nasal Birmingham voice of her youth crept through. It helps in public relations to have a certain amount of charm and Agatha had none. She got results by being a sort of one-woman soft-cop/hard-cop combination; alternately bullying and wheedling on behalf of her clients. Journalists often gave space to her clients just to get rid of her. She was also an expert at emotional blackmail and anyone unwise enough to accept a present or a free lunch from Agatha was pursued shamelessly until they paid back in kind.

She was popular with her staff because they were a rather weak, frivolous lot, the kind of people who build up legends about anyone of whom they are frightened. Agatha was described as "a real character," and like all real characters who speak their mind, she did not have any real friends. Her work had been her social life as well.

As she rose to go through and join the party, a small cloud crossed the horizon of Agatha's usually uncomplicated mind. Before her lay days of nothing: no work from morning till night, no bustle or noise. How would she cope?

She shrugged the thought away and crossed the Rubicon into the outer office to say her farewells.

"Here she comes!" screeched Roy, one of her assistants. "Made some special champagne punch, Aggie. Real knicker-rotter."

Agatha accepted a glass of punch. Her secretary, Lulu,

approached and handed her a gift-wrapped parcel and then the others crowded around with their offerings. Agatha felt a lump rising in her throat. A little insistent voice was chattering in her head, "What have you done? What have you *done?*" There was a bottle of scent from Lulu and, predictably, a pair of crotchless panties from Roy; there was a book on gardening from one, a vase from another, and so it went on. "Speech!" cried Roy.

"Thank you all," said Agatha gruffly. "I'm not going to China, you know. You'll all be able to come and see me. Your new bosses, Pedmans, have promised not to change anything, so I suppose life will go on for all of you much the same. Thank you for my presents. I will treasure them, except for yours, Roy. I doubt if at my age I'll find any use for them."

"You never know your luck," said Roy. "Some horny farmer'll probably be chasing you through the shrubbery."

Agatha drank more punch and ate smoked-salmon sandwiches and then, with her presents packed by Lulu into two carrier bags, she made her way down the stairs of Raisin Promotions for the last time.

In Bond Street, she elbowed a thin, nervous business man aside who had just flagged down a cab, said unrepentantly, "I saw it first," and ordered the driver to take her to Paddington Station.

She caught the 15:20 train to Oxford and sank back into the corner seat of a first-class carriage. Everything was ready and waiting for her in the Cotswolds. An interior decorator had "done over" the cottage, her car was waiting for her at Moreton-in-Marsh station for the short drive to Carsely, a removal firm had taken all her belongings from her London flat, now sold. She was free. She could relax. No temperamental pop stars to handle, no prima-donnaish couture firms to launch. All she had to do from now on was to please herself.

Agatha drifted off to sleep and awoke with a start at the guard's cry of "Oxford. This is Oxford. The train terminates here."

Not for the first time, Agatha wondered about British

3

Rail's use of the word "terminate." One expected the train to blow apart. Why not just say "stops here"? She looked up at the screen, like a dingy television set, which hung over Platform 2. It informed her that the train to Charlbury, Kingham, Moreton-in-Marsh and all further points to Hereford was on Platform 3, and lugging her carrier bags, she walked over the bridge. The day was cold and grey. The euphoria produced by freedom from work and Roy's punch was slowly beginning to evaporate.

The train moved slowly out of the station. Glimpses of barges on one side and straggly allotments on the other and then flat fields flooded from the recent rain lay gloomily in front of her increasingly jaundiced view.

This is ridiculous, thought Agatha. I've got what I always wanted. I'm tired, that's all.

The train stopped somewhere outside Charlbury, gliding to a stop and sitting there placidly in the inexplicable way that British Rail trains often do. The passengers sat stoically, listening to the rising wind whining over the bleak fields. Why are we like sheep that have gone astray? wondered Agatha. Why are the British so cowed and placid? Why does no one shout for the guard and demand to know the reason? Other, more voluble, races would not stand for it. She debated whether to go and see the guard herself. Then she remembered she was no longer in a hurry to get anywhere. She took out a copy of the *Evening Standard,* which she had bought at the station, and settled down to read it.

After twenty minutes the train creaked slowly into life. Another twenty minutes after Charlbury and it slid into the little station of Moreton-in-Marsh. Agatha climbed out. Her car was still where she had left it. During the last few minutes of the journey she had begun to worry that it might have been stolen.

It was market day in Moreton-in-Marsh and Agatha's spirits began to revive as she drove slowly past stalls selling everything from fish to underwear. Tuesday. Market day was Tuesday. She must remember that. Her new Saab purred out of Moreton and then up through Bourton-on-the-Hill. Nearly home. Home! Home at last.

She turned off the A-44 and then began the slow descent to the village of Carsely, which nestled in a fold of the Cotswold Hills.

It was a very pretty village, even by Cotswold standards. There were two long lines of houses interspersed with shops, some low and thatched, some warm gold brick with slate roofs. There was a pub called the Red Lion at one end and a church at the other. A few straggling streets ran off this one main road where cottages leaned together as if for support in their old age. The gardens were bright with cherry blossom, forsythia and daffodils. There was an old-fashioned haberdasher's, a post office and general store, and a butcher's, and a shop that seemed to sell nothing other than dried flowers and to be hardly ever open. Outside the village and tucked away from view by a rise was a council estate and between the council estate and the village proper was the police station, an elementary school, and a library.

Agatha's cottage stood alone at the end of one of the straggling side streets. It looked like a cottage in one of the calendars she used to treasure as a girl. It was low and thatched, new thatch, Norfolk reed, and with casement windows and built of the golden Cotswold stone. There was a small garden at the front and a long narrow one at the back. Unlike practically everyone else in the Cotswolds, the previous owner had not been a gardener. There was little else but grass and depressing bushes of the hard-wearing kind found in public parks.

Inside there was a small dark cubby-hole of a hall. To the right was the living-room; to the left, the dining-room, and the kitchen at the back was part of a recent extension and was large and square. Upstairs were two low-ceilinged bedrooms and a bathroom. All the ceilings were beamed.

Agatha had given the interior decorator a free hand. It was all as it should be and yet . . . Agatha paused at the door of the living-room. Three-piece suite in covered Sanderson's

5

linen, lamps, coffee-table with glass top, fake medieval fire-basket in the hearth, horse brasses nailed to the fireplace, pewter tankards and toby jugs hanging from the beams and bits of polished farm machinery decorating the walls, and yet it looked like a stage set. She went into the kitchen and switched on the central heating. The super-duper removal company had even put her clothes in the bedroom and her books on the shelves, so there was not much for her to do. She went through to the dining-room. Long table, shining under its heat-resistant surface, Victorian dining chairs, Edwardian painting of a small child in a frock in a bright garden, Welsh dresser with blue-and-white plates, another fireplace with a fake-log electric fire, and a drinks trolley. Upstairs, the bed-rooms were pure Laura Ashley. It felt like someone else's house, the home of some characterless stranger, or an expensive holiday cottage.

Well, she had nothing for dinner and after a life of restaurants and take-aways, Agatha had planned to learn how to cook, and there were all her new cookery books in a gleaming row on a shelf in the kitchen.

She collected her handbag and made her way out. Time to investigate what few village shops there were. Many of the shops, the real estate agent had told her, had closed down and had been transformed into "des rezzes," or desirable residences. The villagers blamed the incomers, but it was the motor car which had caused the damage, the villagers themselves preferring to go to the supermarkets of Stratford or Evesham for their goods rather than buy them at a higher price in the village. Most people in the village owned some sort of car.

As Agatha approached the main street, an old man was coming the other way. He touched his cap and gave her a cheerful "arternoon." Then in the main street, everyone she passed greeted her with a few words, a casual "afternoon" or "nasty weather." Agatha brightened. After London, where she had not even known her neighbours, all this friendliness was a refreshing change.

She studied the butcher's window and then decided that cookery could wait for a few days and so passed on to the general store and bought a "very hot" Vindaloo curry to microwave and a can of rice. Again, in the store, she was met with friendliness all round. At the door of the shop was a box of second-hand books. Agatha had always read "improving" books, mostly non-fiction. There was a battered copy of *Gone With the Wind* and she bought it on impulse.

Back in her cottage, she found a basket of pseudo-logs by the fire, little round things made out of pressed sawdust. She piled some up in the grate and set fire to them and soon had a blaze roaring up the chimney. She removed the lace antimacassar which the decorator had cutely draped over the television screen and switched it on. There was some war going on, as there usually was, and it was getting the usual coverage; that is, the anchorman and the reporter were having a cosy talk. "Over to you, John. What is the situation now? Well, Peter . . ." By the time they moved on to the inevitable "expert" in the studio, Agatha wondered why they bothered to send any reporter out to the war at all. It was like the Gulf War all over again, where most of the coverage seemed to consist of a reporter standing in front of a palm tree outside some hotel in Riyadh. What a waste of money. He never had much information and it would surely have been cheaper to place him in front of a palm tree in a studio in London.

She switched it off and picked up *Gone With the Wind*. She had been looking forward to a piece of intellectual slumming to celebrate her release from work, but she was amazed at how very good it was, almost *indecently* readable, thought Agatha, who had only read before the sort of books you read to impress people. The fire crackled and Agatha read until her rumbling stomach prompted her to put the curry in the microwave. Life was good.

But a week passed, a week in which Agatha, in her usual headlong style, had set out to see the sights. She had been to Warwick Castle, Shakespeare's birthplace, Blenheim Palace, and had toured through the villages of the Cotswolds while the wind blew and the rain fell steadily from grey skies, returning every evening to her silent cottage with only a new-found discovery of Agatha Christie to help her through the evenings. She had tried visiting the pub, the Red Lion, a jolly low-raftered chintzy sort of place with a cheerful landlord. And the locals had talked to her as they always did with a peculiar sort of open friendliness that never went any further. Agatha could have coped with a suspicious animosity but not this cheerful welcome which somehow still held her at bay. Not that Agatha had ever known how to make friends, but there was something about the villagers, she discovered, which repelled incomers. They did not reject them. On the surface they welcomed them. But Agatha knew that her presence made not a ripple on the calm pond of village life. No one asked her to tea. No one showed any curiosity about her whatsoever. The vicar did not even call. In an Agatha Christie book the vicar would have called, not to mention some retired colonel and his wife. All conversation seemed limited to "Mawnin'," "Afternoon," or talk about the weather.

For the first time in her life, she knew loneliness, and it frightened her.

From the kitchen windows at the back of the house was a view of the Cotswold Hills, rising up to block out the world of bustle and commerce, trapping Agatha like some baffled alien creature under the thatch of her cottage, cut off from life. The little voice that had cried, "What have I done?" became a roar.

And then she suddenly laughed. London was only an hour and a half away on the train, not thousands of miles. She would take herself up the following day, see her former staff, have lunch at the Caprice, and then perhaps raid the bookshops for some more readable material. She had missed market day in Moreton, but there was always another week.

As if to share her mood, the sun shone down on a perfect spring day. The cherry tree at the end of her back garden, the one concession to beauty that the previous owner had seen fit

8

to make, raised heavy branches of flowers to a clear blue sky as Agatha had her usual breakfast of one cup of black coffee, instant, and two filter-tipped cigarettes.

With a feeling of holiday, she drove up the winding hill that led out of the village and then down through Bourton-on-the-Hill to Moreton-in-Marsh.

She arrived in London's Paddington Station and drew in great lungfuls of polluted air and felt herself come alive again. In the taxi to South Molton Street she realized she did not really have any amusing stories with which to regale her former staff. "Our Aggie will be queen of that village in no time at all," Roy had said. How could she explain that the formidable Agatha Raisin did not really exist as far as Carsely was concerned?

She got out of the taxi in Oxford Street and walked down South Molton Street, wondering what it would be like to see "Pedmans" written up where her own name used to be.

Agatha stopped at the foot of the stairs which led up to her former office over the Paris dress shop. There was no sign at all, only a clean square on the paintwork where "Raisin Promotions" had once been.

She walked up the stairs. All was silent as the grave. She tried the door. It was locked. Baffled, she retreated to the street and looked up. And there across one of the windows was a large board with FOR SALE in huge red letters and the name of a prestigious estate agent.

Her face grim, she took a cab over to the City, to Cheapside, to the headquarters of Pedmans, and demanded to see Mr. Wilson, the managing director. A bored receptionist with quite the longest nails Agatha had ever seen languidly picked up the phone and spoke into it. "Mr. Wilson is busy," she enunciated, picked up the woman's magazine she had been reading when Agatha had arrived and studied her horoscope.

Agatha plucked the magazine from the receptionist's hands. She leaned over the desk. "Move your scrawny butt and tell that shyster he's seeing me."

The receptionist looked up into Agatha's glaring eyes,

gave a squeak, and scampered off upstairs. After some moments during which Agatha had read her horoscope—"Today could be the most important day of your life. But watch your temper"—the receptionist came tottering back on her very high heels and whispered, "Mr. Wilson will see you now. If you will come this way . . ."

"I know the way," snarled Agatha. Her stocky figure marched up the stairs, her sensible low-heels shoes thumping on the treads.

Mr. Wilson rose to meet her. He was a small, very clean man with thinning hair, gold-rimmed glasses, soft hands and an unctuous smile, more like a Harley Street doctor than the head of a public-relations firm.

"Why have you put my office up for sale?" demanded Agatha.

He smoothed the top of his head. "Mrs. Raisin, not *your* office; you sold the business to us."

"But you gave me your word you would keep on my staff."

"And so we did. Most of them preferred the redundancy pay. We do not need an extra office. All the business can be done from here."

"Let me tell you, you can't do this."

"And let me tell you, Mrs. Raisin, I can do what I like. You sold us the concern, lock, stock and barrel. Now, if you don't mind, I am very busy."

Then he shrank back in his chair as Agatha Raisin told him at the top of her voice exactly what he could do to himself in graphic detail before slamming out.

Agatha stood in Cheapside, tears starting to her eyes. "Mrs. Raisin . . . Aggie?"

She swung round. Roy was standing there. Instead of his usual jeans and psychedelic shirt and gold earrings, he was wearing a sober business suit.

"I'll kill that bastard Wilson," said Agatha. "I've just told him what he can do to himself."

Roy squeaked and backed off. "I shouldn't be seen talk-

10

ing to you, sweetie, if you're not the flavour of the month. Besides, you sold him the joint."

"Where's Lulu?"

"She took the redundancy money and is sunning her little body on the Costa Brava."

"And Jane?"

"Working as PR for Friends Scotch. Can you imagine? Giving an alcoholic like her a job in a whisky company? She'll sink their profits down her gullet in a year."

Agatha inquired after the rest. Only Roy had been employed by Pedmans. "It's because of the Trendies," he explained, naming a pop group, one of Agatha's former clients. "Josh, the leader, has always been ever so fond of me, as you know. So Pedmans had to take me on to keep the group. Like my new image?" He pirouetted round.

"No," said Agatha gruffly. "Doesn't suit you. Anyway, why don't you come down and visit me this weekend?"

Roy looked shifty. "Love to, darling, but got lots and lots to do. Wilson is a slave-driver. Must go."

He darted off into the building, leaving Agatha standing alone on the pavement.

She tried to hail a cab but they were all full. She walked along to Bank Station but the tube trains weren't running and someone told her there was a transport strike. "How am I going to get across town?" grumbled Agatha.

"You could try a river boat," he suggested. "Pier at London Bridge."

Agatha stumped along to London Bridge, her anger fading away to be replaced with a miserable feeling of loss. At the pier at London Bridge, she came across a sort of yuppies' Dunkirk. The pier was crammed with anxious young men and women clutching briefcases while a small flotilla of pleasure boats took them off.

She joined the end of the queue, inching forward on the floating pier, feeling slightly seasick by the time she was able to board a large old pleasure steamer that had been pressed into action for the day. The bar was open. She clutched a large

11

gin and tonic and took it up to the stern and sat down in the sunshine on one of those little gold-and-red plush ballroom chairs one finds on Thames pleasure boats.

The boat moved out and slid down the river in the sunshine, seeming to Agatha to be moving past all she had thrown away—life and London. Under the bridges cruised the boat, along past the traffic jams on the Embankment and then to Charing Cross Pier, where Agatha got off. She no longer felt like lunch or shopping or anything else but to get back to her cottage and lick her wounds and think of what to do.

She walked up to Trafalgar Square and then along the Mall, past Buckingham Palace, up Constitution Hill, down the underpass and up into Hyde Park by Deciumus Burton's Gate and the Duke of Wellington's house. She cut across the Park the direction of Bayswater and Paddington.

Before this one day, she thought, she had always forged ahead, always known what she had wanted. Although she was bright at school, her parents made her leave at fifteen, for there were good jobs to be had in the local biscuit factory. At that time, Agatha had been a thin, white-faced, sensitive girl. The crudity of the women she worked with in the factory grated on her nerves, the drunkenness of her mother and father at home disgusted her, and so she began to work overtime, squirrelling away the extra money in a savings account so that her parents might not get their hands on it, until one day she decided she had enough and simply took off for London without even saying goodbye, slipping out one night with her suitcase when her mother and father had fallen into a drunken stupor.

In London, she had worked as a waitress seven days a week so that she could afford shorthand and typing lessons. As soon as she was qualified, she got a job as a secretary in a public-relations firm. But just when she was beginning to learn the business, Agatha had fallen in love with Jimmy Raisin, a charming young man with blue eyes and a mop of black hair. He did not seem to have any steady employment but Agatha thought that marriage was all he needed to make him settle down. After a month of married life, it was finally borne in on

12

her that she had jumped out of the frying pan into the fire. Her husband was a drunk. Yet she had stuck by him for two whole years, being the breadwinner, putting up with his increasing bouts of drunken violence until, one morning, she had looked down at him lying snoring on the bed, dirty and unshaven, and had pinned a pile of Alcoholics Anonymous literature to his chest, packed her things and moved out.

He knew where she worked. She thought he would come in search of her if only for money, but he never did. She once went back to the squalid room in Kilburn which they had shared, but he had disappeared. Agatha had never filed for divorce. She assumed he was dead. She had never wanted to marry again. She had become harder and harder and more competent, more aggressive, until the thin shy girl that she had been slowly disappeared under layers of ambition. Her job became her life, her clothes expensive, her tastes in general those that were expected of a rising public-relations star. As long as people noticed you, as long as they envied you, that was enough for Agatha.

By the time she reached Paddington Station, she had walked herself into a more optimistic frame of mind. She had chosen her new life and she would make it work. That village was going to sit up and take notice of Agatha Raisin.

When she arrived home, it was late afternoon and she realized she had had nothing to eat. She went to Harvey's, the general store-cum-post-office, and ferreted around in the deep freeze wondering if she could face curry again when her eye was caught by a poster pinned up on the wall. "Great Quiche Competition" it announced in curly letters. It was to be held on Saturday in the school hall. There were other competitions listed in smaller letters: fruit cake, flower arrangements, and so on. The quiche competition was to be judged by a Mr. Cummings-Browne. Agatha scooped a Chicken Korma out of the deep freeze and headed for the counter. "Where does Mr. Cummings-Browne live?" she asked.

"That'll be Plumtrees Cottage, m'dear," said the woman. "Down by the church."

13

Agatha's mind was racing as she trotted home and shoved the Chicken Korma in the microwave. Wasn't that what mattered in these villages? Being the best at something domestic? Now if she, Agatha Raisin, won that quiche competition, they would sit up and take notice. Maybe ask her to give lectures on her art at Women's Institute meetings and things like that.

She carried the revolting mess that was her microwaved dinner into the dining-room and sat down. She frowned at the table-top. It was covered with a thin film of dust. Agatha loathed housework.

After her scrappy meal, she went into the garden at the back. The sun had set and a pale-greenish sky stretched over the hills above Carsely. There was a sound of movement from nearby and Angela looked over the hedge. A narrow path divided her garden from the garden next door.

Her neighbour was bent over a flower-bed, weeding it in the failing light.

She was an angular woman who, despite the chill of the evening, was wearing a print dress of the type beloved by civil servants' wives abroad. She had a receding chin and rather bulbous eyes and her hair was dressed in a forties style, pinned back in rolls from her face. All this Agatha was able to see as the women straightened up.

"Evening," called Agatha.

The woman turned on her heel and walked into her house and closed the door.

Agatha found this rudeness a welcome change after all the friendliness of Carsely. It was more what she was used to. She walked back through her own cottage, out the front door, up to the cottage next door, which was called New Delhi, and rapped on the brass knocker.

A curtain at a window near the door twitched but that was the only sign of life. Angela gleefully knocked again, louder this time.

The door opened a crack and one bulbous eye stared out at her.

14

"Good evening," said Agatha, holding out her hand. "I'm your new neighbour."

The door slowly opened. The woman in the print dress reluctantly picked up Angela's hand, as if it were a dead fish, and shook it. "I am Agatha Raisin," said Agatha, "and you are . . . ?"

"Mrs. Sheila Barr," said the woman. "You must forgive me, Mrs. . . . er . . . Raisin, but I am very busy at the moment."

"I won't take up much of your time," said Angela. "I need a cleaning woman."

Mrs. Barr gave that infuriating kind of laugh often described as "superior." "You won't get anyone in the village. It's almost impossible to get anyone to clean. I have my Mrs. Simpson, so I'm very lucky."

"Perhaps she might do a few hours for me," suggested Agatha. The door began to close. "Oh, no," said Mrs. Barr, "I am sure she wouldn't." And then the door was closed completely.

We'll see about that, thought Agatha.

She collected her handbag and went down to the Red Lion and hitched her bottom onto a bar stool. "Evening, Mrs. Raisin," said the landlord, Joe Fletcher. "Turned nice, hasn't it? Maybe we'll be getting some good weather after all."

Screw the weather, thought Agatha, who was tired of talking about it. Aloud she said, "Do you know where Mrs. Simpson lives?"

"Council estate, I think. Would that be Bert Simpson's missus?"

"Don't know. She cleans."

"Oh, ah, that'll be Doris Simpson all right. Don't recall the number, but it's Wakefield Terrace, second along, the one with the gnomes."

Angela drank a gin and tonic and then set out for the council estate. She soon found Wakefield Terrace and the Simpsons because their garden was covered in plastic gnomes, not grouped round a pool, or placed artistically, but just spread about at random.

15

Mrs. Simpson answered the door herself. She looked more like an old-fashioned schoolteacher than a charwoman. She had snow-white hair scraped back in a bun, and pale-grey eyes behind spectacles.

Agatha explained her mission. Mrs. Simpson shook her head. "Don't see as how I can manage any more, and that's a fact. Do Mrs. Barr next to you on Tuesdays, then there's Mrs. Chomley on Wednesdays and Mrs. Cummings-Browne on Thursdays, and then the weekends I work in a supermarket at Evesham."

"How much does Mrs. Barr pay you?" asked Agatha.

"Three pounds an hour."

"If you work for me instead, I'll give you four pounds an hour."

"You'd best come in. Bert! Bert, turn that telly off. This here is Mrs. Raisin what's taken Budgen's cottage down Lilac Lane."

A small, spare man with thinning hair turned off the giant television set which commanded the small neat living room.

"I didn't know it was called Lilac Lane," said Agatha. "They don't seem to believe in putting up names for the roads in the village."

"Reckon that's because there's so few of them, m'dear," said Bert.

"I'll get you a cup of tea, Mrs. Raisin."

"Agatha. Do call me Agatha," said Agatha with the smile that any journalist she had dealt with would recognize. Angela Raisin was going in for the kill.

While Doris Simpson retreated to the kitchen, Agatha said, "I am trying to persuade your wife to stop working for Mrs. Barr and work for me instead. I am offering four pounds an hour, a whole day's work, and, of course, lunch supplied."

"Sounds handsome to me, but you'll have to ask Doris," said Bert. "Not but what she would be glad to see the back of that Barr woman's house."

"Hard work?"

"It's not the work," said Bert, "it's the way that woman

16

do go on. She follows Doris around, checking everything, like."

"Is she from Carsely?"

"Naw, her's an incomer. Husband died a whiles back. Something in the Foreign Office he was. Came here about twenty year ago."

Agatha was just registering that twenty years in Carsely did not qualify one for citizenship, so to speak, when Mrs. Simpson came in with the tea-tray.

"The reason I am trying to get you away from Mrs. Barr is this," said Agatha. "I am very bad at housework. Been a career woman all my life. I think people like you, Doris, are worth their weight in gold. I pay good wages because I think cleaning is a very important job. I will also pay your wages when you are sick or on holiday."

"Now that's more than fair," cried Bert. " 'Member when you had your appendix out, Doris? Her never even came nigh the hospital, let alone gave you a penny."

"True," said Doris. "But it's steady money. What if you was to leave, Agatha?"

"Oh, I'm here to stay," said Agatha.

"I'll do it," said Doris suddenly. "In fact, I'll phone her now and get it over with."

She went out to the kitchen to phone. Bert tilted his head on one side and looked at Agatha, his little eyes shrewd. "You know you'll have made an enemy there," he said.

"Pooh," said Agatha Raisin, "she'll just need to get over it."

As Agatha was fumbling for her door key a half-hour later, Mrs. Barr came out of her cottage and stood silently, glaring across at Agatha.

Agatha gave a huge smile. "Lovely evening," she called.

She felt quite like her old self.

17

TWO

†

PLUMTREES Cottage, where the Cummings-Brownes · lived, was opposite the church and vicarage in a row of four ancient stone houses fronting onto a cobbled diamond-shaped area. There were no gardens at the front of these houses, only narrow strips of earth which held a few flowers.

The door was answered late the next morning to Agatha's knock by a woman whom Agatha's beady eyes summed up as being the same sort of species of ex-patriot as Mrs. Barr. Despite the chilliness of the spring day, Mrs. Cummings-Browne was wearing a print sun-dress which showed tanned middle-aged skin. She had a high autocratic voice and pale-blue eyes and a sort of "colonel's lady" manner. "Yes, what can I do for you?"

Agatha introduced herself and said she was interested in entering the quiche competition but as she was new to the village, she did not know how to go about it. "I am Mrs. Cummings-Browne," said the woman, "and really all you have to do is read one of the posters. They're all over the village, you know." She gave a patronizing laugh which made Agatha want to strike her. Instead Agatha said mildly, "As I say, I am new in the village and I would like to get to know some people. Perhaps you and your husband might care to join me for dinner this evening. Do they do meals at the Red Lion?"

Mrs. Cummings-Browne gave that laugh again. "I wouldn't be seen *dead* in the Red Lion. But they do good food at the Feathers in Ancombe."

"Where on earth is Ancombe?" asked Agatha.

"Only about two miles away. You really don't know your way about very well, do you? We'll drive. Be here at seven-thirty."

The door closed. Well, well, thought Agatha. That was easy. Must be a pair of free-loaders, which means my quiche stands a good chance.

She strolled back through the village, mechanically smiling and answering the greetings of "Mawning" from the passers-by. So there were worms in this charming polished apple, mused Agatha. The majority of the villagers were mainly working- and lower-middle class and extremely civil and friendly. If Mrs. Barr and Mrs. Cummings-Browne were anything to go by, it was the no doubt self-styled upper-class of incomers who were rude. A drift of cherry blossom blew down at Agatha's feet. The golden houses glowed in the sunlight. Prettiness did not necessarily invite pretty people. The incomers had probably bought their dinky cottages when prices were low and had descended to be big fish in this small pool. But there was no impressing the villagers or scoring off them in any way that Agatha could see. The incomers must have a jolly time being restricted to trying to put each other down. Still, she was sure if she won that competition, the village would sit up and take notice.

That evening, Agatha sat in the low-raftered dining-room of the Feathers at Ancombe and covertly studied her guests. Mr. Cummings-Browne—"Well, it's Major for my sins but I don't use my title, haw, haw, haw"—was as tanned as his wife, a sort of orangy tan that led Agatha to think it probably came out of a bottle. He had a balding pointed head with sparse grey hairs carefully combed over the top and odd juglike ears. Mr. Cummings-Browne had been in the British army in Aden, he

20

volunteered. That, Agatha reflected, must have been quite some time ago. Surely the British had left Aden in the sixties. Then it transpired he had done a "little chicken farming," but he preferred to talk about his army days, a barely comprehensible saga of servants he had had, and "chappies" in the regiment. He was wearing a sports jacket with leather patches at the elbow over an olive-green shirt with a cravat at the neck. His wife was wearing a Laura Ashley gown that reminded Agatha of the bedspreads in her cottage.

Agatha thought grimly that her quiche had better win, for she knew when she was being ripped off and the Feathers was doing just that. A landlord who stood on the wrong side of the bar which ran along the end of the dining room drinking with his cronies, a pretentious and dreadfully expensive menu, and sullen waitresses roused Agatha's anger. The Cummings-Brownes had, predictably, chosen the second-most-expensive wine on the menu, two bottles of it. Agatha let them do most of the talking until the coffee arrived and then she got down to business. She asked what kind of quiche usually won the prize. Mr. Cummings-Browne said it was usually quiche lorraine or mushroom quiche. Agatha said firmly that she would contribute her favourite—spinach quiche.

Mrs. Cummings-Browne laughed. If she laughs like that again, I really will slap her, thought Agatha, particularly as Mrs. Cummings-Browne followed up the laugh by saying that Mrs. Cartwright always won. Agatha was to remember later that there had been a certain stillness about Mr. Cummings-Browne when Mrs. Cartwright's name was mentioned, but for the present, she had the bit between her teeth. Her own quiche, said Agatha, was famous for its delicacy of taste and lightness of pastry. Besides, a spirit of competition was what was needed in the village. Very bad for morale to have the same woman winning year in and year out. Agatha was good at emanating emotional blackmail without precisely saying anything direct. She made jokes about how dreadfully expensive the meal was while all the time her bearlike brown eyes hammered home the message: "You owe me for this dinner."

But journalists as a rule belong to the kind of people who are born feeling guilty. Obviously the Cartwright-Brownes were made of sterner stuff. As Agatha was preparing to pay the bill—notes slowly counted out instead of credit card to emphasize the price—her guests stayed her hand by ordering large brandies for themselves.

Despite all they had drunk, they remained as sober-looking as they had been when the meal started. Agatha asked about the villagers. Mrs. Cummings-Browne said they were pleasant enough and they did what they could for them, all delivered in a lady-of-the-manor tone. They asked Agatha about herself and she replied briefly. Agatha had never trained herself to make social chit-chat. She was only used to selling a product or asking people all about themselves to soften them up so that she could eventually sell that product.

They finally went out into the soft dark night. The wind had died and the air held a promise of summer to come. Mr. Cummings-Browne drove his Range Rover slowly through the green lanes leading back to Carsely. A fox slid across the road in front of the lights, rabbits skittered for safety, and bird cherry, just beginning to blossom, starred the hedgerows. Loneliness again gripped Agatha. It was a night for friends, for pleasant company, not a night to be with such as the Cummings-Brownes. He parked outside his own front door and said to Agatha, "Find your way all right from here?"

"No," said Agatha crossly. "The least you could do is to run me home."

"Lose the use of your legs if you go on like this," he said nastily, but after giving an impatient little sigh, he drove her to her cottage.

I must leave a light on in future, thought Agatha as she looked at her dark cottage. A light would be welcoming. Before getting out of the car, she asked him exactly how to go about entering the competition, and after he had told her she climbed down and, without saying good night, went into her lonely cottage.

* * *

22

The next day, as instructed, she entered her name in the quiche-competition book in the school hall. The voices of the schoolchildren were raised in song in some classroom: "To my hey down-down, to my ho down-down." So they still sang "Among the Leaves So Green-O," thought Agatha. She looked around the barren hall. Trestle-tables were set against one wall and there was a rostrum at the far end. Hardly a setting for ambitious achievement.

She then got out her car and drove straight to London this time, much as she loathed and dreaded the perils of the motorways. She parked in the street at Chelsea's World's End where she had lived such a short time ago, glad that she had not surrendered her resident's parking card.

There had been a sharp shower of rain. How wonderful London smelled, of wet concrete, diesel fumes, petrol fumes, litter, hot coffee, fruit and fish, all the smells that meant home to Agatha.

She made her way to The Quicherie, a delicatessen that specialized in quiche. She bought a large spinach quiche, stowed it in the boot of her car, and then took herself off to the Caprice for lunch, where she ate their salmon fish cakes and relaxed among what she considered as "my people," the rich and famous, without it ever crossing her mind that she did not know any of them. Then to Fenwick's in Bond Street to buy a new dress, not print (heaven forbid!) but a smart scarlet wool dress with a white collar.

Back to Carsely in the evening light and into the kitchen. She removed the quiche from its shop wrappings, put her own ready printed label, "Spinach Quiche, Mrs. Raisin," on it, and wrapped it with deliberate amateurishness in thin clear plastic. She surveyed it with satisfaction. It would be the best there. The Quicherie was famous for its quiches.

She carried it up to the school hall on Friday evening, following a straggling line of women bearing flowers, jam, cakes, quiche and biscuits. The competition entries had to be in the school hall the evening before the day of the competition, for some of the women worked at the weekends. As

23

usual, a few of the women hailed her with "Evening. Bit warmer. Maybe get a bit o' sun." How would they cope with some horror like an earthquake or a hurricane? Agatha wondered. Might shut them up in future as the mild vagaries of the Cotswolds weather rarely threw up anything dramatic—or so Agatha believed.

She found she was quite nervous and excited when she went to bed that night. Ridiculous! It was only a village competition.

The next day dawned blustery and cold, with wind tearing down the last of the cherry blossom from the gardens and throwing the petals like bridal showers over the villagers as they crowded into the school hall. A surprisingly good village band was playing selections from *My Fair Lady,* ages of the musicians ranging from eight to eighty. The air smelt sweetly from the flower arrangements and from single blooms set proudly in their thin vases for the flower competition: narcissi and daffodils. There was even a tea-room set up in a side-room with dainty sandwiches and home-made cakes.

"Of course Mrs. Cartwright will win the quiche competition," said a voice near Agatha.

Agatha swung round. "Why do you say that?"

"Because Mr. Cummings-Browne is the judge," said the woman and moved off to be lost in the crowd.

Lord Pendlebury, a thin elderly gentleman who looked like an Edwardian ghost, and who had estates on the hill above the village, was to announce the winner of the quiche competition, although Mr. Cummings-Browne was to be the judge.

Agatha's quiche had a thin slice cut out of it, as had the others. She looked at it smugly. Three cheers for The Quicherie. The spinach quiche was undoubtedly the best one there. The fact that she was expected to have cooked it herself did not trouble her conscience at all.

The band fell silent. Lord Pendlebury was helped up to the platform in front of the band.

"The winner of the Great Quiche Competition is . . ."

24

quavered Lord Pendlebury. He fumbled with a sheaf of notes, picked them up, tidied them, took out a pair of pince-nez, looked again helplessly at the papers, until Mr. Cummings-Browne pointed to the right sheet of paper.

"Bless me. Yes, yes, yes," wittered Lord Pendlebury. "Harrumph! The winner is . . . Mrs. Cartwright."

"Snakes and bastards," muttered Agatha.

Fuming, she watched as Mrs. Cartwright, a gypsy-looking woman, climbed up onto the stage to receive the award. It was a cheque. "How much?" Agatha asked the woman next to her.

"Ten pounds."

"Ten pounds!" exclaimed Agatha, who had not even asked before what the prize was to be but had naïvely assumed it would be in the form of a silver cup. She had imagined such a cup with her name engraved on it resting on her mantelpiece. "How's she supposed to celebrate by spending that? Dinner at McDonald's?"

"It's the thought that counts," said the woman vaguely. "You are Mrs. Raisin. You have just bought Budgen's cottage. I am Mrs. Bloxby, the vicar's wife. Can we hope to see you at church on Sunday?"

"Why Budgen?" asked Agatha. "I bought the cottage from a Mr. Alder."

"It has always been Budgen's cottage," said the vicar's wife. "He died fifteen years ago, of course, but to us in the village, it will always be Budgen's cottage. He was a great character. At least you do not have to worry about your dinner tonight, Mrs. Raisin. Your quiche looks delicious."

"Oh, throw it away," snarled Agatha. "Mine was the best. This competition was rigged."

Mrs. Bloxby gave Agatha a look of sad reproach before moving away.

Agatha experienced a qualm of unease. She should not have been bitchy about the competition to the vicar's wife. Mrs. Bloxby seemed a nice sort of woman. But Agatha had only been used to three lines of conversation: either ordering her staff about, pressuring the media for publicity, or being oily to clients. A faint idea was stirring somewhere in her brain that Agatha Raisin was not a very lovable person.

That evening, she went down to the Red Lion. It was indeed a beautiful pub, she thought, looking about: low-raftered, dark, smoky; with stone floors, bowls of spring flowers, log fire blazing, comfortable chairs and solid tables at proper drinking and eating height instead of those "cocktail" knee-high tables which meant you had to crouch to get the food to your mouth. Some men were standing at the bar. They smiled and nodded to her and then went on talking. Agatha noticed a slate with meals written on it and ordered lasagne and chips from the landlord's pretty daughter before carrying her drink over to a corner table. She felt as she had done as a child, longing to be part of all this old English country tradition of beauty and safety and yet being on the outside, looking in. But had she, she wondered, ever really been part of anything except the ephemeral world of PR? If she dropped dead, right now, on this pub floor, was there anyone to mourn her? Her parents were dead. God alone knew where her husband was, and he would certainly not mourn her. Shit, this gin's depressing stuff, thought Agatha angrily, and ordered a glass of white wine instead to wash down her lasagne, which she noticed had been microwaved so that it stuck firmly to the bottom of the dish.

But the chips were good. Life did have its small comforts after all.

Mrs. Cummings-Browne was preparing to go out to a rehearsal of *Blithe Spirit* at the church hall. She was producing it for the Carsely Dramatic Society and trying unsuccessfully to iron out their Gloucestershire accents. "Why can't any of them achieve a proper accent?" she mourned as she collected her handbag. "They sound as if they're mucking out pigs or whatever one does with pigs. Speaking of pigs, I brought home that horrible Raisin woman's quiche. She flounced off in a huff and said we were to throw it away. I thought you might like

26

a piece for supper. I've left a couple of slices on the kitchen counter. I've had a lot of cakes and tea this afternoon. That'll do me."

"I don't think I'll eat anything either," said Mr. Cummings-Browne.

"Well, if you change your mind, pop the quiche in the microwave."

Mr. Cummings-Browne drank a stiff whisky and watched television, regretting that the hour was before nine in the evening, which meant no hope of any full frontal nudity, the powers-that-be having naïvely thought all children to be in bed by nine o'clock, after which time pornography was permissible, although anyone who wrote in to describe it as such was a fuddy-duddy who did not appreciate true art. So he watched a nature programme instead and consoled himself with copulating animals. He had another whisky and felt hungry. He remembered the quiche. It had been fun watching Agatha Raisin's face at the competition. She really had wanted her dinner back, silly woman. People like Agatha Raisin, that sort of middle-aged yuppie, lowered the tone decidedly. He went into the kitchen and put two slices of quiche in the microwave and opened a bottle of claret and poured himself a glass. Then, putting quiche and wine on a tray, he carried the lot through to the living-room and settled down again in front of the television.

It was two hours later and just before the promised gang rape in a movie called *Deep in the Heart* that his mouth began to burn as if it were on fire. He felt deathly ill. He fell out of his chair and writhed in convulsions on the floor and was dreadfully sick. He lost consciousness as he was fighting his way toward the phone, ending up stretched out behind the sofa.

Mrs. Cummings-Browne arrived home sometime after midnight. She did not see her husband because he was lying behind the sofa, nor did she notice any of the pools of vomit because only one dim lamp was burning. She muttered in

27

irritation to see the lamp still lit and the television still on. She switched both off.

Then she went up to her bedroom—it had been some time since she had shared one with her husband—removed her make-up, undressed and soon was fast asleep.

Mrs. Simpson arrived early the next morning, grumbling under her breath. Her work schedule had been disrupted. First the change-over to cleaning Mrs. Raisin's place, and now Mrs. Cummings-Browne had asked her to clean on Sunday morning because the Cummings-Brownes were going off on holiday to Tuscany on the Monday and Vera Cummings-Browne had wanted the place cleaned before they left. But if she worked hard, she could still make it to her Sunday job in Evesham by ten.

She let herself in with the spare key which was kept under the doormat, made a cup of coffee for herself, drank it at the kitchen table and then got to work, starting with the kitchen. She would have liked to do the bedrooms first but she knew the Cummings-Brownes slept late. If they were not up by the time she had finished the living-room, then she would need to rouse them. She finished cleaning the kitchen in record time and then went into the living-room, wrinkling her nose at the sour smell. She went round behind the sofa to open the window and let some fresh air in and her foot struck the dead body of Mr. Cummings-Browne. His face was contorted and bluish. He was lying doubled up. Mrs. Simpson backed away, both hands to her mouth. She thought vaguely that Mrs. Cummings-Browne must be out. The phone was on the window-ledge. Plucking up her courage, she leaned across the dead body and dialled 999 and asked for the police and an ambulance. She then shut herself in the kitchen to await their arrival. It never occurred to her to check if he was really dead or to go out and get immediate help. She sat at the kitchen table, hands tightly clasped as though in prayer, frozen with shock.

The local policeman was the first to arrive. Police Constable Fred Griggs was a fat, jolly man, unused to coping with much more than looking for stolen cars in the tourist season and charging the odd drunken driver.

He was bending over the body when the ambulance men arrived.

In the middle of all the commotion, Mrs. Cummings-Browne descended the stairs, holding a quilted dressing-gown tightly about her.

When it was explained to her that her husband was dead, she clutched hold of the newel-post at the foot of the stairs and said in a stunned voice, "But he can't be. He wasn't even here when I got home. He had high blood pressure. It must have been a stroke."

But Fred Griggs had noticed the pools of dried vomit and the distorted bluish face of the corpse. "We can't touch anything," he said to the ambulance men. "I'm pretty damn sure it's poisoning."

Agatha Raisin went to church that Sunday morning. She could not remember having been inside a church before, but going to church, she believed, was one of those things one did in a village. The service was early, eight-thirty, the vicar having to go on afterwards to preach at two other churches in the neighbourhood of Carsely.

She saw P.C. Griggs's car standing outside the Cummings-Brownes and an ambulance. "I wonder what happened," said Mrs. Bloxby. "Mr. Griggs is not saying anything. I hope nothing has happened to poor Mr. Cummings-Browne."

"I hope something has," said Agatha. "Couldn't have happened to a nicer fellow," and she marched on into the gloom of the church of St. Jude and left the vicar's wife staring after her. Agatha collected a prayer-book and a hymn-book and took a pew at the back of the church. She was wearing her new red dress and on her head was a broad-brimmed black straw hat decorated with red poppies. As the congregation began to file in, Agatha realized she was overdressed. Everyone else was in casual clothes.

During the first hymn, Agatha could hear the wail of approaching police sirens. What on earth had happened? If one of the Cummings-Brownes had just dropped dead, surely it did not require more than an ambulance and the local policeman. The church was small, built in the fourteenth century, with fine stained-glass windows and beautiful flower arrangements. The old Book of Common Prayer was used. There were readings from the Old and New Testaments while Agatha fidgeted in the pew and wondered if she could escape outside to find out what was going on.

The vicar climbed into the pulpit to begin his sermon and all Agatha's thoughts of escape disappeared. The Reverend Alfred Bloxby was a small, thin, ascetic-looking man but he had a compelling presence. In a beautifully modulated voice he began to preach and his sermon was "Love Thy Neighbour." To Agatha, it seemed as if the whole sermon was directed at her. We were too weak and powerless to alter world affairs, he said, but if each one behaved to his or her neighbours with charity and courtesy and kindness, then the ripples would spread outwards. Charity began at home. Agatha thought of bribing Mrs. Simpson away from Mrs. Barr and squirmed. When communion came round, she stayed where she was, not knowing what the ritual involved. Finally, with a feeling of release, she joined in the last hymn, "My Country 'Tis of Thee," and impatiently shuffled out, giving the vicar's hand a perfunctory shake, not hearing his words of welcome to the village as her eyes fastened on the police cars filling the small space outside the Cummings-Brownes's house.

P.C. Griggs was on duty outside, warding off all questions with a placid "Can't say anything now, I'm sure."

Agatha went slowly home. She ate some breakfast and picked up an Agatha Christie mystery and tried to read, but could not focus on the words. What did fictional mysteries matter when there was a real-live one in the village? Had Mrs.

30

Cummings-Browne hit him on the top of his pointy head with the poker?

She threw down the book and went along to the Red Lion. It was buzzing with rumour and speculation. Agatha found herself in the centre of a group of villagers eagerly discussing the death. To her disappointment, she learned that Mr. Cummings-Browne had suffered from high blood pressure.

"But it can't be natural causes," protested Agatha. "All those police cars!"

"Oh, we likes to do things thoroughly in Gloucestershire," said a large beefy man. "Not like Lunnon, where there's people dropping dead like flies every minute. My shout. What you 'aving, Mrs. Raisin?"

Agatha ordered a gin and tonic. It was all very pleasurable to be in the centre of this cosy group. When the pub finally closed its doors at two in the afternoon, Agatha felt quite tipsy as she walked home. The heavy Cotswolds air, combined with the unusually large amount she had drunk, sent her to sleep. When she awoke, she thought that Cummings-Browne had probably had an accident and it was not worth finding out about anyway. Agatha Christie now seemed much more interesting than anything that could happen in Carsley, and Agatha read until bedtime.

In the morning, she decided to go for a walk. Walks in the Cotswolds are all neatly signposted. She chose one at the end of the village beyond the council houses, opening a gate that led into some woods.

Trees with new green leaves arched above her and primroses nestled among their roots. There was a sound of rushing water from a hidden stream over to her left. The night's frost was slowly melting in shafts of sunlight which struck down through the trees. High above, a blackbird sang a heart-breaking melody and the air was sweet and fresh. The path led her out of the trees and along the edge of a field of new corn, bright green and shiny, turning in the breeze like the fur of some huge green cat. A lark shot up to the heavens, reminding

Agatha of her youth, in the days when even the wastelands of Birmingham were full of larks and butterflies, the days before chemical spraying. She strode out, feeling healthy and well and very much alive.

By following the signs, she walked through fields and more woods, finally emerging onto the road that led down into Carsely. As she walked down under the green tunnels formed by the branches of the high hedges which met overhead and saw the village lying below her, all her euphoria caused by healthy walking and fresh air left, to be replaced by an inexplicable sense of dread. She felt she was walking down into a sort of grave where Agatha Raisin would lie buried alive. Again she was plagued with restlessness and loneliness.

This could not go on. The dream of her life was not what she had expected. She could sell up, although the market was still not very good. Perhaps she could travel. She had never travelled extensively before, only venturing each year on one of the more expensive packaged holidays designed for single people who did not want to mix with the riff-raff: cycling holidays in France, painting holidays in Spain, that sort of thing.

In the village street, a local woman gave her a broad smile and Agatha wearily waited for that usual greeting of "Mawning," wondering what the woman would do or say if she replied, "Get stuffed."

But to her surprise, the woman stopped, resting her shopping basket on one broad hip, and said, "Police be looking for you. Plain clothes."

"Don't know what they want with me," said Agatha uneasily.

"Better go and find out, m'dear."

Agatha hurried on, her mind in a turmoil. What could they want? Her driving licence was in order. Of course, there were those books she had never got around to returning to the Chelsea library . . .

As she approached her cottage, she saw Mrs. Barr standing in her front garden, staring avidly at a small group of three men who were waiting outside Agatha's cottage. When she saw Agatha, she scurried indoors and slammed the door but immediately took up a watching position at the window.

A thin, cadaverous man approached Agatha. "Miss Raisin? I am Detective Chief Inspector Wilkes. May we have a word with you? Indoors."

THREE

†

AGATHA led them indoors. Detective Chief Inspector Wilkes introduced a dark, silent man beside him as Detective Sergeant Friend, and a young tubby oriental who looked like a Buddha as Detective Constable Wong.

Agatha sat in an armchair by the fireplace and the three sat down on the sofa, side by side. "We are here to ask you about your quiche, Mrs. Raisin," said Wilkes. "I understand the Cummings-Brownes took it home. What was in it?"

"What's all this about?" demanded Agatha.

"Just answer my questions," said Wilkes stolidly.

What was in quiche? wondered Agatha desperately. "Eggs, flour, milk and spinach," she volunteered hopefully.

Detective Constable Wong spoke up. He had a soft Gloucestershire accent. "Perhaps it would be best if Mrs. Raisin took us into her kitchen and showed us the ingredients."

The three detectives promptly stood up and towered over Agatha. Agatha got up, registering that her knees were trembling, and led the way into the kitchen while they crowded in after her.

Under their watching eyes, she opened the cupboards. "Strange," said Agatha. "I seem to have used everything up. I am very thrifty."

Wong, who had been watching her with amusement, said suddenly, "If you will write down the recipe, Mrs. Raisin, I'll run down to Harvey's and buy the ingredients and then you can show us how you baked it."

Agatha shot him a look of loathing. She took down a cookery book called *French Provincial Cooking,* opened it, wincing at the faint crack from its hitherto unopened spine, and looked up the index. She found the required recipe and wrote down a list of the ingredients. Wong took the list from her and went out.

"Now *will you* tell me what this is about?" asked Agatha.

"In a moment," said Wilkes stolidly.

Had Agatha not been so very frightened, she would have screamed at him that she had a right to know, but she weakly made a jug of instant coffee and suggested they sit in the living-room and drink it while she waited for Wong.

Having got rid of them, she studied the recipe. Provided she did exactly as instructed, she should be able to get it right. She had meant to take up baking and so she had scales and measures, thank God. Wong returned with a brown paper bag full of groceries.

"Join the others in the living-room," ordered Agatha, "and I'll let you know when it is ready."

Wong sat down in a kitchen chair. "I like kitchens," he said amiably. "I'll watch you cook."

Agatha shot him a look of pure hatred from her little brown eyes as she heated the oven and got to work. There were old ladies being mugged all over the country, she thought savagely. Had this wretched man nothing better to do? But he seemed to have infinite patience. He watched her closely and then, when she finally put the quiche in the oven, he rose and went to join the others. Agatha stayed where she was, her mind in a turmoil. She could hear the murmur of voices from the other room.

It was like being back at school, she thought. She remembered the headmistress telling them that they all must open their lockers for inspection without explaining why. Oh, the dread of opening her own locker in case there was something in it that shouldn't have been there. A policewoman had silently gone through everything. No one explained what was wrong. No one said anything. Agatha could still remember the silent, frightened girls, the stern and silent teachers, the competent policewoman. And then one of the girls was led away. They never saw her again. They assumed she had been expelled because of whatever had been found in her locker. But no one had called at the girl's home to ask her. Judgement had been passed on her by that mysterious world of adults and she had been spirited out of their lives as if by some divine retribution. They had gone on with their schooldays.

Now she felt like a child again, hemmed in by her own guilt and an accusing silence. She glanced at the clock. When had she put it in? She opened the oven door. There it stood, raised and golden and perfect. She heaved a sigh of relief and took it out just as Wong came back into the kitchen.

"We'll leave it to cool for a little," he said. He opened his notebook. "Now about the Cummings-Brownes. You dined with them at the Feathers. What did you have? Mmmm. And then? What did they drink?" And so it went on while out of the corner of her eye, Agatha saw her golden-brown quiche sink slowly down into its pastry shell.

Wong finally closed his notebook and called the others in. "We'll just cut a slice," he said. Agatha wielded a knife and spatula and drew out one small soggy slice.

"What did he die of?" asked Agatha desperately.

"Cowbane," said Friend.

"Cowbane?" Agatha stared at them. "Is that something like mad cow disease?"

"No," said Detective Chief Inspector Wilkes heavily. "It's a poisonous plant, not all that common, but it's found in several parts of the British Isles, including the West Midlands, and we are in the West Midlands, Mrs. Raisin. On examining the contents of the deceased's stomach, it was shown he had eaten quiche and drunk wine just before his death. The green vegetable stuff was identified as cowbane. The poisonous sub-

37

stance it contains is an unsaturated higher alcohol, cicutoxin."

"So you see, Mrs. Raisin," came the mild voice of Wong, "Mrs. Cummings-Browne thinks your quiche poisoned her husband . . . that is, if you ever made that quiche."

Agatha glared out of the window, wishing they would all disappear.

"Mrs. Raisin!" She swung round. Detective Constable Wong's slanted brown eyes were on a level with her own. Wasn't he too small for the police force? she thought inconsequently. "Mrs. Raisin," said Bill Wong softly, "it is my humble opinion that you have never baked a quiche or a cake in your life. Your cookery books had obviously never been opened before. Some of your cooking utensils still had the prices stuck to them. So will you begin at the beginning? There is no need to lie so long as you are innocent."

"Will this come out in court?" asked Agatha miserably, wondering if she could be sued by the village committee for having thrust a Quicherie quiche into their competition.

Wilkes's voice was heavy with threat. "Only if we think it necessary."

Again, Agatha's memory carried her back to her schooldays. She had bribed one of the girls to write an essay for her with two chocolate bars and a red scarf. Unfortunately, the girl, a leading light in the Young People in Christ movement, had confessed all to the headmistress and so Agatha had been summoned and told to tell the truth.

So in a small, almost childish voice, quite unlike her usual robust tones, she confessed going up to Chelsea and buying the quiche. Wong was grinning happily and she could have wrung his neck. Wilkes demanded the bill for the quiche and Agatha found it at the bottom of the rubbish bin under several empty frozen food packets and gave it to him. They said they would check her story out.

Agatha hid indoors for the rest of that day, feeling like a criminal. She would have stayed in hiding the next day had not the cleaner, Mrs. Simpson, arrived, reminding Agatha that she had promised her lunch. Agatha scuttled down to Harvey's and bought some cold meat and salad. Nothing seemed to have changed. People talked about the weather. The death of Cummings-Browne might never have happened.

Agatha returned to find Mrs. Simpson down on her hands and knees, scrubbing the kitchen floor. A sign of her extreme low state was that Agatha's eyes filled with weak tears at the sight. When had she last seen a woman scrubbing a floor instead of slopping it around with a mop? She had hired a succession of cleaning girls through an agency in London, mostly foreign girls or out-of-work actresses who seemed expert at producing an effect of cleanliness without actually ever getting down to the nitty-gritty.

Mrs. Simpson looked up from her cleaning. "I found him, you know," she said. "I found the body."

"I don't want to talk about it," said Agatha hurriedly and Mrs. Simpson grinned as she wrung out the floor cloth. "That's a mercy, for to tell the truth, I don't like talking about it. Rather get on with the work."

Agatha retreated to the living-room and then, when Mrs. Simpson moved upstairs, she prepared her a cold lunch, put it on the kitchen table beside an envelope containing Mrs. Simpson's money, and called upstairs, "I'm going out. I have a spare key. Just lock up and put the key through the letter box," and received a faint affirmative, shouted over the noise of the vacuum cleaner.

Agatha got in her car and drove up and out of the village. Where should she go? Market day in Moreton-in-Marsh. That would do. She battled in the busy town to find a parking place and then joined the throngs crowding the stalls. The Cotswolds appeared to be a very fecund place. There were young women with babies and toddlers everywhere, pushing them in push-chairs, or strollers, as she had heard an American call those chariots which the mothers thrust against the legs of the childless with such aplomb. She had read an article once where a young mother had explained how she had suffered from acute agoraphobia when her child had grown out of the push-chair. It certainly seemed to give the mothers an aggressive edge, as, like so many Boadiceas, they propelled their chariots through the market crowd. Agatha bought a geranium for the kitchen window, fresh fish for dinner, potatoes and cauliflower. She was determined to cook everything herself. No more frozen food. After depositing her shopping in the car, she ate lunch in the Market House Restaurant, bought scent in the chemist's, a blouse at one of the stalls, and then, at four o'clock, as the market was closing down, she reluctantly returned to her car and took the road home.

Mrs. Simpson had left a jug of wildflowers on the middle of the kitchen table. Bless the woman. All Agatha's guilt about having lured her away from Mrs. Barr evaporated. The woman was a queen among cleaners.

The following morning there was a knock at the door and Agatha groaned inwardly. Anyone else, she thought bitterly, would not be depressed, would expect some friend to be standing on the doorstep. But not Agatha Raisin. She knew it could only be the police.

Detective Constable Wong stood there. "This is an informal call," he said. "May I come in?"

"I suppose so," said Agatha ungraciously. "I was just about to have a glass of sherry, but I won't ask you to join me."

"Why not?" he said with a grin. "I'm off duty."

Agatha poured two glasses of sherry, threw some imitation logs on the fire and lit them. "What now?" she asked. "And what do I call you?

"My name is Bill Wong. You may call me Bill."

"An appropriate name. If you were older, I could call you the Old Bill. Now, what about the quiche?"

"You're off the hook," said Bill. "We checked out your story. Mr. Economides, the owner of The Quicherie, remembers selling you that quiche. He cannot understand what happened. He buys his vegetables from the greengrocer's across the road. Greengrocer goes to the new Covent Garden at Vauxhall every morning to buy his stock. Stuff comes from all over the country and abroad. Cowbane must have got in with

40

the spinach. It's a tragic accident. Of course, we had to tell Mrs. Cummings-Browne where the quiche came from."

Agatha groaned.

"She might have accused you of murder otherwise."

"But look here," protested Agatha, "she could have killed her husband by putting cowbane in my quiche."

"Like most of the British population, I'd swear she couldn't tell a piece of cowbane from a palm tree," said Bill. "Also, it couldn't have been you. When you left that quiche, you had no idea it would be taken home and eaten by Cummings-Browne. So it couldn't have been you. And it couldn't have been Mrs. Cummings-Browne. Poisoning like that would need to be a cold-blooded, premeditated act. No, it was a horrible accident. Cowbane was only in part of the quiche."

"I feel sorry for Mr. Economides," said Agatha. "Mrs. Cummings-Browne could sue him."

"She has generously said she will not press charges. She is a very rich woman in her own right. She has the money. She had nothing to gain from his death."

"But why did Cummings-Browne not drop dead at the tasting when he had a slice of it? Perhaps someone substituted another quiche. Or . . . let me think . . . wouldn't there have been some cowbane in that wedge, the juice, for instance?"

"Yes, we wondered about that," said Bill. "Mrs. Cummings-Browne said her husband did feel a bit queasy after the tasting but she put that down to the amount of pre-competition drinks he had been knocking back."

Agatha asked all about the case, all the details she had not asked before. He had been found dead in the morning. Then why, asked Agatha, had Mrs. Cummings-Browne gone straight up to bed?

"Oh, that was because her husband was usually late, drinking at the Red Lion."

"But that precious pair—or rather, it was Mrs. Cummings-Browne—told me they wouldn't be seen dead in the Red Lion. Mind you, that was before they socked me for a disgracefully expensive load of rubbish at the Feathers."

41

"He drinks at the Red Lion, all right, but Mrs. Cummings-Browne owns twenty-five percent of the Feathers."

"The cow! I'll be damned. Anyway, how did you guess I never cooked that quiche? For you did, you know, even before I baked one."

"The minute I saw there wasn't a single baking ingredient in the kitchen I was sure." He laughed. "I asked you to make one to be absolutely sure. You should have seen your face!"

"Oh, *very* funny."

He looked at her curiously. What an odd woman she was, he thought. Her shiny brown, well-groomed hair was not permed but cut in a sort of Dutch bob that somehow suited her square, rather truculent face. Her body was square and stocky and her legs surprisingly good. "What, asked Bill, "was so special to a recently ex-high-powered business woman like yourself about winning a village competition?"

"I felt out of place," said Agatha bleakly. "I wanted to make my mark on the village."

He laughed happily, his eyes closing into slits. "You've done just that. Mrs. Cummings-Browne knows now you cheated and so does Fred Griggs, the local bobby, and he's a prize gossip."

Agatha felt too humiliated to speak. So much for her dream home. She would need to sell up. How could she face anyone in the village?

He looked at her sympathetically. "If you want to make your mark on the village, Mrs. Raisin, you could try becoming popular."

Agatha looked at him in amazement. Fame, money and power were surely the only things needed to make one's mark on the world.

"It comes slowly," he said. "All you have to do is start to like people. If they like you back, regard it as a bonus."

Really, what odd types they had in the police force these days, thought Agatha, surprised. Did she dislike people? Of course she didn't. Well, so far the only people she had taken a dislike to in Yokel Country, she thought savagely, were old

42

fart-face next door and Mrs. Cummings-Browne and the dear deceased.

"How old are you?" she asked.

"Twenty-three," said Bill.

"Chinese?"

"Half. Father is Hong Kong Chinese and Mother is from Evesham. I was brought up in Gloucestershire." He rose to go but for some reason Agatha wanted him to stay.

"Are you married?" she asked.

"No, Mrs. Raisin."

"Well, sit down for a moment," said Agatha urgently, "and tell me about yourself."

Again a flicker of sympathy appeared in his eyes. He sat down and began to talk about his short career in the police force and Agatha listened, soothed by his air of certainty and calm. Unknown to her, it was the start of an odd friendship. "So," he said at last, "I really must go. Case finished. Case solved. Nasty accident. Life goes on."

The next day, to escape from the eyes of the villagers, eyes that would accuse her of being a cheat, Agatha drove to London. She was anxious about Mr. Economides. Agatha, a regular take-away eater, had frequented Mr. Economides's shop over the years. Perhaps some of Bill Wong's remarks had struck home, but Agatha had realized Mr. Economides, although their relationship had been that of customer and salesman, was as near a friend as she had got. The shop contained two small tables and chairs for customers who liked to have coffee, and when the shop was quiet, Mr. Economides had often treated Agatha to a coffee and told her tales of his numerous family.

But when she arrived, the shop was busy and Mr. Economides was guarded in his answers as his competent hairy hands packed quiche and cold cuts for the customers. Yes, Mrs. Cummings-Browne had called in person to assure him that she would not be suing him. Yes, it had been a tragic accident. And now, if Mrs. Raisin would excuse him . . . ?

Agatha left, feeling rather flat. London, which had so

43

recently enclosed her like a many-coloured coat, now stretched out in lonely streets full of strangers all about her. She went to Foyle's bookshop in the Charing Cross Road and looked up a book on poisonous plants. She studied a picture of cowbane. It was an innocuous-looking plant with a ridged stem and flower heads composed of groups of small white flowers. She was about to buy the book when she suddenly thought, why bother? It had been an accident, a sad accident.

She pottered around a few other shops in London before returning to her car and joining the long line of traffic that was belching its way out of London. Reluctant to return to the village before dark, she cut off the motorway and headed for Oxford and parked her car in St. Giles and made her way to the Randolph Hotel for tea. She was the only customer, odd in that most popular of hotels. She settled back in a huge sofa and drank tea and ate crumpets served to her by a young maiden with a Pre-Raphaelite face. Faintly from outside came the roar of traffic ploughing up Beaumont Street past the Ashmoleum Museum. The hotel had a dim ecclesiastical air, as if haunted by the damp souls of dead deans. She pushed the last crumpet around on her plate. She did not feel like eating it. She needed a purpose in life, she thought, an aim. Would it not be marvelous if Cummings-Browne turned out to have been murdered after all? And she, Agatha Raisin, solved the case? She would become known throughout the Cotswolds. People would come to her. She would be respected. Had it been an accident? What sort of marriage had the Cummings-Brownes really had where she could come home and trot off to bed while her husband lay dead behind the sofa? Why separate bedrooms? Bill Wong had told her that. Why should Mr. Economides's excellent and famous quiche suddenly contain cowbane when over the years he had not had one complaint? Perhaps she could ask around. Just a few questions. No harm in that.

Feeling more cheerful than she had for a long time, she paid the bill and tipped the gentle waitress lavishly. The sun was sinking low behind the trees as she motored through the village and turned off at Lilac Lane. She fished out the spare door key and then she heard her phone ringing, sharp and insistent.

She swore under her breath as she fumbled with the key. It was the first time her phone had rung. She tumbled in the door and felt her way towards it in the gloom.

"Roy here," came the familiar mincing voice of her ex-assistant.

"How lovely to hear from you," cried Agatha in tones she had never used before to the young man.

"Fact is, Aggie, I was hoping I could come down and see you this weekend."

"Of course. You're welcome."

"I've got this Australian friend, Steve, wants to see the countryside. Do you mind if he comes too?"

"More the merrier. Are you driving here?"

"Thought we'd take the train and come down Friday night."

"Wait a bit," said Agatha, "I've got a timetable here." She fumbled in her bag. "Yes, there's a through train leaves Paddington at six-twenty in the evening. Don't need to change anywhere. Gets in at Moreton-in-Marsh—"

"Where?"

"Moreton-in-Marsh."

"Too Agatha Christie for words, darling."

"And I'll meet you at the station."

"It's the May Day celebrations at the weekend, Aggie, and Steve wants to look at maypoles and morris dancers and all that sort of thing."

"I haven't had time to look at any posters, Roy. I've been involved in a death."

"Did one of the clodhoppers try to mumble with you with his gruttock, luv?"

"Nothing like that. I'll tell you all about it when I see you."

Angela whistled to herself as she cracked open one of her cookery books and began to prepare the fish she had bought the day before. There seemed to be so many exotic recipes. Surely one just fried the stuff. So she did and by the time it was ready, realized she had not put the potatoes on to boil or cooked the cauliflower. She threw a packet of mircrowaveable chips in the micro and opened a can of bright-green peas. It all tasted delicious to Agatha's undemanding palate when she finally sat down to eat.

The next day, she called in at Harvey's and studied the posters at the door. Yes, there was to be morris dancing, maypole dancing, and a fair in the village on the Saturday. People nodded and smiled to her. No one said "quiche" or anything dreadful like that. Cheerfully Agatha trotted home but was waylaid by Mrs. Barr before she could get to her own garden gate.

"I thought you would have been at the inquest yesterday at Mircester," said Mrs. Barr, her eyes cold and watchful.

"No one asked me," said Agatha. "It was an accident. I suppose the police evidence was enough."

"Not enough for me," said Mrs. Barr coolly. "Nothing came out about the way you cheated at that competition."

Curiosity overcame rancour in Agatha's bosom. "Why not? Surely it was mentioned that it had been bought in a shop in Chelsea?"

"Oh, yes, *that* came out but not a word of condemnation for you being a cheat and a liar. Poor Mrs. Cummings-Browne broke down completely. We don't need your sort in this village."

"And what was the verdict?"

"Accidental death, but you killed him, Agatha Raisin. You killed him with your nasty foreign quiche, just as much as if you had knifed him."

Agatha's eyes blazed. "I'll kill you, you malicious harridan, if you don't bugger off."

She marched to her own cottage, blinking tears from her eyes, appalled at her own shock and dismay and weakness.

Thank God Roy was coming. Dear Roy, thought Agatha sentimentally, forgetting she had always considered him a tiresomely effeminate young man whom she would have sacked had he not had a magic touch with the peculiar world of pop music.

There came a knock at the door and Agatha cringed, wondering if some other nasty local was about to berate her. But when she opened it, it was Bill Wong who stood on the step.

"Came to tell you about the inquest," he said. "I called yesterday but you were out."

"I was seeing *friends,*" said Agatha loftily. "In fact, two of them are coming to stay with me for the weekend. But come in."

"What was the Barr female on about?" he asked curiously as he followed Agatha into her kitchen.

"Accusing me of murder," mumbled Agatha, putting groceries away in the cupboards. "Like a coffee?"

"Yes, please. So the inquest is over and Mr. Cummings-Browne is to be cremated and his ashes cast to the four winds on Salisbury Plain in memory of his army days."

"I believe Mrs. Cummings-Browne collapsed at the inquest," said Agatha.

"Yes, yes, she did. Two sugars please and just a dash of milk. Most affecting."

Agatha turned at looked at him, her interest suddenly quickening. "You think she was acting?"

"Maybe. But I was surprised he was so generally mourned. There were quite a lot of ladies there sobbing into their handkerchiefs."

"With their husbands? Or on their own?"

"On their own."

Agatha put a mug of coffee down in front of him, poured one for herself and sat down at the kitchen table opposite him.

"Something's bothering you," said Agatha.

"Oh, the case is closed and I have a lot of work to do. There's an epidemic of joy-riders in Mircester."

"What time did Mrs. Cummings-Browne go to bed, the night her husband died?" asked Agatha.

47

"Just after midnight or thereabouts."

"But the Red Lion closes sharp at eleven and it's only a few minutes' walk away."

"She said he often stayed out late, drinking with friends."

Agatha's eyes were shrewd. "Oho! And weeping women at the inquest. Don't tell me old jug ears was a philanderer."

"There's no evidence of that."

"And yet Mrs. Cartwright always won the competition. Why?"

"Perhaps her baking was the best."

"No one bakes quiche better than Mr. Economides," said Agatha firmly.

"But you are the incomer. More natural to give a prize to one of the locals."

"Still . . ."

"I can see from the look in your eye, Mrs. Raisin, that you would like it to be murder after all and so clear your conscience."

"Why did you call to tell me about the inquest?"

"I thought you would be interested. There's a paragraph about it in today's *Gloucestershire Telegraph*."

"Have you got it?" demanded Agatha. "Let me see."

He fished in his pocket and pulled out a crumpled newspaper. "Page three."

Agatha turned to page three.

At the coroner's court in Mircester yesterday [she read], a verdict of accidental death by eating poisoned quiche was pronounced. The victim was Mr. Reginald Cummings-Browne, fifty-eight, of Plumtrees Cottage, Carsely. Giving evidence, Detective Chief Inspector Wilkes said that cowbane had been introduced into a spinach quiche by accident. The quiche had been bought by a newcomer to the village, Mrs. Agatha Raisin. She had bought the quiche from a London delicatessen and had entered it in a village competition as her own baking,

48

a competition at which the late Mr. Cummings-Browne was the judge.

The owner of the delicatessen, Mr. Economides, had stated to the police that the cowbane must have become mixed with the spinach by accident. It was stressed that no blame fell on the unfortunate Mr. Economides, a Greek immigrant, aged forty-five, who owns The Quicherie at the World's End, Chelsea.

Mrs. Vera Cummings-Browne, fifty-two, collapsed in court.

Mr. Cummings-Browne was a well-known figure in the Cotswolds . . .

"And blah, blah, blah," said Agatha, putting the paper down. "Hardly a paragraph."

"You're lucky," said Bill Wong. "If there hadn't been riots on that estate in Mircester and two deaths, I am sure some enterprising reporter would have been around to find out about the cheating incomer of Carsley. You got off lucky."

Agatha sighed. "I'll never live it down, unless I can prove it was murder."

"Don't go looking for more trouble. That's why there's a police force. Best let everyone forget about your part in the death. Economides is lucky as well. With all this going on in Russia, not one London paper has bothered to pick up the story."

"I still wonder why you came?"

He drained the last of his coffee and stood up.

"Perhaps I like you, Agatha Raisin."

Agatha blushed for about the first time in her life. He gave her an amused look and let himself out.

FOUR

†

AGATHA felt quite nervous as she waited for the Cotswold Express to pull in at Moreton-in-Marsh Station. What would this friend of Roy's be like? Would she like him? Agatha's main worry was that the friend might not like her, but she wasn't even going to admit to that thought.

The weather was calm but still cold. The train, oh, miracle of miracles, was actually on time. Roy descended and rushed to embrace her. He was wearing jeans and a T-shirt which bore the legend I HAVE BEEN USED. Following him came a slight young man. He had thick black hair and a heavy moustache and wore a light-blue denim jacket, jeans, and high-heeled cowboy boots. Butch Cassidy comes to Moreton-in-Marsh. This then was Steve. He gave her a limp handshake and stood looking at her with doggy eyes.

"Welcome to the Cotswolds," said Agatha. "Roy tells me you're Australian. On holiday?"

"No, I am a systems analyst," said Steve in the careful English accents of an Eliza Doolittle who hadn't yet quite got it. "I work in the City."

"Come along, then," said Agatha. "The car's parked outside. I thought I would take you both out for dinner tonight. I'm not much of a cook."

"And neither you are, ducks," said Roy. "He turned to Steve. "We used to call her the queen of the microwave. She ate most of her meals in the office and kept a microwave oven there, awful things like the Rajah's Spicy Curry and things like that. Where are we going to eat, Aggie?"

"I thought maybe the Red Lion in the village."

She unlocked the car door but Roy stood his ground. "Pub grub?" he asked.

"Yes."

"Steak and kidney pie and chips, sausage and chips, fish and chips and lasagne and chips?"

"Yes, so what?"

"So what? My delicate little stomach cringes at the thought, that's what. My friend Jeremy said there was ever such a good restaurant in the Horse and Groom at Bourton-on-the Hill. Don't you just love these place names, Steve? See, he's drooling already." Steve looked impassive. "They're Basque and do all those sort of fishy dishes. I say, Aggie, have you heard the one about the fire at the Basque football game? They all rushed to get out of the stadium and all got crushed in the exit and do you know what the moral of that is, my loves? Don't put all your Basques in one exit. Get it?"

"Stop wittering," said Agatha. "All right. We'll try the place, although if it's that good they may not have a table left."

But it turned out the Horse and Groom had just received a cancellation before they arrived. The dining-room was elegant and comfortable and the food was excellent. Agatha asked Steve to tell her about his work and then regretted it bitterly as he began a long and boring description of his job in particular and computers in general.

Even Roy grew weary of his friend's monologue and cut across it, saying, "What's all this about you being involved in a death, Aggie?"

"It was an awful mistake," said Agatha. "I entered a spinach quiche in a village competition. One of the judges ate it and died of poisoning."

Roy's eyes filled with laughter. "You never could cook, Aggie dear."

"It wasn't my cooking," protested Agatha. "I bought a quiche from The Quicherie in Chelsea and entered that."

Steve looked at her solemnly. "But surely in these sort of home-baking competitions you're supposed to cook the thing yourself."

"Yes, but—"

"But she was trying to pull a fast one as usual," crowed Roy. "Who was the judge and what did he die of?"

"Mr. Cummings-Browne. Cowbane poisoning."

"Struck down by a bane of cows? What is it? One of those peculiar agricultural diseases like swine fever or violet-root rot?"

"No, cowbane is a plant. It must have got mixed up in the spinach that Mr. Economides of the deli used."

Steve put down his fork and looked gravely at Agatha. "So you murdered him."

Roy screeched with laughter. He kicked his heels in the air, fell off the chair and rolled around the dining-room carpet, holding his stomach. The other diners studied him with the polite frozen smiles the English use for threatening behaviour.

"Oh, Aggie," wheezed Roy when his friend had picked up his chair and thrust him back into it, "you are a one."

Patiently Agatha explained the whole sorry business. It had been a sad accident.

"What do they think about you in the village?" asked Roy, mopping his streaming eyes. "Are they calling you the Borgia of the Cotswolds?"

"It's hard to know what they think," said Agatha. "But I had better sell up. The whole move to Carsely was a terrible mistake."

"Wait a minute," said Steve. He carefully extracted a piece of lobster and popped it in his mouth. "Where does this cowbane grow?"

"In the West Midlands, and this, as the police pointed out, is the West Midlands."

53

Steve frowned. "Does it grow in farms among the regular vegetables?"

Agatha searched her memory for what she had read about cowbane in the book in Foyle's. "It grows in marshy places."

"I've heard the Cotswolds are famous for asparagus and strawberries . . . oh, and plums and things like that," said Steve. "I read up on it. But not spinach. And how could a marshy plant get in among a field of spinach?"

"I don't know," said Agatha, "but as I recall, it grows in other parts of the British Isles as well. I mean, the stuff at Covent Garden comes from abroad and all over the place in Britain."

Steve shook his head slowly, his mouth open as he contemplated another piece of lobster. "Are you wondering if there's an aargh in the month?" demanded Roy. "You look like one of those faces at the fairground where you've to try and toss a ball into the mouth."

"It just doesn't happen," said Steve.

"What?"

"Well, look here. A field of spinach is harvested. For some reason a marshy plant gets caught up with the spinach. Right? So how come no one else dropped dead? How come it all got into one spinach quiche? Just the one. Surely a bit of it would have got into *another* quiche. Surely another one of this Economides's customers would bite the dust."

"Oh, the police will have looked into all that," said Roy a trifle testily. He felt Steve was taking up too much of the conversation.

Steve shook his head slowly from side to side.

"Look," said Agatha. "Be sensible. Who was to know I would walk off in a huff and leave that quiche? Who would even know that the Cummings-Brownes would take it home? The vicar could have taken it and given it to some old-age pensioner. Lord Pendlebury could have taken it."

"When did you take your quiche to the competition?" asked Steve.

54

"The night before," said Agatha.

"So it was just lying there all night, unattended, in this hall? Someone could have baked another quiche with cowbane in it and substituted it for Agatha's quiche."

"We're back to motive," said Agatha. "So say someone replaced a poisoned quiche for mine. Who's to know Cummings-Browne would take it? I didn't even know I was going to walk off and leave it until the last minute."

"But it could have been meant for you," said Steve. "Don't you see? Even if you had won that competition, only a little slice was taken out for the judging, and then you would have taken the rest home." He leaned forward. "Who hates you enough?"

Agatha thought uneasily of Mrs. Barr and then shrugged. "This is ridiculous. Do you read Agatha Christie?"

"All the time," said Steve.

"Well, so do I, but delightful as those detective stories are, believe me, murders are usually sudden and violent and take place in cities, some drunken lout of a husband bashing his wife to death. Don't you see, I would *like* it to be murder."

"Yes, I can see that," said Steve, "because you have been exposed as a cheat."

"Here, wait a minute—"

"But it all looks very odd."

Agatha fell silent. If only she had never tried to win that stupid competition.

Again a feeling of loneliness assailed her as she paid the bill and ushered her guests out into the night. She had a whole weekend in front of her entertaining this precious pair, and yet their very presence emphasized her loneliness. Roy had no real affection for her of any kind. His friend had wanted to see rural England and so he was using her.

Roy pranced around the cottage, looking at everything. "Very cute, Aggie," was his verdict. "Fake horse brasses! Tch! Tch! And all that farm machinery."

"Well, what would you have?" said Agatha crossly.

"I dunno, sweetie. Looks like a stage set. Nothing of Aggie here."

"Perhaps that's understandable," said Steve. "There are people who do not have personalities that transfer to interior decorating. You need to be a homebody."

"You can go off people, you know," commented Agatha waspishly. "Off to bed with both of you. I'm tired. The village festivities don't begin until noon, so you can have a long lie."

The next morning Roy took over the cooking when he found Agatha was about to microwave the sausages for breakfast. He whistled happily as he went about the preparations and Agatha told him he would make someone a good wife. "More than you would, Aggie," he said cheerfully. "It's a wonder your health hasn't crumbled under a weight of microwaved curries."

Steve came down wrapped in a dressing-gown, gold and blue stripes and with the badge of a cricket club on the pocket. "He got it at a stall in one of the markets," said Roy. "Don't bother talking to him, Aggie. He doesn't really wake up until he's had a jug of coffee."

Agatha read through the morning papers, turning the pages rapidly to see if there was anything further about the quiche poisoning, but there wasn't a word.

The morning passed amicably if silently and then they went out to the main street, Roy doing cart-wheels down the lane past Mrs. Barr's cottage. Agatha saw the lace curtains twitch.

Steve took out a large notebook and began to write down all about the festivities, which started off with the crowning of the May Queen, a small pretty schoolgirl with a slimly old-fashioned figure. In fact all the schoolchildren looked like illustrations in some long-forgotten book with their innocent faces and underdeveloped figures. Agatha was used to seeing schoolgirls with busts and backsides. The Queen was drawn by the morris men in their flowered top hats, the bells at their knees jingling. Roy was disappointed in the morris dancers, possibly because, despite the flowered hats, they looked like a

56

boozy Rugby team and were led by a white-haired man who struck various members of the audience with a pig's bladder. "Supposed to make you fertile," said Steve ponderously and Roy shrieked with laughter and Agatha felt thoroughly ashamed of him.

They wandered around the stalls set up in the main street. Every one seemed to be selling wares in support of some charity or other. Agatha winced away from the home-baking stand. Roy won a tin of sardines at the tombola and got so carried away, he bought ticket after ticket until he managed to win a bottle of Scotch. There was a game of skittles which they all tried, a rendering of numbers from musicals by the village band, and then the morris dancers again, leaping up into the sunny air, accompanied by fiddle and accordion. "Don't you know you are living in an anachronism?" said Steve ponderously, scribbling away in his notebook.

Roy wanted to try his luck at the tombola again and he and Steve went off. Agatha flicked through a pile of second-hand books on a stall and then looked sharply at the woman behind the stall. Mrs. Cartwright!

She was, as Agatha had already noticed, a gypsy-looking woman, swarthy-skinned among all the pink-and-white complexions of the villagers. Her rough hair hung down her back and her strong arms were folded across her generous bosom.

"Mrs. Cartwright?" said Agatha tentatively. The woman's dark eyes focused on her. "Oh, you be Mrs. Raisin," she said. "Bad business about the quiche."

"I can't understand it," said Agatha. "I shouldn't have bought it, but on the other hand, how on earth would cowbane get into a London quiche?"

"London is full of bad things," said Mrs. Cartwright, straightening a few paperbacks that had tumbled over.

"Well, the result is that I will have to sell up," said Agatha. "I can't stay here after what happened."

" 'Twas an accident," said Mrs. Cartwright placidly. "Reckon you can't go running off after an accident. Besides,

57

I was ever so pleased a London lady should think she had to buy one to compete with me."

Agatha gave her an oily smile. "I did hear you were the best baker in the Cotswolds. Look, I would really like to talk about it. May I call on you?"

"Any time you like," said Mrs. Cartwright lazily. "Judd's cottage, beyond the Red Lion on the old Station Road."

Roy came prancing up and Agatha moved on quickly, afraid that Roy's chattering and posturing might put Mrs. Cartwright off. Agatha began to feel better. Mrs. Cartwright hadn't accused her of cheating, nor had she been nasty.

But then, after Steve and Roy had rejoined her and as they were leaving the May Day Fair, they came face to face with Mrs. Barr. She stopped in front of Agatha, her eyes blazing. "I am surprised you have the nerve to show your face in the daylight," she said.

"What's got your knickers in a twist, sweetie?" asked Roy.

"This woman"—Mrs. Barr bobbed her head in Agatha's direction, "caused the death of one of our most respected villagers by poisoning him."

"It was an accident," said Roy, before Agatha could speak. "Bugger off, you old fright. Come on, Aggie."

Mrs. Barr stood opening and shutting her mouth in silent outrage as Roy propelled Agatha past her.

"Miserable old cow," said Roy as they turned into Lilac Lane. "What got up her nose?"

"I lured her cleaning woman away."

"Oh, that's a capital crime. Murder has been committed for less. Take us to Bourton-on-the-Water, Aggie. Steve wants to see it and we don't need to eat yet after that enormous breakfast."

Agatha, although she still felt shaken by Mrs. Barr, patiently got out the car. "Stow-on-the-Wold," screamed Roy a quarter of an hour later as Agatha was about to bypass that village. "We must see it." So Agatha turned round and went into the main square, thrusting her car head first into the one

58

remaining parking place, which a family car had been just about to reverse into.

She had never seen so many morris dancers. They seemed to be all over the place and of a more energetic type than the ones in Carsely as they waved their handkerchiefs and leaped in the air like so many Nijinskys.

"I think," said Roy, "that if you've seen one lot of morris dancers, you've seen the lot. Put away your notebook, Steve, for God's sake."

"It is all very interesting," said Steve. "Some say that morris dancing was originally Moorish dancing. What do you think?"

"I think . . . yawn, yawn, *yawn*," said Roy pettishly. "Let's go and sample the cosmopolitan delights of Bourton-on-the Water."

Bourton-on-the-Water is certainly one of the prettiest villages in the Cotswolds, with a glassy stream running through the centre under stone bridges. The trouble is that it is a famous beauty spot and always full of tourists. That May Day they were out in force and Agatha thought longingly of the peaceful streets of London. There were tourists everywhere: large family parties, sticky crying children, busloads of pensioners from Wales, muscle-bound men with tattoos from Birmingham, young Lolitas in white slit skirts and white high-heeled shoes, tottering along, eating ice cream and giggling at everything in sight. Steve wanted to see all that was on offer, from the art galleries to the museums, which depressed Agatha, because a lot of the village museum displays were items from her youth and she felt only really old things should go into museums. Then there was the motor museum, also jammed with tourists, and then, unfortunately, someone had told Steve about Birdland at the end of the village and so they had to go there, and stare at the birds and admire the penguins. Agatha had often wondered what it would be like to live in Hong Kong or Tokyo. Now she knew. People everywhere. People *eating* everywhere: ice cream, chocolate bars, hamburgers, chips, munch, munch, munch went all those English

59

jaws. They seemed to enjoy being in such a crowd, except the many small children who were getting tired and bawled lustily, dragged along by indifferent parents.

The air was turning chilly when Steve with a sigh of pleasure at last closed his notebook. He looked at his watch. "It's only half past three," he said. "We can make it to Stratford-on-Avon. I must see Shakespeare's birthplace."

Agatha groaned inwardly. But not so long ago Agatha Raisin would have told him to forget it, that she was bored and tired, but the thought of Carsely and Mrs. Barr made her meekly walk with them to the car-park and set out for Stratford.

She parked in the multi-storey Birthplace Car-Park and plunged into the crowds of Stratford with Roy and Steve. So many, many people, all nationalities this time. They shuffled along with the crowds through Shakespeare's home, a strangely soulless place, thought Agatha again. It had been so restored, so *sanitized* that she could not help feeling that some of the old pubs in the Cotswolds had more of an air of antiquity.

Then down to look at the River Avon. Then a search by Steve for tickets to the evening's showing of *King Lear* by the Royal Shakespeare Company which, to Agatha's dismay, he managed to get.

In the darkness of the theatre with her stomach rumbling, for she had had nothing to eat since breakfast, Agatha's mind turned back to the . . . murder? It would surely do no harm to find out a little more about Mr. Cummings-Browne. Then Mrs. Simpson had found the body. How had Mrs. Cummings-Browne reacted? The first act passed unheeded before Agatha's eyes. Two large gins at the interval made her feel quite tipsy. Once more, she imagined solving the case and earning the respect of the villagers. By the last act, she was fast asleep and all the glory of Shakespeare fell on her deaf ears.

It was only as they were walking out—crowds, more crowds—that Agatha realized she had nothing at home for them to eat and it was too late to find a restaurant. But Steve, who had, at one point of the day, been lugging a carrier bag, said he had planned to cook them dinner and had bought fresh trout at Birdland.

"You really ought to dig in your heels and stay here," said Roy, as he got out of the car in front of Agatha's cottage. "No people. Quiet. Calm. You're lucky you don't live in a tourist village. Do any tourists come at all?"

"The Red Lion's got rooms, I believe," said Agatha. "A few let out their cottages. But not many come."

"Let's have a drink while Steve does the cooking," said Roy. He looked around Agatha's living-room. "If I were you, I would junk all those cutesy mugs and fake horse brasses and farm machinery, and get some paintings and bowls of flowers. It's not the thing to have a fire-basket, particularly a fake medieval one. You're supposed to burn the logs on the stone hearth."

"I dig my heels in over the fire-basket," said Agatha, "but I might get rid of the other stuff." She thought, They collect a lot for charity in this village. I could load up the car with the stuff on Tuesday and take it along to the vicarage. Ingratiate myself a bit there.

Dinner was excellent. I must learn to cook, thought Agatha. I've got little else to do. Steve opened his notebook. "Tomorrow, if you do not think it too much, Agatha, I would like to visit Warwick Castle."

Agatha groaned. "Warwick Castle's like Bourton-on-the-Water, wall-to-wall tourists from one year's end to the other."

"But it says here," said Steve, fishing out a guidebook, "that it is one of the finest medieval castles in England."

"Well, I suppose that's true but—"

"I would very much like to go."

"All right! But be prepared for an early start. See if we can get in there before the crowds."

Warwick Castle is a tourist's dream. It has everything from battlements and towers to a torture chamber and dungeon. It has rooms peopled by Madame Tussaud's waxworks depicting a Victorian house party. It has signs in the drive

61

saying: DRIVE SLOWLY, PEACOCKS CROSSING. It has a rose garden and a peacock garden. It takes a considerable amount of time to see everything and Steve wanted to see everything. With unflagging energy and interest, he climbed up the towers and along the battlements and down to the dungeons. Oblivious to the tourists crowding behind, he lingered in the staterooms, writing busily in his notebook. "Are you going to write about all this?" asked Agatha impatiently.

Steve said only in letters. He wrote a long letter home each week to his mother in Sydney. Agatha hoped they could finally escape, but the tyranny of the notebook was replaced by the tyranny of the video camera. Steve insisted they all climb back up to the top of one of the towers and he filmed Agatha and Roy standing at the edge leaning against the crenellated parapet.

Agatha's feet were aching by the time she climbed back in her car. They had lunch at a pub in Warwick and Agatha, numb with fatigue, found herself agreeing to take them round the Cotswold villages they had not seen, the ones whose names intrigued Steve, like Upper and Lower Slaughter, Aston Magna, Chipping Campden, and so on. Steve found shops open in Chipping Campden and bought groceries, saying he would cook them dinner that evening.

She was so tired when dinner was over that all Agatha wanted to do was go to bed, but it turned out that Steve's camera was the type you could plug in to the TV and show the film taken.

Agatha leaned back and half-closed her eyes. She hated seeing herself on film anyway. Then she heard Roy exclaim, "Wait a minute. At Warwick Castle. On top of the tower. That woman. Look, Aggie. Run it again, Steve."

The film flickered back and then began to roll again. There she was with Roy on top of the tower. Roy was giggling and clowning. The camera then slowly panned over the surrounding countryside, inch, it seemed, by inch, Steve obviously trying to avoid the amateur's failing of camera swing. And then suddenly it focused on a woman, standing a little way from Agatha and Roy. She was a spinsterish creature in a tweed jacket, drooping tweed skirt and sensible shoes. But she was glaring at Agatha with naked venom in her eyes and her fingers were curled like claws. The film moved back to Agatha and Roy.

"Enter First Murderer," said Roy. "Anyone you know, Aggie?"

Agatha shook her head. "I've never seen her before, not in the village anyway. Run it again."

Again those hate-filled eyes loomed up. "Perhaps it wasn't me she was glaring at," said Agatha. "Perhaps her husband had just come up the stairs." Steve shook his head. "There was no one else there. I remember seeing just that woman when I was filming. Then, just as I'd finished, a whole lot of tourists appeared."

"How odd." Roy stared blankly at the television screen. "How could she know you enough to hate you? What were we saying?"

"Roy was clowning," said Agatha slowly. "It's a pity you haven't any sound on that film, Steve."

"I forgot. There is. Usually I don't bother about it and tape some music to go with the English travelogue and then send it home to my mother."

"Turn the sound up," said Roy eagerly.

Into the room came the sound of the wind on the top of the battlements. Then Roy's voice. "Do you want Aggie to throw herself off the battlements like Tosca?" And Agatha saying, "Oh, do give over, Roy. Gosh, it's cold here."

And then, in sepulchral tones, Roy said, "As cold as the grave into which you drove Mr. Cummings-Browne with your quiche, Agatha."

Agatha's voice was replying testily, "He's not in a grave. He's scattered to the four winds on Salisbury Plain. Are you finished yet, Steve?"

Then Steve's voice saying, "Just a bit longer," and then the shot of the glaring woman.

"And you said nobody hated you!" mocked Roy. "That

63

one looked as if she wanted to kill you. Wonder who she is?"

"I'll photograph her from the screen," said Steve, "and send you a print. Might be an idea to find out. She must have known about the death of Cummings-Browne."

Agatha sat silent for a few moments. She thought she would never forget that spinsterish face and those glaring eyes.

"Beddy-byes," said Roy. "Which train should we catch tomorrow?"

Agatha roused herself. "Trains might not be very good on a holiday Monday. I'll run you to Oxford and take you both for lunch and you can get the train from there."

She had thought she would be glad to see the last of the pair of them, but when she finally stood with them on Oxford Station to say goodbye, she suddenly wished they weren't going.

"Come again," she said. "Any time."

Roy planted a wet kiss on her cheek. "We'll be back, Aggie. Super weekend."

The guard blew his whistle, Roy jumped aboard to join Steve, and the train moved out of the station.

Agatha stood forlornly for several minutes, watching the train disappearing round the curve, before trailing out to the car-park. She felt slightly frightened and wished she had been able to go to London with them. Why had she ever left her job?

But home was waiting for her in Carsely, down in a fold of the Cotswold Hills, Carsely where she had disgraced herself, where she did not belong and never would.

FIVE

†

AGATHA loaded up the car with the toby jugs, pewter mugs, fake horse brasses and bits of farm machinery the next day and drove the short distance to the vicarage.

Mrs. Simpson was busy cleaning the cottage. Agatha planned to talk to her over lunch. Perhaps it was because of the poisoning, but Mrs. Simpson called Agatha Mrs. Raisin and Agatha felt compelled to call her Mrs. Simpson, not Doris. The cleaner was efficient and correct but exuded a certain atmosphere of wariness. At least she had not brought her own lunch.

Mrs. Bloxby, the vicar's wife, answered the door herself. Frightened of a rebuff, Agatha gabbled out that she had brought some items she hoped the church might be able to sell to benefit some charity.

"How very good of you," said Mrs. Bloxby. "Alf," she called over her shoulder, "Mrs. Raisin has brought us some items for charity. Come and lend a hand." Agatha was startled. Vicars should not be called plain Alf but something like Peregrine, Hilary, or Aloysius. The vicar appeared wearing an old gardening shirt and corduroy trousers.

All three carried the boxes into the vicarage living-room. Agatha took out a few of the items. "My dear Mrs. Raisin," exclaimed Mrs. Bloxby, "are you sure? You could sell this stuff yourself for quite a bit of money. I don't mean the horse brasses, but the jugs are good and the farm-machinery pieces are genuine. This"—she held up a shiny instrument of torture—"is a genuine mole trap. You don't see many of those around today."

"No, I'll be happy if you get some money. But try to choose some charity which won't spend it all on cocktail parties or politics."

"Yes, of course. We're very keen on supporting Cancer Research and Save the Children," said the vicar. "Perhaps you would like a cup of coffee, Mrs. Raisin?"

"That would be nice."

"I'll leave my wife to look after you. I have Sunday's sermons to prepare."

"Sermons?"

"I preach in three churches."

"Why not use the same sermon for all?"

"Tempting, but it would hardly show a sign of caring for the parishioners."

The vicar retreated to the nether regions and his wife went off to the kitchen to make coffee. Agatha looked about her. The vicarage must be very old indeed, she thought. The window-frames sloped and the floor sloped. Here was no fitted carpet such as she had in her own cottage but old floor-boards polished like black glass and covered in the centre by a brightly coloured Persian rug. Logs smouldered in the cavernous fireplace. There was a bowl of pot-pourri on one small table. A vase of flowers stood on another, and there was a bowl of hyacinths at the low window. The chairs were worn, with—Agatha shifted her bottom experimentally—feather cushions. In front of her was a new coffee-table of the kind you buy in Do-It-Yourself stores and put together, and yet, covered as it was with newspapers and magazines, and the beginnings of a tapestry cushion-cover, it blended in with the rest of the room. Above her head were low beams black with age and centuries of smoke. There was a faint smell of lavender and

66

wood-smoke mixed with the smells of hyacinths and pot-pourri.

Also, there was an air of comfort and *goodness* about the place. Agatha decided that the Reverend Bloxby was a rare bird in the much-maligned aviary of the Church of England—a man who believed what he preached. For the first time since she had arrived in Carsely, she felt unthreatened and, as the door opened, and the vicar's wife appeared, filled with a desire to please.

"I've toasted some teacakes as well," said Mrs. Bloxby. "It's still so cold. I do get tired of keeping the fires burning. But of course you have central heating, so you don't have that problem."

"You have a beautiful home," said Agatha.

"Thank you. Milk and sugar?" Mrs. Bloxby had a small, delicate, lined face and brown hair threaded with grey. She was slim and fragile with long, delicate hands, the sort of hands that portrait painters used to love to give their subjects.

"And how are you settling in, Mrs. Raisin?"

"Not very well," said Agatha. "I may have to settle *out?*"

"Oh, because of your quiche," said Mrs. Bloxby tran-quilly. "Do try a teacake. I make them myself and it is one of the few things I do well. Yes, a horrible affair. Poor Mr. Cummings-Browne."

"People must think I am a dreadful person," said Agatha.

"Well, it was unfortunate that wretched quiche should have cowbane in it. But a lot of cheating goes on in these village affairs. You're not the first."

Agatha sat with a teacake dripping butter and stared at the vicar's wife. "I'm not?"

"No, no. Let me see, there was Miss Tenby five years ago. An incomer. Set her heart on winning the flower-arranging competition. She ordered a basket of flowers from the florist over at St. Anne's. Quite blatant about it. It was a very pretty display but the neighbours had seen the florist's van arriving and so she was found out. Then there was old Mrs. Carter. *She* bought her strawberry jam and put her own label on it and

67

won. No one would ever have known if she had not got drunk in the Red Lion and bragged about it. Yes, your deception would have occasioned quite a lot of comment in the village, Mrs. Raisin, had it not all happened before, or, for that matter, if the judging had been fair."

"Do you mean Mr. Cummings-Browne cheated?"

Mrs. Bloxby smiled. "Let us say he was apt to give prizes to favourites."

"But if this was generally known, why do the villagers bother to enter anything at all?"

"Because they are proud of what they make and like to show it off to their friends. Besides, Mr. Cummings-Browne judged competitions in neighbouring villages and it is estimated he had only one favourite in each. Also, there is no disgrace in losing. Alf often wanted to change the judge, but the Cummings-Brownes did give quite a lot to charity and the one year Alf was successful and got someone else to judge, the judge gave the prize to his sister, who did not even live in the village."

Agatha let out a long slow breath. "You make me feel less of a villain."

"It was all very sad. You must have had a frightful time."

To Agatha's horror, her eyes filled with tears and she dabbed at them fiercely while the vicar's wife looked tactfully away.

"But be assured"—the vicar's wife addressed the coffee-pot—"that your deception did not occasion all that much comment. Besides, Mr. Cummings-Browne was not popular."

"Why?"

The vicar's wife looked evasive. "Some people are not, you know."

Agatha leaned forward. "Do you think it was an accident?"

"Oh, yes, for if it were not, then one would naturally suspect the wife, but Vera Cummings-Browne was a most devoted wife, in her way. She has a great deal of money and he had very little. They have no children. She could have walked off and left him any time at all. I had to help comfort her on the day of her husband's death. I have never seen a woman more grief-stricken. It is best to put the whole matter behind you, Mrs. Raisin. The Carsely Ladies' Society meets tonight here at the vicarage at eight o'clock. Do come along."

"Thank you," said Agatha humbly.

"Have you got rid of that dreadful woman?" asked the vicar ten minutes later when his wife walked into his study.

"Yes. I don't think she's really so bad and she is genuinely suffering about the quiche business. I've invited her to the women's get-together tonight."

"Then thank goodness I won't be here," said the vicar and bent over his sermon.

Agatha felt cleansed of sin as she drove back to her cottage. She would go to church on Sunday and she would try to be a good person. She put a Linda McCartney's frozen Ploughman's Pie in the microwave for Mrs. Simpson's lunch, hoping the ex-Beatle's wife knew about cooking but wondering whether she had just sold her name to be used on the product.

Mrs. Simpson picked at the hot mess tentatively with her fork and all Agatha's saintliness evaporated. "It's not poisoned," she snapped.

"It's just I don't much care for frozen stuff," said Mrs. Simpson.

"Well, I'll get you something better next time. Was Mrs. Cummings-Browne very upset about the death of her husband?"

"Oh, dreadful it was," said Doris Simpson. "Real shook, her were. Numb with shock at first and then crying and crying. Had to fetch the vicar's wife to help."

Guilt once more settled on Agatha's soul. She felt she had to get out. She walked to the Red Lion and ordered a glass of red wine and sausage and chips.

Then she remembered her intention of calling on Mrs.

Cartwright. It all seemed a bit pointless now but it was something to do.

Judd's Cottage where the Cartwrights lived was a broken-down sort of place. The garden gate was hanging on its hinges and in the weedy front garden was parked a rusting car. Agatha looked this way and that, wondering how the car had got in but could see no way it could have been achieved short of lifting it bodily over the fence.

The glass pane on the front door was cracked and stuck in place with brown paper tape. She rang the bell and nothing happened. She rapped at the side of the door. Mrs. Cartwright's blurred figure loomed up on the other side of the glass.

"Oh, it's you," she said when she opened the door. "Come in."

Agatha followed her into a sour-smelling cluttered living-room. The furniture was soiled and shiny with wear. There was a two-bar electric fire in the grate with imitation plastic coals on the top. A bunch of plastic daffodils hung over a chipped vase on the window. There was a cocktail cabinet in one corner ornamented with pink glass and strips of pink fluorescent lighting.

"Drink?" asked Mrs. Cartwright. Her coarse hair was wound up in pink foam rollers and she was wearing a pink wrap-over dress which gaped when she moved to reveal a dirty petticoat.

"Thank you," said Agatha, wishing she had not come.

Mrs. Cartwright poured two large glasses of gin and then tinged them pink with Angostura. Agatha looked nervously at her own glass, which was smeared with lipstick at the rim.

Mrs. Cartwright sat down and crossed her legs. Her feet were encased in dirty pink slippers. All this pink, thought Agatha nervously. She looks like some sort of debauched Barbara Cartland.

"Did you know Mr. Cummings-Browne well?" asked Agatha.

Mrs. Cartwright lit a cigarette and studied Agatha through the smoke. "A bit," she said.

"Did you like him?"

"Some. Can't think straight at the moment."

"Because of the death?"

"Because of the bingo over at Evesham. John, that's my husband, he's cut off my money on account he doesn't want me to go there. Men are right bastards. I brought up four kids and now they've left home and I want a bit o' fun, all he does is grumble. Yes, give me a bit o' money for the bingo and I can 'member most things."

Agatha fished in her handbag. "Would twenty pounds help?"

"Would it ever!"

Agatha passed the money over. Then there came the sound of the front door being opened. Mrs. Cartwright thrust the note down into her bosom, grabbed Agatha's glass and ran with that and her own to the kitchen.

"Ella?" called a man's voice.

The door opened and a strongly built apelike man walked in just as his wife came back from the kitchen. "Who's she?" he demanded, jerking a thumb at Agatha. "I told you not to let them Jehovahs in."

"This is Mrs. Raisin from down Lilac Lane, called social-like."

"What do you want?" he snarled.

Agatha stood up. Mrs. Cartwright's large dark eyes flashed a warning. "I am collecting for charity," said Agatha.

"Then you can bugger off. Haven't got a penny to spare. *She's* seen to that."

"Sit down, John, and shut up. I'll see Mrs. Raisin out."

Agatha nervously edged past John Cartwright. Mrs. Cartwright opened the front door. "Come tomorrow," she whispered. "Three in the afternoon."

Was there some sinister mystery or had she just been conned out of twenty pounds? Agatha walked thoughtfully down the road.

71

When she got back to her cottage, Mrs. Simpson was hard at work in the bedrooms. Agatha washed a load of clothes and carried them out to the back garden where there was one of those whirligig devices for hanging clothes. Feeling more relaxed than she had for some time and quite domesticated, Agatha pinned out the clothes. As she moved around to the other side of the whirligig, she saw Mrs. Barr. She was leaning on her garden fence, staring straight at Agatha with a look of cold dislike on her face. Agatha finished pinning the clothes, raised two fingers at Mrs. Barr and went indoors.

"Post came," shouted Mrs. Simpson from upstairs. "I put it on the kitchen table."

Agatha noticed a flat brown envelope for the first time. She tore it open. There was a large print of the woman on the tower at Warwick Castle. Agatha shuddered. Those staring eyes, that hatred reminded her of Mrs. Barr. Pinned to the enlargement was a note: "Thank you for a splendid weekend, Steve."

She put the photograph away in the kitchen drawer, feeling even after she had closed the drawer that those eyes were still staring at her.

Overcome by the need for some escapist literature, she drove down to Moreton-in-Marsh, swearing under her breath as she remembered it was market day. By driving round and round the car-park, she was able to secure a place when some shopper drove off.

Walking through the Old Market Place, as the new mini shopping arcade was called, she crossed the road and walked between the crowded stalls to the row of shops on the far side where she knew there was a second-hand bookshop. In the back room were rows and rows of paperbacks. She bought three detective stories—one Ruth Rendell, one Colin Dexter, and one Colin Watson—and then returned to her car. She flipped open the Colin Watson one and was caught by the first page. Oh, the joys of detective fiction. Time rolled past as Agatha sat in the car-park and read steadily. Finally it dawned on her that it was ridiculous to sit reading in a car-park when

she had the comfort of her own home and so drove back to
Carsely just in time to meet Bill Wong, who was standing on
her doorstep.

"Now what?" demanded Agatha uneasily.

Bill smiled. "Just called to see how you were."

At first Agatha felt gratified as she unlocked the door and
let herself in, picking up the other key from the kitchen floor
where it had fallen when Mrs. Simpson had popped it through
the letter-box. Then she felt a twinge of unease. Could Bill
Wong be checking up on her for any reason?

"Coffee?" she asked.

"Tea will do." In the sitting-room, Bill looked slowly
around. "Where did all the bits and pieces go?"

"I didn't think they were *me*," said Agatha, "so I gave
them to the church to sell for charity."

"What is *you* if toby jugs and farm machinery are not?"

"Don't know," mumbled Agatha. "Something a bit more
homy."

"The lighting's wrong," said Bill, looking at the spot-
lights on the beams. "Spots are out."

"You sound like someone talking about acne," snapped
Agatha. "And why is everyone suddenly so arty-farty about
interior decoration these days?"

"Ah, your friends who came at the weekend, the prancing
one and the one with the cowboy boots?"

"You've been spying on me!"

"Not I. I was off duty and took a girl-friend to Bourton-
on-the-Water. A great mistake. I'd forgotten about the holiday crowds."

"I can't imagine you having a girl-friend."

"Oh! Why?"

"I don't know. I always imagine you as never being off
duty."

"In any case," said Bill, "I hope you haven't decided to
become the Miss Marple of Carsely and are still trying to
prove accident as murder."

Agatha opened her mouth to tell him about Mrs. Cartwright and then decided against it. He would criticize her for interfering and he would point out, probably correctly, that Mrs. Cartwright had nothing to tell and was simply out for money.

Instead she said, "An odd thing happened at Warwick Castle. Steve, the young man with the cowboy boots, took a video film of me and Roy, that's the other young man, on the top of one of the towers. He showed the video on television in the evening and there on the tower was this woman glaring at me with hatred."

"Interesting. But you could have jostled her on the stairs or trod on her foot."

"He took a photograph from the television set and it's quite clear, and we were talking about the death when he filmed. Would you like to see it?"

"Yes, might be someone I know."

Agatha brought in the print and handed it to him. He studied it carefully. "No one I've seen before," he said, "but if you took that nasty look off her face, she would look like hundreds of other women in the Cotswold villages: thin, spinsterish, wispy hair, indeterminate features, false teeth . . ."

"How do you know about the false teeth, Sherlock?"

"You can always tell by the drooping corners of the mouth and by the way the jaw sags. Mind if I keep this?"

"Why?" demanded Agatha.

"Because I might find out who it is and do you a favour by revealing to you that Miss Prim here was merely offended by your friends or perhaps you reminded her of someone she hated in her past and then you can be easy."

"That is kind of you," said Agatha gruffly. "I'm beginning to get edgy what with her next door glaring at me over the garden fence because I took her char away."

"I wouldn't worry about her. Taking someone's cleaning woman away is like mugging them. The trouble with business women like yourself, Mrs. Raisin, is that your normally very active brain has nothing left to feed on but trivia. After a few

74

months, believe me, you will settle down and get involved in good works."

"Heaven forbid," said Agatha with a shudder.

"Why? Had I suggested bad works, would you have been pleased?"

"I'm going to a meeting of the Carsely Ladies' Society at the vicarage tonight," said Agatha.

"That should be fun," said Bill with his eyes twinkling. "And now I'd better go. I'm on late duty."

After a meal at the Red Lion—giant sausage and chips liberally doused with ketchup—Agatha walked to the vicarage and rang the bell. From inside came the hum of voices. She felt suddenly nervous and yes, a little timid.

Mrs. Bloxby answered the door. "Come in, Mrs. Raisin. Most people have arrived." She led Agatha into the sitting-room, where about fifteen women were seated about. They stopped talking and looked curiously at Agatha. "I'll introduce you," said Mrs. Bloxby. Agatha tried to remember the names but they kept sliding out of her mind as soon as each was announced. Mrs. Bloxby offered Agatha tea, cakes and sandwiches. Agatha helped herself to a cucumber sandwich.

"Now, if we are all ready," said Mrs. Bloxby, "our chairwoman, Mrs. Mason, will begin. The floor is yours, Mrs. Mason."

Mrs. Mason, a large woman in a purple nylon dress and large white shoes like canoes, surveyed the room. "As you know, ladies, our old people in the village do not get out much. I am appealing to any of you with cars to step in and volunteer to take some of them on an outing when you can manage it. I will read out the names of the old people and volunteer if you can manage some free time."

There seemed to be no shortage of volunteers as Mrs. Mason went through a list in her hand. Agatha looked around at the other women. There was something strangely old-fashioned about them with their earnest desire to help. All were middle-aged apart from a thin, pale-looking girl in her twenties who was seated next to Agatha. "Ain't got no car," she whispered to Agatha. "Can hardly take them on me bike."

"And now," said Mrs. Mason, "last but not least, we have old Mr. and Mrs. Boggle at Culloden."

There was a long silence. The fire behind Mrs. Mason's ample figure crackled cheerfully, spoons clinked against teacups, jaws munched. No volunteers.

"Come now, ladies. Mr. and Mrs. Boggle would love a trip somewhere. Needn't be too far. Even just into Evesham and around the shops."

Agatha thought she felt the vicar's wife's eyes resting on her. Her voice sounded odd in her own ears as she heard herself saying, "I'll take them. Would Thursday be all right?"

Did she sense a feeling of relief in the room? "Why, thank you, Mrs. Raisin. How very good of you. Perhaps you do not know the village very well, but Culloden is number 28, Moreton Road, on the council estate. Shall we say nine o'clock on Thursday, and I shall take it on myself to tell Mr. and Mrs. Boggle?"

Agatha nodded.

"Good. They will be *so* pleased. Now, as you know, next week we are to be hosted by the Mircester Ladies' Society and they have promised us an exciting time. I will pass around a book and sign your names in it if you wish to go. Retford Bus Company is giving us a bus for the day."

The book was passed round. After some hesitation, Agatha signed her name. It would be something to do.

"Right," said Mrs. Mason. "The coach will leave from outside here at eleven in the morning. I am sure we will all be awake by that time." Dutiful laughter. "And so I will get our secretary, Miss Simms, to read out the minutes of your last meeting in case any of you missed it.

To Agatha's surprise, the young girl next to her rose and went to face the company. In a droning nasal voice she read out the minutes. Agatha stifled a yawn. Then the treasurer gave a lengthy report of money raised at the last fête in aid of Cancer Research.

Agatha was nearly asleep when she heard her own name. The treasurer had been replaced by Mrs. Bloxby. "Yes," said the vicar's wife, "when our new member, Mrs. Raisin, came with boxes and boxes of stuff and gave them all away to be sold for charity, I thought I would show you some of the items. I think they warrant a special sale."

Agatha felt gratified as oohs and ahs greeted the toby jugs and bits of burnished farm machinery. "Reckon I'd buy some o' that meself," said one of the women.

"I am glad you share my enthusiasm," said Mrs. Bloxby. "I suggest we should take the school hall for the tenth of June, that's a Saturday, and put these items on display. The week before the sale, we will have a special pricing meeting. That will also give us time to find some extra items. Mrs. Mason, can I ask you to run the tea-room as usual?"

Mrs. Mason nodded.

"Mrs. Raisin, perhaps you might like to take command of the main stall?"

"Tell you what," said Agatha. "I'll auction them. I'll be auctioneer. People always pay more when they are bidding against each other."

"What a good idea. All in favour?" Hands were raised.

"Excellent. The money will go to Save the Children. Perhaps, if we are lucky, some of the local papers might put in an item."

"I'll see to that," said Agatha, feeling better by the minute. This was like old times.

Her happiness was dimmed when the business was over; and the women were gathering up their coats and handbags when Miss Simms nudged her and said, "Better you than me."

"You mean the auction?"

"Naw, them Boggles. Grouchiest old miseries this side o' Gloucester."

But somehow Mrs. Bloxby was there and had heard the remark. She smiled into Agatha's eyes and said, "What a good deed to give the Boggles an outing. Old Mrs. Boggle has bad arthritis. It will mean so very much to them."

77

Agatha felt weak and childlike before the simple, uncomplicated goodness in Mrs. Bloxby's eyes and filled again with that desire to please.

And the women as they were leaving spoke to her of this and that and not one mentioned quiche.

With a feeling of belonging, Agatha walked home. Lilac Lane was beginning to live up to its name. Lilac trees, heavy with blossom, scented the evening air. Wisteria hung in purple profusion over cottage doors.

Must do something about my own garden, thought Agatha.

She unlocked and opened her front door and switched on the light. One sheet of paper lay on the doormat, the message scrawled on it staring up at her: "Stop nosey-parking, you innerfering old bich."

Picking it up with the tips of her fingers, Agatha stared at it in dismay. For the first time she realized how very quiet the village was in the evening. She was surrounded by silence, a silence that seemed ominous, full of threat.

She dropped the note into the rubbish bin and went up to bed, taking the brass poker with her, propping it up by the bedside where she could reach it easily.

Old houses creak and sigh as they settle down for the night. For a long time Agatha lay awake, starting at every sound, until she suddenly fell asleep, one hand resting on the knob of the poker.

SIX

†

THE next morning, the rough winds were shaking the darling buds of May. Sunlight streamed in Agatha's windows. It was a day of movement and bright, sharp, glittering colour. She took the threatening note out of the rubbish. Why not show this to Bill Wong? What did it mean? She had not been doing any investigating to speak of. But he would ask a lot of questions and she might slip up and tell him of her visit to Mrs. Cartwright and that Mrs. Cartwright had told her to call again.

She smoothed out the note and tucked it in with the cookery books. Perhaps she should keep it just in case.

After breakfast, there was a knock at her door. She had a little scared feeling it might be Mrs. Barr. Damn the woman! She was nothing but a warped middle-aged frump, and such should not cause a stalwart such as Agatha Raisin any trouble at all.

But it was Mrs. Bloxby who stood there, and behind her, to Agatha's dismay, Vera Cummings-Browne.

"May we come in?" asked Mrs. Bloxby.

Agatha led the way into the kitchen, bracing herself for tears and recriminations. Mrs. Bloxby refused Agatha's offer of coffee and said, "Mrs. Cummings-Browne has something to say to you."

Vera Cummings-Browne addressed the table-top rather than Agatha. "I have been most distressed, most upset about the death of my husband, Mrs. Raisin. But I am now in a calmer frame of mind. I do not blame you for anything. It was an accident, a strange and unfortunate accident." She raised her eyes. "You see, I have always believed that when one dies, it is *meant*. It could have been a car driven by a drunken driver which mounted the pavement. It could have been a piece of fallen masonry. The police pathologist felt that Reg could have survived the accidental poisoning had he been stronger. But he had high blood pressure and his heart was bad. So be it."

"I am so very sorry," said Agatha weakly. "How very generous of you to call on me."

"It was my Christian duty," said Mrs. Cummings-Browne.

Behind the mask of her face, which Agatha hoped was registering sorrow, sympathy, and concern, her mind was rattling away at a great rate. "So be it . . . Christian duty?" How very *stagy*. But then Mrs. Cummings-Browne buried her face in her hands and wept, gasping through her sobs, "Oh, Reg, I do miss you so. Oh, Reg!"

Mrs. Bloxby led the weeping Mrs. Cummings-Browne out. No, thought Agatha, the woman was genuinely broken up. Mrs. Cummings-Browne had forgiven her. All Agatha had to do was to get on with life and forget about the whole thing.

She set about phoning up the editors of local newspapers to raise publicity for the auction. Local editors were used to timid, pleading approaches from ladies of the parish. Never before had they experienced anything like Agatha Raisin on the other end of the phone. Alternately bullying and wheedling, she left them with a feeling that something only a little short of the crown jewels was going to be auctioned. All promised to send reporters, knowing they would have to keep their word, for Agatha threatened each that she would phone on the morning of the auction to see if they had indeed dispatched someone.

That passed the morning happily. But by the afternoon and after a snack of Farmer Giles' Steak and Kidney Pie ("Suitable for Microwaves"), Agatha found her steps leading her in the direction of the Cartwrights'.

Mrs. Cartwright answered the door herself, her hair back in pink rollers, her body in a pink dressing-gown.

"Come in," she said. "Drink?"

Agatha nodded. Pink gin again. Where had Mrs. Cartwright learned to drink pink gins? she wondered suddenly. Surely Babycham and brandy, lager and lime, rum and Coke would have been more to her taste.

"How was bingo?" asked Agatha.

"Not a penny," said Mrs. Cartwright bitterly. "But tonight's my lucky night. I saw two magpies in the garden this morning."

Agatha reflected that as magpies were a protected species, one saw the wretched black-and-white things everywhere. Surely it would have been more of a surprise if Mrs. Cartwright had not seen any magpies at all.

"I wanted to know about Mr. Cummings-Browne," said Agatha.

"What, for example?" Mrs. Cartwright narrowed her eyes against the rising smoke from the cigarette she held in one brown hand.

From the living-room where they sat, Agatha could see through to the cluttered messy kitchen—hardly the kitchen of a dedicated baker.

"Well, as you won the prize year after year, I thought you might have known him pretty well," she said.

"As much as I know anyone in the village." Mrs. Cartwright took a slug of her gin.

"Do you bake a lot?"

"Naw. Used to. Occasionally do some baking for Mrs. Bloxby. Terrible woman she is. Can't say no to her. Come in the kitchen and I'll show you."

Dirty dishes were piled in the sink. A tattered calendar showing a picture of a blonde in nothing but a wisp of gauze and sandals leered down from the wall. But on a cleared corner of the kitchen table beside the half-empty milk bottle, the pat of butter smeared with marmalade, lay a tray of delicate fairy cakes. They looked exquisite. There was no doubt Mrs. Cartwright could bake.

"So I'd make a quiche and get a tenner for it," said Mrs. Cartwright. "Silly waste of time if you ask me. My husband doesn't like quiche. Used to make them for the Harveys and they'd sell them down at the shop for me. Went well, too. But I can't seem to find the time these days." She tottered back to the living-room in her pink high-heeled mules.

Agatha decided to get down to some hard business. "I paid you twenty pounds for information yesterday," she said bluntly, "information which I have not yet received."

"I spent it."

"Yes, but how you spent it or what you spent it on is not my affair," snapped Agatha.

Mrs. Cartwright put a finger to her brow. "Now what was it? Dammit, my bloody memory's gone wandering again."

Her eyes gleamed darkly as Agatha fished in her capacious handbag. Agatha held up a twenty. "No, you don't," she said as Mrs. Cartwright reached for it. "Information first. Is your husband liable to come in?"

"No, he's up at Martin's farm. He works there."

"So what have you got to tell me?"

"I was surprised," said Mrs. Cartwright, "when Mr. Cummings-Browne died."

"Oh, weren't we all," commented Agatha sarcastically.

"I mean, I thought *he* would've murdered *her*."

"What, why?"

"He spoke to me a bit. People are always telling me their troubles. It's because I'm the maternal type." Mrs. Cartwright yawned, reached inside her dressing-gown and scratched one of her generous bosoms. A smell of sour sweat came to Agatha's nostrils and she thought inconsequently how rare it was

82

to meet a really dirty woman in these hygienic days. "Couldn't stand Vera, Reg couldn't. She held the purse-strings and he said she made him jump through hoops or sit up and beg just to get some drinking money. The only money he had of his own was his pension and that didn't go very far. He used to say to me, 'Ella,' he'd say, 'one day I'm going to wring that woman's neck and be rid of her for once and for all.' "

Agatha looked bewildered. "But he died, not her!"

"Maybe she got there first. She hated him."

"But I had dinner with the pair of them and they seemed quite a devoted couple; in fact, quite alike."

"Naw, you could have a laugh with Reg, but Mrs. Snobby was always turning her nose up at me. That was no accident. That was murder."

"But how could she do it? I mean, it was my quiche."

"Dunno, but I feel it here." Mrs. Cartwright struck her bosom and another waft of sweat floated across to Agatha's nostrils.

"Mrs. Cartwright called on me this morning," said Agatha firmly, "and forgave me. But she was broken up about her husband's death, quite genuinely so."

"She acts in the Carsely Dramatic Society," said Mrs. Cartwright cynically, "and bloody good she is, too. Right little actress."

"No," said Agatha stubbornly. "I know when people are being straight with me, and you are not one of those people, Mrs. Cartwright."

"Told you what I know." Mrs. Cartwright stared at the twenty-pound note, which Agatha still held in her hand.

The broken gate outside creaked and Agatha started nervously. She did not want another confrontation with John Cartwright. She thrust the note at Mrs. Cartwright. "Look," she said urgently, "you know where to find me. If there's anything at all you can tell me, let me know."

"I certainly will," said Mrs. Cartwright, looking happy now that she had the money in her possession.

Agatha was just leaving by stepping round the broken

83

garden gate when she saw John Cartwright lumbering down the road. She hurried on, but he had seen her. He caught up with her and roughly seized her arm and swung her round. "You've been snooping around about Cummings-Browne," he snarled. "Ella told me. I'm telling you for the last time, you go near her again and I'll break your neck. That fart Cummings-Browne got what was coming to him and so will you."

Agatha wrenched her arm free and hurried on, her face flaming. She went straight home and put the threatening note in an envelope along with a letter and addressed it to Detective Constable Wong at Mircester Police Station. She felt sure now that John Cartwright had written that note.

As she approached her cottage, she saw a couple arriving at New Delhi, Mrs. Barr's house. They turned and stared at her. They looked vaguely familiar. With a wrench of memory, Agatha realized they had been among the other diners in the Horse and Groom that evening when she had been discussing the "murder" with Roy and Steve.

She went into her own cottage and stood in her sitting-room, looking about her. She had never furnished anything in her life before, living as she had in a succession of furnished rooms until she made her first real money, and then renting a furnished flat and finally buying one, but that too had been furnished, for she had bought the contents as well.

She screwed up her eyes and tried to visualize what she would like but no ideas came except that the three-piece suite annoyed her. She wanted something more in the lines of the vicarage living-room. Well, antiques could be bought, and that was as good a reason as any to get out of Carsely for the remainder of the day.

She drove to Cheltenham Spa and after cruising about that town's irritating and baffling one-way system until she got her bearings, she stopped a passer-by and asked where she could buy antique furniture. She was directed to a network of streets behind Montpelier Terrace. She drove there and managed to find a parking space in a private parking lot outside someone's house. Her first good find was in an old

84

cinema now used as a furniture warehouse. She bought an old high-backed wing armchair in soft green leather and a Chesterfield sofa with basketwork and soft dull-green cushions. Then, to the increasing delight of the salesman, who had feared it was going to be a slow day, she also bought a wide Victorian fruitwood chair, running her fingers appreciatively over the carving. She paid for the lot without a blink and said she would pick them up after the tenth of June. Agatha now planned to amaze the village by adding her living-room furniture to the sale. Two elegant lamps caught her eye as she was leaving and she purchased them as well. Agatha remembered when she was at school, she had vowed that when she had her first pay cheque, she would walk into a sweet-shop and buy all the chocolate she wanted. But by the time that happened, her desires had focused on a pair of purple high-heeled shoes with bows. She enjoyed having enough money to enable her to buy what she wanted.

Then, before she left Cheltenham, she went to Marks and Spencer and bought giant prawns in garlic butter and a packet of lasagne, both of which she could cook in the microwave. It was still not her own cooking, but a cut above what she could get at the village shop.

Later, after a good meal, she settled down to read a detective story, wondering idly whether she should take the television set up to the bedroom. The vicarage living-room did not boast a television set.

It was only when she was preparing for bed that she remembered the Boggles with a sinking heart. With any luck, they would not expect her to drive them about all day.

In the morning, she presented herself at the Boggles's home. Why Culloden? Were they Scottish?

But Mr. Boggle was a small, spry, wrinkled man with a Gloucestershire accent and his wife, an old creaking harridan, was undoubtedly Welsh.

Agatha waited for either of the pair to say it was very kind of her, or to evince any sign of gratitude, but they both

85

climbed into the back seat and Mr. Boggle said, "We're going to Bath."

Bath! Agatha had been hoping for somewhere nearer, like Evesham.

"It's quite a bit away," she protested.

Mrs. Boggle jabbed her in the shoulder with one horny forefinger. "You said you was takin' us out, so take us."

Agatha fished out her road atlas. The easiest would be to get on the Fosse Way to Cirencester and then on to Bath.

She heaved a sigh. It was a glorious day. Summer was edging its way into England. Hawthorn flowers were heavy with scent, pink and white along the winding road out of Carsely. On either side of the Fosse Way, obviously a Roman road, for it runs straight as an arrow up steep hills and down the other side, lay fields of oilseed rape, bright yellow, Van-Gogh yellow, looking too vulgarly bright among the gentler colours of the English countryside. Queen Anne's lace frothed along the roadside. There was no sound from the passengers in the back. Agatha began to feel more cheerful. Perhaps her ancient passengers would be content to go off on their own in Bath.

But in Bath, Agatha's troubles started. The Boggles pointed out that they had no intention of walking from any car-park to the Pump Room where, it appeared, they meant to "take the waters." It was Agatha's duty to drive them there and then go and park the car herself. She sweated her way round the one-way system, congested with traffic, trying to turn a deaf ear to Mr. Boggle's comments of "Not a very good driver, are you?"

"Well?" demanded Mrs. Boggle when they had reached the colonnaded entrance to the Pump Room. "Aren't you going to help a body out?"

Mrs. Boggle was small and round, dressed in a tweed coat and a long scarf that seemed to be inextricably wound around the seat-belt. She smelt very strongly of cheap scent. "Stop pushin' me. You're hurtin' me," she grumbled as Agatha tried to release her from bondage. Her husband elbowed Agatha

86

aside, produced a pair of nail scissors and hacked through the scarf. "Now look what you've done," moaned Mrs. Boggle.

"Quit your frettin', woman," said Mr. Boggle. He jerked a thumb at Agatha. "Her'll buy you another one."

Like hell, thought Agatha when she finally parked near the bus station. She deliberately took a long time returning to the Pump Room, an hour, in fact. She found the Boggles in the tea-room beside an empty coffee-pot and plates covered in cake crumbs.

"So you've finally decided to show up," said Mr. Boggle, handing her the bill. "You're a fine one."

"The trouble is, no one don't care nothing about old folks these days. All they want is discos and drugs," said Mrs. Boggle. They both stared fiercely at Agatha.

"Have you taken the waters yet?" asked Agatha.

"Going to now," said Mrs. Boggle. "Help me up."

Agatha raised her to her feet, gagging slightly at the wafts of cheap scent and old body. The Boggles drank cups of sulphurous water. "Do you want to see the Roman Baths?" asked Agatha, remembering Mrs. Bloxby and determined to please. "I haven't seen them."

"Well, we've seen them scores of times," whined Mrs. Boggle. "We wants to go to Polly Perkin's Pantry."

"What's that?"

"That's where we's having dinner."

The Boggles belonged to that generation which still took dinner in the middle of the day.

"It's only ten to twelve," pointed out Agatha, "and you've just had coffee and cakes."

"But you've got to go and get the car," said Mr. Boggle. "Pantry's up in Monmouth Road. Can't expect us to walk there. No consideration."

The idea of a short break from the Boggles while she got the car prompted Agatha to accept her orders docilely. Again she took her time, returning to pick up the Boggles at one o'clock and ignoring their cries and complaints that Mrs. Boggle's joints were stiffening with all the waiting.

No one could accuse Agatha Raisin of having a delicate or refined palate, but she had a sharp eye for a rip-off and as soon as she sat down with the horrible pair in Polly Perkins' Pantry, she wondered if they were soul mates of the Cummings-Brownes. Waitresses dressed in laced bodices and mob caps flitted about at great speed, therefore being able to ignore all the people trying to get served.

The menu was expensive and written in that twee kind of prose which irritated Agatha immensely. The Boggles wanted Beau Nash cod fritters to start—"sizzling and golden, on a bed of fresh, crunchy lettuce"—followed by Beau Brummell escalopes of veal—"tender and mouth-watering, with a white wine sauce and sizzling aubergine sticks, tender new carrots, and succulent green peas." "And a bottle of champagne," said Mr. Boggle.

"I'm not made of money," protested Agatha hotly.

"Champagne's good for my arthuritis," quavered Mrs. Boggle. "Not often we gets a treat, but if you' goin' to count every penny . . ."

Agatha caved in. Get them sozzled and they might sleep on the way home.

The waitresses were now grouped in a corner by the till, chatting and laughing. Agatha rose and marched over to them. "I have no intention of waiting for service. Get a move on," she snarled. "I want cheerful and polite and *fast* service *now*. And don't give me those looks of dumb insolence. Jump to it!"

A now surly waitress followed Agatha over to her table and took the order. The champagne was warm when it arrived. Agatha cracked. She rose to her feet and glared at the pale, shy English faces of the other diners. "Why do you sit there and put up with this dreadful service?" she howled. "You're *paying* for it, dammit."

"You're right," called a meek-looking little man. "I've been here for half an hour and no one's come near this table."

Cries of rage and frustration rose from the other diners. The manager was hurriedly summoned from some office abovestairs. An ice bucket was produced like lightning. "On the house," muttered the manager, bending over Agatha. Waitresses flew backwards and forwards, serving the customers this time, long skirts swinging, outraged bosoms heaving under laced bodices, mob caps nodding.

"They'll be worn out by the time they get home," said Agatha with a grin. "Never moved so much in all their lives."

Mrs. Boggle speared a cod fritter and popped the whole thing in her mouth. "We've never 'ad trouble afore," she said through a spray of codflakes. "Have we, Benjamin?"

"No, people respect *us*," said Mr. Boggle.

Agatha opened her mouth to blast the horrible pair when Mr. Boggle added, "Were you one o' his fancy women?"

She looked at him dumbfounded.

"Who?"

"Reg Cummings-Browne, him what you poisoned."

"I didn't poison him," roared Agatha and then dropped her voice as the other diners stared. "It was an accident. And what the hell makes you think I was having an affair with Cummings-Browne?"

"You was seen up at Ella Cartwright's. Like to like, I allus say."

"You mean Mrs. Cartwright was having an affair with Cummings-Browne?"

"Course. Everybody knew that, 'cept her husband."

"How long had this been going on?"

"Dunno. Must have gone off her, though, for he was arter some bit in Ancombe, or so I heard."

"So Cummings-Browne *was* a philanderer," said Agatha.

Enlivened by champagne, Mr. Boggle suddenly giggled. "Got his leg over half the county, if you ask me."

Agatha's mind raced. She remembered having dinner with the Cummings-Brownes. She remembered Mrs. Cartwright's name being mentioned and the sudden stillness between the pair. Then there were those sobbing women at the inquest.

"O' course," said Mrs. Boggle suddenly, "we all knew it was you that was meant to be poisoned, if anyone."

"Why would anyone want to poison me?" demanded Agatha.

"Look what you did to Mrs. Barr. Lured Mrs. Simpson away from her with promises of gold. Heard Mrs. Barr down in Harvey's talking about it."

"Don't try to tell me that Mrs. Barr would try to poison me because I took her cleaning woman away."

"Why not? Reckon her has a point. Said you brought down the tone of the village."

"Are you usually so rude to people who give up a day to take you out?" asked Agatha.

"I tell it like it is," said Mrs. Boggle proudly.

Agatha was about to retort angrily when she remembered herself saying exactly the same thing on several occasions. Instead she said, after they had demolished their main course, "Do you want any pudding?"

Silly question. Of course they wanted pudding. Prince Regent fudge cake with ice cream—"devilishly good."

Agatha's mind returned to the problem of Cummings-Browne's death. Mr. Cummings-Browne had been a judge at competitions in other villages. He had had favourites. Had those favourites been his mistresses? And what of the burning animosity of Mrs. Barr? Was it all because of Mrs. Simpson? Or did Mrs. Barr enter home-baking, jam-making, or flower-arranging in the village competitions?

"Don't want coffee," Mrs. Boggle was saying. "Goes straight for me bowels."

Agatha paid the pill but did not leave a tip, free champagne or no free champagne.

"If you would both like to wait here," she said, "I'll get the car." Freedom from this precious pair was close at hand. Agatha felt quite cheerful as she brought the car round.

As she was heading out of Bath, Mrs. Boggle poked her in the shoulder. "Here! Where you going?"

"Home," said Agatha briefly.

90

"We wants to hear the band in the Parade Gardens," said Mr. Boggle. "What sort of a day out is it if you can't hear the band?"

Only the thought of Mrs. Bloxby's gentle face made Agatha turn the car round. The couple had to be deposited at the gardens while Agatha wearily parked the car again, a long way away, and then walked back. Deck chairs had to be found for the Boggles.

The sun shone, the band played its way through a seemingly endless repertoire as the afternoon wore on. Then the Boggles wanted afternoon tea at the Pump Room. Did they always eat so much? wondered Agatha. Or were they storing up food inside for some long hibernation before the next outing?

At last they allowed her to take them home. All went well until she reached the Fosse Way and again that horny finger prodded her back. "I have ter pee," said Mrs. Boggle.

"Can't you wait until I reach Bourton-on-the-Water or Stowe?" called Agatha over her shoulder. "Bound to be public toilets there."

"I gotta go *now*," wailed Mrs. Boggle.

Agatha pulled into the side of the road, bumping the car onto the grassy verge.

"You'd best help her," said Mr. Boggle.

Mrs. Boggle had to be led into a field and behind the shelter of some bushes. Mrs. Boggle produced toilet paper from her handbag. Mrs. Boggle needed help getting her knickers down, capacious pink cotton knickers with elastic at the knee.

It was all very stomach-churning for Agatha, who felt quite green when she finally shepherded her charge back to the car. It would be a cold day in hell, thought Agatha, before she ever let herself in for a day like this again.

She felt quite limp and weepy when she arrived outside Culloden. "Why Culloden?" she asked.

"When we bought our council house," said Mr. Boggle,

91

"we went down to the nursery where they sell house signs. I wanted Rose Cottage, but she wanted Culloden."

Agatha got out and heaved Mrs. Boggle onto the pavement beside her husband. Then she fairly leaped back into the driving seat and drove off with a frantic crunching of gears.

Detective Constable Wong was waiting on Agatha's doorstep.

"Out enjoying yourself?" he asked as Agatha let him into the house.

"I've had a hellish time," said Agatha, "and I don't want to talk about it. What brings, you here?"

He sat down at the kitchen table and spread out the anonymous letter. "Have you any idea who sent this?"

Agatha plugged in the electric kettle. "I thought it might be John Cartwright. He's been threatening me."

"And why should John Cartwright threaten you?"

Agatha looked shifty. "I called on his wife. He didn't seem to like it."

"And you were asking questions," said Bill.

"Well, do you know that Cummings-Browne was having an affair with Ella Cartwright?"

"Yes."

Agatha's eyes gleamed. "Well, there's a motive . . ."

"In desperately trying to prove this a murder, you are going to land into trouble. No one likes anyone poking into their private life. This note, now. It interests me. No finger-prints."

"Everyone knows about fingerprints," scoffed Agatha.

"And everyone also knows that if you do not have a criminal record, there is no way the police can trace you through your fingerprints. The police are not going to finger-print a whole village just because of one nasty letter. Then it was, I think, written by someone literate trying to sound semi-literate."

"How do you come by that?"

"Even in the broadest Gloucestershire dialect, interfering comes out sounding just that, not "innerfering." Might be

92

interferin' with the dropped g, but that's all. Also, strangely enough, everyone appears to know how to spell bitch. Apart from the Cartwrights, who else have you been questioning?"

"No one," said Agatha. "Except that I was discussing the murder in the Horse and Groom with my friends, and two friends of her next door were there."

"Not murder," he said patiently. "Accident. I'll keep this note. I haven't found anyone who recognizes the woman in your photograph. The reason I have called is to warn you, Agatha Raisin, not to go messing about in people's lives, or soon there might be a real-live murder, with you as the corpse!"

SEVEN

†

AGATHA'S figure, though stocky, had hitherto carried very little surplus fat. As she tried to fasten her skirt in the morning, she realized she had put on about an extra inch and a half around the waistline. In London, she had walked a lot, walking being quicker than sitting in a bus crawling through the traffic. But since she had come to Carsely, she had been using the car to go everywhere apart from short trips along the village. Carsely was not going to make Agatha Raisin let herself go!

She drove to a bicycle shop in Evesham and purchased a light, collapsible bicycle of the kind she could carry around in the boot of her car. She did not want to experiment cycling near the village until she felt she had remastered the knack. She had not cycled since the age of six.

She parked off the road next to one of the country walks, took out the little bicycle, and pushed it to the beginning of the grassy path. She mounted and wobbled off very nervously, climbed a small rise, and then, with a feeling of exhilaration, cruised downhill through pretty woods dappled with sunlight. After a few miles, she realized she was approaching the village, and with a groan, she turned back. Her well-shaped legs, although fairly sturdy with London walking, were not up to cycling the whole way back up the hill and so she got off and pushed. Clouds covered the sun very quickly and it began to rain, fine, soft, drenching rain.

In London, she could have gone into a bar or café and waited for the rain to stop, but there was nothing here but fields and woods and the steady drip of water from the trees above.

She thankfully reached her car and stowed away the bicycle. She was just moving off when a car passed her. She stared at it in amazement. Surely it was that rusting brown thing she had recently seen trapped in the Cartwrights' front garden. On impulse, she swung her own car round and set off in pursuit. Her quarry wound through narrow lanes, heading for Ancombe. Agatha tried to keep out of sight, but there were no other cars on the road. She could just make out that Mrs. Cartwright was driving the rusty car.

As Agatha approached Ancombe, she noticed large signs and arrows directing drivers to the ANCOMBE ANNUAL FAIR. Mrs. Cartwright appeared to be heading for it. Now there were other cars and Agatha let a mini get between her and Mrs. Cartwright.

Mrs. Cartwright parked her car in a large wet field. Agatha, ignoring a steward's waving arm, parked a good bit away. As abruptly as it had started, the rain stopped and the sun shone down. Feeling damp and creased, Agatha got out. There was no sign of Mrs. Cartwright. Her car, an old Ford Vauxhall, Agatha noted as she passed it, was empty.

Agatha walked towards the fair and paid the ten pence admission charge and an additional ten pence for a programme. She flicked through it until she found the Home-Baking Competition tent on the map in the centre.

Just as she was about to enter the tent, Agatha came face to face with Mrs. Cartwright. "What you doin' here?" demanded Mrs. Cartwright suspiciously.

"How did you get your car out of the garden?" asked Agatha.

"Push the fence over, drive off, push the fence up again.

Been like that for years, but will my John fix it? Nah. Why are you here?"

"I heard there was a fair on," said Agatha vaguely. "Are you entering anything?"

"Quiche," said Mrs. Cartwright laconically. She suddenly grinned. "Spinach quiche. Better prizes here than you get at Carsely."

"Think you'll win?"

"Bound to. Haven't any competition really."

"Did Mr. Cummings-Browne judge the home-baking here as well?"

"Nah. Dogs. Best of breed and all that. Look . . ." Mrs. Cartwright glanced furtively around. "Want a bit of info?"

"I've paid you forty pounds to date and I haven't yet got my money's worth," snapped Agatha. "And you can tell that husband of yours to stop threatening me."

"He's always threatening people and he thinks you're a nosy old tart. Still, if you don't want to know what went on at Ancombe . . . ."

She began to move away.

"Wait," said Agatha. "What can you tell me?"

Mrs. Cartwright's dark eyes rested greedily on Agatha's handbag.

Agatha clicked it open and took out her wallet. "Ten if I think it's worth it."

Mrs. Cartwright leaned forward. "The dog competition's always won by a Scottie."

"So?"

"And the woman who shows the Scotties is Barbara James from Combe Farm. At the inquest her were, and crying fit to bust."

"Are you saying . . . ?"

"Our Reg had to have a bit before he would favour someone year in and year out."

Agatha handed over ten pounds. She studied her programme. The dog judging was due to begin in an arena near the tent. When she looked up from her programme, Mrs. Cartwright had gone.

Agatha sat on a bench just outside the roped-off arena. She opened her programme again. The Best of Breed competition was to be judged by a Lady Waverton. She looked up. A stout woman in tweeds and a deerstalker was sitting on a shooting-stick, her large tweed-encased bottom hanging down on either side of it, studying the dogs as they were paraded past her. A fresh-faced woman of about thirty-five with curly brown hair and rosy cheeks was walking a Scotch terrier past Lady Waverton. Must be this Barbara James, thought Agatha.

It was all so boring, Agatha felt quite glassy-eyed. How nervous and pleading the contestants looked, like parents at prize-giving. Lady Waverton wrote something down on a piece of paper and a messenger ran with it to a platform, where a man seated on a chair was holding a microphone. "Attention, please," said the man. "The awards for Best of Breed are as follows. Third place, Mr. J. G. Feathers for his Sealyham, Pride of Moreton. Second, Mrs. Comley, for her otter hound, Jamesy Bright Eyes. And the first is . . ."

Barbara James picked up her Scottie and cuddled it and looked expectantly towards the two local newspaper photographers. "The first prize goes to Miss Sally Gentle for her poodle, Bubbles Daventry of the Fosse."

Miss Sally Gentle looked remarkably like her dog, having curly white hair dressed in bows. Barbara James strode from the arena, her face dark with fury.

Agatha rose to her feet and followed her. Barbara went straight to the beer tent. Agatha hovered in the background until the disappointed competitor had got herself a pint of beer. Agatha detested beer but she gamely ordered a half pint and joined Barbara at one of the rickety tables that were set about the beer tent.

Agatha affected surprise. "Why, it's Miss James," she cried. She leaned forward and patted the Scottie, who nipped her hand. "Playful, isn't he?" said Agatha, casting a look of loathing at the dog. "Such a good head. I was sure he would win."

"It's the first time in six years I've lost," said Barbara. She stretched her jodphurred legs moodily out in front of her and stared at her toe-caps.

Agatha fetched up a sigh. "Poor Mr. Cummings-Browne."

"Reg knew a good dog when he saw one," said Barbara. "Here, go on. Walkies." She put the dog down. It strolled over to the entrance to the tent and lifted its leg against a rubbish bin. "Did you know Reg?"

"Only slightly," said Agatha. "I had dinner with the Cummings-Brownes shortly before he died.

"It should never have happened," said Barbara. "That's the trouble with these Cotswold villages. Too many people from the cities coming to settle. Do you know how he died? Some bitch of a woman called Raisin bought a quiche and tried to pass it off at the competition as her own."

Agatha opened her mouth to admit she was that Mrs. Raisin when it started to rain again, suddenly, as if someone had switched on a tap. It was a long walk to where she had parked her car. A chill wind blew into the tent.

"Terrible," said Agatha feebly. "Did you know Mr. Cummings-Browne well?"

"We were very good friends. Always good for a laugh, was Reg."

"Have you entered anything in the home-baking competition?" asked Agatha.

Barbara's blue eyes were suddenly suspicious. "Why should I?"

"Most of the ladies seem very talented at these shows."

"I can't bake, but I know a good dog. Dammit, I should have won. What qualifications does this Lady Muck have for judging a dog show? I'll tell you . . . none. The organizers want a judge and so they ask any fool with a title. She couldn't even judge her own arse."

As Barbara picked up her beer tankard, Agatha noticed the woman's rippling muscles and decided to retreat.

But at that moment, Ella Cartwright looked into the beer tent, saw Agatha and called out, "Enjoying yourself, Mrs. Raisin?"

Barbara slowly put down her tankard. "You!" she hissed. She lunged across the table, her hands reaching for Agatha's throat.

Agatha leaped backwards, knocking her flimsy canvas-and-tubular-steel seat over. "Now, don't get excited," she said weakly.

But Barbara leaped on her and seized her by the throat. Agatha was dimly aware of the grinning faces of the drinkers in the tent. She got her knee into Barbara's stomach and pushed with all her strength. Barbara staggered back but then came at her again. She was blocking the way out. Agatha fled behind the serving counter, screaming for help while the men laughed and cheered. She seized a large kitchen knife and held it in front of her. "Get away," she said breathlessly.

"Murderer!" shrieked Barbara but she backed off. Then there came a blinding flash and the click of a camera. One of the local photographers had just snapped Agatha brandishing the kitchen knife.

Still holding the knife, Agatha edged around to the exit. "Don't come near me again or I'll *kill* you," shouted Barbara.

Agatha dropped the knife outside the tent and ran. Once in the safety of her car and with the doors locked, she sat panting. She thrust the key in the ignition and then paused, dismay flooding her. That photograph! She could already see it in her mind's eye on the front of some local paper. What if the London papers picked it up? Oh, God. She was going to have to get that film.

She felt shaken and tired as she reluctantly climbed out again and trekked across the rain-sodden field.

Keeping a sharp eye out for Barbara James, she threaded her way through the booths selling old books, country clothes, dried flowers, local pottery, and, as usual, home-baking. In

100

addition to the usual stands, there was one selling local country wines. The photographer was standing there with a reporter sampling elderberry wine. Agatha's heart beat hard. His camera case was on the ground at his feet, but the camera which had taken the photo of her was still around his neck. Agatha backed off in case he should see her. He stood there, sampling wine for a long time until the terrier racing was announced, He said something to the reporter and they headed off to the arena. Agatha followed them and waited until they were in the arena. She retreated to a stand and bought herself a wax-coat and a rain-hat. The rain was still drumming down. It was going to be a long day. The terrier racing was followed by show jumping. Agatha lurked at the edge of the thinning crowd, but feeling that the hat and coat she had just put on disguised her somewhat.

At the end of the show jumping, the rain stopped again and a chill yellow sunlight flooded the fair. Heart beating hard, Agatha saw the photographer wind the film from his camera, pop it in his case, and then reload with another. Slowly she took off her coat. The photographer and reporter headed out of the arena and back to the local wine-stand. "Try the birch wine," the woman serving was urging them as Agatha crept closer. She dropped her coat over the camera case, mumbled something and bent and seized the handle of the camera case and lifted it up and scurried off round the back of a tent. She opened the case and stared down in dismay at all the rolls of film. Too bad. She took them all out after putting on her coat again so that she could stuff the rolls of film into her pocket.

She heard a faint yell of "Police!" and hurried off, leaving the camera case on the ground. She felt sure that the woman serving the wine had not noticed her and the photographer and reporter had not even turned round. She felt lucky in that they were not from a national paper, otherwise they would have concentrated on her and Barbara James and would have referred back to the quiche poisoning. But local photographers and reporters knew that their job at these fairs was to get

101

as many faces and prize-winners on their pages as possible so as to boost circulation. But if the picture of her brandishing a knife in the beer tent had turned out well, she knew they would use it, along, no doubt, with quotes from the enraged Barbara James.

She was just driving out of the car-park when a policeman flagged her down. Agatha let down the window and looked at him nervously. "A photographer has had his camera case stolen," said the policeman. "Did you notice anything suspicious?" He peered into the car, his eyes darting this way and that. Agatha was painfully conscious of her coat pockets bulging with film. "No," she said. "What a terrible thing to happen."

There came a faint cry of "We've found it." The policeman straightened up. "That's that," he said with a grin. "These photographers are always drinking too much. Probably just forgot where he left it."

He stood back. Agatha let in the clutch and drove off. She did not once relax until she was home and had lit a large fire. When it was blazing, she tipped all the rolls of film onto it and watched them burn merrily. Then she heard a car drawing up.

She looked out of the window. Barbara James!

Agatha dived behind the sofa and lay there, trembling. The knocking at the door, at first mild, became a fusillade of knocks and kicks. Agatha let out a whimper. Then there was silence. She was just about to get up when something struck her living-room window and she crouched down again. She heard what she hoped was Barbara's car driving off. Still she waited.

After ten minutes, she got up slowly. She looked at the window. Brown excrement was stuck to it, along with wisps of kitchen paper. Barbara must have thrown a wrapper full of the stuff.

She went through to the kitchen and got a bucket of water and took it outside and threw it at the window, returning to get more water until the window was clean. She was going back inside when she saw Mrs. Barr standing at her garden gate, watching her, her pale eyes alight with malice.

Her rumbling stomach reminded Agatha that she had not eaten. But she did not have the courage to go out again. At least she had bread and butter. She made herself some toast.

The phone rang shrilly. She approached it and gingerly picked up the receiver. "Hullo," came Roy's mincing voice. "That you, Aggie?"

"Yes," said Agatha, weak with relief. "How are you?"

"Bit fed up."

"How's Steve?"

"Haven't seen him. Gone all moody on me."

"Buy him a book on village customs. That'll make his eyes light up."

"The only way to make that one's eyes light up," said Steve waspishly, "is to shine a torch in his ear. I've been given the Tolly Baby Food account."

"Congratulations."

"On what?" Roy's voice was shrill. "Baby food's not my *scene*, ducky. They're doing it deliberately. Hoping I'll fail. More your line."

"Wait a bit. Isn't Tolly Baby Food the stuff that some maniac's been putting glass in and then blackmailing the company?"

"They've arrested someone, but now Tolly wants to restore their image."

"Try going Green," suggested Agatha. "Suggest to the advertising people a line of healthy baby food, no additives, and with a special safety cap. Get a cartoon figure to promote it. Throw a press party to show off the new vandal-proof top. 'Only Tolly Baby Food keeps baby safe,' that sort of thing. And don't drink yourself. Take any journalist who has a baby out for lunch separately."

"They don't have babies," complained Roy. "They give birth to bile."

"There are a few fertile ones." Agatha searched her memory. "There's Jean Hammond, she's got a baby, and Jeffrey

103

Constable's wife has just had one. You'll find out more if you try. Anyway, women journalists feel obliged to write about babies to show they're normal. They have to keep trying to identify with the housewives they secretly despise. You know Jill Stamp who's always rambling on about her godson? Hasn't got one. All part of the image."

"I wish you were doing it," said Roy. "It was fun working for you, Aggie. How's things in Rural Land?"

Agatha hesitated and then said, "Fine."

This was greeted by a long silence. It suddenly struck Agatha with some amazement that Roy might possibly want an invitation.

"You know all that tat in my living-room?"

"What, the fake horse brasses and things?"

"Yes, I'm auctioning them all off in the name of charity. On the tenth of June, a Saturday. Like to come down and see me in action?"

"Love to."

"All right. I'll meet the train on Friday evening, on the ninth. Wonder you can bear to leave London."

"London is a *sink*," said Roy bitterly.

"Oh, God, there's a car outside," yelped Agatha. She looked out of the window. "It's all right, it's only the police."

"What *have* you been up to?"

"I'll tell you when I see you. Bye."

Agatha answered the door to Bill Wong. "Now what?" she asked. "Or is this just a friendly call?"

"Not quite." He followed her into the kitchen and sat down at the table.

"You were at the Ancombe Fair, I gather," said Bill.

"So?"

"You were seen in the beer tent waving a knife at Miss Barbara James."

"Self-defence. The woman tried to strangle me."

"Why?"

"Because I believe she had been having an affair with Cummings-Browne and she learned my name and saw red."

104

He flipped open a small notebook and consulted it. "Photographer Ben Birkin of the *Cotswold Courier* snapped a picture and lo and behold, his camera case was snatched. No cameras taken but all the rolls of film."

"Odd," said Agatha. "Coffee?"

"Yes, please. Then I had a call from Fred Griggs, your local bobby. He had a report that a woman answering to Barbara James's description threw shit at your windows."

"She's mad," said Agatha, thumping a cup of instant coffee in front of Bill. "Quite mad. And you still claim the death of Cummings-Browne was an accident. I regret that scene in the beer tent. I'm glad that photographer lost his film. I've suffered enough without having my photo on the front of some local rag. Oh, God, I suppose they'll run the story even if they don't have the picture to go with it."

He looked at her speculatively. "You are a very lucky woman. The editor was so furious with Ben Birkin that he didn't want to know about two women fighting in the beer tent. Furthermore, it so happens that John James, Barbara's father, owns shares in the company which owns the newspaper. The editor's only interested in cramming as many names and pictures of the locals into his paper as he can. Luckily, there were several amateur photographers at the fair and Bill was able to buy their film. Do you wish to charge Barbara James with assault or with throwing what possibly was dog-do at your window?"

Agatha shuddered. "I never want to see that woman again. No."

"I've been making more inquiries about Cummings-Browne," said Bill. "Seems he was quite a Lothario. You wouldn't think it to look at him, would you? Pointy head and jug ears. Oh, I've found the identity of the woman who was glaring at you at Warwick Castle."

"Who is she?"

"Miss Maria Borrow, spinster of the parish, not this parish, Upper Cockburn."

"And was *she* having an affair with Cummings-Browne?"

105

"Seems hardly believable. Retired schoolteacher. Gone a bit batty. Taken up witchcraft. Sixty-two."

"Oh, well, sixty-two. I mean, even Cummings-Browne could hardly—"

"But for the past three years she has won the jam-making competition at Upper Cockburn, and Mr. Cummings-Browne was the judge. Now don't go near her. Let well alone, Mrs. Raisin. Settle down and enjoy your retirement."

He rose to his feet, but instead of going to the front door he veered into the living-room and stood looking at the fire. He picked up the long brass poker and shifted the blazing wood. Little black metal film spools rattled through the fire-basket and onto the hearth.

"Yes, you are *very* lucky, Mrs. Raisin," said Bill. "I happen to detest Ben Birkin."

"Why?" asked Agatha.

"I was having a mild flirtation with a married lady and I was giving her a cuddle behind the abbey in Mircester. Ben took a photograph and it was published with the caption: 'Safe in the Arms of the Law.' Her husband called on me and I had a job to talk my way out of that one."

Agatha rallied. "I'm not quite sure what you are getting at. I found a pile of old unused film in my luggage and I was burning it."

Bill shook his head in mock amazement. "One would think all your years in public relations would have taught you how to lie better. Mind your own business in future, Agatha Raisin, and leave any investigation to the law."

The squally rain disappeared and clear blue skies shone over the Cotswolds. Agatha, shaken by the fight with Barbara James, put her bicycle in her car and went off to drive around the Cotswolds, occasionally stopping at some quiet lane to change over to her bicycle. Huge festoons of wisteria hung over cottage doors, hawthorn blossoms fell in snowy drifts beside the road, the golden stone of houses glowed in the warm sun and London seemed very far away.

At Chipping Campden, she forgot her determination to slim and ate steak and kidney pie in the antique cosiness of the Eight Bells before sauntering down the main street of the village with its green verges and houses of golden stone with gables, tall chimneys, archways, pediments, pillars, mullioned or sash windows, and big flat stone steps. Despite the inevitable groups of tourists, it had a serene, retiring air. Full of steak and kidney pie, Agatha began to feel a little sense of peace. In the middle stood the Market Hall of 1627 with its short strong pillars throwing black shadows onto the road. Life could be easy. All she had to do was to forget about Cummings-Browne's death.

During the next few days, the sun continued to shine and Agatha continued to tour about, occasionally cycling, occasionally walking, returning every evening with a new feeling of health and well-being. It was with some trepidation that she remembered she was to accompany the Carsely ladies to Mircester.

But no angry faces glared at her as she climbed aboard the bus. Mrs. Doris Simpson was there, to Agatha's relief and surprise, and so she sat beside the cleaning woman and chatted idly of this and that. The women in the bus were mostly middle-aged. Some had brought their knitting, some squares of tapestry. The old bus creaked and clanked along the lanes. The sun shone. It was all very peaceful.

Agatha assumed that the entertainment to be provided for them by the ladies of Mircester would take the form of tea and cakes, and meant to indulge herself to the full, feeling all the exercise she had taken in the past few days merited a binge on pastry. But when they alighted at a church hall it was to find that a full-scale lunch with wine had been laid on. The wine had been made by members of the Mircester Ladies' Society and was extremely potent. Lunch consisted of clear soup, roast chicken with chips and green peas, and sherry trifle, followed by Mrs. Rainworth's apple brandy. Applause for Mrs. Rainworth, a gnarled old crone, was loud and appreciative as the brandy went the rounds.

The chairwoman of the Mircester Ladies' Society got to her feet. "We have a surprise for you." She turned to Mrs. Bloxby. "If your ladies would take their bus to the Malvern Theatre, they will find seats have been booked for them."

"What is the entertainment?" asked Mrs. Bloxby.

There were raucous shouts from the Mircester ladies of "Secret! You'll see."

"I wonder what it is," said Agatha to Doris Simpson as they climbed aboard their coach again. It was now Doris and Agatha. "I don't know," said Doris. "There was some children's theatre giving a show. Might be that."

"I've drunk so much," said Agatha, "I'll probably sleep through the lot."

"Now that is a surprise," exclaimed Doris when their ancient bus clanked to a halt outside the theatre. "It says, 'All-American Dance Troupe. The Spanglers.' "

"Probably one of these modern ballet companies," groaned Agatha. "Everyone in black tights dancing around what looks like a bomb site. Oh, well, I hope the music's not too loud."

Inside, she settled herself comfortably with the other members of the Carsely Ladies' Society.

To a roll of drums, the curtain rose. Agatha blinked. It was a show of male strippers. The music beat and pulsated and the strobe lights darted here and there. Agatha sank lower in her seat, her faced scarlet with embarrassment. Mrs. Rainworth, the inventor of the apple brandy, stood up on her seat and shouted hysterically, "Get 'em orf." The women were yelling and cheering. Agatha was dimly glad of the fact that Doris Simpson had taken out some knitting and was working away placidly, seemingly oblivious to what was going on on the stage or in the audience. The strippers were tanned and well-muscled. They did not strip completely. They had an arch teasing manner, more like bimbos than men. Naughty but nice. But most of the women were beside themselves. One middle-aged dyed blond, one of the Mircester ladies, made a wild rush to the stage and had to be pulled back.

108

Agatha suffered in silence. But when the show finished, her agony was not over. Members of the audience who wanted their photographs taken with one of the strippers could do so for a mere fee of ten pounds. And with a few exceptions, the Carsely ladies all wanted photographs taken.

"Did you enjoy the show, Mrs. Raisin?" asked the vicar's wife, Mrs. Bloxby, as Agatha shakily got on board the bus. "I was shocked," said Agatha.

"Oh, it was only a bit of fun," said Mrs. Bloxby. "I've seen worse on television."

"I'm surprised *you* should find it amusing," said Agatha.

"They're such good boys. Do you know they did a special show for the Kurdish refugees and raised five thousand pounds? And all that money for the photographs goes towards restoring the abbey roof."

"How clever of them," said Agatha, who recognized good PR when she heard it. By donating occasionally to charity, the troupe of male strippers had made themselves respectable and allowed licensed lust to flourish in the breasts of the Cotswold ladies, who would turn up by the busload to cheer them on. Perhaps these Americans had started an English tradition, mused Agatha sourly. Perhaps in five hundred years' time there would be male strippers performing in the squares of the Cotswold villages while tour guides lectured their clients on the beginnings of this ancient ritual.

Back to the church hall and down to business. Once more they were a large group of staid worthy women, discussing the arrangements of this fête and that to raise funds for charity. Mrs. Bloxby got to her feet and said, "Our Mrs. Raisin is running an auction on June tenth to raise money for charity. I hope you will all come and help to drive up the bidding. We are very grateful to Mrs. Raisin and hope you will all do your best to support her." Agatha cringed, waiting for someone to say, "Not *that* Mrs. Raisin, not the one who poisoned poor Mr. Cummings-Browne," but all she got was a warm-hearted round of applause. Agatha felt quite weepy as she stood up and bowed in acknowledgement. Bill Wong was right. Retirement would be highly enjoyable just so long as she forgot all about Reg Cummings-Browne and that wretched quiche.

EIGHT

†

AGATHA kept to her determination to mind her own business as far as the death of Cummings-Browne was concerned. Instead, she turned her energies again on the local newspapers and dealers, rousing interest in the auction. The editors published paragraphs about the auction just to keep Agatha quiet, as journalists had done in the not so very long ago when she was selling some client or product.

In their good-natured way, the Carsely Ladies' Society contributed books, plates, vases and other worn-looking items which they had bought over the years at other sales and were now recycling. As the day of the auction approached, Agatha began to receive more and more visitors. Mrs. Mason, the chairwoman of the group, called regularly with several of the other ladies with their contributions, until Agatha's living-room began to look more and more like a junk shop.

She was so engrossed in all this that she almost forgot about Roy's visit and had to rush to meet the train on the Friday evening. She wished he were not coming. She was beginning to feel part of this village life and did not want outrageous Roy to damage her new image of Lady Bountiful.

To her relief, he descended from the train looking as much a businessman as several of the other London commuters. He had a conventional hair-style, no ear-rings, and wore a business suit. Hanging baskets of flowers were ornamenting Moreton-in-Marsh Station and roses bloomed in flower-beds on the platform. The sun was blazing down on a perfect evening.

"Like another world," said Roy. "I thought you'd made a ghastly mistake coming here, Aggie, but now I think you're lucky."

"How's the baby-food thing going?" asked Agatha as he got in the car.

"I did what you said and it was a great success, so I've leaped to respectability with the firm. Do you know who the latest client is?"

Agatha shook her head.

"Handley's nursery chain."

Agatha looked bewildered. "More babies?"

"No, dear. Gardens. They've even given me a dress allowance, tweed sports jacket, cords and brogues, can you believe it? Do you know, I thought I quite liked flowers, but they've got all these poisonously long latin names, like chemical formulas, and I never took Latin at school. It's all so *boring;* garden sheds and gnomes and crazy paving as well."

"I might like a gnome," said Agatha. "No, not for me," she added, thinking of Mrs. Simpson.

"We'd better sit in the kitchen," she said when they arrived home. "The living-room is chock-a-block with all the stuff for the sale."

"Are you cooking?" asked Roy nervously.

"Yes, one of the members of the Carsely Ladies' Society, Mrs. Mason, has been giving me some lessons."

"What is this ladies' society?"

Agatha told him and then gave him a description of her outing to Mircester and he laughed till he cried.

The dinner consisted of vegetable soup, followed by shepherd's pie and apple crumble. "Keep it simple," Mrs. Mason had said.

"This is remarkably good," said Roy. "You're even wearing a print dress, Aggie."

"It's comfortable," said Agatha defensively. "Besides, I'm battling with a weight problem."

" 'Wider still and wider, shall her bounds be set,' " quoted Roy with a grin.

"I never believed in the middle-aged spread before," said Agatha. "I thought it was just an excuse for indulgence. But the very air seems to make me fat. I'm tired of bicycling and exercise routines. I feel like giving up and becoming really fat."

"You can't get thin eating like this," said Roy. "You're supposed to snack on lettuce leaves like a rabbit."

After dinner, Agatha showed him the pile of goods in the living-room. "A delivery van is coming first thing in the morning," she said, "and then, after they've dropped the whole lot off at the school hall, they'll go to Cheltenham and pick up the new stuff. Perhaps when you learn about plants you can tell me what to do about the garden."

"Not too late even now to put things in," said Roy, airing his new knowledge. "What you want is instant garden. Go to one of the nurseries and load up with flowers. A cottage garden. All sorts of old-fashioned things. Climbing roses. Go for it, Aggie."

"I might. That is, if I really decide to stay."

Roy looked at her sharply. "The murder, you mean. What's been happening?"

"I don't want to talk about it," said Agatha hurriedly. "Best to forget about the whole thing."

In the morning, Agatha stood with her hands on her hips and surveyed the school hall with dismay. All the contents of her living-room looked sparse now. Hardly an event. Mrs. Bloxby appeared and said in her gentle voice, "Now this looks really nice."

"The hell it does," said Agatha. "No suggestion of an

113

occasion. Not enough stuff. What about if the ladies put some more stuff in, anything at all? Any old junk."

"I'll do what I can."

"And the band, the village band, should be playing. Give a festive air. What about some morris dancers?"

"You should have thought of this before, Mrs. Raisin. How can we organize all that in such a short time?"

Agatha glanced at her watch. "Nine o'clock," she said. "The auction's at three." She took out a notebook. "Where does the bandmaster live? And the leader of the morris dancers?"

Bewildered, Mrs. Bloxby supplied names and addresses. Agatha ran home and roused Roy, who had been sleeping peacefully. "You've got to paint some signs quick," said Agatha. "Let me see, the signs for the May Day celebrations are stored at Harvey's, because I saw them in the back room of the shop. Get them and paint over them. Put, 'Bargains, Bargains Bargains. Great Auction. Three o'Clock. Teas. Music. Dancing.' Put the signs up on the A-44 where the drivers can see them and have a big arrow pointing down to Carsely, and then you'll need more signs in the village itself pointing the way."

"I can't do that," protested Roy sleepily.

"Oh yes, you can," growled the old Agatha. "Hop to it."

She got out the car and drove to the bandmaster's and ruthlessly told him it was his duty to have the band playing. "I want last-night-of-the-prom stuff," said Agatha, " 'Rule, Britannia,' 'Land of Hope and Glory,' 'Jerusalem,' the lot. All the papers are coming. You wouldn't want them to know that you wouldn't do anything for charity."

The leader of the morris dancers received similar treatment. Mrs. Doris Simpson was next on the list. To Agatha's relief, she had taken a day off work for the auction. "It's the hall," said Agatha feverishly. "It looks so drab. It needs flowers."

"I think I can get the ladies to do that," said Doris placidly. "Sit down, Agatha, and have a cup of tea. You'll give yourself a stroke going on like this."

But Agatha was off again. Round the village she went, haranguing and bullying, demanding any items for her auction until her car was piled up with, she privately thought, the most dismal load of tat she had ever seen.

Roy, sweating in the already hot sun, crouched up on the A-44, stabbing signs into the turf. The paint was still wet and his draughtsmanship was not of the best, but he had bought two pots of paint from Harvey's, one red and one white, and he knew the signs were legible. He trudged back down to the village, thinking it was just like Agatha to expect him to walk, and started putting up signs around the village.

With a happy feeling of duty done, he returned to Agatha's cottage, meaning to creep back to bed for a few hours' sleep.

But Agatha fell on him. "Look!" she cried, holding up a jester's outfit, cap and bells and all. "Isn't this divine? Miss Simms, the secretary, wore it in the pantomime last Christmas, and she's as slim as you. Should be a perfect fit. Put it on."

Roy backed off. "What for?"

"You put it on, you stand up on the A-44 beside the signs and you wave people down to the village. You could do a little dance."

"No, absolutely not," said Roy mulishly.

Agatha eyed him speculatively. "If you do it, I'll give you an idea for those nurseries which will put you on the PR map for life."

"What is it?"

"I'll tell you after the auction."

"Aggie, I *can't*. I'd feel ever such a fool."

"You're meant to look like a fool, man. For heaven's sake, you parade through London in some of the ghastliest outfits I've ever seen. Do you remember when you had pink hair? I asked you why and you said you liked people staring at you. Well, they'll all be staring at you. I'll get your photo in the papers and make them describe you as a famous public-relations executive from London. Look, Roy, I'm not *asking* you to do it. I'm telling you!"

"Oh, all right," mumbled Roy, thinking that at times like this Agatha Raisin reminded him forcefully of his own bullying mother.

"I'll tell you one thing," he said, making a bid for some sort of independence, "I'm not walking all that way back in all this heat. I'll need your car."

"I might need it. Take my bike."

"Cycle all the way up that hill? You must be mad."

"Do it!" snapped Agatha. "I'll get you the bike while you put on your costume."

Well, it wasn't too bad. It wasn't too bad at all, thought Roy later as he capered beside the road and waved his jester's sceptre in the direction of Carsely. Motorists were honking and cheering, a busload of American tourists had stopped to ask him about it, and hearing the auction was "chockful of rare antiques," they urged their tour guide to take them to it.

At ten minutes to three, he got on Agatha's bike and free-wheeled down the long winding road to the village. He had meant to remove his outfit, but everyone was looking at him and he liked that, so he kept it on. Outside, the morris dancers were leaping high in the sunny air. Inside, the village band was giving "Rule, Britannia" their best effort, and lo and behold, a sturdy woman dressed as Britannia was belting out the lyric. The school hall was jammed with people.

Then the band fell silent and Agatha, in a Royal Garden Party sort of hat, white straw embellished with blue asters, and wearing a black dress with a smart blue collar, stood at the microphone.

Agatha planned to start with the least important items and work up.

She sensed that the crowd had a slightly inebriated air, no doubt thanks to old Mrs. Rainworth from Mircester, who had set up a stand outside the auction and was selling her apple brandy at fifty pence a glass.

Mrs. Mason handed Agatha the first lot. Agatha looked down at it. It was a box of second-hand books, mostly paperback romances. There was one old hardback book on top.

116

Agatha picked it up and looked at it. It was *Ways of the Horse,* by John Fitzgerald, Esquire, and all the *S*'s looked like *F*'s, so Agatha knew it was probably eighteenth century but still worthless. She opened it up and looked at the title page and affected startled surprise. Then she put the book back hurriedly and said, "Nothing here. Perhaps we should start with something more interesting."

She looked across the hall at Roy, who instinctively picked up his cue. "No, you don't," he shouted. "Start with that one. I'll bid ten pounds."

There was a murmur of surprise. Mrs. Simpson, who, along with others, had been asked to do her best to force up the bidding, cheerfully called, "Fifteen pounds." A small man who looked like a dealer looked up sharply. "Who'll offer me twenty?" said Agatha. "All in a good cause. Going, going . . ." Mrs. Simpson groaned audibly. The little man flapped his newspaper. "Twenty," said Agatha gleefully. "Who'll give me twenty-five?"

The Carsely ladies sat silent, clutching their handbags. Another man raised his hand. "Twenty-five it is," said Agatha. The box of worthless books was finally knocked down for fifty pounds. Agatha was unrepentant. All in a good cause, she told herself firmly.

The bidding went on. The tourists joined in. More people began to force their way in. Villagers began to bid. It was such a big event that they all wanted now to say they had contributed. The sun beat down through the windows of the school hall. Occasionally from outside came the sound of fiddle and accordion as the morris dancers danced on, accompanied by the occasional raucous cry of old Mrs. Rainworth, "Apple brandy. Real old Cotswold recipe."

Midlands Television turned up and Agatha spurred herself to greater efforts. The bidding was running wild. One by one, all the junk began to disappear. Her sofa and chairs went to a Gloucestershire dealer, even the fake horse brasses disappeared and the Americans bid hotly for the farm machinery, recognizing genuine antiques in their usual irritatingly sharp way.

When the auction was over, Agatha Raisin had made £25,000 for Save the Children. But she knew that she now had to soothe the savage breasts of those who felt they had been cheated.

"I must thank you all," she said with a well-manufactured break in her voice. "Some of you may feel you have paid more than you should. But remember, you are helping charity. We of Carsely thank you from the bottom of our hearts. Now, if you will all join me in singing 'Jerusalem.' "

The famous hymn was followed by Mrs. Mason leading the audience in "Land of Hope and Glory." The vicar then said a prayer, and everyone beamed happily in a euphoric state.

Agatha was surrounded by reporters. No nationals, she noticed, but what did it matter? She said to them, facing the Midlands Television camera, "I cannot take the credit for all this. The success of this venture is thanks to the freely given services of a London public-relations executive, Roy Silver. Roy, take a bow."

Flushed with delight, Roy leaped nimbly up onto the stage and cavorted in his cap and bells for the camera. The band then played selections from *Mary Poppins* as the crowds dispersed, some to the tea-room, some back to the apple-brandy stall, the rest to watch the morris dancing.

Agatha felt a pang of regret and half wished she had not given Roy the credit. He was beside himself with joy and, followed by the television camera, had gone out to join the morris dancers, where he was turning cartwheels and showing off to his heart's content.

"Pity it won't make the nationals," mourned Roy as he and Agatha sat later on Agatha's new furniture.

"If you make the locals, you'll be lucky," said Agatha, made waspish by fatigue. "We'll need to wait now until Monday. I don't think there's a local Sunday paper, and then

118

there's hardly any news coverage on television at the week-ends."

"Put on the telly," said Roy. "They do the Midlands news for a few minutes after the national."

"They only do about three minutes in all," said Agatha, "and they're hardly going to cover a local auction."

Roy switched on the television. The local news covered another murder in Birmingham, a missing child in Stroud, a pile-up on the M-6, and then, "On a lighter note, the pictur-esque village of Carsely raised a record sum . . ." And there was Roy on the road waving down motorists and then a shot of Agatha running the auction, the singing of "Jerusalem" and then a quick shot of Roy with the morris dancers, "Roy Silver, a London executive," and Roy stopping his cavorting to say seriously, "One does what one can for charity."

"Well," said Agatha, "even I'm surprised."

"There's another news later," said Roy, searching through the newspaper. "Must video it and show it to old Wilson."

"I looked fat," said Agatha dismally.

"It's the cameras, love, they always put *pounds* on. By the way, did you ever discover who that woman was, the one on the tower of Warwick Castle?"

"Oh, her. Miss Maria Borrow of Upper Cockburn."

"And?"

"And nothing. I've decided to let the whole thing rest. Bill Wong, a detective constable, seems to think that the attacks on me have been caused by my Nosy-Parkering."

Roy looked at her curiously. "You'd better tell me about it."

Wearily, Agatha told him what had been happening since she had last seen him.

"I wouldn't just let it go," said Roy. "Tell you what, if you can borrow a bicycle for me, we could both cycle over to this village, Upper Cockburn, and take a look-see. Get exer-cise at the same time."

"I don't know . . ."

119

"I mean, we could just ask around, casual like."

"I'll think about it after church," said Agatha.

"Church!"

"Yes, church service, Roy. Early tomorrow."

"I'll be glad to get back to the quiet life of London," said Roy with feeling. "Oh, what about the idea for my nurseries?"

"Oh, that! Well, what about this. Get some new plant or flower and name it after Princess Di."

"Isn't there a rose or something already?"

"There's a Fergie, I think. I don't know if there's a Di."

"And they usually do things like that at the Chelsea Flower Show."

"Don't be so defeatist. Get them to find some new plant of any kind. They're always inventing new things. Fake it if necessary."

"Can't give gardeners fakes."

"Then don't. Find something, call it the Princess Diana, hold a party in one of the nurseries. Anything to do with Princess Diana gets in the papers."

"Wouldn't I need permission?"

"I don't know. Find out. Phone up the press office at the palace and put it to them. Take it from me, they're not going to object. It's a flower, for God's sake, not a Rottweiler."

His eyes gleamed. "Might work. When does Harvey's open in the morning to sell newspapers?"

"They open for one hour on Sundays. Eight till nine. But you won't find anything, Roy. The nationals weren't at the auction."

"But if the locals have a good photo, they send it to the nationals."

Agatha stifled a yawn. "Dream on. I'm going to bed."

When they walked to church the next morning, Agatha felt she ought to tie Roy down before he floated away. A picture of him had appeared in the *Sunday Times*. He was dancing with the morris men. Three old village worthies with highly photographable wizened faces were watching the dancing. It was a

120

very good photo. It looked like a dream of rural England. The caption read, "London PR executive, Roy Silver, 25, entertaining the villagers of Carsely, Gloucestershire, after running a successful auction which raised £25,000 for charity."

It was all *my* work, thought Agatha, regretting bitterly having given Roy the credit.

But at the morning service, the vicar gave credit where credit was due and offered a vote of thanks to Mrs. Agatha Raisin for all her hard work. Roy looked sulky and clutched the *Sunday Times* to his thin chest.

After the service, Mrs. Bloxby when appealed to said she had an old bicycle in the garden shed which Roy could use. "The least I can do for you, Mrs. Raisin," said Mrs. Bloxby gently. "Not only did you do sterling work but you let your young friend here take all the credit."

Roy was about to protest that he had stood for hours on the main road looking like an idiot in the name of charity, but something in Mrs. Bloxby's gentle gaze silenced him.

Upper Cockburn was six miles away and they pedalled off together under the hot sun. "Going to be a scorcher of a summer," said Roy. "London seems thousands of miles away from all this." He took one hand off the handlebars and waved around at the green fields and trees stretched out on either side.

Agatha suddenly wished they were not going to Upper Cockburn. She wanted to forget about the whole thing now. There had been no further attacks on her, no nasty notes.

The tall steeple of Upper Cockburn church came into view, rising over the fields. They cycled into the sun-washed peace of the main street. "There's a pub," said Roy, pointing to the Farmers Arms. "Let's have a bite to eat and ask a few questions. Did this Miss Borrow go in for village competitions?"

"Yes, jam-making," said Agatha curtly. "Look, Roy, let's just have lunch and go home."

"Think about it."

The pub was low and dark, smelling of beer, with a

121

flagged floor and wooden settles dark with age. They sat in the lounge bar. From the public bar Tina Turner was belting something out on the juke-box and there came the click of billiard balls. A waitress, in a very short skirt and with long, long legs and a deep bosom revealed by the low neck of her skimpy dress, bent over them to take their orders. Roy surveyed her with a frankly lecherous look. Agatha gazed at him in dawning surprise.

"What's made your friend, Steve, moody?" she asked.

"What? Oh, woman trouble. Got involved with a married woman who's decided that hubby is better after all."

Well, thought Agatha, these days, with women looking more like men and men looking more like women, you never can tell. Perhaps in thousands of years' time there would be a unisex face and people would have to go around with badges to proclaim their gender. Or maybe the women could wear pink and the men blue. Or maybe . . .

"What are you thinking about?" demanded Roy.

Agatha gave a guilty start. "Oh, about the Borrow woman," she said mendaciously.

Roy took her now empty gin glass and went to the bar to get her a refill. Agatha saw him talking to the landlord.

He came back, looking triumphant. "Miss Maria Borrow lives in Pear Trees, which is the cottage to the left of this pub. There!"

"I don't know, Roy. It's such a lovely day. Couldn't we just take a look around the village and then go back?"

"I'm doing this for your own good," said Roy severely. "Gosh, this steak-and-kidney pudding is great. You know, there's nothing like these English dishes when they're done well."

"I should have had a salad," mourned Agatha. "I can feel every calorie."

"I'm weak-willed, she thought when she had eaten every scrap of the steak-and-kidney pudding and she realized she had let Roy talk her into a helping of hot apple pie with cream, real cream, and not that stuff like shaving soap.

The waitress came up when they had finished the pie, her high heels clacking on the stone flags of the floor. "Anything else?" she asked.

"Just coffee," said Roy. "That was an excellent meal."

"Yes, I reckon the part-timer on Sundays does a better job than our Mrs. Moulson during the week," she said.

"Who's your part-timer?"

"That's John Cartwright from over Carsely way."

She clacked off. "What's the matter?" asked Roy, seeing Agatha's startled face.

"John Cartwright's the husband of Ella Cartwright, who was having an affair with Cummings-Browne. Who ever would have thought he could cook? He's a great dirty ape of a man. You see, it could have been done. Someone could have replaced my quiche with one of their own."

"Again, I have to point out that you would be intended as the victim," said Roy patiently.

"Wait a bit. Maybe it was intended for Cummings-Browne. Why not? Everyone knew he was to be the judge. Perhaps there wasn't enough cowbane in that little piece he nibbled at the show."

"I'm sure any murderer would have thought of that."

"But John Cartwright struck me as having the IQ of a plant."

The waitress brought coffee. When she had gone again, Roy said, "Have you ever wondered about Economides?"

"What? Why should the owner of The Quicherie, who didn't even know Cummings-Browne or where I was taking the quiche, decide to put cowbane in it?"

"But from what I've gathered," said Roy, "Economides didn't shriek and complain. Did he demand to see the quiche?"

"I don't think so. But he would want to let the matter drop. Perhaps the John Cartwright in the kitchen is another John Cartwright?"

"Finish your coffee," urged Roy, "and let's stroll round the back of the pub and take a look in the kitchen door."

Agatha paid the bill and they walked together into the sunlight. "How do you know the kitchen's at the back?" she asked.

"Just a guess. We'll try to the right because the car-park's to the left."

They walked round the building. Agatha was about to enter a small area of dustbins and outhouses when she drew back with a yelp and collided into Roy. "It *is* John Cartwright," she said. "He's standing outside the kitchen door smoking a cigarette."

"Let me see." Roy pushed her aside and peered cautiously round the corner of the building. John Cartwright was leaning against the doorway, holding a home-made cigarette in one large dirty hand. His apron was stained with grease and gravy. The sun shone on the tattoos on his black hairy arms.

"I feel sick," said Roy, retreating. "He looks filthy. Food poisoning oozing out of every dirty pore."

"I think we've done enough for one day," said Agatha. "Let's leave this Borrow woman alone."

"No," said Roy stubbornly. "We're so close."

Maria Borrow's cottage was low and thatched and very old. The small diamond-paned windows winked in the sunlight and the little garden was a riot of roses, honeysuckle, snapdragons, delphiniums and busy Lizzies. Roy nudged Agatha and pointed to the brass door-knocker, which was in the shape of a grinning devil.

"What are we going to say?" asked Agatha desperately.

"Nothing like the truth," retorted Roy, seizing the door-knocker.

The low door creaked open, and Miss Maria Borrow stood there. Her greyish hair was scraped up into a knot on the top of her head. Her eyes were pale. They looked past Roy to where Agatha stood cringing behind him.

"I knew you would come," she said and she stood aside to let them enter.

They found themselves in a low-beamed living-room crowded with furniture and photographs in silver frames.

From the beams hung bunches of dried herbs and flowers. On a low table in front of a chair on which Maria Borrow placed herself was a crystal ball.

Roy giggled nervously. "See us coming in that?" he asked.

Maria nodded her head several times. "Oh, yes." She was wearing a long purple woollen gown despite the heat of the day. "You have come to make amends," she said, turning to Agatha. "You and *your* fancy man."

"Mr. Silver is a young friend," said Agatha. "In fact, Mr. Silver is *considerably* younger than I."

"A lady is as young as the gentleman she feels," said Roy and cackled happily. "Look," he said, becoming serious, "we were visiting Warwick Castle and took a video on one of the towers. When we ran it, there you were, glaring at Aggie here like poison. We want to know why."

"You poisoned my future husband," said Maria.

There was a silence. A trapped fly buzzed against one of the windows and from the village green outside came muted shouts and the thud of cricket ball on bat.

Agatha cleared her throat. "You mean Mr. Cummings-Browne."

Maria nodded her head madly. "Oh, yes, yes; we were engaged to be married."

"But he was married already," exclaimed Roy.

Maria waved a thin hand. "He was divorcing her."

Agatha shifted uneasily. Vera Cummings-Browne was not much of a looker, but she was streets ahead of Maria Borrow, with her greyish face, thin lips, and pale eyes.

"Had he told her?" asked Roy.

"I believe so."

Agatha looked at her uneasily. Maria seemed so calm.

"Were you lovers?" asked Roy.

"Our union was to be consummated on Midsummer's Eve," said Maria. Her pale eyes shifted to Agatha. "I am a white witch but I know evil when I see it. You, Mrs. Raisin, were an instrument of the devil."

125

Agatha rose to her feet. "Well, we needn't keep you any longer," she said. She felt claustrophobic. All she wanted to do was to escape into the sunlight, into the sights and sounds of ordinary village life.

"But you will be punished," went on Maria, as if Agatha had not spoken. "Evil deeds are always punished. I will see to that."

Roy forced a light note. "So if anything happens to Aggie here, we'll know where to look."

"You will not know where to look," said Maria Borrow, "for it will be done by the supernatural powers I conjure up."

Agatha turned on her heel and walked out. There was a game of cricket taking place on the village green, leisurely, placid, with little knots of spectators standing about.

"I'm scared," she said when Roy joined her. "The woman's barking mad."

"Let's walk away from the cottage a bit," said Roy. "I'm beginning to think that Reg Cummings-Browne would have screwed the cat."

"He probably took what he could," said Agatha. "He was hardly an Adonis. We shouldn't have come, Roy. Something always happens to me after I've been asking questions. Let's just enjoy the rest of the day."

They went to get their bikes, which were chained to a fence beside the pub. As they were mounting, John Cartwright came around the side of the pub. Lunch-time was over. He had discarded his apron. He stopped short at the sight of them and glowered. They pedalled off as fast as they could.

On the road home, Roy struck a rock and catapulted over the handlebars, fortunately landing on the soft grass at the side of the road. He was winded but unhurt. "You see what can happen?" he said. "You really ought to wear a cycling helmet, Aggie."

The rest of the day passed pleasantly, until Agatha ran him into Oxford and waved goodbye to him at the station.

* * *

126

The next day, she remembered his remark about cycling helmets and bought one at a shop in Moreton-in-Marsh. Although she had a cottage-cheese salad for lunch and a chicken salad for dinner, she still felt fat. Exercise was called for. She put on her new helmet and got out her bike and pedalled up out of the village, having to get off several times and push. The light was fading as clouds were beginning to build up in the evening sky. At the top of the road, Agatha turned her bike about, looking forward to the long free-wheeling ride down into Carsely. The air was warm and sweet. Tall hedges and trees flew past. She felt she was flying, flying like a witch on her broomstick.

So exhilarated was she by the feeling of speed and freedom that she did not see the thin wire stretched chest-high across the road. Her bike went flying on as she crashed on her head on the road. She was dimly aware of rapid footsteps approaching her and her terrified mind registered that the wire had been no accident and that someone was probably coming now to kill her.

NINE

†

DAZED, Agatha sensed rather than saw her assailant coming nearer and something made her summon up all her efforts and roll across the hard surface of the road just as some weapon smashed down where she had been lying.

"Stop!" shouted a voice. Agatha's attacker ran off just as she dizzily hoisted herself up on one elbow. She got a glimpse of a dark figure breaking through a gap in the hedge at the side of the road and then she was blinded with the light of a bicycle lamp.

Bill Wong's voice came loud and clear. "Where did he go?"

"Over there," said Agatha faintly, waving an arm in the direction in which her assailant had fled. Bill left his bike by the side of the road and then plunged off through the hedge.

Agatha slowly moved her arms and legs, then she sat up and groggily took off her helmet. Her first coherent thought was, Damn Roy, why didn't he let me leave things as they were? She slowly got up on her feet and then was violently sick. Shakily she inched along the road until she came to her bike. She picked it up and then stood trembling. An owl sailed across in front of her and she yelped with fear. The heavy silence of the countryside pressed in on her. Suddenly she knew she could not wait for Bill Wong to return. Hoping her bike was undamaged, she mounted and free-wheeled slowly down into Carsely. No one was about the deserted village. She turned into Lilac Lane, noticing that there were no lights burning in Mrs. Barr's cottage.

She let herself into her own and then shut and locked the door. How flimsy that Yale lock now looked. She would get some security firm to put in burglar alarms and those lights which came on the minute anyone even approached the cottage. She went into her living-room and poured herself a stiff brandy and lit a cigarette. She tried to think but her mind seemed numb with fright. A knocking at the door made her start and spill some of her brandy. She didn't even have a spyhole. "Who is it?" she quavered.

"Me. Bill Wong."

Agatha opened the door. Bill Wong stood there with Fred Griggs, the local policeman, behind him. "There'll be reinforcements along soon," said Bill. "Fred, you'd best get back and block off that bit of the road where the attack took place. I'm slipping. I should have thought of that. Wilkes will have my guts for garters."

Bill and Agatha went into the living-room. "Thank God you happened along," said Agatha. "What were *you* doing on a bike?"

"I'm too fat," said Bill. "I saw you on yours and took a leaf out of your book. I was coming to pay you a visit. Now, I happen to know you were over in Upper Cockburn asking where Miss Maria Borrow lives, and Miss Borrow was the woman in that photograph you gave me. Not only that, you had lunch in the pub where John Cartwright acts as part-time cook."

"You've been checking up on me," said Agatha hotly.

"Not I. Word gets around."

Agatha shivered. "It was that Borrow woman, I'll swear. She's quite mad. She says Cummings-Browne promised to marry her."

"I'm beginning to think Cummings-Browne was a bit

130

touched himself," said Bill drily. "Anyway, Wilkes will soon be here and you will be asked all sorts of questions. But I think I can tell you now who had a go at you."

"Barbara James? Maria Borrow?"

"No, I think it was John Cartwright, and do you know why?"

"Because he killed Cummings-Browne."

"No, because you've been ferreting about. I swear he knows his wife had an affair with Cummings-Browne and he doesn't want it to get out."

"Then the logical way to put a stop to it would have been to kill Cummings-Browne in the first place!"

"But he is not a logical man. He's a great ape. Now begin at the beginning and tell me what happened."

So Agatha told him about the wire stretched across the road, about how someone had brought something crashing down near her which would have struck her if she hadn't rolled away.

"But look," ended Agatha, "the horrible Boggles, a couple of pensioners I took out for the day, they knew about the affair, so surely it was generally known in the village about the goings-on between Ella Cartwright and Cummings-Browne."

"Look at it this way. Cartwright may have suspected something was going on but he could never prove it. She would deny it. Then Cummings-Browne dies, so that's over. But you turn up asking questions, and he gets scared. That sort of man couldn't bear the idea of his wife having an affair—no, I mean the idea of anyone else *knowing*. Pride does not belong exclusively to the upper classes, you know. Here's the rest of them arrived. You'll need to answer questions all over again."

Detective Chief Inspector Wilkes and Detective Sergeant Friend came in. "We did as you suggested and went straight to Cartwright's house," said Wilkes. "He's gone. Dived in the door, the wife says, grabbed a few clothes, shoved them in a bag, and off he went. Took that old car of theirs. She says she doesn't know what's going on. She says he was getting a bee in his bonnet about Mrs. Raisin here and kept saying he would shut her mouth. Anyway, we searched the house. She said we needed a warrant but I told her I could get that, so she may as well let us save time. In the bedroom upstairs we found a stack of cash in a box, a sawn-off shotgun, and one of those giant bottles filled with change, the kind they have in bars for charity. This one was for Spastics. There was a robbery last month from the Green Man over at Twigsley. Masked man with sawn-off shotgun emptied the till and swiped the charity bottle off the bar. Looks like Cartwright did it. Ella Cartwright broke down. Her husband thought Mrs. Raisin here was on to that and that was the reason she was snooping around. So much for all your theories about the cheated husband. We've put out a call for him but I'll bet that car of his is found abandoned quite near. He did time over in Chelmsford in Essex ten years ago for armed robbery, and it was assumed he'd gone straight. Funny, we'd never have got on to him if this hadn't happened. It was Ella Cartwright who told us about the prison sentence."

"But when Mr. Cummings-Browne died," exclaimed Agatha, "surely you looked to see if anyone in the village had a record."

"Even then, it would have meant nothing. Before we knew it was an accident, we would have been looking for a more domestic poisoner."

Agatha stared at him. It was as if the blow to her head had cleared her brains. "Of course," she said, "Vera Cummings-Browne did it. She saw the opportunity when I left my quiche at the competition. She took it home, threw it away, and substituted one of her own."

Wilkes gave her a pitying look. "That was the first thing we thought of. We had her garbage checked, her cooking utensils, every surface of her kitchen, and her drains. Nothing had been cooked in that kitchen the day before Cummings-Browne was found dead. Now, will you just describe to us what happened this evening, Mrs. Raisin?"

Wearily, Agatha went over it all again.

At last Wilkes was finished. "We should be thankful to you, Mrs. Raisin, for leading us to Cartwright. He might have killed you, although I suspect he only meant to beat you up."

"Thanks a lot," said Agatha bitterly.

"On the other hand, I am sure we would have caught up with him sooner or later. You really must leave investigations to the police. Everyone has something to hide, and if you are going to go around shoving your nose into affairs which do not concern you, you are going to be hurt. Now, do you wish to be taken to hospital for an examination?"

Agatha shook her head. She hated and feared hospitals quite illogically, for she had never been treated in one.

"Very well. If we have any further questions, we will call on you tomorrow. Have you some friend who can stay the night with you?"

Again, Agatha shook her head. She wanted to ask Bill to stay, but off duty or not, he was obviously expected to leave with his superiors. He threw her a sympathetic look as he went out.

When they had gone, she switched on every light in the house. She felt as weak as a kitten. She turned on the television and then switched it off again, fearing that the sound would drown out the sounds of anyone creeping up on the house. She sat by the fire, clutching the poker, too frightened to go to bed.

And then she thought of Mrs. Bloxby, the vicar's wife. She rang up the vicarage. The vicar answered. "Could I speak to your wife? It's Agatha Raisin."

"It's a bit late," said the vicar, "and I don't know . . . oh, here she is."

"Mrs. Bloxby," said Agatha in a timid voice, "I wonder if you can help me."

"I hope so," said the vicar's wife in her gentle voice.

So Agatha told her of the assault and ended up bursting into tears.

"There, there," said Mrs. Bloxby. "You must not be alone. I will be along in a minute."

Agatha put down the phone and dried her eyes. She felt

suddenly silly. What had come over her, crying like a child for help, she who had never asked anyone for help before?

But soon she heard a car drawing up outside and immediately all her fears left her. She knew it was Mrs. Bloxby.

The vicar's wife came in carrying a small case. "I'll just stay the night," she said placidly. "You must be very shaken. Why don't you go to bed and I'll bring you up a drink of hot milk and sit with you until you go to sleep?"

Gratefully Agatha agreed. Soon she lay upstairs until Mrs. Bloxby came into the bedroom carrying a hot-water bottle in one hand and a glass of hot milk in the other. "I brought along the hot-water bottle," she said, "because when you have had a fright, no amount of central heating seems to warm you up."

Agatha, with the hot water bottle on her stomach and the hot milk inside her, and Mrs. Bloxby sitting on the end of her bed, felt soothed and secure. She told the vicar's wife all about John Cartwright and how they had found the money from the robbery in his house. "Poor Mrs. Cartwright," said Mrs. Bloxby. "We will all need to call on her tomorrow to see what we can do. She will need to get a job now. He did not allow her very much money but it would be very good for her to have something to do, other than playing bingo. We will all rally round. Try to sleep now, Mrs. Raisin. The weather forecast is good and things look so much simpler when the sun is shining. We have a meeting of the Carsely Ladies' Society at the vicarage tomorrow night. You must come. Mr. Jones— you do not know him, such a charming man and a gifted photographer—is going to give us a slide show of the village past and present. We are all looking forward to it."

Agatha's eyelids begin to droop and with the sound of Mrs. Bloxby's gentle voice in her ears, she fell fast asleep.

She awoke once during the night, immediately gripped with terror. Then she remembered the vicar's wife was in the spare bedroom across the landing and felt the fear and tension leaving her body. Mrs. Bloxby's goodness was a bright shining weapon against the dark things of the night.

The next day, Agatha went along to Mrs. Cartwright's, mindful of her promise to Mrs. Bloxby that morning to help out. But in the clear light of a sunny day, she felt sure Ella Cartwright would be more interested in money than sympathy.

"Come in," said Ella Cartwright wearily. "Coppers are crawling around upstairs. Have a gin."

"This must have been a sad blow," said Agatha, finding it hard to find the right words after a lifetime of not bothering.

"It's a bloody relief." Mrs. Cartwright lit a cigarette and then rolled up the sleeve of her cotton dress. "See these bruises? That was him, that was. Never marked my face, the cunning sod. I hope the p'lice catch him before he comes snooping back round here. I told him you only wanted to know about Reg, but he thought you'd got wind of the robbery. Fair paranoid, he was."

Agatha accepted a pink gin. "I felt guilty about Mr. Cummings-Browne's death, that was all," she said. "And there was a rumour that you and he were . . . friends."

Mrs. Cartwright grinned. "Oh, Reg liked his bit o' slap and tickle. No harm in it, is there? Took me out to a few posh restaurants. Said he'd marry me. I laughed like a drain. He wanted women to be crazy about him, so he usually made a pass at spinsters and widows. Didn't quite know what to make of me at first. We was good pals, for he knew I didn't believe a word he said."

"Weren't you worried about his wife finding out?"

"Nah. I s'pose her knew. Didn't bother her, none of it, I reckon."

"But you said they hated each other."

"I was trying to give you your money's worth. Tell you something, though. You never can tell what a married couple really think about each other. One says one thing, t'other says something else. Fact is, they got along pretty well. They was two of a kind."

"You mean, she had affairs as well?"

"Nah. She liked to play lady of the manor and he liked

135

to play Lord Muck, judging competitions, trying to rub shoulders with the aristocracy. You should have seen the pair of them if someone had a title. Scraping and simpering and my-lording the chap to death."

"What will you do now?"

"Get a job, I reckon. Mrs. Bloxby's coming to run me over to Mircester. There's a new Tesco's supermarket and they're hiring people. Don't want to go but you find you're doing what Mrs. Bloxby wants whether you wants to do it or not."

Agatha finished her gin and took her leave. Somehow what Ella had said about the Cummings-Browne's marriage made sense. There was no reason for any further investigation. Agatha realized that deep in her heart, she must have thought Vera Cummings-Browne the murderess all along. No one had murdered anybody. This time she really would take Bill Wong's advice.

But as she walked back to her own cottage, she saw to her surprise that there was a large FOR SALE notice outside Mrs. Barr's cottage. Mrs. Barr saw her coming and stood at her garden gate waiting for her.

"You have driven me away," said Mrs. Barr. "I cannot continue to live next door to a murderess."

"Fat chance you'll have of selling it," said Agatha. "Nobody's buying these days, and who the hell is going to want a twee cotage called New Delhi anyway?"

She marched to her own cottage and went in and slammed the door.

But Agatha felt bleak. She had poked a stick into the village ponds and stirred up a lot of mucky feelings.

That evening, before the Carsely Ladies' Society meeting, she went to the Red Lion for dinner. The landlord, Joe Fletcher, gave her a cheerful good evening and then asked her what all this business about John Cartwright trying to kill her had been. Immediately several of the villagers crowded around to hear the story. Agatha told them everything—about the wire across the road and how Bill Wong had come to her

rescue and how the police had found the money from the
robbery in Cartwright's house—while they all pressed closer,
occasionally making sure her glass was refilled. "I gather his
last crime was in Essex," said Agatha. "Does that mean he
wasn't from here?"

"Born and brought up here," said a large farmer called
Jimmy Page. "Decent people, his folks were. Lived down the
council houses. Died a whiles back. Couldn't do a thing with
him, not since he was so high. Got Ella in the family way and
her father came after him with a shotgun and that's how they
got married. Kept going off to make his fortune, he said, and
sometimes he'd come back flush and sometimes he wouldn't.
Bad lot."

Agatha realized dimly that she had not eaten but she did
not want to leave the bar and the company. She knew also that
she was sinking an unusually large amount of gin.

"I see Mrs. Barr has put her house up for sale," she
remarked.

"Oh, aye, her's been left a bigger cottage over Ancombe
way," said the farmer. "Aunt of hers died."

"What!" Agatha stared. "She let me believe it was to get
away from me."

"Wouldn't pay no heed to her," said farmer Page comfortably. A small man popped his head over Mr. Page's beefy
shoulder. "Her hasn't been the same since that play." His
voice rose to a falsetto. 'Oh, Reg, Reg, kiss me.' "

"That be enough now, Billy," admonished another man.
"We all makes a fool o' ourself sometime or t'other. No cause
to throw stones. Turning into a scorcher of a summer, ain't
it?"

In vain did Agatha try to find out about Mrs. Barr.
Gossip was over for the night. Farming and the weather were
the subjects allowed. The old grandfather clock in the corner
of the pub gave a small apologetic cough and then chimed out
the hour.

"Goodness!" Agatha scrambled down from the bar stool.
"I'm late."

She felt very tipsy as she hurried to the vicarage. "You're not terribly late," whispered Mrs. Bloxby after she had opened the door to her. "Miss Simms has just finished reading the minutes."

Agatha accepted a cup of tea and two dainty sandwiches and sat down as near to the rest of the eats as she could get.

"Now," said Mrs. Mason, "our guest of the evening, Mr. Jones."

Polite applause while Mr. Jones set up a screen and a slide projector.

He was a small spry man with white hair and horn-rimmed glasses.

"For my first slide," he said, "here is Bailey's grocery store in the 1920s." A picture, at first fuzzy, came into focus: a store with striped awnings, and grinning villagers standing in front of it. Delighted cries from the older members. "Reckon that's Mrs. Bloggs; you see that liddle girl standing to the right?"

Agatha stifled a yawn and slowly reached out in the gloom for a hefty slice of plum cake. She felt sleepy and bored. All the frights of the past few weeks which had kept her adrenalin flowing had faded away. The attacks on her had been made by a burglar who was now on the run. Maria Borrow was a crazy old fright. Barbara James was a pain in the neck. Something nasty had happened in the wood-shed of Mrs. Barr's past. Who gave a damn? And what was she, the high-powered Agatha Raisin, doing sitting in a vicarage eating plum cake and being bored to death?

Slide followed slide. Even when photos of "our village prize-winners" jerked onto the screen, Agatha remained in a stupor of boredom. There was Ella Cartwright being presented with a ten-pound note by Reg Cummings-Browne, looking as long dead as the old photos of villagers she had already seen. Then Vera Cummings-Browne getting a prize for flower arranging, then Mrs. Bloxby getting a prize for jam. Mrs. Bloxby? Agatha looked at the photo of the vicar's wife standing with Reg Cummings-Browne and then relapsed back into her torpor. Mrs. Bloxby? Not in a hundred years!

And then she fell asleep and in her dreams she cycled down into Carsely in the fading light and standing in the middle of the road waiting for her and brandishing a double-barrelled shotgun was Mrs. Barr. Agatha awoke with a shriek of fear and found the slide show was over and everyone was looking at her.

"Sorry," she mumbled.

"Don't worry," said Miss Simms, who was next to her. "It was that nasty fright you had."

When Agatha made her way homeward, she decided to get some sort of alarm system installed the very next day and then wondered why. Somewhere at the back of her mind, she had decided to leave the village.

The next day, she phoned a security firm and placed an order for their best of everything in the way of burglar-proofing and then went around opening the doors and the windows to try to get a breath of cool air. The heat was building up. Before, when it had been fine, the days had been sunny and the nights cool, but now the sky burnt blue, deep blue above the twisted cottage chimneys and the sun beat down. By lunch-time, the heat was fierce. She took a small thermometer outside and watched as it shot up over the one-hundred-degrees Fahrenheit mark and disappeared. Mrs. Simpson was vacuuming busily upstairs, having changed her cleaning day to fit in a dentist's appointment. Agatha remembered the talk about Mrs. Barr and climbed the stairs. "Can I have a word with you?" she shouted over the noise of the vacuum. Mrs. Simpson reluctantly turned the machine off. She was proud of doing a good job and felt she had already wasted too much time earlier hearing Agatha's adventures.

"I was asking in the pub last night why Mrs. Barr was selling up and I heard an aunt had died and left her a larger cottage over Ancombe way."

"Yes, that's right." Doris Simpson's hand hovered longingly over the vacuum switch.

"Why don't you come down to the kitchen and have a cup of coffee, Doris?"

"Got too much to do, Agatha."

"Skip for once. I'm still getting over my fright and I want to talk," said Agatha firmly.

"I meant to clean the windows."

"It's too hot. I'll hire a window cleaner. Doris!"

"Oh, all right," said Doris ungraciously.

Would anyone in this day and age believe you had to beg a cleaner to leave her work? marvelled Agatha.

Once in the kitchen and with coffee poured, Agatha said, "Now tell me about Mrs. Barr."

"What's to tell?"

"Someone in the pub said something about her having disgraced herself and then said in a high voice as if imitating her, 'Reg, Reg, kiss me.' "

"Oh, that!"

"Oh, what, Doris? I'm dying of curiosity."

"Curiosity killed the cat," said Doris sententiously. "Well, there was this young chap over at Campden and he wrote a play, sort of old-fashioned type thing it were, you know, where they has long cigarette holders and talks like them old British war films. He was a protegé of Vera Cummings-Browne. Anyway, Mrs. Cummings-Browne said she would get the dramatic society to put it on. Two of the parts were about a middle-aged couple remembering the passion of their youth, or that's how the programme put it. This was played by Mrs. Barr and Mr. Cummings-Browne. Dead boring that whole play was. Anyway, they were supposed to be on a liner and there they was sat, in deck chairs and with travel rugs over their knees saying things like, 'Remember India, darling?' "

"Sort of fake Noël Coward?"

"I s'pose. I wouldn't know. Anyways, Mrs. Barr suddenly turns to him and says, 'Reg, Reg, kiss me.' Well, that

140

waren't in the scrip' and what's more, the character Mr. Cummings-Browne was playing was called Ralph. He muttered something and she threw herself at him, his deck chair went over, and we all cheered and laughed, thinking it was the first funny thing that evening, but the playwright screamed awful words and tried to climb up on the stage and Mrs. Cummings-Browne closed the curtains. We could hear the most awful row going on backstage and then Mrs. Cummings-Browne came out in front of the curtains and said the rest of the play was cancelled."

"So Mrs. Barr must have been having an affair with Cummings-Browne!"

"You know, I often wonder if that one did more than have a bit of a kiss and cuddle. I mean, take Ella Cartwright; for all she looks like a slut, all she really cares about is getting money for the bingo. Now can I go back to work?"

The security firm arrived and Agatha paid over a staggering sum and then they began to fit lights and alarms and pressure pads.

"Going to be like Fort Knox here," grumbled Doris.

Agatha went out and sat in the garden to get away from the workmen, but the sun was too fierce. The air of the Cotswolds is very heavy and on that day the sun seemed to have burnt all the oxygen out of it. She felt as isolated as if she were on a desert island, even with Doris working away and men bustling about fixing the alarm system. She moved her chair into a patch of shade. She would not make any rash decisions. She would see how quickly Mrs. Barr sold her house and try to find out how much she got for it. If the sale was a healthy one, then she would put her own cottage on the market. She would move back to London and start all over again in the PR business. She would try to lure Roy away from Pedmans. He was shaping up nicely.

Although the news bulletins said the tar was melting on the streets of London under the heat, she saw it under rainy skies with the pavements glistening in the wet, reflecting the colours of the goods in the shop windows. She had become

141

used to the international population of London, to the different-coloured faces, to the exotic restaurants. Here she was surrounded by Anglo-Saxon faces and Anglo-Saxon ways. The scandal of John Cartwright was over, she knew that. Already plans were being made for the annual village band concert, money to Famine Relief this time. Apart from sending money off to the distressed of the outside world, the villagers were not much concerned with anything that went on which disturbed the slow, easy tenor of their days. Suffocating! That's what it was. Suffocating, thought Agatha, striking the arm of her chair.

"Someone to see you," called one of the workmen.

Agatha went into the house. Bill Wong was standing at the front door. "Come in," called Agatha. "Have they caught him?"

"Not yet. See you're getting every security system going."

"They've started, so they may as well finish," said Agatha. "Let's hope it adds to the price of the house, for I mean to leave." He followed her into the kitchen and sat down. "Leave? Why? Anyone else been trying to murder you?"

"Not yet." Agatha sat down opposite him. "I'm bored."

"Some would think you were leading a very exciting life in the country."

"I don't fit in here," said Agatha. "I mean to go back to London and start in business again."

His almond-shaped eyes studied her without expression. Then he said, "You know, you haven't given it much time. It takes about two years to settle in anywhere. Besides, you're a different person. Less prickly, less insensitive."

Agatha sniffed. "Weak, you mean. No, nothing will change my mind now. Why are you here?"

"Just to ask after your health." He fished in the pocket of the jacket which he had been carrying over his arm when he arrived and which was now on the back of the chair. He produced a jar of home-made jam. "It's my mother's," he said awkwardly. "Thought you might like some. Strawberry."

142

"Oh, how lovely," said Agatha. "I'll take it up to London with me."

"You're surely not leaving right away!"

"No, but I thought while you were talking that it would do me good to take a short holiday from Carsely—book into some hotel in London."

"How long for?"

"I don't know. Probably a week."

"So this means your life as an amateur detective is over."

"It never really got started," said Agatha. "I thought the fuss I was causing was because there was a murderer in the village. But all I was doing was riling people up."

Bill studied her for a few moments and then said, "Perhaps you might find you have changed. Perhaps you will find London doesn't suit you anymore."

"Now, that I very much doubt," laughed Agatha. "I tell you what I'll do when I get back. I'll invite you for dinner." She looked at him, suddenly shy. "That is, if you want to come."

"I'd like that . . . provided it isn't quiche."

After he had gone, Agatha paid Doris Simpson and told her she would be away the following week but gave her a spare key and got the head workman to instruct both of them in the mysterious working of the burglar alarms. Then she phoned up a small but expensive London hotel and booked herself in for a week. She was lucky they had just received a cancellation, and as it was, she had to reserve a double room.

Then she began to pack. The evening brought little respite from the heat and a good deal of nuisance. The news that all the lights outside Agatha's cottage went on when anyone passed on the road quickly spread amongst the village children, who ran up and down with happy swooping screams like giant swallows until the local policeman turned up to drive them away.

Agatha went along to the Red Lion. "We all need air-conditioning," she said to the landlord.

"Happen you're right," he said, "but what's the point of

the expense? Won't see another summer like this in England for years. Fact is, maybe we'll get a bad winter. Old Sam Sturret was just in here and he was saying how the winter's going to be mortal bad. We'll be snowed up for weeks, he says."

"Don't the snow-ploughs come around?"

"Not from the council, they don't, Mrs. Raisin m'dear. Us relies on the farmers with their tractors to try to keep the roads clear."

Agatha was about to protest that considering what they paid in poll-tax, they ought to have proper gritting and salting lorries, not to mention council snow-ploughs, and was about to say she would get up a petition to hand into the council when she remembered she would probably be living in London by the winter.

One by one, the locals began to drift into the pub. The landlord told them all he had put out tables in the garden and so they moved out there and Agatha was asked to join them. One man had brought along an accordion and he began to play and soon more villagers came in, drawn by the sound of the music, and then all began to sing along. Agatha was surprised, when the last orders were called, to realize she had been out in the pub garden all evening.

As she walked home, she felt muddled. That very afternoon, the burning ambition she had lived with so long had returned in full force and she had felt her old self again. Now she began to wonder whether she wanted to be her old self again. Her old self didn't sit singing in pubs or, she thought, as she saw Mrs. Bloxby outside her cottage door under the glare of the new security lights, get visits from the vicar's wife.

"I heard you were leaving for London tomorrow," said Mrs. Bloxby, "and came to say goodbye."

"Who told you?" asked Agatha, unlocking her front door.

"That nice young detective constable, Bill Wong."

"He always seems to be about. Doesn't he have any work to do in Mircester?"

144

"Oh, he often calls round the villages," said Mrs. Bloxby vaguely. "He also said something very distressing—about you leaving us for good."

"Yes, I plan to go back into business. I should never have retired so early."

"Well, that's a great pity for Carsely. We planned to make more use of your organizing skills. You will be back by next Saturday afternoon?"

"I doubt it," said Agatha, when they were both seated in the living-room. "Why next Saturday afternoon?"

"That's the day of the village band concert. Mrs. Mason is doing the cream teas. Quite an event."

Agatha gave her a rather pitying smile, thinking that it was a sad life if all you had to look forward to was a concert by the village band.

The talked for a little longer and then Mrs. Bloxby left. Agatha packed a suitcase, carefully putting the pot of strawberry jam in one corner. She lay awake for a long time with the bedroom windows wide open, hoping for a breath of air, but buoyed up by the thought of London and a return from the grave that was Carsely.

TEN

✝

LONDON! And how it smelt! Awful, thought Agatha, sitting in the dining-room of Haynes Hotel. She lit a cigarette and stared bleakly out at the traffic grinding past through Mayfair.

The man at the table behind her began to cough and choke and flap his newspaper angrily. Agatha looked at her burning cigarette and sighed. Then she raised a hand and summoned the waiter. "Remove that man from the table behind me," she said, "and find him somewhere else. He's annoying me."

The waiter looked from the man's angry face to Agatha's pugnacious one and then bent over the man and said soothingly that there was a nice table in the corner away from the smoke. The man protested loudly. Agatha continued to smoke, ignoring the whole scene, until the angry man capitulated and was led away.

Imagine living in London and complaining about cigarette smoke, marvelled Agatha. One had only to walk down the streets to inhale the equivalent of four packs of cigarettes.

She finished her coffee and cigarette and went up to her room, already suffocatingly hot, and phoned Pedmans and asked for Roy.

At last she was put through to him. "Aggie," he cried. "How are things in the Cotswolds?"

"Hellish," said Agatha. "I need to talk to you. What about lunch?"

"Lunch is booked. Dinner?"

"Fine. I'm at Haynes. See you at seven-thirty in the bar."

She put down the phone and looked around. Muslin curtains fluttered at the window, effectively cutting off what oxygen was left in the air. She should have gone to the Hilton or somewhere American, where they had air-conditioning. Haynes was small and old-fashioned, like a country house trapped in the middle of Mayfair. The service was excellent. But it was a very English hotel and very English hotels never planned on a hot summer.

She decided, for want of anything better to do, to go over to The Quicherie and see Mr. Economides. The traffic was congested as usual and there wasn't a taxi in sight, so she walked from Mayfair along through Knightsbridge to Sloane Street, down Sloane Street to Sloane Square, and so along the Kings Road to the World's End.

Mr. Economides gave her a guarded greeting, but Agatha had come to expect friendship and set herself to please in a way that was formerly foreign to her. The shop was quiet and relatively cool. It was the slack part of the day. Soon the lunch-time rush of customers would build up, buying coffee and sandwiches to take back to their offices. Agatha asked about Mr. Economides's wife and family and he began to relax perceptibly and then asked her to take a seat at one of the little marble-topped tables while he brought her a coffee.

"I really should apologize for having brought all that trouble down on your head," said Agatha. "If I hadn't decided to cheat at that village competition by passing one of your delicious quiches off as one of my own, this would never have happened."

Suddenly, for some reason, the full shock of the attack on her by John Cartwright suddenly hit her and her eyes shone with tears.

148

"Now, then, Mrs. Raisin," said Mr. Economides. "I'll tell you a little secret. I cheat, too."

Agatha dabbed at her eyes. "You? How?"

"You see, I have a sign up there saying 'Baked on the Premises,' but I often visit my cousin in Devon at the weekends. He has a delicatessen just like mine. Well, you see, sometimes if I'm going to be back late on a Sunday night after visiting him and I don't want to start baking early on Monday, I bring a big box of my cousin's quiches back with me if he has any left over. He does the same if he's visiting me, for his trade, unlike mine, is at the weekends with the tourists, while mine is during the week with the office people. So it was one of my cousin's quiches you bought."

"Did you tell the police this?" asked Agatha. The Greek looked horrified. "I didn't want to put the police onto my cousin." He looked at Agatha solemnly.

Agatha stared at him in bafflement and then the light dawned. "Is it the immigration police you're frightened of?"

He nodded. "My cousin's daughter's fiancé came on a visitor's visa and they married in the Greek Orthodox Church but haven't yet registered with the British authorities and he is working for his father-in-law without a work permit and so . . ." He gave a massive shrug.

Agatha did not know anything about work permits but she did know from her dealings with foreign models in the past that they were paranoid about being deported. "So it was just as well Mrs. Cummings-Browne didn't sue," she said.

A shutter came down over his eyes. Two customers walked into the shop and he said a hurried goodbye before scuttling back behind the counter.

Agatha finished her coffee and took a stroll around her old haunts. She had a light lunch at the Stock Pot and then decided an air-conditioned cinema would be the best way to pass the afternoon. A little voice in her head was telling her that if she was determined to move back to London, she should start looking for a flat to live in and business premises to work from, but she shrugged the voice away. There was

149

time enough, and besides, it was too hot. She bought an *Evening Standard* and discovered that a cinema off Leicester Square was showing a rerun of Disney's *Jungle Book*. So she went there and enjoyed the film and came out with the pleasurable prospect of seeing Roy, feeling sure that he would galvanize her into starting her new business.

It was hard, she thought, when she descended to the hotel bar at seven-thirty, to get used to the new Roy. There he was with one of the latest flat-topped haircuts and a sober business suit and an imitation of a Guard's regimental tie.

He hailed her affectionately. Agatha bought him a double gin and asked him how his nursery project was going and he said it was coming along nicely and that they had made him a junior executive and had given him a private office and a secretary because they were so impressed by his getting his photo in the *Sunday Times*. "Have another gin," said Agatha, wishing that Roy were still unhappy at Pedmans.

He grinned. "You forget I've seen the old Aggie in action. Fill 'em up with booze and then go in for the kill over coffee. Break the habit, Aggie. Hit me with whatever is on your mind before we get to dinner."

"All right," said Agatha. She looked around. The bar was getting crowded. "Let's take our drinks to that table over there."

Once they were both settled, she leaned forward and looked at him intently. "I'll come straight out with it, Roy. I'm coming back to London. I'm going to set up in business again and I want you to be my partner."

"Why? You're through with the mess. You've got that lovely cottage and that lovely village . . ."

"And I'm dying of boredom."

"You haven't given it time, Aggie. You haven't settled in yet."

"Well, if you're not interested," said Agatha sulkily.

"Aggie, Pedmans is big, one of the biggest. You know that. I've got a great future in front of me. I'm taking it serious now instead of camping about a few pop groups. I want to get

150

out of pop groups. One of them hits the charts and then, two weeks later, no one wants to know. And you know why? The pop business has become all hype and no substance. No tunes. All thump, thump, thump for the discos. Sales are a fraction of what they used to be. And do you know why I want to stick with Pedmans? I'm on my way up and fast. And I plan to get what you've got—a cottage in the Cotswolds.

"Look, Aggie, no one wants to live in cities anymore. The new generation is getting Americanized. Get up early enough in the morning and you don't need to live in London. Besides, I'm thinking of getting married."

"Oh, pull the other one," said Agatha rudely. "I don't think you've ever taken a girl out in your life."

"That's all you know. The thing is that Mr. Wilson likes his execs to be married."

"And who's the lucky girl?"

"Haven't found her yet. But some nice quiet girl will do. There are lots around. Someone to cook the meals and iron the shirts."

Really, thought Agatha crossly, under the exterior of every effeminate man beats the heart of a real chauvinist pig. He would find a young girl, meek, biddable, a bit common so as not to make him feel inferior. She would be expected to learn to host little dinner parties and not complain when her husband only came home at weekends. They would learn to play golf. Roy would gradually become plump and stuffy. She had seen it all happen before.

"But as my partner, you could earn more," she said.

"You've lost your clients to Pedmans. It would take ages to get them back. You know that, Aggie. You'd have to start small again and build up. Is that what you really want? Let's go in for dinner and talk some more. I'm famished."

Agatha decided to leave the subject for the moment and began to tell him about the attack on her by John Cartwright and how he had turned out to be a burglar.

"Honestly, Aggie, don't you see—London would be *tame*

151

by comparison. Besides, a friend tells me you're never alone in the country. The neighbours care what happens to you."

"Unless they're like Mrs. Barr," said Agatha drily. "She's selling up. The cow had the cheek to claim I had driven her off, but in fact she was left a bigger cottage by an aunt in Ancombe."

"I thought she was an incomer," said Roy. "Now you tell me she's had at least one relative living close by."

"If you haven't been born and brought up in Carsely itself, take it from me, you're an incomer," reported Agatha. "Oh, something else about her."

She told Roy about the play and he shrieked with laughter. "Oh, it must be murder, Aggie," he gasped.

"No, I don't think it was any more, and I don't care now. I visited Economides today and the reason he's glad to let the whole business blow over is that the quiche he sold me was actually baked on his cousin's premises down in Devon and the cousin has a new son-in-law working for him who doesn't have a work permit."

"Ah, that explains that, and the burglaring John Cartwright explains his behavior, but what of the women that Cummings-Browne was philandering with? What of the mad Maria?"

"I think she's just mad, and Barbara James is a toughie and Ella Cartwright is a slut and Mrs. Barr has a screw loose as well, but I don't think any of them murdered Cummings-Browne. Here I go again. It wasn't murder, Roy. Bill Wong was right."

"Which leaves Vera Cummings-Browne."

"As for her, I was suddenly sure she had done it, that it was all very simple. She suddenly thought of the murder when I left my quiche. She went home and dumped mine and baked another."

"Brilliant," said Roy. "And she wasn't found out because Economides was so frightened about work permits and things that he didn't look at or examine the quiche that was supposed to be his!"

152

"That's a good theory. But the police exploded that. They checked everything in her kitchen, her pots and pans, her groceries and even her drains. She hadn't been baking or cooking anything at all on the day of the murder. Let it go, Roy. You've got me calling it murder and I had just put it all behind me. To get back to more interesting matters . . . Are you determined to stay with Pedmans?"

"I'm afraid so, Aggie. It's all your fault in a way. If you hadn't arranged that publicity for me, I wouldn't have risen so fast. Tell you what I'll do, though. You get started and I'll drop a word in your ear when I know any client who's looking for a change . . . not one of mine, of course. But that's all I can do."

Agatha felt flat. The ambition which had fueled her for so long seemed to be draining away. After she had said goodbye to Roy, she went out and walked restlessly about the night-time streets of London, as if searching for her old self. In Piccadilly Circus, a couple of white-faced drug addicts gazed at her with empty eyes and a beggar threatened her. Heat still seemed to be pulsing up from the pavements and out from the buildings.

For the rest of the week, she took walks in the parks, a sail down the Thames, and went to theatres and cinemas, moving through the stifling heat of London feeling like a ghost, or someone who had lost her cards of identity. For so long, her work had been her character, her personality, her identity.

By Friday evening, the thought of the village band concert began to loom large in her mind. The women of the Carsely Ladies' Society would be there, she could trot along to the Red Lion if she was lonely, and perhaps she could do something about her garden. Not that she was giving up her idea! A pleasant-looking garden would add to the sale price of the house.

She arose early in the morning and settled her bill and made her way to Paddington Station. She had left her car at Oxford. Once more she was on her way back. "Oxford. This

153

is Oxford," intoned the guard. With a strange feeling of being on home ground, she eased out of the car-park and drove up Worcester Street and then Beaumont Street and so along St. Giles and the Woodstock Road to the Woodstock Roundabout, where she took the A-40 bypass to Burford, up over the hills to Stowe-on-the-Wold, along to the A-44 and so back down into Carsely.

As she drove along Lilac Lane to her cottage, she suddenly braked hard outside New Delhi. SOLD screamed a sticker across the estate agent's board.

Wonder how much she got, mused Agatha, driving on to her own cottage. That was quick! But good riddance to bad rubbish anyway. Hope someone pleasant moves in. Not that it matters for I'm leaving myself, she reminded herself fiercely.

Urged by a superstitious feeling that the village was settling around her and claiming her for its own, she left her suitcase inside the door and drove off again to the estate agent's offices in Chipping Campden, the same estate agent who had sold Mrs. Barr's house.

She introduced herself and said she was putting her house on the market. How much for? Well, the same amount as Mrs. Barr got for hers would probably do. The estate agent said he was not allowed to reveal how much Mrs. Barr had got but added diplomatically that she had been asking for £150,000 and was very pleased with the offer she had received.

"I want one hundred seventy-five thousand pounds for mine," said Agatha. "It's thatched and I'll bet it's in better nick than that tart's."

The estate agent blinked, but a house for sale was a house for sale, and so he and Agatha got down to business.

I don't need to sell to just anyone, thought Agatha. After all, I owe it to Mrs. Bloxby and the rest to see that someone nice gets it.

The village band was playing outside the school hall. Before Agatha went to hear it, she carried a present she had bought for Doris Simpson along to the council estate. When she pushed open the gate of Doris's garden, she noticed to her

154

surprise that all the gnomes had gone. But she rang the bell
and when Doris answered, put a large brown paper parcel in
her arms.

"Come in," said Doris. "Bert! Here's Agatha back from
London with a present. It's ever so nice of you. You really
shouldn't have bothered."

"Open it, then," said Bert, when the parcel was placed on
the coffee-table in their living-room.

Doris pulled off the wrappings to reveal a large gnome
with a scarlet tunic and green hat. "You really shouldn't have
done it," said Doris with feeling. "You really shouldn't."

"You deserve it," said Agatha. "No, I won't stay for
coffee. I'm going to hear the band."

Inside the school hall, stalls had been set up. Agatha went
in and wandered about, amused to notice that some of the
items from her auction were being recycled. And then she
stopped short in front of a stall run by Mrs. Mason. It was
covered in garden gnomes.

"Where did you get all these?" asked Agatha, filled with
an awful suspicion.

"Oh, that was the Simpsons," she said. "The gnomes
were there when they moved into that house and they've been
meaning to get rid of them for ages. Can I interest you in
buying one? What about this jolly little fellow with the fishing
rod? Brighten up your garden."

"No, thanks," said Agatha, feeling like a fool. And yet
how could she have known the Simpsons didn't like gnomes?

She wandered into the tea-room, which was off the main
hall, to find Mrs. Bloxby helping Mrs. Mason. "Welcome
back," cried Mrs. Bloxby. "What can I get you?"

"I haven't had lunch," said Agatha, "so I'll have a couple
of those Cornish pasties and a cup of tea. You must have been
up all night baking."

"Oh, it's not all mine, and when we have a big affair like
this, we do it in bits and pieces. We bake things and put them
in the freezer, that big thing over there, and then just defrost
them in the microwave on the day of the event."

Agatha picked up her plate of pasties and her teacup and sat down at one of the long tables. Farmer Jimmy Page joined her and introduced his wife. Various other people came over. Soon Agatha was surrounded by a group of people all chatting away.

"You'll know soon enough," she said at last. "I'm putting my cottage up for sale."

"Well, that's a pity," said Mr. Page. "You off to Lunnon again?"

"Yes, going to restart in business."

"S'pose it's different for you, Mrs. Raisin," said his wife. "I once went up there and I was so lonely. Cities are lonely places. Different for you. You must have scores of friends."

"Yes," lied Agatha, thinking bleakly that the only friend she had was Roy and he had only become a friend since she had moved to the Cotswolds. The heat was still fierce. Agatha felt too lazy to think what to do next and somehow she found she had accepted an invitation to go back to Jimmy Page's farm with a group of them. Once at the farm, which was up on a rise above the village, they all sat outside and drank cider and talked idly about how hot the weather was and remembered summers of long ago, until the sun began to move down the sky and someone suggested they should move to the Red Lion and so they did.

Walking home later, slightly tipsy, Agatha shook off doubts about selling the house. Once the winter came, things in Carsely would look different, bleaker, more shut off. She had done the right thing. But Jimmy Page had said her cottage was seventeenth century. Nothing fake about it, he had said, apart from the extension.

She kicked off her shoes and reached out a hand to switch on the lights when the security lights came on outside the house, brilliant and dazzling. She stood frozen. There came soft furtive sounds as though someone were retreating quietly from the door. All she had to do was to fling open the door and see who it was. But she could not move. She felt sure something dark and sinister was out there. It could not be

156

children. Young people in Carsely went to bed at good old-fashioned times of the evening, even on holiday.

She sank down onto the floor and sat there with her back against the wall, listening hard. And then the security lights went off again, plunging the house into darkness.

She sat there for a long time before slowly rising and switching on the house lights, moving from room to room, switching them all on as she had done before when she was frightened.

Agatha wondered whether to call Mrs. Bloxby. It was probably one of the young men of the village, or someone walking a dog. Slowly her fear left her, but when she went up to bed, she left all the lights burning.

In the morning she was heartened to see a huge removal van outside New Delhi and the removal men hard at work. Obviously Mrs. Barr did not see anything wrong in moving house on the Sabbath. Agatha was just wondering whether to go to church or not when the phone rang. It was Roy.

"I've got a surprise for you, love."

Agatha felt a sudden surge of hope. "You've decided to leave Pedmans?"

"No, I've bought a car, a Morris Minor. Got it for a song. Thought I'd drive down and bring the girl-friend to see you."

"Girl-friend? You haven't got one."

"I have now. Can we come?"

"Of course. What's her name?"

"Tracy Butterworth."

"And what does she do?"

"She's one of the typists in the pool at Pedmans."

"When will you get here?"

"We're leaving now. Hour and a half if the roads aren't bad. Maybe two."

Agatha looked in the fridge after she had rung off. She hadn't even any milk. She went to a supermarket in Stow-on-the-Wold which opened on Sundays and bought milk, lettuce and tomatoes for salad, minced meat and potatoes to make

157

shepherd's pie, onions and carrots, peas, a frozen apple pie and some cream.

There was no need to do any cleaning when she returned. Doris had been in while she had been in London and the place was impeccable. As she drove down into Carsely, the removal van passed her, followed by Mrs. Barr in her car. They must have been at it since six in the morning, thought Agatha, making a mental note of the removal firm.

She put away her groceries when she got home, found a pair of scissors, edged through the hedge at the back into Mrs. Barr's garden, and cut bunches of flowers to decorate her cottage.

She prepared the shepherd's pie after she had arranged the flowers, thinking that she really must do something about the garden. It would look lovely in the spring if she put in a lot of bulbs—but, of course, she would not be in Carsely in the spring.

Being still an inexperienced cook, the simple shepherd's pie took quite a long time and she was just putting it in the oven when she heard a car draw up.

Tracy Butterworth was all Agatha had expected. She was thin and pallid, with limp brown hair. She was wearing a white cotton suit with a pink frilly blouse and very high-heeled white shoes. She had a limp handshake and said, "Please ter meet you," in a shy whisper and then looked at Roy with devotion.

"I see a removal van outside that awful woman's cottage," said Roy.

"What!" Agatha cast an anguished look at the vases of flowers. "I thought she'd gone."

"Relax. Someone's moving in, not out. Say something, Tracy. She won't eat you."

"You've got ever such a lovely cottage," volunteered Tracy. She dabbed at her forehead with a scrap of lace-edged handkerchief.

"It's too hot to be dressed up," said Agatha. Tracy winced and Agatha said with new kindness, "Not that you

158

don't look very smart and pretty. But make yourself at home. Kick off your shoes and take off your jacket."

Tracy looked nervously at Roy.

"Do as she says," he ordered.

Tracy had very long thin feet, which she wriggled in an embarrassed way once her shoes were off. Poor thing, thought Agatha. He'll marry her and turn her into the complete Essex woman. Two children called Nicholas and Daphne at minor public schools, house in some twee builder's close called Loam End or something, table-mats from the Costa Brava, ruched curtains, Jacuzzi, giant television set, boredom, out on Saturday night to some road-house for chicken in a basket washed down with Beaujolais nouveau and followed by Black Forest gateau. Yes, Essex it would be and not the Cotswolds. Roy would be happier with his own kind. He too would change and take up weight-lifting and squash and walk around with a portable telephone glued to his ear, speaking very loudly into it in restaurants.

"Let's go along to the pub for a drink," said Agatha, after Roy had been talking about the days when he worked for her, elaborating every small incident for Tracy's benefit. Agatha wondered whether to offer Tracy a loose dress to wear but decided against it. The girl would take it as a criticism of what she was wearing.

In the pub, Agatha introduced them to her new-found friends and Tracy blossomed in the undemanding company which only expected her to talk about the weather.

The heat was certainly bad enough to be exciting. The sun beat down fiercely outside. One man volunteered that a temperature of 129 degrees Fahrenheit had been recorded at Cheltenham.

Back at the cottage and Tracy helped with the lunch, her high heels stabbing little holes into the kitchen linoleum until Agatha begged her to take them off. There was some shade in the garden after lunch and so they moved there, drinking coffee and listening idly to the sounds of the new neighbour moving in.

"Don't you even want to peek over the hedge or take a cake along or something?" asked Roy. "Aren't you curious?"

Agatha shook her head. "I've seen the estate agent and this house goes up for sale next week."

"You're selling?" Tracy looked at her in amazement. "Why?"

"I'm going back to London."

Tracy looked around the sunny garden and then up to the Cotswold Hills above the village, shimmering in a heat haze. She shook her head in bewilderment. "Leave all this? I've never seen anywhere more beautiful in all me life." She looked back at the cottage and struggled to express her thoughts. "It's so old, so settled. There's somethink peaceful about it, know what I mean? Of course, I s'pose it's diff'rent for you, Mrs. Raisin. You've probably travelled and seen all sorts of beautiful places."

Yes, Carsely *was* beautiful, thought Agatha reluctantly. The village was blessed with many underground springs, and so, in the middle of all the drought around, it glowed like a green emerald.

"She doesn't like it," crowed Roy, "because people keep trying to murder her."

Tracy begged to be told all about it and so Agatha began at the beginning, talking at first to Tracy and then to herself, for there was something nagging at the back of her mind.

That evening, Roy took them out for dinner to a pretentious restaurant in Mircester. Tracy only drank mineral water, for she was to drive Roy home. She seemed intimidated by the restaurant but admiring of Roy, who was snapping his fingers at the waiters and, as far as Agatha was concerned, behaving like a first-class creep. Yes, thought Agatha, Roy will marry Tracy and she will probably think she is happy and Roy will turn out to be someone I can't stand. I wish I had never got him that publicity.

When she waved goodbye to them, it was with a feeling of relief. The time was rapidly approaching when Roy would phone expecting an invitation and she would make some excuse.

But of course she wouldn't need to bother. For she would be back in London.

ELEVEN

†

ON Monday morning, Agatha rose late, wondering why she had slept so long and wishing she had risen earlier to catch any coolness of the day. She put on a loose cotton dress over the minimum of underwear, went downstairs and took a mug of coffee out into the garden.

She had been plagued with dreams of Maria Borrow, Barbara James, and Ella Cartwright, who had appeared as the three witches in *Macbeth*. "I have summoned the evil spirits to kill you," Maria Borrow had croaked.

Agatha sighed and finished her coffee and went for a walk to the butcher's which was near the vicarage. The sign saying "New Delhi" had been taken down. There was no evidence of the new owner, but Mrs. Mason and two other women were standing on the step, carrying cakes to welcome the newcomer. Agatha walked on, reflecting that nobody had called on *her* when she had first arrived.

She was about to go into the butcher's when she stiffened. A little way away, Vera Cummings-Browne was standing talking to Barbara James, who had a Scottie on a leash. Agatha dived for cover into the butcher's shop and almost collided with Mrs. Bloxby.

"Seen your new neighbour yet?" asked Mrs. Bloxby.

"No, not yet," said Agatha, keeping a wary eye on the door in case Barbara should leap in and savage her. "Who is he?"

"A retired colonel. Mr. James Lacey. He doesn't use his title. Very charming."

"I'm not interested," snapped Agatha. Mrs. Bloxby looked at her in pained surprise and Agatha coloured.

"Sorry," she mumbled. "I just saw Vera Cummings-Browne with Barbara James. Barbara James tried to attack me."

"She always had a dreadful temper," said Mrs. Bloxby placidly. "Mrs. Cummings-Browne is just back from Tuscany. She is very brown and looks fit."

"I didn't even know she was away," commented Agatha. "I'm wondering what to buy. My cooking skills are still very limited."

"Get some of those lamb chops," advised the vicar's wife, "and put them under the grill with a little mint. I have fresh mint in the garden. Come back with me for a coffee and I'll give you some. You just cook the chops slowly on either side until they are brown. Very simple. And I shall give you some of my mint sauce, too."

Agatha obediently bought the chops but hesitated in the doorway. "Do you mind seeing if the coast is clear?"

Mrs. Bloxby looked out. "They've both gone."

Over the coffee-cups in the vicarage garden, under the shade of a cypress tree, Mrs. Bloxby asked, "Are you still determined to move?"

"Yes," said Agatha bleakly, wishing some of her old ambition and drive would come back to her. "The estate agents should be putting a 'For Sale' board up this morning."

Mrs. Bloxby looked at her over the rim of her coffee-cup. "Strange how things work out, Mrs. Raisin. I thought your being here had something to do with Divine Providence."

Agatha gave a startled grunt.

"First I felt you had been brought here for your own benefit. You struck me as a lady who had never known any

164

real love or affection. You seemed to carry a weight of loneliness about with you."

Agatha stared at her in deep embarrassment.

"Then of course there is the death of Mr. Cummings-Browne. My husband, like the police, maintains it was an accident. I felt that God had sent you here to find out the culprit."

"Meaning you think it's murder!"

"I've tried not to. So much more comfortable to believe it an accident and settle back into our ways. But there is something, some atmosphere, something *wrong*. I sense evil in this village. Now you are going, no one will ask questions, no one will care, and the evil will remain. Call me silly and superstitious if you like, but I believe the taking of a human life is a grievous sin which should be punished by law." She gave a little laugh. "So I shall pray that if murder has been done, then the culprit will be revealed."

"But you've got nothing concrete to go on?" asked Agatha.

She shook her head. "Just a feeling. But you are going, so that is that. I feel that Bill Wong shares my doubts."

"He's the one that has been urging me to leave the whole thing alone!"

"That is because he is fond of you and does not want to see you get hurt."

Agatha turned the conversation over in her mind. The "For Sale" notice was up when she got back, giving her a temporary feeling, as if she had already left the village.

She got out a large notebook and pen and sat down at the kitchen table and began to write down everything that had happened since she came to the village. The long hot day wore on and she wrote busily, going back and back over her notes, looking for some clue. Then she tapped the pen on the paper. For a start, there was one little thing. The body had been found on Sunday. On Tuesday—it must have been Tuesday, for on the Wednesday the police had told her that Mrs. Cummings-Browne did not mean to sue The Quicherie—the bereaved widow had gone to Chelsea *in person*. Agatha sat back and chewed the end of her pen. Now wasn't that odd behaviour? If your husband has just been murdered and you are collapsing about the place with grief and everyone is talking about how stricken you are, how do you summon up the energy to go all the way to London? She could just as easily have phoned. Why? Agatha glanced at the kitchen clock. What exactly had Vera Cummings-Browne *said* to Mr. Economides? She went to the phone, lifted the receiver and put it back down again. Despite his confession about his relative without the work permit, the Greek had still looked guarded. The shop didn't close till eight. Agatha decided to motor up to London and catch him before he shut the shop for the evening.

She had just locked the door behind her when she found on turning round that a family consisting of ferrety husband, plump wife, and two spotty teenagers were surveying her.

"We've come to look round the house," said the man.

"You can't." Agatha pushed past the family.

"It says 'For Sale,' " he complained.

"It's already sold," lied Agatha. She heaved the board out of the ground and dropped it on the grass. Then she got into her car and drove off, leaving the family staring after her.

The hell with it, thought Agatha, I wouldn't want to inflict that lot on the village anyway.

She made London in good time, for most of the traffic was going the other way.

She parked on a double yellow line outside The Quicherie.

She went into the shop. Mr. Economides was clearing his cold shelf of quiche for the night. He looked at Agatha and again that wariness was in his eyes.

"I want to talk to you," said Agatha bluntly. "Don't worry," she lied. "I've got friends in the Home Office. You won't come to any harm."

He took off his apron and walked around the counter.

The both sat down at one of his little tables. There was no offer of coffee. His dark eyes surveyed her mournfully.

"Look, tell me exactly what happened between you and Mrs. Cummings-Browne when she called on you."

"Can't we forget the whole thing?" he pleaded. "All ended well. No bad publicity in the London papers."

"A man was poisoned," said Agatha. "Don't worry your head about immigration. I'll keep you out of it. Just tell me."

"All right. She came in in the morning. I forget what day it was. But mid-morning. She started shouting that I had poisoned her husband and that she would sue me for every penny I'd got. She told me about the quiche you had bought. I cried and pleaded innocence. I threw myself on her mercy. I told her the quiche was not one of mine but had come down from Devon. I told her my cousin grew all the vegetables for his shop in his own market garden. Some of that cowbane must have got mixed in with the spinach. I told her about my cousin's son-in-law. She went very quiet. Then she said she was overwrought. She said she hardly knew what she was saying. She was a different woman, calm and sad. No action would be taken against me or my cousin, she said.

"But the next day, she came back."

"What!"

Agatha leaned forward, clenching her hands in excitement.

"She said that if I ever told anyone that the quiche had come from Devon, then she would change her mind and sue and she would also report my relative to the Home Office and get him deported."

"Goodness!" Agatha looked at him in bewilderment. "She must be mad." Two people came into the shop. Mr. Economides rose to his feet. "You will not tell? I only told you before because I thought the whole thing was over."

"No, no," gabbled Agatha.

She went out into the heat and drove off, heading automatically back to the Cotswolds, her brain in a turmoil. Vera

Cummings-Browne didn't want the police to know that the quiche had come from Devon. Why?

And then the light dawned. A phrase from the book on poisonous plants leaped into her mind. "Cowbane is to be found in marshy parts of Britain . . . East Anglia, West Midlands, and southern Scotland." But not Devon.

But, wait a bit. The police had been thorough. They had searched her kitchen and even her drains for traces of cowbane. And they had said that Vera Cummings-Browne probably didn't know cowbane from a palm tree. But couldn't she just have looked up a book, as she, Agatha, had done? If she had, she would not only know what it looked like and where to get it, she would know it did not grow in Devon.

When she got home, Agatha wondered whether to phone Bill Wong but then decided against it. He would have all the answers. There had been no trace of cowbane in Vera's house. Her brain had been unhinged by the death and that was why she had gone to see Economides.

She put the estate agent's display board back in place and then tried to get a good night's sleep, but the days and days of heat had made the old stone walls of her cottage radiate like a furnace.

Agatha awoke, tired and listless, but dutifully got out her notes again and added what she had found out.

Cowbane. What about the local library? she thought with a jolt. Would they know whether Vera Cummings-Browne had taken out a book on poisonous plants? Would there be a record? Of course there must be! How else could they write to people who had failed to return books?

As she trudged along to the library, Agatha reflected that her standard of dressing was slipping. In London, she had used Margaret Thatcher as a role model, rather than Joan Collins or any other British beauty, favouring crisp dresses and business suits. Now her loose print dress flopped about her and her bare feet were thrust into sandals.

The library was a low stone building. A plaque above the door stated it had been originally the village workhouse. Agatha pushed open the door and went in. She recognized the lady behind the desk as being Mrs. Josephs, one of the members of the Carsely Ladies' Society.

Mrs. Josephs smiled brightly. "Were you looking for anything in particular, Mrs. Raisin? We've got the latest Dick Francis."

Agatha plunged in. "I was upset by Mr. Cummings-Browne's death," she said.

"As were we all," murmured Mrs. Josephs.

"I'd hate a mistake like that to happen again," said Agatha. "Have you a book on poisonous plants?"

"Now, let me see." Mrs. Josephs extracted a microfiche nervously from a pile and slotted it into the viewing screen. "Yes, Jerome on *Poisonous Plants of the British Isles.* Number K-543. Over to your left by the window, Mrs. Raisin."

Agatha searched the shelves until she found the book. She opened it at the front and studied the dates stamped there. It had last been taken out a whole ten days before the death. Still . . .

"Could you tell me who was the last to take this out, Mrs. Josephs?"

"Why?" The librarian looked anxious. "I hope it wasn't Mrs. Boggle. She *will* leave the pages stuck together with marmalade."

"I was thinking of getting up a lecture on local poisonous plants," said Agatha, improvising. "Whoever had it out before might show equal interest," said Agatha, looking at the illustrations in the book as she spoke.

"Oh, well, let me see. We still have the old-fashioned card system." She drew out long drawers and flicked through the listed book cards until she drew out the one on poisonous plants. "That was last taken out by card holder number 27. We don't have many members. I fear this is a *television* village. Let me see. Number 27. Why, that's Mrs. Cummings-Browne!" Her mouth fell a little open and she stared through her glasses at Agatha.

And at that moment, the library door opened and Vera

Cummings-Browne walked in. Agatha seized the book and returned it to the shelves and then said brightly to Mrs. Josephs, "I'll let you know about the Dick Francis."

"You'll need to join the library first, Mrs. Raisin. Would you like a card?"

"Later," muttered Agatha. She looked over her shoulder. Vera was standing some distance away, looking through the returned books. "Not a word," hissed Agatha and shot out.

So she did know about cowbane, thought Agatha triumphantly. And she certainly knew what it looked like. She saw clearly in her mind's eye the coloured illustration in the book. Then she stopped in the middle of the main street, too shocked to notice that a handsome middle-aged man had come out of the butcher's and was looking at her curiously.

She had seen cowbane recently, but in black and white. What? Where? She began to walk home, cudgelling her brains.

And then, just at her garden gate, she had it. The slide show. Mr. Jones's slide show. Mrs. Cummings-Browne getting the prize for the best flower arrangement, an arty thing of wild flowers and garden flowers and, snakes and bastards, *with a piece of cowbane right in the middle of it!*

The handsome middle-aged man was turning in at the gate of what had so recently been Mrs. Barr's cottage. He was the new tenant, James Lacey.

"Must find Jones," said Agatha aloud. "Must find Jones."

Batty, thought James Lacey. I don't know that I like having a neighbour like that.

Into Harvey's went Agatha. "Where do I find Mr. Jones, the one who takes the photographs?"

"That'll be the second cottage along Mill Pond Edge," said the woman behind the till. "Do be uncommon hot, Mrs. Raisin."

"Screw the weather," said Agatha furiously. "Where's Mill Pond Edge?"

"Second lane on your right as you go out the door."

"I know the heat's getting us down," said the woman in

Harvey's to Mrs. Cummings-Browne later, "but there was no need for Mrs. Raisin to be so rude. I was only trying to tell her where Mr. Jones lives."

Agatha was fortunate in finding Mr. Jones at home because he was also a keen gardener and liked to spend most of the day touring the local nurseries. He had all his photographs neatly filed and found the one Agatha asked for without any trouble.

She looked greedily at the flower arrangement. "Mind if I keep this for a few days?"

"No, not at all," said Mr. Jones.

And Agatha shot off without warning him not to say anything to Mrs. Cummings-Browne.

She went to the Red Lion, clutching the photo in a brown manila envelope, her brain buzzing with thoughts.

She ordered a double gin and tonic. "Someone said as how he'd seen that detective, the Chinese one, heading your way with a basket," said the landlord.

Agatha frowned. She did not want to tell Bill anything. Not now. Not until she had it all worked out.

Bill Wong turned away from Agatha's cottage, disappointed. He glared up at the "For Sale" sign. He felt sure she was making a mistake. A faint miaow came from inside the basket. "Shh," he said gently. He had brought Agatha a cat. His mother's cat had produced a litter and Bill, as usual, could not bear to see the little creatures drowned, so had started to inflict them on his friends as presents.

He was walking past the cottage next door when he saw James Lacey. "Good morning," said Bill. He eyed the newcomer to Carsely shrewdly and wondered what Agatha thought of him. James Lacey was surely handsome enough to strike any middle-aged woman all of a heap. He was over six feet tall, with a strong tanned face and bright blue eyes. His thick black hair, fashionably cut, had only a trace of grey. "I was looking for your neighbour, Mrs. Raisin," said Bill.

"I think the heat's got to her," said James in a clear

171

upper-class voice. "She went past me muttering, 'Mr. Jones, Mr. Jones.' Whoever Mr. Jones is, I feel sorry for him."

"Anyway, I've brought her this cat," said Bill, "as a present, and a litter tray. It's house-trained. Would you be so good as to give it to her when she returns? My name is Bill Wong."

"All right. Do you know when that will be?"

"Shouldn't be long," said Bill. "Her car's outside."

He handed over the cat in its carrying basket and the litter tray and went off. Jones, he thought. What's she up to now?"

He went into Harvey's to buy a bar of chocolate and asked the woman behind the till, "Who's Mr. Jones?"

"Not you too," she said crossly. "Mrs. Raisin was in here to find out, and quite rude she was. We're all suffering from this heat, but there's no call to behave like that."

Bill waited patiently until the complaints were over and he could find out about Mr. Jones. He didn't really know why he was bothering except that Agatha Raisin had a way of stirring things up.

Agatha was quite depressed as she walked home. She thought she had solved the case, as she had begun to call it in her mind, but while in the pub, that great stumbling block had risen up in front of her again. There was no way Vera Cummings-Browne could have cooked a poisoned quiche in her kitchen without the police forensic team finding a trace of it.

She let herself wearily into her hot house. Better put the whole business to the back of her mind and go down to Moreton and buy a fan of some kind.

There was a knock at the door. She looked through the new spyhole installed by the security people and found herself looking at the middle of a man's checked shirt. She opened the door on the chain.

"Mrs. Raisin," said the man. "I am your new neighbour, James Lacey."

"Oh." Agatha took in the full glory of James Lacey and her mouth dropped open.

"A Mr. Wong called but you were out."

"What do the police want now?" demanded Agatha crossly.

"I did not know he was from the police. He was plain clothes. He asked me to give you this cat."

"Cat!" echoed Agatha, amazed.

"Yes, cat," he said patiently, thinking, she really is nuts.

Agatha dropped the chain and opened the door. "Come in," she said, suddenly aware of her loose print dress and her bare, unshaven legs.

They walked into the kitchen. Agatha knelt down and opened the basket. A small tabby kitten strolled out, looked around and yawned. "That's a sweet little fellow," he said, edging towards the door. "Well, if you'll excuse me, Mrs. Raisin . . ."

"Won't you stay? Have a cup of coffee?"

"No, I really must go. Oh, there's someone at your door."

"Could you wait just for a moment," said Agatha, "and watch the kitten until I see who that is?"

She left the kitchen before he could reply. She opened the door. A woman stood there, looking as fresh as a spring day despite the heat. She was wearing a white cotton dress with a red leather belt around her slender waist. Her legs were tanned and unhairy. Her expensively dyed blonde hair shone in the sunlight. She was about forty, with a clever face and hazel eyes. She was exactly the sort of woman, Agatha thought, who would be bound to catch the eye of this glamorous new neighbour.

"What is it?" demanded Agatha.

"I've come to view the house."

"It's sold. Goodbye." Agatha slammed the door.

"If your house is sold," said James Lacey when she returned to the kitchen, feeling more of a frump than ever, "you should get the estate agents to put a 'Sold' sign up."

"I didn't like the look of her," muttered Agatha.

"Indeed? I thought she looked very pleasant."

Agatha looked at the wide-open kitchen door, which gave

173

a perfect view of whoever was standing at the front door, and blushed.

"Now you really must excuse me," he said, and before Agatha could protest, he had made his escape.

The cat made a faint pleading sound. "What am I going to do with you?" demanded Agatha, exasperated. "What is Bill Wong thinking of?"

She poured the cat some milk in a saucer and watched it lapping it up. Well, she would need to feed it until she decided how to get rid of it. She went back into the heat. Her neighbour was working in his front garden. He saw her coming, smiled vaguely, and retreated into his cottage.

Damn, thought Agatha angrily. No wonder all these women were crawling onto his doorstep with gifts. She went to Harvey's, where the woman behind the till gave her a hurt look, and bought cat food, extra milk, and cat litter for the tray.

She returned home and fed the kitten and then took a cup of coffee into the garden. Her handsome neighbour had knocked all thoughts of murder out of her head. If only she had been properly dressed. If only he hadn't heard her being so rude to that woman who wanted to see the house.

The kitten was rolling over in the sun. She watched it moodily. She, too, could have taken along a cake. In fact, she still could. She scooped up the kitten and carried it inside and then went back to Harvey's to find that it was early-closing day.

She could go down to Moreton and buy a cake, but one should really take home-baking along. Then she remembered the freezer in the school hall. That was where the ladies of Carsely stored their home-baking for fêtes to come. There would be no harm in just *borrowing* something. Then she could go home and put on something really pretty and take along the cake.

The school hall was fortunately empty. She went through into the kitchen and gingerly lifted the lid of the freezer. There were all sorts of goodies: tarts, angel cakes, chocolates cakes, sponges and—she shuddered—even quiche.

She took out a large chocolate cake, feeling every bit the thief she was, looking about her, expecting any moment to be surprised. She gently lowered the lid and slipped the frozen cake into a plastic bag she had brought with her for the purpose. Back home again.

She took a shower and washed her hair, dried it and brushed it until it shone. She put on a red linen dress with a white collar and tan high-heeled sandals. Then she gave the kitten some more milk and defrosted the cake in the microwave after taking it out of its cellophane wrapper. She arranged it on a plate and marched along to James Lacey's cottage.

"Oh, Mrs. Raisin," he said when he opened the door and reluctantly accepted the cake. "How good of you. Perhaps you would like to come in, or," he added hopefully, "perhaps you are too busy."

"No, not at all," said Agatha cheerfully.

He led the way into his living-room and Agatha's curious eyes darted from side to side. There were books everywhere, some already on banks of shelves, some in open boxes on the floor, waiting to be stored away.

"It's like a library," said Agatha. "I thought you were an army man."

"Ex. I am settling down in my retirement to write military history." He waved a hand to a desk in the corner which held a word processor. "If you'll excuse me a moment, I'll make some coffee to go with that delicious cake. You ladies are certainly champion bakers."

Agatha settled herself carefully in a battered old leather armchair, hitching her skirt up slightly to show her legs to advantage.

It had been years since Agatha Raisin had been interested in any man. In fact, up until she had set eyes on James Lacey, she would have sworn that all her hormones had lain down and died. She felt excited, like a schoolgirl on her first date.

She hoped the cake was a good one. How fortunate she had remembered that kitchen in the school hall.

And then she froze and clutched tightly at the leather arms of the chair. The kitchen. Did it have a cooker? It had a microwave oven, for that was where they defrosted the goodies when they were setting up the tea-room for one of their endless charity drives.

She had to go back. She shot out of her chair and out of the door of the cottage just as James Lacey entered his living-room, carrying a tray with a coffee-pot and two mugs.

He carefully set down the tray and walked to his front door and looked out.

Agatha Raisin, with her skirts hitched up, was running down Lilac Lane as if all the fiends of hell were after her.

Might be inbreeding, he thought. He sat down and cut a slice of cake.

Agatha ran into the school-hall kitchen and looked feverishly about. There it was, what she had been hoping to see—a large gas cooker. She opened the low cupboards next to the sink. They were full of cups and saucers, mixing bowls, pie dishes, pots and pans.

She sat down suddenly. That's how it could have been done. That's how it must have been done.

She racked her memory. Mrs. Mason had been in the kitchen on the day of the auction, for example, beating up a fresh batch of cakes. The kitchen was also used for cooking. But wouldn't people remember if Vera Cummings-Browne had been in there on the day of the quiche competition, cooking quiche?

But she didn't have to be, thought Agatha. All she had to do was cook it any time before and put it in the freezer and keep an eye on it to make sure it was not used until she needed it. The remains of her, Agatha's quiche, would have been dumped with all the other rubbish left over from the tea-room. All Vera had to do was take out her poisoned quiche, take it home, pop it in the microwave, cut a slice out of it to match

176

the missing slice that had been taken out at the competition, wrap it up and take it with her when she went out and dump it somewhere. Agatha was willing to bet the forensic men hadn't gone through the widow's clothes looking for poisoned crumbs.

How to prove it?

Confront her with it, thought Agatha, and get myself wired for sound. Trap her into a confession.

●

TWELVE

†

MR. James Lacey looked uneasily out of his window. There was that Agatha Raisin woman, hurrying back. Her lips were moving soundlessly. He shrank back behind the curtains, but to his relief she went on, and shortly afterwards he heard her front door slam.

He thought she would be back at his door, but the day wore on and there was no sign of her. Early in the evening, he heard her car starting up and soon he saw her drive past. She did not look at him or wave.

He continued to work steadily, straightening up as he heard someone hurrying down the road. He looked over the hedge. And there came Agatha, on foot this time. He ducked below the hedge. On she went and again he heard her door slam.

An hour later, just as he was about to go inside for the night, a police car raced past and stopped outside Agatha's door and three men got out, one of whom he recognized as Bill Wong. They hammered at the door but for some reason the mysterious Mrs. Raisin did not answer it. He heard Bill Wong say, "Her car's gone. Maybe she's gone to London."

All very odd. He wondered if Agatha was wanted for

some crime or had simply been discovered missing from some lunatic asylum.

Inside her cottage, Agatha crouched down until the police car had gone. She had deliberately hidden her car off one of the side roads at the top of the hill out of Carsely in case Bill Wong came calling. She had no intention of seeing him until she presented him with full proof that Vera Cummings-Browne was a murderess. She was slightly thrown when she looked out of her bedroom window to see the three of them, but assumed that it was because John Cartwright had been found. All that could wait. Agatha Raisin, detective, was going to solve The Great Quiche Mystery all by herself.

The next morning James Lacey found he was persuading himself that his front garden needed more attention, although he had already pulled up every single weed. He did find, however, that the small patch of grass needed edging and got out the necessary tools, all the while keeping a curious eye on the cottage next door.

Soon he was rewarded. Out came Agatha and walked along the road. This time he leaned over the garden gate.

"Good morning, Mrs. Raisin," he called.

Agatha focused on him, gave him a brief "Good morning," and walked on. Love could wait, thought Agatha.

She located her car and drove to Oxford through Moreton-in-Marsh, Chipping Norton, and Woodstock while the brassy sun glared down. She parked the car in St. Giles and walked along Cornmarket and down to the Westgate Shopping Centre until she found the shop she wanted. She bought a small but expensive tape recorder which she could wear strapped to her body and which could be activated by switches concealed in her pockets. She then bought a loose man's blouson with inside pockets.

"Now for it," she muttered as she drove back to Carsely. "I hope the bitch hasn't gone back to Tuscany."

As she topped a rise on the road after leaving Chipping Norton, she saw that black clouds were piling up on the horizon. She decided to drive straight home and run the risk of being visited by the police.

When she let herself into her cottage, the kitten scampered about in welcome, and Agatha found she was delaying her preparations by giving the little kitten milk and food and then letting it out into the garden to play in the sun. She strapped on the tape recorder and arranged the switches in her pockets and then tested the machine to make sure it worked properly, which it did.

Now for Vera Cummings-Browne!

It came as a let-down to find there was no answer to her knock at the door of Vera's cottage. She asked at Harvey's if anyone had seen her and one woman volunteered that Mrs. Cummings-Browne had said she was going out of the village to do some shopping. Agatha groaned. All she could do was wait.

At Mircester Police Headquarters, Detective Chief Inspector Wilkes stopped at Bill Wong's desk. "Have you phoned your friend, Mrs. Raisin, to tell her we caught John Cartwright?"

"I forgot about it," said Bill. "I was more interested in this." He held up a black-and-white photograph of Vera Cummings-Browne receiving first prize for her flower arrangement.

"What's that?"

"That is what Mrs. Raisin was after yesterday. I heard she had called on a Mr. Jones and thought I would call on him too to find out if she had stirred anything up. She had taken a photograph from him but he gave me the negative. I've just had it printed. And that"—Bill stabbed a stubby finger in the middle of the flower arrangement—"looks exactly like cowbane, the plant Mrs. Cummings-Browne professed to know nothing about. Mrs. Raisin's hit on something. Maybe I'd better get over there."

How many times, wondered Agatha, had she trekked through the stifling heat up to Vera's cottage, only to find it locked and silent? She was sweating under her blouson.

And then, at last, she saw Vera's Range Rover parked on the cobbles outside the door.

With a quickening feeling of excitement, Agatha knocked at the cottage door.

There was a long silence punctuated by a rumble of thunder from overhead. Agatha knocked again. A curtain at a side window twitched and then the door was opened.

"Oh, Mrs. Raisin," said Mrs. Cummings-Browne blandly. "I was just going out."

"I want to talk to you," said Agatha pugnaciously.

"Well, wait a moment while I put the car away. I think it's going to rain at last."

A stab of doubt assailed Agatha. Vera looked completely calm. But then Vera could not possibly know why she had called.

To be on the safe side, she followed her out and watched her put the car away in a garage at the end of the row of cottages.

Vera came back with a brisk step. "I've just got time for a cup of tea, Mrs. Raisin, and then I really must go. I am setting up a flower-arranging competition at Ancombe and someone needs to show these silly village women what to do."

She bustled into the kitchen to make tea. "Take a seat in the drawing-room, Mrs. Raisin. Won't be long."

Agatha sat down in the small living-room and looked about. Here was where it had all happened. A bright flash of lightning lit up the dark room and then there was a tremendous crash of thunder.

"How dark it is in here!" exclaimed Vera, coming in with a tray of tea-things. She set them down on a low table. "Milk and sugar, Mrs. Raisin?"

"Neither," said Agatha gruffly. "Just tea." Now it had come to it, she felt almost too embarrassed to begin. There was something so *normal* about Vera as she poured tea—from her well-coiffed hair to her Liberty dress.

"Now, Mrs. Raisin," said Vera brightly. "What brings you? Starting another auction? Do you know, it's actually getting *cold*. The fire's made up. I'll just put a match to it. In fact, the fire's been made up for *weeks*. Hasn't this weather been fierce? But it's broken now, thank goodness. Just listen to that storm."

Agatha nervously sipped her tea and wished Vera would settle down so that she could get the whole distasteful business over and done with.

Trickles of sweat were running down inside her clothes. How on earth could Vera find the room cold? The fire crackled into life.

Vera sat down, crossed her legs and looked with bright curiosity at Agatha.

"Mrs. Cummings-Browne," said Agatha, "I know you murdered your husband."

"Oh, really?" Vera looked amused. "And how am I supposed to have done that?"

"You must have had it planned for some time," said Agatha heavily. "You had already baked a poisoned quiche and put it in the freezer in the school hall along with the other goodies that the ladies use when the tea-room is in operation. You were waiting for a good chance to use it. Then I gave you that chance. You naturally did not want your husband to die after appearing to eat one of your own quiches. When I said I was leaving mine, you saw your chance and took it. You got rid of mine with the rest of the rubbish left over after the competition. You took your own quiche home, defrosted it, and left two slices for your husband's supper. I don't know whether you actually checked to see whether he had died when you came home.

"Then you heard I had actually bought that quiche in London. You're a greedy woman, I know that, from the way I was conned into paying for that expensive meal in a lousy restaurant in which you own part of the business. You saw an opportunity of getting money out of poor Mr. Economides, and so you went straight to London to tell him you were suing him. Who knows? You probably hoped he would settle out of court. But he confessed that the quiche had come from his

183

cousin's shop in Devon. His cousin grew his own vegetables and there is no cowbane in Devon. So you told the police you had decided to forgive him and not press charges. You said you did not know what cowbane looked like. But you borrowed a book on poisonous plants from the library, and furthermore, I found out from a photo Mr. Jones had given me that you had used cowbane already in one of your floral arrangements. So that's how it was done!"

Agatha trumphantly drained her teacup and stared defiantly at Vera.

To her surprise, Vera's only reaction was to get up and put coal on the blazing wood on the fire.

Vera sat down again. She looked at Agatha.

"As a matter of fact, you are quite right, Mrs. Raisin." She raised her voice above the noise of the thunder. "You just had to go and cheat in that competition, didn't you, you silly bitch? So I thought I'd get some financial mileage out of it and yes, I did hope that Greek would volunteer to settle out of court. Then he let fall the bit about Devon. But at least I had him so frightened, he didn't even examine his own supposed quiche closely. I had a bad moment thinking he would and that he would say it wasn't his. So everything looked safe. I was tired of Reg's bloody philandering, but I turned a blind eye to it until that Maria Borrow came on the scene. She turned up here one day and told me Reg was going to marry her. Her! Pathetic mad old spinster. It was the ultimate shame. I knew he didn't mean to divorce me but sooner or later this Borrow fright was going to tell everyone he did and I wasn't standing for that. Do you know I thought it hadn't worked? I came home and saw the lights burning and the television on but no sign of Reg. I was a bit relieved. He'd gone out before and left everything on. So I just went to bed. When they told me in the morning he was dead, I couldn't believe I had caused it. I used to dream of getting rid of him and I almost thought that the baking of that poisoned quiche and the substitution for yours had all been in my mind and that they would tell me

184

he'd died of a stroke. What's the matter, Mrs. Raisin? Feeling drowsy?"

Agatha felt her head swimming. "The tea," she croaked.

"Yes, the tea, Mrs. Raisin. Think you're so bloody clever, don't you? Well, only a crass fool would drop in to accuse a poisoner and drink tea."

"Cowbane," gasped Agatha.

"Oh, no, dear. Just sleeping pills. I found out from Jones what you had been asking, and from that woman in the library. I followed you to Oxford. I had seen your car the night before parked up in one of the lanes. I was waiting for you when you drove off. So I went to Oxford, too, to a quack I'd heard of, a private doctor who gives all sorts of pills to anyone. I said I was Mrs. Agatha Raisin and couldn't sleep. Here are the pills." Vera dug in a pocket of her dress and held up a pharmacist's bottle. And with your name on them."

She stood up. "And so I just spread a few of these leaflets advertising the flower-arranging competition about the floor, and I help a live coal to roll out of the fire on top of them. I will tell everyone that I told you to make yourself comfortable and wait until I returned. Such a sad accident. Everything is tinder-dry with the heat. You'll have quite a funeral pyre. I'll just drop what's left of these sleeping pills into your handbag and put it in the kitchen by the window and hope it survives the blaze."

It was like a dream of hell, thought Agatha. She could not move. But she could see . . . just. Vera spread the leaflets about, frowned down at them, and then went into the kitchen and returned with a bottle of cooking oil. She sprinkled some of that about and then took the bottle back to the kitchen. "Such a good thing this cottage is heavily insured," she remarked.

She picked up a glowing coal from the fire with the brass tongs and dropped it on the leaflets and then stood patiently while it smouldered on the floor. With a click of annoyance, Vera struck a match and dropped it on the leaflets, which leaped into flame. She edged towards the door. There was a stack of magazines in a rack by the fire. It burst into flames. Then she locked the living-room windows. With a little smile, Vera said, "Bye, Mrs. Raisin," and let herself out of the cottage. She walked to her garage, glancing over her shoulder. She had taken the precaution of closing the curtains. She would have to get away quickly all the same.

With one superhuman effort, Agatha shoved one finger down her throat and was violently sick. She fell off the chair onto the blazing carpet. Whimpering and sobbing, she crawled away from the roaring fire, dragging herself to the kitchen. Vera had locked the front door. No use trying that way. Agatha feebly kicked the kitchen door closed behind her. The noise in her ears was deafening. The thunder was crashing outside, the fire was roaring inside.

Agatha's weak hands scrabbled upwards until she grasped the edge of the kitchen sink. Sinks had water and behind the sink was the kitchen window, which that hellcat might have forgotten to lock.

But despite the fact she had been sick, Agatha had swallowed quite a large amount of sleeping pills, or draught, or whatever it was that Vera had put in her tea. Blackness overcame her and she made one last effort heaving herself up, gazing out of the window, her mouth silently opening to form the word "help," before she fell back onto the kitchen floor, unconscious.

"I don't see why we're working overtime on this Raisin woman, Bill," grumbled the detective chief inspector. "The fact that Mrs. Cummings-Browne had cowbane in her flower arrangement could be coincidence."

"I've always been sure she had done it," said Bill. "I told Mrs. Raisin to mind her own business because I didn't want her getting hurt. We've got to ask Vera Cummings-Browne about this photograph. What a storm!"

They were cruising in the police car slowly along Carsely's main street. Bill peered through the windscreen. A flash of lightning lit up the street, lit up the approaching Range Rover, and lit up the startled face of Vera behind the wheel. Almost without thought, Bill swung the wheel and blocked the street.

"What the hell!" shouted Wilkes.

Vera jumped out of her car and began to run off down one of the lanes leading off the main street. "It's Mrs. Cummings-Browne. After her," shouted Bill. Wilkes and Detective Sergeant Friend scrambled out of the car, but Bill ran instead through the pounding rain towards Vera's cottage, cursing under his breath as he saw the fierce red glow of a fire behind the drawn curtains of the living-room.

The kitchen window was to the left of the door. He ran to it to try to force a way in and was just in time to see the white staring face of Agatha Raisin rising above the kitchen sink and disappearing again.

There was a narrow strip of flower-bed outside the cottage, edged with round pieces of marble rock. He seized one of these and threw it straight at the kitchen window, thinking wildly that it was only in films that the whole window shattered, for the rock went straight through, leaving a jagged hole.

He seized another one and hammered furiously at the glass until he had broken a hole big enough to crawl through.

Agatha was lying on the kitchen floor. He tried to pick her up. At first she seemed too heavy. The roar of the fire from the other room was tremendous. He got Agatha up on her feet and shoved her head in the kitchen sink. Then he got hold of her ankles and heaved, so that her heels went over her head and out through the window. He seized her by the hair and, panting and shoving, thrust the whole lot of her through the broken glass and out onto the cobbles outside and then dived through the window himself just as the kitchen door fell in and raging tongues of flames scorched through the room.

He lay for a moment on top of Agatha while the rain drummed down on both of them. Doors were opening, people were coming running. He heard a woman shout, "I phoned the

187

fire brigade." His hands were bleeding and Agatha's face was cut from where he had shoved her through the broken glass. But she was breathing deeply. She was alive.

Agatha recovered consciousness in hospital and looked groggily around. There seemed to be flowers everywhere. Her eyes focused on the Asian features of Bill Wong, who was sitting patiently beside the bed.

Then Agatha remembered the horror of the fire. "What happened?" she asked feebly.

From the other side of the bed came the stern voice of Detective Chief Inspector Wilkes. "You nearly got burnt to a crisp, that's what," he said, "and would have been if Bill here hadn't saved your life."

"You've got to lose weight, Mrs. Raisin," said Bill with a grin. "You're a heavy woman. But you'll be pleased to know that Vera Cummings-Browne is under arrest, although whether she'll stand trial is another matter. She went barking mad. But you did a silly and dangerous thing, Mrs. Raisin. I gather you went to accuse her of murder and then you calmly drink a cup of tea which she had made."

Agatha struggled up against the pillows. "It's thanks to me you got her. I suppose you found her taped confession on my body."

"We found a blank tape on your body," said Bill. "You had forgotten to switch the damn thing on."

Agatha groaned. "So how did you get her to confess?" she said.

"It was like this," said Bill. "I wondered what you were up to seeing this Mr. Jones. I found out about the photograph you had taken, he gave me the negative, I got it developed and found the cowbane in it. We were heading to her cottage to ask her a few questions when we saw her driving along. I blocked the street. She got out and ran for it, and when Mr. Wilkes caught up with her, she broke down and confessed and said it would be all worth it if you died in the fire. I managed to get you out."

188

"What put you on to her in the first place?" asked Wilkes crossly. "Surely not one piece of cowbane in a photograph?"

Agatha thought quickly. She had not switched on the tape. There was no need for them to know that her quiche had come from Devon or anything about Mr. Economides's cousin. So instead, she told them about the school-hall kitchen and the library book.

"You should have brought information like that straight to us," said Wilkes crossly. "Bill here got his hands cut badly rescuing you and you were nearly killed. For the last time, leave investigations to the police."

"Next time I won't be so amateur," said Agatha huffily.

"Next time?" roared Wilkes. "There won't *be* a next time."

"The thing that puzzles me," said Agatha, "is why didn't I notice the taste of the sleeping pills in the tea? I mean, if she had ground all those pills up, at least it surely would have tasted gritty."

"She got gelatine capsules of Dormaron, a very powerful sleeping pill, from some quack in Oxford who is being questioned. The stuff's tasteless. She simply cut open the capsules and put the liquid in your tea," said Wilkes. "I'll be back when you get home to question you further, Mrs. Raisin, but don't ever try to play detective again. By the way, we got John Cartwright. He was working on a building site in London."

He stomped out. "I'd better be going as well," said Bill. For the first time Agatha noticed his bandaged hands.

"Thank you for saving my life," she said. "I'm sorry about your hands."

"I'm sorry about your face," he said. Agatha raised her hands to her face and felt strips of sticking plaster. "There's a couple of stitches in a cut in your cheek. But the only way I could get you out was by shoving you through the window, and I'm afraid I tore a handful of your hair out as well."

"I've given up worrying about my appearance," said Agatha. "Oh, my kitten. How long have I been here?"

"Just over night. But I called on your neighbor, Mr. Lacey, and he offered to keep the cat until your return."

"That's good of you. Mr. Lacey? Does he know what happened?"

"I hadn't time to explain. I simply handed over the cat and said you'd had an accident."

Agatha's hands flew up to her face again. "Do I look awful? Did you tear out much hair? Is there a mirror in here?"

"I thought you didn't care about your appearance."

"And all those flowers? Who are they from?"

"The big one is from the Carsely Ladies' Society, the small bunch of roses is from Doris and Bert Simpson, the elegant gladioli from Mrs. Bloxby, the giant bouquet from the landlord of the Red Lion and the regulars, and that weedy bunch is from me."

"Thank you so much, Bill. Er . . . anything from Mr. Lacey?"

"Now how could there be? You barely know the man."

"Is my handbag around? I must look a fright. I need powder and lipstick and a comb and I've some French perfume in there."

"Relax. They're letting you home tomorrow. You can paint your face to your heart's content. Don't forget that dinner invitation."

"Oh, what? Oh, yes, that. Of course you must come. Next week. Perhaps I might be able to help you with some of your cases?"

"No," said Bill firmly. "Don't ever try to solve a crime again." Then he relented. "Not but what you haven't done me a favour."

"In what way?"

"I confess I'd been following you around on my time off and getting the local bobby to report anything to me. Like you, I never could really believe it to be an accident. But Wilkes is more or less crediting me with solving the case because he would rather die than admit a member of the public could do anything to help. So when's that dinner?"

"Next Wednesday? Seven o'clock, say?"

"Fine. Go back to sleep. I'll see you then."

"Am I in Moreton-in-Marsh?"

"No, Mircester General Hospital."

After he had gone, Agatha fished in the locker beside her bed and found her handbag. The pills had been taken out of it, she noticed. She opened her compact and stared at her face in the mirror and let out a squawk of dismay. She looked a wreck.

" 'Ere!" Agatha looked across at the next bed. It contained an elderly woman who looked remarkably like Mrs. Boggle. "What you done?" she asked avidly. "All them police in 'ere."

"I solved a case for them," said Agatha grandly.

"Garn," said the old horror. "Last one in that bed thought she was Mary Queen of Scots."

"Shut up," snarled Agatha, looking in the mirror and wondering whether the sticking plaster did not look, in fact, well, heroic.

The day wore on. The television set at the end of the beds flickered through soap opera after soap opera. No one else called. Not even Mrs. Bloxby.

Well, that's that, thought Agatha bleakly. Why did they bother to send flowers? Probably thought I was dead.

THIRTEEN

†

AGATHA was told next day that an ambulance would be leaving the hospital at noon to take her home. She was rather pleased about that. Her home-coming in an ambulance should make the village sit up and take notice.

She took the greetings cards off the bouquets of flowers around her bed to keep as a souvenir of her time in the Cotswolds. How odd that she had volunteered to help Bill with his cases, just as if she meant to stay. She asked a nurse to take the flowers to the children's ward and then got dressed and went downstairs to wait for the ambulance. There was a shop in the entrance hall selling newspapers. She bought a pile of the local ones but there was no mention of Vera Cummings-Browne's arrest. But perhaps it all leaked out too late for them to do anything about it.

To her dismay, the "ambulance" turned out to be a mini bus which was taking various geriatric patients back to their local villages. Why does the sight of creaking old people make me feel so cruel and impatient? thought Agatha, watching them fumbling and stumbling on board. I'll be old myself all too soon. She forced herself to get up to help an old man who was trying to get into the bus. He leered at her. "Keep your hands to yourself," he said. "I know your sort."

The rest of the passengers were all old women who shrieked with laughter and said, "You are a one, Arnie," and things like that, all of them evidently knowing each other very well.

It was a calm, cool day with great fluffy clouds floating across a pale-blue sky. The old woman next to Agatha caught her attention by jabbing her painfully in the toes with her stick. "What happened to you then?" she asked, peering at Agatha's sticking-plaster-covered face. "Beat you up, did he?"

"No," said Agatha frostily. "I was solving a murder case for the police."

"It's the drink," said the old woman. "Mine used ter come home from the pub and lay into me something rotten. He's dead now. It's one thing you've got to say in favour of men, they die before we do."

" 'Cept me," said Arnie. "I'm seventy-eight and still going strong."

More cackles. Agatha's announcement about solving a murder case had bit the dust. The mini bus rolled lazily to a stop in a small hamlet and the woman next to Agatha was helped out. She looked at Agatha and said in farewell, "Don't go making up stories to protect him. I did that. Different these days. If he's bashing you, tell the police."

There was a murmur of approval from the other women.

The bus moved off. It turned out to be a comprehensive tour of Cotswold villages as one geriatric after another was set down.

Agatha was the last passenger. She felt dirty and weary as the bus rolled down into Carsely. "Where to?" shouted the driver.

"Left here," said Agatha. "Third cottage along on the left."

"Something going on," called the driver. "Big welcome. You been in the wars or something?"

The ambulance stopped outside Agatha's cottage. There was a big cheer. The band began to play "Hello Dolly." They

194

were all there, all the village, and there was a banner hanging drunkenly over her doorway which said, WELCOME HOME.

Mrs. Bloxby was the first with a hug. Then the members of the Carsely Ladies' Society. Then the landlord, Joe Fletcher, and the regulars from the Red Lion.

Local photographers were busy clicking their cameras, local reporters stood ready.

"Everyone inside," called Agatha, "and I'll tell you all about it."

Soon her living-room was crowded, with an overflow stretching into the dining-room and kitchen as she told a rapt audience how she had solved The Case of the Poisoned Quiche. It was highly embroidered. But she did describe in glorious Technicolor how the brave Bill Wong had dragged her from the burning house, "his clothes in flames and his hands cut to ribbons."

"Such bravery," said Agatha, "is an example of the fine men we have in the British police force."

Some reporters scribbled busily; the more up-to-date used tape recorders. Agatha was about to hit the nationals, or rather, Bill Wong was. There had been two nasty stories recently about corrupt policemen, but the newspapers knew there was nothing more the British liked to read about than a brave bobby.

Next door, James Lacey stood in his front garden, burning with curiosity. The visit from Agatha had been enough. He had called on the vicarage and told Mrs. Bloxby sternly that although he was grateful for the welcome to the village, he now wanted to be left strictly alone. He enjoyed his own company. He had moved to the country for peace and quiet. Mrs. Bloxby had done her work well. So although he had watched the preparations for Agatha's return, he did not know what she had done or what it had all been about. He wanted to walk along and ask someone but felt shy of doing so because he had said he wanted to be alone and he remembered he had added that he had no interest in what went on in the village or in anyone in it.

One by one Agatha's fan club was leaving. Doris Simpson was among the last to go. She handed Agatha a large brown paper parcel.

"Why, what's this, Doris?" asked Agatha.

"Me and Bert got talking about that gnome you gave us," said Doris firmly. "Those things are expensive and we don't really have much interest in our garden and we know you must have liked it because you bought it. So we decided to give it back to you."

"I couldn't possibly accept it," said Agatha.

"You must. We haven't felt right about it."

Agatha, who had long begun to suspect that her cleaning lady had a will of iron, said feebly, "Thank you."

"Anything else?" called Joe Fletcher from the doorway.

Agatha made a sudden decision. "Yes, there is," she said. "Take that 'For Sale' sign down."

At last they had all gone. Agatha sat down, suddenly shivering. The full horror of what had happened to her at Vera's hit her. She went upstairs and took a hot bath and changed into a night-gown and an old shabby blue wool dressing-gown. She peered in the bathroom mirror. There was a bald sore red patch at the front of her hair where Bill had pulled it out. She switched on the central heating and then threw logs on the fire, lit a match and then shuddered and blew the match out. It would be a while before she could bear the sight of a fire.

There was a tentative knock at the door. Still shivering and holding her dressing-gown tightly about her, she went to open it. James Lacey stood there, holding the kitten in its basket and the litter tray.

"Bill Wong asked me to look after the cat for you," he said. He eyed her doubtfully. "I could look after it for another day if you're not up to it."

"No, no," babbled Agatha. "Come in. I wonder how Bill got the cat? Of course, he would have taken the keys out of my bag in the hospital. How very good of you."

She caught a glimpse of herself in the hall mirror. How awful she looked, and not a scrap of make-up on either!

She carried the cat into the living-room and stooped and let it out of its basket and then took the litter tray into the kitchen. When she returned, James was sitting in one of her chairs staring thoughtfully at the large gnome which Doris had returned and Agatha had unwrapped. It was standing on the coffee-table leering horribly, like old Arnie on the mini bus.

"Would you like a gnome?" asked Agatha.

"No, thank you. It's an unusual living-room ornament."

"It's not really mine. You see . . ."

There was a hammering at the door. Agatha swore under her breath and went to answer it. Midlands Television and the BBC. "Can't you come back later?" pleaded Agatha, casting a longing look back towards the living-room. But then she saw the police car driving up as well. Detective Chief Inspector Wilkes had called.

The television interviewers had a more modified version of Agatha's story than the villagers had heard. Detective Chief Inspector Wilkes was interviewed saying sternly that the public should leave police matters to the police, as Mrs. Raisin had nearly been killed and he had nearly lost one of his best officers, Agatha shrewdly guessing that when that appeared on the screens, his comments would be cut down to the simple fact that he had nearly lost one of his best officers. Everyone wanted a hero, and Bill Wong was to be the hero. Somehow in the middle of it all, James Lacey had slipped out. The television teams rushed off to find Bill Wong in Mircester, a policewoman with a recorder came in from the police car, and Wilkes got down to exhaustive questioning.

At last they left, but the phone rang and rang as various nationals phoned up to add to the stories sent in by the local men. By eleven o'clock, the phone fell silent. Agatha fed the cat and then carried it up to bed. It lay on her feet, purring gently. I'd better think of a name for it, she thought sleepily.

The phone rang downstairs. "Now what?" groaned Agatha aloud, gently lifting the cat off her feet and wondering why she had not bothered to get a phone extension put in the bedroom. She went downstairs and picked up the receiver.

"Aggie!" It was Roy, his voice sharp with excitement. "I thought I'd never get through. I saw you on the telly."

"Oh, that," said Agatha. She shivered. "Can I call you back tomorrow, Roy?"

"Look, sweetie, there seems to be more publicity comes out of that little village than out of all the streets of London. The idea is this. Maybe the telly will be back for a follow-up. I'll run down there tomorrow and you can tell them how I helped you to solve the mystery. I phoned Mr. Wilson at home and he thinks it's a great idea."

"Roy, the story will be dead tomorrow. You know it, I know it. Let me go back to bed. I won't be up to seeing visitors for some time."

"Well, I must say I thought you might have mentioned me," complained Roy. "Who was it went with you to Ancombe? I've phoned round all the papers but the night-desks say if you want to volunteer a quote about me, fine, but they're not interested in taking it from me, so be a sweetie and phone them, there's a dear."

"I am going to bed, Roy, and that's that. Finish."

"Aren't we being just a bit of a selfish bitch hogging all the limelight?"

"Good night, Roy," said Agatha and put down the receiver and then turned back and lifted it off the hook.

"Well, I want to meet this Raisin woman," said James Lacey's sister, Mrs. Harriet Camberwell, a week later. "I know you want to be left alone. But I'm dying of curiosity. They gave a lot of play to that detective, Wong, but she solved it, didn't she?"

"Yes, I suppose she did, Harriet. But she's very odd. Do you know she keeps a garden gnome on her coffee-table as an ornament? She walks down the street muttering and talking to herself."

"How sweet. I simply must meet her. Run along and ask her to drop by for a cup of tea."

"If I do that, will you go back to your husband and leave me alone?"

"Of course. Go and get her and I'll make the tea and cut some sandwiches."

Agatha was still recovering from the shock of being nearly burnt to death. She had not bothered about trying to see James, waiting until her cuts healed up and her hair grew back. When that happened, she thought, she would plan a campaign.

The weather had turned pleasantly warm instead of the furnace heat of the days before the storm. She had the doors and windows open and was lying in her old loose cotton dress on the kitchen floor, tossing balls of foil into the air to amuse the kitten, when James walked in.

"I should have knocked," he said awkwardly, "but the door was open." Agatha scrambled to her feet. "I wonder whether you would like to step along for a cup of tea."

"I must change," said Agatha wildly.

"I've obviously come at a bad moment. Maybe another time."

"No! I'll come now," said Agatha, frightened he would escape.

They walked along to his cottage. No sooner was she seated, no sooner was Agatha admiring his handsome profile, which was turned towards the kitchen door, when an elegant woman walked in carrying a tea-tray.

"Mrs. Raisin, Mrs. Camberwell. Harriet, darling, this is Mrs. Raisin. Harriet's dying to hear all about your adventures, Mrs. Raisin."

Agatha felt small and dingy. But then women like Harriet Camberwell always made her feel small and dingy. She was a very tall woman, nearly as tall as James, slim, flat-chested, square hunting shoulders, clever upper-class face, expensive hair-style, tailored cotton dress, cool amused eyes.

Agatha began to talk. The villagers would have been

199

amazed to hear her dull rendering of her adventures. She stayed only long enough to briefly recount her story, drink one cup of tea, eat one sandwich, and then she firmly took her leave.

At least Bill Wong was coming for dinner. Be thankful for small comforts, Agatha, she told herself sternly. But she had thought of James Lacey a lot and her days had taken on life and colour. Still, there was no need to look a fright simply because her guest was only Bill.

She changed and did her hair and put on make-up and put on the dress she had worn for the auction. Dinner—taught this time by Mrs. Bloxby—was to be simple: grilled steaks, baked potatoes, fresh asparagus, fresh fruit salad and cream. Champagne on ice for the celebration, for Bill Wong had been elevated to detective sergeant.

It was a new, slimmer Bill who walked in the door at seven o'clock. He had been keeping in shape rigorously ever since he had seen his rather chubby features on television.

He talked of this and that, noticing that Agatha's bearlike eyes were rather sad and she seemed to have lost a great deal of animation. He reflected that the attempt on her life must have hit her harder than he would have expected.

She was not contributing much to the conversation and so he searched around for another topic to amuse her. "Oh, by the way," he said as she slid the steaks under the grill, "your neighbour has given breaking up hearts in the village. He told Mrs. Bloxby he wanted to be left alone and was quite sharpish about it. Then, when the ladies of Carsely back off, he is visited by an elegant woman whom he introduces to all and sundry in Harvey's as Mrs. Camberwell. He calls her 'darling.' They make a nice pair. Mrs. Mason was heard to remark crossly that she had always thought him an odd sort of man anyway and that she had only taken around a cake to be friendly.

"And guess what?"

"What?" said Agatha testily.

"Your old persecutor, Mrs. Boggle, ups and asks him

point-blank in the middle of Harvey's if he means to marry Mrs. Camberwell, everyone thinking her a widow. And *he* replies in surprise, 'Why the devil should I marry my own sister?' So I gather the ladies of Carsely are now thinking that although they cannot really call on him after what he said to Mrs. Bloxby, perhaps they can get up a little party or dinner and lure him into one of their homes." Bill laughed heartily.

Agatha turned around, her face suddenly radiant. "We haven't opened the champagne and we must celebrate!"

"Celebrate what?" asked Bill in sudden suspicion.

"Why, your promotion. Dinner won't be long."

Bill opened the champagne and poured them a glass each.

"Is there anything you would like me to do, Mrs. Raisin, before dinner? Lay the table?"

"No, that's done. But you could start off by calling me Agatha, and there is something else. There's a sign in the front garden and a sledge hammer beside it. Could you hammer it into the ground?"

"Of course. Not selling again, are you?"

"No, I'm naming this cottage. I'm tired of everyone still calling it Budgen's cottage. It belongs to me."

He went out into the garden and picked up the sign and hammered its pole into the ground and then stood back to admire the effect.

Brown lettering on white, it proclaimed boldly: RAISIN'S COTTAGE.

Bill grinned. Agatha was in Carsely to stay.

The author wishes to thank her pet vet, Anne Wombill, of Cirencester for all her help. This book is for Anne and her husband, Robin, with love.

THE
VICIOUS VET

ONE

†

AGATHA Raisin arrived at London's Heathrow Airport with a tan outside and a blush of shame inside. She felt an utter fool as she pushed her load of luggage towards the exit.

She had just spent two weeks in the Bahamas in pursuit of her handsome neighbour, James Laccy, who had let fall that he was going to holiday there at the Nassau Beach Hotel. Agatha in pursuit of a man was as ruthless as she had been in business. She had spent a great deal of money on a fascinating wardrobe, had slimmed furiously so as to be able to sport her rejuvenated middle-aged figure in a bikini, but there had been no sign of James Lacey. She had hired a car and toured the other hotels on the island to no avail. She had even called at the British High Commission in the hope they had heard of him. A few days before she was due to return, she had put a long-distance call through to Carsely, the village in the Cotswolds in which she lived, to the vicar's wife, Mrs. Bloxby, and had finally got around to asking for the whereabouts of James Lacey.

She still remembered Mrs. Bloxby's voice, strengthening and fading on a bad line, as if borne towards Agatha on the tide. "Mr. Lacey changed his plans at the very last minute. He decided to spend his vacation with a friend in Cairo. He did say he was going to the Bahamas, I remember, and Mrs. Mason said, 'What a surprise! That's where our Mrs. Raisin is going.' And the next thing we knew this friend in Egypt had invited him over."

How Agatha had squirmed and was still squirming. It was plain to her that he had changed his plans simply so as not to meet her. In retrospect, her pursuit of him had been rather blatant.

And there was another reason she had not enjoyed her holiday. She had put her cat, Hodge, a present from Detective Sergeant Bill Wong, into a cattery and somehow Agatha found she was worrying that the cat might have died.

At the Long-Stay Car-Park, she loaded in her luggage and then set out to drive to Carsely, wondering again why she had ever retired so young—well, these days early fifties *was* young—and sold her business to bury herself in a country village.

The cattery was outside Cirencester. She went up to the house and was greeted ungraciously by the thin rangy woman who owned the place. "Really, Mrs. Raisin," she said, "I am just going out. It would have been more considerate of you to phone."

"Get my animal . . . *now,*" said Agatha, glaring balefully, "and be quick about it."

The woman stalked off, affront in every line of her body. Soon she came back with Hodge mewling in his

2

carrying basket. Totally deaf to further recriminations, Agatha paid the fee.

Being reunited with her cat, she decided, was a very comforting thing, and then wondered if she was reduced to the status of village lady, drooling over an animal.

Her cottage, crouched under its heavy weight of thatch, was like an old dog, waiting to welcome her. When the fire had been lit, the cat fed, and with a stiff whisky inside her, Agatha felt she would survive. Bugger James Lacey and all men!

She went to the local store, Harveys', in the morning to get some groceries and to show off her tan. She ran into Mrs. Bloxby. Agatha felt uncomfortable about that phone call but Mrs. Bloxby, ever tactful, did not remind her of it, merely saying that there was a meeting of the Carsely Ladies Society at the vicarage that evening. Agatha said she would attend, although thinking there must be more to social life than tea at the vicarage.

She had half a mind not to go. Instead she could go to the Red Lion, the local pub, for dinner. But on the other hand, she had promised Mrs. Bloxby that she would go, and somehow one did not break promises to Mrs. Bloxby.

When she made her way out that evening, a thick fog had settled down on the village, thick, freezing fog, turning bushes into crouching assailants and muffling sound.

The ladies were all there among the pleasant clutter of the vicarage sitting-room. Nothing had changed. Mrs. Mason was still the chairwoman—chairpersons did not exist in Carsely because, as Mrs. Bloxby pointed out, once you started that sort of thing you didn't know where

3

to stop, and things like manholes would become person-holes—and Miss Simms, in Minnie Mouse white shoes and skimpy skirt, still the secretary. Agatha was pressed for details about her holiday and so she bragged about the sun and the sand until she began to feel she had actually had a good time.

The minutes were read, raising money for Save The Children was discussed, an outing for the old folks, and then more tea and cake.

That was when Agatha heard about the new vet. The village of Carsely had a veterinary surgery at last. An extension had been built on to the library building. A vet, Paul Bladen, from Mircester, held a surgery there twice a week on Tuesday and Wednesday afternoons.

"We weren't going to bother at first," said Miss Simms, "because we usually go to the vet at Moreton, but Mr. Bladen's ever so good."

"And ever so good-looking," put in Mrs. Bloxby.

"Young?" asked Agatha with a flicker of interest.

"Oh, about forty, I think," said Miss Simms. "Not married. Divorced. He's got these searching eyes, and such beautiful hands."

Agatha was not particularly interested in the vet, for her thoughts were still on James Lacey. She wished he would return so that she could show him she did not care for him at all. So, as the ladies gushed their praise for the new vet, she sat writing scripts in her head about what he would say and what she would say, and imagining how surprised he would be to find out that ordinary neighbourly friendliness on her part had been mistaken on his for pursuit.

4

But as the fates would have it, Agatha was destined to meet Paul Bladen the very next day.

She decided to go to the butcher's and get herself a steak and buy some chicken livers for Hodge. "Marnin,' Mr. Bladen," said the butcher, and Agatha turned round.

Paul Bladen was a good-looking man in his early forties with thick wavy fair hair dusted with grey, light-brown eyes which crinkled up as though against the desert sun, a firm, rather sweet mouth, and a square chin. He was slim, of medium height, and wore a tweed jacket with patches and flannels and, for it was a freezing day, an old London University scarf about his neck. He reminded Agatha of the old days when university students dressed like university students, before the days of T-shirts and frayed jeans.

For his part, Paul Bladen saw a stocky middle-aged woman with shiny brown hair and small, bearlike eyes in a tanned face. Her clothes, he noticed, were very expensive.

Agatha thrust out her hand and introduced herself, welcoming him to the village in her best lady-of-the-manor voice. He smiled into her eyes, holding on to her hand, and murmuring something about the dreadful weather. Agatha forgot all about James Lacey. Or nearly. Let him rot in Egypt. She hoped he'd got gippy tummy, she hoped a camel bit him.

"As a matter of fact," cooed Agatha, "I was coming to see you. With my cat."

Did a frost settle momentarily on those crinkled eyes? But he said, "There is a surgery this afternoon. Why don't you bring the animal along? Say, two o'clock?"

"How lovely to have our own vet at last," enthused Agatha.

He gave her that intimate smile of his again and Agatha went out treading on air. Fog was still holding the countryside in its grip although, far, far above, a little red disk of a sun struggled to get through, casting a faint pink light on the frost-covered landscape, which reminded Agatha of the Christmas calendars of her youth where the winter scenes were decorated with glitter.

She hurried past James Lacey's cottage without a glance, thinking what to wear. What a pity all those new clothes had been meant for hot weather.

While the tabby, Hodge, watched curiously, she studied her face in the dressing-table mirror. A tan was all very well, but there was a lot to be said for thick make-up on a middle-aged face. There was a pouchy softness under her chin which she did not like and the lines down the side of her mouth appeared more pronounced since before she had gone away, reminding her of all the dire warnings about what sun-bathing did to the skin.

She slapped on skin-food and then rummaged through her wardrobe, settling at last on a cherry-red dress and black tailored coat with a velvet collar. Her hair was shiny and healthy, so she decided not to wear a hat. It was a bitterly cold day and she should wear her boots, but she had a new pair of Italian high heels and she knew her legs were good.

It was only after two hours of diligent preparation that she realized she had first to catch her cat, eventually running the animal to earth in a corner of the kitchen and shoving him ruthlessly in the wicker carrying basket. Hodge's wails rent the air. But deaf for once to her pet, Agatha tripped along to the surgery in her high heels. By the time she

6

reached the surgery, her feet were so cold she felt she was walking on two lumps of pain.

She pushed open the surgery door and went into the waiting-room. It seemed to be full of people: Doris Simpson, her cleaning woman, with her cat; Miss Simms with her Tommy; Mrs. Josephs, the librarian, with a large mangy cat called Tewks; and two farmers, Jack Page, whom she knew, and a squat burly man she only knew by sight, Henry Grange. There was also a newcomer.

"Her be Mrs. Huntingdon," whispered Doris. "Bought old Droon's cottage up back. Widow."

Agatha eyed the newcomer jealously. Despite the efforts of Animal Liberation to stop women from wearing furs, Mrs. Huntingdon sported a ranch mink coat with a smart mink hat. A delicate French perfume floated from her. She had a small pretty face like that of an enamelled doll, large hazel eyes with (false?) eyelashes, and a pink-painted mouth. Her pet was a small Jack Russell which barked furiously, swinging on the end of its lead as it tried to get at the cats. Mrs. Huntingdon seemed unaware of the noise or of the baleful looks cast at her by the cat owners. She was also sitting blocking the only heater.

There were "No Smoking" signs all over the walls, but Mrs. Huntingdon lit up a cigarette and blew smoke up into the air. In a doctor's waiting-room, where patients had only themselves to worry about, there would have been protests. But a vet's waiting-room is a singularly unmanning or unwomanning place, people made timid by worry about their pets.

Along one side of the waiting-room was a desk with a nurse-cum-receptionist behind it. She was a plain girl with lank brown hair and the adenoidal accents of Birmingham. Her name was Miss Mabbs.

Doris Simpson was the first to go in and was only out of sight for five minutes. Agatha surreptitiously rubbed her cold feet and ankles. This would not take long.

But Miss Simms was next and she was in there for half an hour, emerging at last with her eyes shining and her cheeks pink. Mrs. Josephs had her turn. After a very long time she came out, murmuring, "Such a firm hand Mr. Bladen does have," while her ancient cat lay supine in its basket as one dead.

Agatha went to the counter after Mrs. Huntingdon was ushered in and said to Miss Mabbs, "Mr. Bladen told me to call at two. I have been waiting a considerable time."

"Surgery starts at two. That's probably what he meant," said Miss Mabbs. "You'll need to wait your turn."

Determined not to have got all dressed up for nothing, Agatha sulkily picked up a copy of *Vogue*, June 1988, and retreated to her hard plastic chair.

She waited and waited for the merry widow plus dog to reappear, but the minutes ticked past and Agatha could hear a ripple of laughter from the surgery and wondered what was going on in there.

Three quarters of an hour went by while Agatha finished the copy of *Vogue* and a well-preserved 1981 copy of *Good Housekeeping* and was absorbed in a story in an old *Scotch Home* annual about the handsome laird of the Scottish highlands who forsook his "ain true love" Morag of the glens for Cynthia, some painted harlot from London. At last Mrs. Huntingdon came out, holding her dog. She smiled vaguely all around before leaving and Agatha glowered back.

There were only the two farmers and Agatha left. "Reckon I won't be coming here again," said Jack Page. "Waste a whole day, this would."

But he was dealt with very quickly, having come to collect a prescription for antibiotics, which he handed over to Miss Mabbs. The other farmer also wanted drugs and Agatha brightened as he reappeared after only a few moments. She had meant to berate the vet on having kept her waiting so long but there was that sweet smile again, that firm clasp of the hand, those searching, intimate eyes.

Feeling quite fluttery and at the same time guilty, for there was nothing up with Hodge, Agatha smiled back in a dazed way.

"Ah, Mrs. Raisin," said the vet, "let's have the cat out. What's his name?"

"Hodge."

"Same as Dr. Johnson's cat."

"Who's he? Your partner at Mircester?"

"Dr. *Samuel* Johnson, Mrs. Raisin."

"Well, how was I to know?" demanded Agatha crossly, her private opinion being that Dr. Johnson was one of those old farts like Sir Thomas Beecham that people always seemed to be quoting loftily at dinner parties. James Lacey had suggested the name.

To hide her irritation, she raised Hodge's basket onto the examining table and undid the latch and opened the front. "Come on now, out you come," cooed Agatha to a baleful Hodge who crouched at the back of the basket.

"Let me," said the vet, edging Agatha aside. He thrust a hand in and brutally dragged Hodge out into the light and then held the squirming, yowling animal by the scruff up in the air.

9

"Oh, don't do that! You're scaring him," protested Agatha. "Let me hold him."

"Very well. He looks remarkably healthy. What's up with him?"

Hodge buried his head in the opening of Agatha's coat. "Er, he's off his food," said Agatha.

"Any sickness, diarrhoea?"

"No."

"Well, we'd best take his temperature. Miss Mabbs!"

Miss Mabbs came in and stood with head lowered. "Hold the cat," ordered the vet.

Miss Mabbs detached the cat from Agatha and pinned him down with one strong hand on the examining table.

The vet advanced on Hodge with a rectal thermometer. Could it be, wondered Agatha, that the thermometer was thrust up poor Hodge's backside with unnecessary force? The cat yowled, struggled free, sprang from the table and crouched in a corner of the room.

"I've made a mistake," said Agatha, now desperate to get her pet away. "Perhaps if he shows any severe signs I'll bring him back."

Miss Mabbs was dismissed. Agatha tenderly put Hodge back in the basket.

"Mrs. Raisin."

"Yes?" Agatha surveyed him with bearlike eyes from which the love-light had totally fled.

"There is quite a good Chinese restaurant in Evesham. I've had a hard day and feel like treating myself. Would you care to join me for dinner?"

Agatha felt gratified warmth coursing through her middle-aged body. Bugger all cats in general and Hodge in particular. "I'd love to," she breathed.

10

"Then I'll meet you there at eight o'clock," he said, smiling into her eyes. "It's called the Evesham Diner. It's in an old house in the High Street, seventeenth century, can't miss it."

Agatha emerged grinning smugly into the now empty waiting-room. She wished she had been the first "patient" so she could have told all those other women she had a date.

But she stopped at the store on the road home and bought Hodge a tin of the best salmon to ease her conscience.

By the time she had reached home and cosseted Hodge and settled him in front of a roaring fire, she had persuaded herself that the vet had been firm and efficient with the cat, not deliberately cruel.

The desire to brag about her date was strong, so she phoned the vicar's wife, Mrs. Bloxby.

"Guess what?" said Agatha.

"Another murder?" suggested the vicar's wife.

"Better than that. Our new vet is taking me out for dinner this evening."

There was a long silence.

"Are you there?" demanded Agatha sharply.

"Yes, I'm here. I was just thinking . . ."

"What?"

"Why is he taking you out?"

"I should have thought that was obvious," snarled Agatha. "He fancies me."

"Forgive me. Of *course* he does. It's just that I feel there is something cold and calculating about him. Do be careful."

"I am not sweet sixteen," said Agatha huffily.

"Exactly."

11

That "exactly" seemed to Agatha to be saying, "You are a middle-aged woman easily flattered by the attentions of a younger man."

"In any case," Mrs. Bloxby went on, "do go very carefully on the roads. It's starting to snow."

Agatha rang off, feeling flat, and then she began to smile. Of course! Mrs. Bloxby was jealous. All the women in the village were smitten by the vet. But what was that she had said about snow? Agatha twitched back the curtain and looked out. Wet snow was falling, but it was not lying on the ground.

At seven-thirty she drove off in all the discomfort of a tight body stocking under a black wool Jean Muir dress embellished with a rope of pearls. Her heels were very high, so she kicked them off and drove up the hill from the village in her stockinged feet.

The snow was getting thicker and suddenly, near the top of the hill, she crossed over a sort of snow-line and found herself driving over thick snow. But ahead lay the tempting vision of dinner with the vet.

She pressed her foot on the brake to slow down as she neared the A44 and quite suddenly the car went into a skid. It was all so quick, so breathlessly fast. Her headlights whirled crazily round the winter landscape, and then there was a sickening crunch as she hit a stone wall on her left. She switched off the lights and the engine with a trembling hand and sat still.

A car going the other way, towards the village, stopped. A door opened and closed. Then a dark figure loomed up on Agatha's side of the car. She opened the window. "Are you all right, Mrs. Raisin?" came James Lacey's voice.

Before the vet, before the fiasco of the Bahamas, Agatha had often fantasized about James Lacey rescuing her from some accident. But all she could think about now was that precious date.

"I think nothing's broken," said Agatha and then struck the wheel in frustration. "Bloody, bloody snow. I say, can you run me into Evesham?"

"You must be joking. It's to get worse, or so the weather forecast said. Fish Hill will be closed."

"Oh, no," wailed Agatha. "Maybe we could go another way. Maybe through Chipping Camden."

"Don't be silly. Does your engine still work?"

Agatha switched it on and it sprang into life.

"What about the lights?"

Agatha switched them on, glaring out at a snow-covered wilderness.

James Lacey inspected the damage to the front of the car. "The glass in your headlamps is all shattered and you'll need a new bumper, radiator, and number-plate. You'd best back out and follow me down to the village."

"If you won't run me, then I'll get a cab."

"You can try." He walked off to his own car and Agatha heard him starting up. She reversed and followed him. He parked outside his own house, waved to her, and strode indoors.

Agatha leaped out of her own car, forgetting she was in her stockinged feet, and ran into the house. She seized the phone and, looking at a list of taxi-cab companies pinned to the wall, she began to phone them one after the other, but no taxi driver was prepared to go to Evesham or anywhere else on such a night.

Dammit, thought Agatha furiously, my car still works. I'm going.

She pulled on a pair of boots over her wet feet and went out again. But she was half-way up the hill again when both her headlamps blew, leaving her crawling along in snowy darkness.

Wearily, she turned the car and headed back down to the village again. Back indoors, she phoned the Chinese restaurant. No, came a voice at the other end, Mr. Bladen had not turned up. Yes, he had booked a table. No, he had definitely not arrived.

Feeling very flat, Agatha phoned directory inquiries and got a Mircester number for the vet. A woman answered the phone. "I am afraid Mr. Bladen is busy at the moment." The voice was cool and amused.

"This is Agatha Raisin," snapped Agatha. "He was to meet me in a restaurant in Evesham tonight."

"You could hardly have expected him to drive in such weather."

"Who is speaking, please?" demanded Agatha.

"This is his wife."

"Oh!" Agatha dropped the receiver like a hot coal.

So he was still married after all! What was it all about? But if he were married, then he should not have asked her out. Agatha had very firm views about dating married men.

She felt somehow as if he had set out to deliberately make a fool of her. Men! And James Lacey! He had simply gone indoors without calling to see if she were indeed un-harmed after her accident.

Agatha felt silly and now she had only a ruined car to show for her dreams of a date with a handsome man. She passed the rest of the evening filling in an accident claim form, the purring Hodge on her lap.

The next day dawned foggy as well as snowy. Once more Agatha felt that old trapped feeling. She waited and waited for the phone to ring, sure that Paul Bladen would call her to say *something*. But it sat there, squat in its silence.

At last she decided to pay a visit to her neighbour, James Lacey, if only to explain to him, subtly, that she had not been pursuing him. But although a thin column of smoke rose from his chimney, although his snow-covered car was parked outside, he did not answer the door.

Agatha felt well and truly snubbed. She was sure he was in there.

Hodge, in the selfish way of cats, played happily in the snow in the garden, stalking imaginary prey.

In the afternoon, the doorbell went. Agatha peered at herself in the hall mirror, grabbed a lipstick she always kept ready on the hall table and painted her mouth. Then, smoothing down her dress, she opened the door.

"Oh, it's you," she said, looking down into the round oriental features of Detective Sergeant Bill Wong.

"That's not much of a greeting," he said. "Any chance of a cup of coffee?"

"Come in," said Agatha, leaning over his shoulder and peering hopefully up and down the lane.

"Who were you expecting?" he asked, when they were seated in the kitchen.

"I was expecting an apology. Our new vet, Paul Bladen, invited me out for dinner in Evesham last night, but I had a skid at the top of the road and couldn't make it. But as it turned out, he didn't even get to the restaurant. I phoned his home and a woman answered it. She said she was his wife."

"Couldn't be," said Bill. "He was separated from his wife for about five years and the divorce came through last year."

"What's he playing at?" cried Agatha, exasperated.

"You mean, who's he playing with. Snowy night, no way of getting to Evesham, had a bit of fun at home instead."

"Well, he should have phoned anyway," said Agatha.

"Talking about your love life, how did you get on in the Bahamas?"

"Nice," said Agatha. "Got some sun."

"See anything of Mr. Lacey?"

"Didn't expect to. He'd gone to Cairo."

"And you knew that before you left?"

"What is this?" exclaimed Agatha. "A police interrogation?"

"Just friendly questions. Glad to see Hodge is happy. Looking very fit."

"Oh, Hodge is in the best of health."

The almond-shaped eyes studying her so intently glittered slightly in the white light from the snow coming in the kitchen window.

"Then why did poor Hodge have to go on to this vet?"

"Have you been spying on me?"

"No, I just happened to be passing yesterday and I saw you carrying Hodge in a basket to the surgery. You should wear more sensible footwear in this weather."

"I just wanted to check the cat had all his shots," said Agatha, "and what I choose to wear on my feet is my business."

16

He raised his hands and let them fall. "Sorry. Funny thing about Bladen, though."

"What?"

"He went into partnership with Peter Rice, the vet in Mircester, some time ago. What a queue of women there were during the first weeks! Right out in the street. But then they stopped coming. Seems Bladen is no good with pets. He's a whiz with farm animals and horses, but he loathes cats and small dogs."

"I don't want to talk about the man," said Agatha hotly. "Haven't you got anything else to talk about?"

So Bill told her all about the trouble with the increase in car theft in the area and how a lot of the crime was being increasingly committed by juveniles, while Agatha listened with half an ear and hoped the phone would ring to salve her pride. But by the time Bill left, the wretched machine was still silent.

She phoned the local garage and told them to come and tow her broken car away and give her an estimate, and then, after she had seen her vehicle carried off down the street on the back of a truck, she decided to go down to the Red Lion. There was no reason to dress up anymore. For months now she had worn only her best and smartest clothes when passing James Lacey's door. She put on a thick sweater, a tweed skirt and boots. But just as she was shrugging herself into a sheepskin coat, the telephone suddenly shrilled, making her jump.

She picked it up, sure it would be Paul Bladen at last, but a voice she did not recognize said tentatively, "Agatha?"

"Yes, who is it?" said Agatha, made cross by disappointment.

17

"It's Jack Pomfret. Remember me?"

Agatha brightened. Jack Pomfret had run a rival public-relations company to her own, but they had always been on amicable terms.

"Of course. How's things?"

"I sold out about the same time as you," he said. "Decided to take a leaf out of your book, have early retirement, have a bit of fun. But it get's boring, know what I mean?"

"Oh, yes," said Agatha with feeling.

"I'm thinking of starting up again and wondered if you would like to be my partner."

"Bad time," said Agatha cautiously. "Middle of a recession."

"Big companies need PR and I've got two lined up, Jobson's Electrics and Whiter Washing Powder."

Agatha was impressed. "Are you anywhere near here?" she asked. "We need to sit down together and discuss this properly."

"What I thought," he said eagerly, "was if you could take a trip up to London, we could get down to business."

The thought of fleeing the village, of getting away from lost romantic hopes, made Agatha say, "I'll do that. I'll book a place in town. What's your number? I'll call you back."

She wrote down his phone number and then, about to phone her favourite hotel, paused. Damn Hodge. She couldn't really dump that poor animal back in the cattery. Then she remembered a block of expensive service flats into which she had once booked visiting foreign clients and

18

phoned them and managed to get a flat for two weeks. She was sure they did not allow pets but she wasn't even going to ask them. Hodge could survive indoors for two weeks. The weather was lousy anyway.

TWO

†

AGATHA could not immediately plunge into business affairs, for Hodge, who had kept all his destruction to the outdoors in Carsely, had started to scratch the furniture in the service flat in Kensington, and so Agatha had to buy a scratching post and spend some time crouched on the floor in front of it, raking it with her fingernails, to show the cat what to do.

Having seen her pet settled at last, she phoned Jack Pomfret, who said he would meet her at the Savoy Grill for lunch.

Carsely was whirling away to a small speck in Agatha's mind. She was back in London, part of it again, not visiting, back in business.

Jack Pomfret, a slim Oxbridge type, fighting the age battle in denim and hair-weave, enthused over Agatha's appearance. Agatha curiously asked him why he had really decided to sell up.

"Just like you," he said with a boyish grin. "Thought retirement would suit me. Actually we, that's my wife, Marcia, and I, moved to Spain for a bit, but the climate didn't suit us. Down in the south. Too hot. But tell me all about yourself and what you've been doing."

Agatha settled back and bragged about her part in a murder investigation, highly embroidered.

"But village life must be absolutely stultifying for you, darling," he said, smiling into her eyes in a way that reminded Agatha of the vet. "All those dead brains and clodhoppers."

"I must admit I get bored," said Agatha, and then felt a pang of guilt as the faces of the village women rose before her eyes. "Actually, everyone's very nice, very kind. It's not them. It's me. I'm just not used to country life."

They talked on until the coffee arrived and then got down to business. Jack said that there was an office up at Marble Arch they could rent. All they really needed to kick off were three rooms. Agatha studied the figures. He seemed to have gone into everything very carefully.

"This rent is very high," said Agatha. "We would be better to get the end of a lease somewhere. Then, before we even start thinking about it, we should be sure we had enough clients."

"Would those two biggies I mentioned to you, Jobson's Electronics and Whiter Washing Powder, convince you?"

"Of course."

"The managing directors of both companies happen to be in London for a business conference. Tell you what. Lay on some drinks and fiddly bits and I'll bring them round to your flat. I'll phone you later today and give you a time."

"I must say, if you have contacts like this, we'll shoot to the top of the league in a few weeks," said Agatha.

He did phone later, the managing directors came round to Agatha's the following day and it was a jolly meeting, particularly for Agatha, as both men flirted with her.

As Jack got up to leave, having stayed on for an extra drink after the businessmen had left, he kissed Agatha on the cheek and said, "I'll give you a round figure for your share of the concern, you give me a cheque and leave all the nitty-gritty business side to me. You're the whiz with the clients, Agatha. Always were. Look the way you had those two eating out of your hand!"

"How much?" demanded Agatha.

He named a figure which made her blink. He sat down again and took out sheaves of facts and figures. Agatha thought hard. The sum he had named would take away all her savings. She still had the cottage in Carsely, but she wouldn't need that anymore now she was back in business.

"Let me sleep on it," she said. "Leave the papers with me."

After he had gone, she wished she had not drunk so much. She stared down at the figures. They needed all the basic things like computers and fax machines, desks and chairs. Party to launch it. Paper and paper-clips. "I'm not sure," she said slowly. "What do you think, Hodge? Hodge?"

But there was no sign of the cat. She searched the small flat, under the bed, in the cupboards and closets, but no Hodge.

The cat must have slipped out when her guests were leaving.

She threw on her coat and went down by the stairs, not the lift, calling "Hodge! Hodge!" A woman opened a door and said in glacial tones, "Do you mind keeping that noise down?"

"Get stuffed," snarled Agatha, sick with worry. If this were Carsely, said a voice in her head, the whole village would turn out to help you. She opened the street door. Outside lay anonymous, uncaring London. She trekked round and round the squares and gardens of Kensington while the traffic often drowned the sound of her frantically calling voice.

"If I was you, dear," said a woman's voice at her elbow, "I'd wait till after the traffic dies down. Cat, is it? Well, the traffic scares them."

But Agatha ploughed on, her feet cold and aching. She asked in all the shops up the Gloucester Road, but she was just another woman looking for a lost pet and no one had seen the cat, nor did they look at all interested or concerned.

She wandered dismally back into Cornwall Gardens. Someone was stumbling through a Chopin sonata in an amateurish way. Someone else was having a party, a press of people standing shoulder to shoulder in a front room.

And then Agatha saw a cat walking slowly towards her, a tabby cat. She advanced slowly, praying under her breath. Hodge was a tabby, striped grey and black, hardly an original-looking animal.

"Hodge," said Agatha gently.

The cat stopped and looked up at her. "Oh, it *is* you," said Agatha gratefully and scooped the cat up into her arms.

"I'm glad someone's picked up that poor stray," said a man who was walking his dog. "I was going to phone the

24

RSPCA. Been living in these gardens for about two weeks. In this cold, too. Still, cats are great survivors."

"It's *my* cat," said Agatha, and clutching the animal as fiercely as a mother does her hurt child, she stalked off to her flat.

She opened the door and closed it firmly behind her, put the cat on the floor and said, "Hot milk is what you need."

Agatha went into the minuscule kitchen. Hodge rose from a kitchen chair and stretched and yawned.

"How did you get there?" demanded Agatha, bewildered. She swung round. The tabby she had picked up in Cornwall Gardens came into the kitchen, mewing softly. In the full glare of the fluorescent light, Agatha saw that it was a skinny thing, not at all like Hodge.

"Two of them," groaned Agatha. She couldn't keep two. One was worry enough. Where had Hodge been? thought Agatha, who was not yet well enough versed in the ways of cats and did not know they could appear to vanish into thin air. She thought of putting the new cat back out in the gardens. But that would be cruel. She could take it to the RSPCA but they would probably gas it, for who would want a plain tabby cat?

She warmed milk and put down two bowls of it and then two bowls of cat food. Hodge seemed to have placidly accepted the newcomer. Agatha changed the litter in the tray, hoping the new animal was house-trained.

When she went to bed, the cats settled down on either side of her. It was comforting. What would they say in Carsely when she returned with two? But then, she would only be returning to Carsely to pack up.

* * *

25

But the village was still fresh in her mind when she awoke the next morning. She decided to phone Bill Wong and tell him her news.

At police headquarters in Mircester, they said it was his day off and so Agatha phoned his home.

Bill listened carefully while she outlined all her plans and told him of the visit of the two managing directors.

There was a silence. Then he said in his soft Gloucester accent, "That's odd."

"What is?" demanded Agatha.

"I mean, *two* managing directors of big companies turning up just like that. I don't know much about business . . ."

"No, you don't," put in Agatha.

"But I would have thought a meeting would have been set up for you, liaison with the advertising department, the firms' public-relations officers, that sort of thing."

"Oh, they both happened to be in town for some business meeting."

"And what do you really know about this Jack Pomfret? You're not just going to hand over any money or anything like that?"

"I'm not stupid," said Agatha, angry now, for she was beginning to think she was.

"A good way to find out about people," said Bill, "is to call at their home. You can usually get an idea of how flush they are from where they live and what the wife is like."

"So you think I should spy on him? And you're always telling me I don't know how to mind my own business."

"I think you're a Nosy Parker when you don't have to be and touchingly naïve when you do have to be," said Bill.

"Look, copper, I ran a successful business for years."

"Maybe Carsely's made you forget what an evil place the world can be."

"What? After all that murder and mayhem?"

"Different sort of thing."

"Well, I've finished with Carsely."

There was an amused chuckle from the other end of the phone. "That's what you think."

Agatha settled down with a coffee and cigarette to go through the papers Jack had given her again. Did he really expect her just to hand over a cheque without seeing his equal contribution? The new cat and Hodge were chasing each other over the furniture, the stray seeming to have recovered amazingly.

Agatha opened her brief-case and found a clipboard and put the papers on it. She phoned Roy Silver, the young man who had once worked for her.

"Aggie, love," his voice lilted down the line. "I was thinking of coming down to see you. What are you up to?"

"I need some help. Do you remember Jack Pomfret?"

"Vaguely."

"You wouldn't happen to have an address for him?"

"As a matter of fact I have, sweetie. I pinched your business address book when I left. Don't squawk! You'd probably have forgotten about it. Let me see . . . aha, 121, Kynance Mews, Kensington. Do you want the phone number?"

"I've got that, but it doesn't seem like a Kensington one. Never mind. I'll walk round. It's only round the corner."

"How long are you in London? I gather you are in London. Want to meet up?"

27

"Maybe later," said Agatha. "Did you get married?"

"No, why?"

"What about that girl, what's-her-name, you brought down to meet me?"

"Ran off and left me for a lager lout."

"I'm sorry."

"I'm not," said Roy waspishly. "I can do better than that."

"Look, I'll call you. I've got something to deal with first." Agatha said goodbye and put the phone down. Why hadn't Jack said he was living just round the corner?

She walked along to the end of Kynance Mews to 121 and pressed the bell.

A thin, tweedy woman answered the door, the kind Agatha didn't like, the kind who wore cultured pearls and green wellies in London.

"Mr. Pomfret?" asked Agatha.

"Mr. Pomfret no longer lives here," said the woman acidly. "I bought the house from him. But I am not his secretary and I refuse to send any more letters on to him. All he needs to do is to pay a small amount of money to the post office in order to get his mail redirected."

"If you give me his address, I can take any letters to him," said Agatha.

"Very well. Wait there and I'll write it down."

Agatha stood in the freezing cold on the frost-covered cobbles of the mews. A skein of geese flew overhead on their way from the Round Pond in Kensington Gardens to St. James's Park. Her breath came out in a little cloud of steam in front of her face. Two dog lovers stood at the entrance to the mews and unleashed their animals, which peed their way down from door to door and then both squatted down

28

and defecated, before the satisfied owners called them to heel. There was no more selfish animal lover than a Kensington animal lover, thought Agatha.

"Here you are," said the woman, "and here's the address." She handed Agatha a slip of paper and a pile of letters. Agatha thanked her and put the letters in her briefcase and then looked down in surprise at the address as the woman firmly closed the door: 8A Ramillies Crescent, Archway. Well, there were some mansions in Archway and some rich people left in that declining suburb, but 8A suggested a basement flat.

She headed off to the Gloucester Road tube, and not wanting to make a lot of changes took the District Line to Embankment and then the Northern Line to Archway. Once she was settled on the Northern Line, she took out the letters. They were mostly junk mail but there was one from the income tax.

Agatha's heart sank down to her cold feet. Lawabiding, financially secure people were the ones that kept in touch with the Inland Revenue.

She then took out a pocket atlas of London and looked up Ramillies Crescent, which was in a network of streets behind the hospital.

Everyone at the main road junction in Archway at the exit to the tube looked depressed. You could, thought Agatha bleakly, take the lot and dump them on the streets of Moscow and no one would notice they were foreigners. She ploughed up the steep hill from the tube and turned off towards Ramillies Crescent when she got to the hospital.

It turned out to be a run-down crescent of Victorian houses. No one here was obviously feeling the recession, for no one had ever got to any point from which to recess *to*.

The gardens were untended and most of them had been concreted over to make space for some rusting car. Agatha arrived at Number 8. Sure enough, 8A was the basement flat. Edging her way around a broken pram which looked as if it had been thrown there rather than left to rot, she rang the doorbell. Marcia Pomfret, she vaguely remembered, was a statuesque blonde.

At first she did not recognize Marcia in the woman who opened the door to her, a woman with a faded, lined face and black roots, who looked at her without a spark of recognition.

"What are you selling?" asked Marcia in a weary, nasal voice.

Agatha made up her mind to lie. "I'm not selling anything," she said brightly. "Your name was given to me because I believe you and your husband lived in Spain. I am doing research for the Spanish government. They would like to know why various British families did not settle in Spain but returned."

Agatha scooped the clipboard and papers out of her briefcase and stood waiting.

"You may as well come in," said Marcia. "I usually stand talking to the walls here, and that's a fact."

She led the way into a dark living-room. Agatha's sharp eyes recognized what she called landlord's furniture and sat down on a worn sofa in front of a low glass-and-chrome coffee-table.

"Now," she said brightly, "what took you to Spain?"

"It was my husband, Jack," said Marcia. "He'd always wanted to run a bar. Thought he could do it. So he sold the business and the house and we bought this little bar on the Costa Del Sol. He called it Home from Home. Made it

30

British-like. San Miguel beer and steak-and-kidney pud. We had a little flat above the bar. Slave labour, it was. While he was out chatting up the birds in the bar, I was in the kitchen, wasn't I, turning out those hot English meals when it was cooking-hot outside."

"And were you successful?" asked Agatha, pretending to take notes.

"Naw. We was just another English bar among all them other English bars. Couldn't get help. The Spanish'll only work for top wages. Nearly died with the heat, I did. 'Soon it'll be all right,' Jack said. 'Spend the days on the beach and let someone do the work for us.' But the place never really got off the ground. Once the tourist season was over, that was that. I said to Jack he'd have been better to make it Spanish, get the locals and the better-class tourists who don't come all this way for English muck, but would he listen? So we sold up and came back to nothing."

Agatha asked a few more questions about Spain and the Spanish to keep up the pretence. Then she put the clipboard away and rose to go. "I hope you will soon be on your feet again."

Marcia shrugged wearily and Agatha suddenly remembered what she had looked like ten years ago at a party, blonde and beautiful. Jack's latest bimbo, they had called her, but he had married her.

"Have you any children?" Agatha asked.

Marcia shook her head. "Just as well," she said sadly. "Wouldn't want to bring them up here."

And just as well, indeed, thought Agatha miserably as she trailed off down the street. For when he finds I haven't been suckered, he'll search around for a new wife, and one with money this time. She remembered his letters and

31

stopped beside a pillar-box, readdressed the lot and popped them in.

Jack Pomfret was standing on the up escalator at Archway tube when he saw the stocky figure of Agatha Raisin on the down escalator and opened his copy of *The Independent* and hid behind it. He ran all the way home once he was out in the street.

"Was that Raisin woman here?" he demanded.

"What Raisin woman?" demanded Marcia. "There was only some woman from the Spanish government asking questions about British who had left Spain."

"What did she look like?"

"Straight brown hair, small brown eyes, bit of a tan."

"You silly bitch, that was Agatha Raisin smelling out God knows what kind of rats. What did you tell her?"

"I told her how we couldn't make that bar work. How was I to know . . . ?"

Jack paced up and down. The money he'd spent feeding that old cow at the Savoy! The money he'd paid to those two actor friends to impersonate businessmen! Perhaps he could still save something.

Agatha packed up her stuff and left the rented flat for a new one, sacrificing the money she'd paid in advance. She moved to another rented service flat in Knightsbridge, behind Harrods. She would see a few shows and eat a few good restaurant meals before returning to that grave called Carsely.

She knew Jack would come looking for her and she did not relish the confrontation, for like all people who have been tricked, she felt ashamed of her own gullibility.

So when Jack Pomfret, sweating lightly despite the cold, called at her old flat, he did not find anyone there. The owners did not know she had left, for she had not returned her keys, and assumed she was out, and so Jack called and called desperately in the ensuing days until even he had to admit to himself that there was little hope of getting any money out of Agatha Raisin.

Apart from going to shows and restaurants, Agatha took the new cat to the Emergency Veterinary Clinic in Victoria, learned it was female, got it its shots, named it Boswell despite its gender, with some idea of keeping up the literary references, and decided that two cats were as easy to keep as one.

One evening, walking home from the theatre through Leicester Square, she was just priding herself at how easily she fitted back into city life when a youth tried to seize her handbag. Agatha hung on like grim death, finally managing to land a hefty kick on her assailant's shins. He ran off. Passers-by stared at her curiously but no one asked her if she was all right. When one lived in town, thought Agatha, one became street-wise, developed an instinct for danger. But in sleepy Carsely, where she often did not bother to lock her car at night, such instincts had gone. She walked on purposefully, striding out with a confident step which declared, don't mug me, I'm loaded for bear, the step of the street-wise.

At the end of a week, she headed back to Carsely, carrying two cat baskets this time.

For the first time, she had an odd feeling of coming home. It was a sunny day, with a faint hint of warmth in

33

the air. Snowdrops were fluttering shyly at village door-steps.

She thought of the vet, Paul Bladen, again. Now she had a new cat, she had every excuse to take it to the vet for a check-up. On the other hand, if Bill Wong was to be believed, Paul Bladen did not like cats. She decided to go along and say she needed some eye ointment.

She had really only half believed Bill, however, and was surprised to find the waiting-room empty. Miss Mabbs looked up listlessly from a torn magazine and said Mr. Bladen was up at Lord Pendlebury's racing stable but would be back soon. Agatha waited and waited.

After an hour, Paul Bladen walked into the waiting-room, nodded curtly to Agatha and disappeared into the surgery. Agatha had half a mind to leave.

But after only a few moments, Miss Mabbs told her to go through.

He listened to Agatha's tale of the cat's eye infection and then scribbled out a prescription, saying they were out of the ointment, but that she could get it at the chemist's in Moreton-in-Marsh. He then obviously waited for Agatha to leave.

"Don't you think you owe me an explanation?" demanded Agatha. "I tried to go to that restaurant in Evesham but the snow was so bad, I crashed. I tried to phone you but some woman answered the phone, saying she was your wife. I thought you might have had the decency to phone *me*."

He was suddenly all charm. "Mrs. Raisin, I am very sorry. The weather was so dreadful, I was sure you would not even try to make it. The woman on the phone was my sister, being silly. Do forgive me. Look, what about to-

34

night? There's a new Greek restaurant in Mircester, just near the abbey. We could meet there at eight." But when he smiled into her eyes, Agatha was reminded bitterly of Jack Pomfret.

She hesitated, looking out of the surgery window. It was then that she saw James Lacey, looking the same as ever. He was a very tall, well-built man with a handsome, tanned face and bright blue eyes. His thick black hair had only a trace of grey at the sides. He was strolling past with that easy, rangy stride of his, James Lacey without a care in the world.

"I'd love to go," she said. "See you then."

When Agatha got home, the phone was ringing and she picked up the receiver. Jack Pomfret's voice sounded down the line. "Agatha, Agatha, I can explain . . ."

Agatha slammed the receiver back on its stand. The phone immediately began to ring again.

She snatched it up. "Look, bugger off, you useless con," she snarled. "If you think   "

"Mrs. Raisin, it's me, Bill."

"Oh! I told you to call me Agatha."

"Sorry. Agatha. So business wasn't business?"

"No," said Agatha curtly.

"Pity. What about dinner tonight?"

"What?"

"You, me, dinner."

Bill Wong was in his twenties, so any invitation to dinner was prompted by pure friendship. Nonetheless she was flattered and almost tempted to dump the vet. But the vet was nearer her age.

"I've got a date, Bill. "What about next week?"

"Right. I'll probably see you before then. Who's your date with? Lacey?"

"No, the vet."

"Out of the frying pan into the fire."

"What the hell does that mean? You mean he's after my *money*? Well, let me tell you, Bill Wong, that a lot of men find me attractive."

"Sure, sure. Talking off the top of my head. See you soon. Only joking. He's probably loaded."

THREE

†

AGATHA tried on one dress after the other, gave up and changed into an old skirt and blouse, was about to leave and hurried back indoors to put on the body stocking, the Jean Muir dress, the pearls, and gummed on a pair of false eyelashes she had bought in London.

James Lacey saw her drive off. He noticed that she no longer went slowly past his house, looking eagerly out of the car window.

Agatha drove along the Fosse to Mircester, an old cobbled town dominated by a great medieval abbey. She found the restaurant without difficulty. It was more like a dingy shop with closed curtains rather than a restaurant, but she was sure all would be warmth and elegance inside.

The Stavros Restaurant came as a bit of a shock to her when she walked inside. There was cracked linoleum on the floor and checked plastic table-cloths covered the tables. A few rather dingy enlarged photographs of views of Greece, the Acropolis, Delphi, and so on stared down from the walls.

Paul Bladen rose to meet Agatha. He was wearing his old tweeds and an open-necked shirt.

"You look very grand," he said by way of greeting.

"I didn't know it would be such a . . . quaint . . . restaurant," said Agatha, sitting down.

"The food makes up for the decor." He poured her a glass of retsina from a carafe, and Agatha took a swig, mentally damning it as lighter fuel but hoping the alcohol content was enough to give courage.

A skinny waitress with dead-white *Return of the Mutant Women* make-up came up with a notebook.

"Watyerwant?" she asked laconically.

Agatha, who would normally have told her to buzz off and give her time to choose something had, that evening, decided to play the feminine and submissive woman, so she batted her false eyelashes at Paul and said, "You choose for me."

The dish was supposed to be stuffed vine leaves. Agatha, poking at it after it had arrived at their table with depressing speed, decided the vine leaves were cabbage and the filling was watery rice.

She found that by dint of breaking the little packets open and spreading them about her plate she could actually make it look as if she had at least eaten some of it.

Paul Bladen talked all the while about his hopes to supply Carsely with a really good veterinary service and ordered another large carafe of retsina, as Agatha was making up in drink what she was not getting in the way of food.

"Now," he said, smiling into her eyes, "tell me all

38

about yourself. How is it that such a sophisticated lady ends up in a Cotswold village?"

A sober Agatha might have remembered that the Cotswolds, being fashionable, abound in quite a lot of interesting people, but the tipsy Agatha was flattered and told him all about her childhood dream of owning a cottage in the country, how she had built up a successful business, sold it and retired early. "*Very* early," said Agatha.

He reached across the table and took her hand. "You haven't mentioned your husband."

Agatha shrugged. "I left him years and years ago. I suppose he's dead." Agatha had never even bothered to get a divorce. Paul's hand was warm and dry and firm. She felt fluttery and breathless, almost as if she were on a first date.

"I'm doing all the talking," she said. "What about you?"

"I am working on a dream," he said. He released her hand as the waitress came up and put two Levantine sticky cakes, oozing watery honey, in front of them and two cups of black sludge masquerading under the name of Greek coffee.

"I plan to create a really good veterinary hospital," he said, "but that takes money."

"You should ask the Carsely Ladies Society," said Agatha. "They're terribly good at fund-raising."

"Unlike you, I think they are all too provincial to grasp such a grand concept."

"I wouldn't say that." Agatha thought of Mrs. Bloxby. "They're really dedicated workers . . . I tell you what. I'll give you a contributuon to start your fund off."

Twenty pounds, thought Agatha charitably. After all, he is paying for this quite hideous dinner.

He seized her hand again. "You don't seem to like your coffee."

"I like filter coffee."

"Then let's go to my place and have some." He stroked his thumb over the palm of her hand.

Well, this is it, thought Agatha, as she drove after his car through the dark winding streets of the old town, this is what I got all dressed up for. But the euphoria induced by all she had drunk was leaving her.

Paul, in the car in front, stopped outside a small Victorian villa on the outskirts of the town.

As Agatha followed him into a gloomy hall, she was suddenly seized with panic as he turned and smiled slowly and intimately at her. Sex! Here it was and here were all the fears. She hadn't shaved her armpits. What if she wasn't . . . er . . . gymnastic enough? The house was cold. One of her false eyelashes was beginning to slip. She could feel it. What if she had to undress in front of him and he saw her trying to get out of that body stocking?

"I've got to go," she said suddenly. "I forgot to leave the cats any water."

"Agatha, Agatha, they'll be all right. Come here."

"And I'm expecting an important phone call from New York and . . . I mean, thanks for the dinner. My treat next time. Honestly, got to rush."

Agatha fled down the garden path, stumbling on her high heels.

She unlocked her car and dived into the driving seat and then drove off, not feeling the panic ebb until she was safely back out of the town and on her road home. Along the Fosse, a police car loomed up in her rear-view mirror. She thought of all she had drunk and prayed they would not stop her and breathalyse her. She dropped her speed to thirty and the police car moved out and passed her.

She felt bewildered by her reactions to the handsome vet. She had not had an affair with anyone in quite a long time. What a fool she had been. Not once did she allow the thought to form in her head that the idea of love-making without love had become repugnant to her. That was too old-fashioned an idea to admit to, and Agatha Raisin was determinedly modern.

The next day Paul Bladen went back to Lord Pendlebury's racing stables. He was to perform Hobday's operation on a racehorse to stop its roaring. This involved cutting the vocal cords. He filled a syringe with a drug called Immobilon to anaesthetize the animal. Beside him on a small rickety table which he had carried into the stable for the purpose, he placed a glass bottle of Revivon to inject the horse when the operation was over, and also a glass bottle of Narcon, a powerful antidote in case he got any of the Immobilon into his bloodstream by mistake.

"There now, boy, easy," he said, patting the horse on the nose as it shuffled and whinnied. He felt irritated that Lord Pendlebury had not even bothered to supply him with a stable-boy to help. The sun was shining in through the open stable door, casting a huge gold rectangle on the cobbles at his feet. He raised the syringe to inject the horse in the jugular vein. The gold at his feet darkened as if a cloud had passed over the face of the sun. Then something struck him savagely on the back of the head and he fell sprawling.

41

Winded but not unconscious, he twisted round on the cobbles. "What the hell are you . . . ?" he began.

A hand twisted the syringe out of his grasp and the next thing he knew, the syringe had been plunged into his chest. He scrabbled desperately at the table where the antidote lay. Even Revivon, the drug to revive the horse, would work if he couldn't reach the Narcon, but the table was kicked over and he died a few seconds later.

Agatha heard about his death the following day from Bill Wong, and her first feeling was one of selfish relief that the vet was no longer around to gossip about the way she had fled from his house.

Agatha had replaced the electric cooker in her kitchen with an Aga stove. The door of the stove was open and a wood fire burning briskly. A jug of early daffodils from the Channel Islands stood on the window-ledge. The square plastic table was gone and now there was a solid wooden one with a scrubbed top.

"It was a tragic accident," said Bill. "Some vets won't work with Immobilon. It's deadly. There was a case not long ago where the vet put the syringe full of the stuff in his breast pocket and approached the horse. The horse nudged him on the chest, the syringe pricked the vet and that was enough. He died almost instantly."

"You'd think they'd have some sort of antidote," said Agatha.

"Oh, they do, but there's not often time to reach it. In Paul Bladen's case, it was on a little table, but either he kicked it over in his death agonies, or the horse kicked it over."

"You mean it's like cyanide? You writhe about?"

"Come to think of it, you don't," said Bill. "Good way to commit suicide . . . quick and painless. There was one curious thing."

"Yes?" Agatha's eyes brightened.

"No, not that curious. Not murder. But there was a lump on the back of his head, but of course it was assumed he got that striking his head when he fell, although he was found lying on his side. His fingerprints were on the edge of the table, as if he'd made an attempt to get to the antidote."

"And he was all alone?"

"Yes. The reason for that, reading between the lines of old Lord Pendlebury's statement, is that he high-handedly demanded help. Lord Pendlebury said his stable staff were all too busy and then made sure they were. It was an operation to stop the horse roaring. A lot of the racehorses make a roaring sound on the course."

"Seems brutal."

"Everything to do with animals is brutal."

James Lacey hovered outside Agatha's door. She had baked him a pie two months ago and he knew he should have returned the pie dish. He had been putting it off. But the fact that Agatha had apparently ceased to pursue him had given him courage. He rang the bell, thinking that with any luck she might be out around the village, and then he could safely leave the pie dish on the doorstep.

But Agatha answered the door. "Come in and have coffee," she said, taking the pie dish. "We're in the kitchen."

That "we" encouraged James Lacey to step inside. He

was writing a military history, and like most writers spent his days looking for excuses not to work.

He knew Bill Wong and nodded a greeting. James settled down over a cup of coffee, relieved that Agatha was not staring at him in the intense way she usually did.

"We've just been talking about Paul Bladen's death," said Agatha. She described what had happened.

The retired colonel despised what he called "women's gossip" and would have been amazed had anyone pointed out to him that he was just like the rest of the human race, a gossip himself.

"I'm not surprised," he said cheerfully, "that a man so generally loathed should be bumped off."

"But he wasn't bumped off," protested Agatha.

The people who claim not to be gossips are usually the worst kind, and James Lacey weighed in. "How can you be sure?" he demanded. "For a start, did you hear about poor Mrs. Josephs? You know she was devoted to that old cat of hers, Tewks. Well, she kept going to Bladen with one excuse or another. One day he asked her to leave the cat with him for a full examination. When she went back to collect her beloved pet, he had put it to death. He said the cat was too old and needed to be put out of its misery. Mrs. Josephs was distraught.

"Then there was Miss Simms. She kept going along on one pretext or another. The last time she went, she said, and I believe her, it was because the cat had a genuine complaint. It was scratching and scratching. Bladen told her coldly the cat had fleas, and not to waste his time and be more thorough with her housekeeping. She took her cat back to her former vet, who told her the animal had an allergy. Miss Simms returned to Bladen and ripped him up and down. You could hear it all over the village. But then Bladen had told Jack Page, the farmer, that he was sick of those women and their dreary pets. He only had time for working animals."

"This must have all happened when I was in London," said Agatha. "I mean, they all went to him when he first came."

"They were all in love with him," said James. "Then for some reason he started to get nasty to a few of them. There are still some who think he's the best vet ever . . . or was."

"Who are they?" asked Bill.

"Mrs. Huntingdon, the pretty newcomer with the Jack Russell; Mrs. Mason, the chairwoman of the Carsely Ladies Society; Mrs. Harriet Parr from the lower village; and Miss Josephine Webster, who runs that shop which seems to sell nothing other than dried flowers."

"How did you learn all this?" exclaimed Agatha, and then turned pink, for she realized in that moment that he was every bit as much pursued by the village women as Paul Bladen had been.

"Oh, people talk to me," he said vaguely.

"You had a dinner date with Bladen," said Bill Wong, looking at Agatha. "The night before his death, in fact, for I asked you out for dinner and you told me you couldn't go because you had a date with him."

"So what?" demanded Agatha.

James Lacey looked at her curiously. She was quite attractive, he supposed, in a pugnacious sort of way. In fact, now that she was not oiling all over him, he could see that

45

she did have certain good points. She had a trim, if rather stocky figure, excellent legs, rather small, intelligent brown eyes, and shiny healthy brown hair, worn straight but cut by some no doubt expensive hairdressing master.

"So I'm interested," Bill was saying. "Where did you go for dinner?"

"That new Greek place in Mircester."

"Horrible dump," said James. "Took someone there for dinner myself. Never again."

Agatha wondered immediately whom he had taken for dinner, but she said, "I didn't find out all that much about him. Oh, he said his dream was to open a veterinary hospital."

"Aha," said Bill maliciously. "Tried to get money out of you, did he?"

"NO, HE DID NOT!" yelled Agatha, and added in a quieter voice. "It may come as a surprise to you, but he fancied me."

"I'm glad about that. I mean, you'd suffered enough already with that chap in London trying to cheat you," said Bill.

"More coffee?" said Agatha, glaring at him.

"Yes, please," said James Lacey.

"Not for me," said Bill. "Back to work." And he left the kitchen too quickly for James to change his mind and escape.

Determined to be as remote and cool as possible, Agatha served James with another cup of coffee and then sat at the far end of the table from him. More for something to say than because she was interested, she said, "So you think someone might have murdered Paul Bladen?"

46

"It did cross my mind," he said. "I mean, it would be so easy to do. Creep up on him when he had a syringe full, knock him on the head . . . No that won't do. He hadn't been knocked on the head."

"But he might have been," said Agatha. "I mean, he had a lump on his head. They decided he might have got it falling on the floor, but he was lying on his side."

"I suppose the police know what they are doing," said James. "I mean, if anyone else had been around Lord Pendlebury's racing stables, he or she would have been seen. This is the country. You can't sneak around places quietly like you can in the city."

"I wonder," said Agatha. "I would like to see those racing stables. Do you know Lord Pendlebury?"

"No. But all you have to do is go up there and ask him to contribute to one of those charities you're always raising money for. Then, when you leave the house, all you have to do is to go to the stables and take a look around."

"I wish you would come with me," said Agatha. He looked at her nervously, but she had not said it in any flirtatious way.

He thought of the work he had to do, he thought of the joys of writing and found himself saying, "I don't see why not. We could go up this afternoon, say, about two."

"That is very kind of you," said Agatha calmly.

She saw him to the door, ushered him out, and then performed a war dance in her little hall. The impossible was about to happen. She was going to spend an afternoon with James Lacey.

* * *

47

By two o'clock, Agatha, weary of trying on clothes, had settled for a cherry-red sweater, a neat tweed skirt, brogues, and a sheepskin coat.

She stood by the window of the dining-room, which faced the front of the house so that she could watch him arriving. And there he came with his long rangy stride. Although in his fifties, he was a handsome man, over six feet tall, with crisp dark hair with only a trace of grey, humorous eyes and a powerful nose. He was wearing a moth-eaten old shooting sweater with worn suede patches on the shoulders over a checked shirt and olive-green cords. Agatha had a good stare at him to compensate for the fact that she intended to remain cool and detached when she actually met him again.

Lord Pendlebury's home, Eastwold Park, lay at the end of a long drive which led off the road from the village. Agatha felt quite elated. The only time she had been inside the doors of a grand house before was as a tourist. She wondered if she should curtsy—no, that was for royalty— and should she call him "my lord"? Best to watch how James Lacey went on and copy him.

They drove up and parked outside the front of one of those rambling Cotswold mansions which cover quite a bit of ground without appearing to do so. The door was answered not by a butler, but by one of the village women, Mrs. Arthur, wearing an overall and brushing wisps of grey hair from her eyes. Mrs. Arthur was a member of the Carsely Ladies Society, but Agatha had not known she worked for Lord Pendlebury.

"I wanted to ask Lord Pendlebury if he would contribute to our fund-raising for Save the Children," said Agatha.

"You can *ask*," said Mrs. Arthur. "No harm in *asking*, I always say." She stayed put.

"Why don't you ask Lord Pendlebury then if we may see him?" demanded James Lacey.

"On your own heads be it," said Mrs. Arthur. "He's in the study, over there." She jerked a thumb towards a door at the end of the hall.

It was all very disappointing, thought Agatha, as she followed James Lacey across the hall. There should have been a butler to take a visiting card on a silver tray. But James was already holding open the study door for her.

Lord Pendlebury was seated in a battered leather armchair before a dying wood fire. He was fast asleep.

"Well, that's that," whispered Agatha.

James crossed to the window. "The stable block is out the back," he said, not bothering to lower his voice. "You can see it from here."

"Shhh," urged Agatha. The room was so silent, book-lined, dim, with two walls of calf-bound books, a large desk, bowls of spring flowers on odd little tables, and the solemn tick of clocks intensifying the silence.

"Who are you?" Lord Pendlebury was awake now and staring straight at her.

Agatha jumped and said, "I am Agatha Raisin from Carsely. The gentleman there is Mr. Lacey." She longed to call him colonel but was sure James would object. "I am collecting money on behalf of the Carsely Ladies Society for Save the Children."

Like an American swearing the oath of allegiance, Lord Pendlebury put an arm across his chest, no doubt to protect his wallet.

49

"I have already given money to Cancer Research," he said.

"But this is Save the Children."

"I don't *like* children," said Lord Pendlebury petulantly. "Too many of them. Go away."

Agatha opened her mouth to blast him, but James Lacey said quickly, "Fine-looking stables you have, sir. Mind if we walk over and take a look?"

"Doesn't matter if I mind, does it?" said Lord Pendlebury. "A landowner no longer has any privacy. If it's not busybodies like you, it's those damn environmentalists, walking over my land with their rucksacks, eating health-food nut bars and farting. Do you know what causes the damage to the ozone layer? It's health fanatics, eating ghastly bran and nut bars and farting about the landscape. Sending out poisonous gases and wind. Ought to be put down."

"Quite," said James indifferently while Agatha glared at Lord Pendlebury.

"You don't seem a bad sort of chap," said Lord Pendlebury, peering at James in the gloom of the study. "But that woman looks like one of those hunt saboteurs, slavering on about the darling foxes."

"Listen, you," said Agatha, advancing on him.

James took her firmly by the arm and guided her towards the door. "Thank you for your kind invitation, Lord Pendlebury," he said over his shoulder. "We shall enjoy seeing your stables."

"Rude old bugger," raged Agatha when they were out in the hall.

James shrugged. "He's old. Leave him be. We get to see the racing stables and that's why we came."

But Agatha was still smarting. She felt she had been grossly insulted. Worse than that, she thought Lord Pendlebury had been able to see right through her expensive sheepskin and sweater, right down into her working-class soul.

"I'm going to have a firm talk with Mrs. Arthur," said Agatha as they walked together towards the stable block. "She could probably earn more working in a factory or a supermarket."

"She and her husband work for Lord Pendlebury," pointed out James Lacey. "They get a rent-free cottage on the estate and all the free vegetables they want from the market garden. Anyway, you want to persuade Mrs. Arthur to leave to get your revenge on the old man because he thought you were a flatulent fox preserver."

This was the truth, and so Agatha decided James was really quite an uninteresting and charmless man after all.

The other thing that was irritating was that although James Lacey had spent less time in and around the village compared to herself, he seemed to know a remarkable number of people. He hailed Lord Pendlebury's trainer, Sam Stodder, and introduced him to Agatha.

"Lord Pendlebury said we could take a look around the stables, Mr. Stodder," said James. "Sad thing about that vet's death, wasn't it?"

"Sad, for sure. Happened right over there. He were doing that operation to stop Sparky roaring."

"And no one else was about at the time?"

"No. Lord Pendlebury had a new filly out in the paddock and took us all off to have a look. We was all talking and smoking and admiring the filly, 'cos it's not often the old man lets us slack. Devil for work, he is. Then Bob

Arthur, him what does for my lord, he strolls off and says he's going for to see how the vet is getting on and next thing he comes out, yelling and crying that Bladen is dead. 'Looks like someone's done fer him,' he says, so his lordship says for to call the police."

"And it was in here?" asked Agatha, approaching the right wing of the stable block.

Both men followed her in. There was nothing to be seen. The row of loose boxes stretched off into the gloom, the horses' heads poking out. "Oldest bit of the stables," said Sam. "In the rest of it, the loose boxes open right out onto the courtyard, not inside like here."

Agatha stared at the floor, but there was nothing to be seen, not even a sliver of glass.

"Why did Mr. Arthur say that it looked like someone had done for him?" she asked.

"Reckon he waren't none too popular, like. Wizard with horses, mind. Lord Pendlebury thought him a cheeky sort and wanted Mr. Rice, Bladen's partner from Mircester, but Mr. Rice don't like Lord Pendlebury and that's a fact, and so he do make excuses not to come."

"I don't suppose anyone likes Lord Pendlebury, horrible old man that he is," said Agatha.

"You're entitled to your opinion, I'm sure," said Sam, "but don't expect none of us here to say a word against the old man. Course you haven't been as long in these parts as Mr. Lacey here, or you'd know that criticism of his lordship is not welcome; no, that it's not."

"I've been here a considerable time longer than Mr. Lacey," said Agatha huffily.

"Well, there's folks that fit in and folks that don't,"

52

said Sam. "Afternoon." He touched his cap and strolled off."

"What a feudal peasant," said Agatha.

"Sam's a good man, and we're the peasants in this case."

"What?"

"Vulgarly poking our noses in where they don't belong. What on earth are we doing here, Mrs. Raisin?"

"Agatha."

"Agatha. The man died because of an unfortunate accident."

"I'm not so sure," said Agatha, more out of a desire to be contrary than because she believed it.

They strolled round to the front of the house where Agatha's car was parked. It looked new and shiny after all the expensive repairs. Lord Pendlebury came towards them.

His tall, thin, heron-like figure loped up to them. "What do you think you're doing?" he said angrily. "There's an open day once a year, on June first; otherwise keep off private property."

"It's us," said James Lacey patiently. "You gave us permission to go and look at your stables."

His pale watery eyes blinked at them and then focused on Agatha. "Oh, the hunt saboteur," he said. "The people one has to put up with these days."

He headed off towards the stables, leaving James amused and Agatha fuming.

"You're hardly the flavour of the month," said James.

"The man's senile," snapped Agatha. She had often lingered longingly while on the tour of some stately home outside the roped-off private part hoping a member of the

53

family would recognize her as one of their own kind and ask her to tea. That fantasy seemed totally ridiculous now.

She drove James back to the village, feeling hurt and gauche and inadequate. He glanced at her sideways and something prompted him to say, "I haven't been to the Red Lion for ages. Fancy a drink there this evening?"

Agatha's spirits rocketed like the pheasant which rose up before the wheels of her car and over the hedge beside the road. But she kept her voice light and casual. "That would be nice. What time?"

"Oh, about eight. I have to go to Moreton for something, so I'll see you there."

He was already regretting his invitation, and yet there was no sign of any return of that predatory look he had noticed before in Agatha's eyes.

Agatha, guessing that he would not bother to change, restrained herself from changing her own clothes. She fed the cats and played with them and tried not to watch the clock. Excitement built up in her as eight o'clock approached. Although she had, with the help of Mrs. Bloxby, been training herself to cook, she put a frozen lasagne in the microwave for her dinner so as not to waste more time on elaborate preparations. It tasted foul. How could she ever have eaten such stuff?

As she walked to the Red Lion, a full moon was shining down, washing everything with silver, outlining the skeletal arms of trees against the starry sky. White and pink verbena flowers scented the air, reminding Agatha unromantically of expensive bath soap. At exactly three minutes past eight, she pushed open the door of the Red Lion.

James Lacey was there in the low-raftered pub, standing at the bar, talking to the landlord. "What'll you have?" he asked by way of greeting.

"Gin and tonic," said Agatha, settling herself happily on a bar stool.

"I was wondering," he began as he paid for her drink. But Agatha was never to know what he was wondering, for the pub door opened and the yapping of a Jack Russell and a heavy smell of French perfume heralded the arrival of Mrs. Huntingdon, Carsely's newest incomer.

To Agatha's dismay, James said, "Evening, Freda. What'll you have? Do you know Agatha Raisin? Agatha, this is Freda Huntingdon."

So it was Freda, was it? thought Agatha gloomily. The widow was wearing a cherry-red sleeveless jacket over a black cashmere sweater and short black wool skirt. Her legs in fine black stockings were very good.

"Let's sit at that table over there," said James after he had bought Freda a whisky and water.

"Perhaps Freda is meeting someone," suggested Agatha hopefully.

"No," she said in a husky voice, "all on my lonesome. Thought I might find you here, James. How's the writing going?"

James! Freda! Rats! Agatha plumped herself down at the table by the log fire and tried not to let her bitter disappointment show on her face.

"The writing's not going at all well," said James. "I look for every excuse not to get started. This morning I defrosted the fridge, and this afternoon Mrs. Raisin—"

"Agatha, please."

"Sorry, Agatha and I went to see Lord Pendlebury."

"Isn't he an old duck?" murmured Freda. "Quite one of the old school."

"How do you know him?" asked Agatha.

"I talked to him outside the church last Sunday," said Freda. "I found him quite charming."

"I don't think Agatha found him at all charming," said James. "He mistook her for a hunt saboteur."

Freda Cunningham laughed merrily. Her dog peed against the leg of the table and she said "Tut-tut" and picked up the revolting yapping creature and cuddled it on her lap.

"Have you seen the latest *Star Trek* movie, James?" asked Freda. She lit a cigarette and blew a cloud of smoke in Agatha's direction.

"I haven't seen any *Star Trek* movie, let alone the latest," replied James.

"But you should! They're tremendous fun. The new one's on at Mircester. Tell you what, come with me tomorrow."

At that moment, Agatha saw Jack Page, the farmer, come in. She felt she could not bear any more of Freda and James. She rose and picked up her unfinished drink. "Just going to have a drink with Jack."

Jack Page hailed her. "Nights are drawing out, Agatha," he said. "Be spring before you know it. Sorry to hear about that crash you had."

He was a cheerful man with an easy manner. Agatha told him at length about her crash. He bought her another drink. Agatha sat down on a bar stool next to him and tried to forget about the pair in the corner.

"Bad thing about that vet," said Jack.

"You went to him, didn't you?" said Agatha. "I saw

you there the first time I took my cat along. What did you make of him?"

"The surgery was handy to nip down and get antibiotics and things," said Jack. "Never thought about him much one way or t'other. Then I heard what he done to poor Mrs. Josephs's cat, so I stopped going. That was right cruel."

"You don't think someone bumped him off, do you?"

"Ah, you're looking for another murder to solve," he teased. "Sad accident, it were. Funeral's next Monday in Mircester, at St. Peter's.

"I might go," said Agatha.

"Was you friendly with him then?"

"Had dinner with him one night," replied Agatha, "but not really friendly."

He drained his tankard and set the empty glass down on the bar. "I'd best be getting back. I told the wife I'd only stop for the one. Why not come back and say hullo?"

Agatha had a sudden longing to turn round. But Mrs. Huntingdon let out a trill of laughter and her dog gave a volley of barks.

"I'd like that," said Agatha, picking up her handbag.

She turned at last and gave a casual wave to James before leaving with the farmer.

James Lacey watched her go with some surprise. And he had thought she was pursuing him!

FOUR

†

SNOW was falling as Agatha entered the church of St. Peter in Mircester the following Monday. She was already wishing she had not come. A doggedness to find out something about the vet's death had prompted this visit. So long as she was worrying about the vet's death, Agatha did not need to worry about James Lacey.

The church was very old, with fine stained-glass windows and a dreadful seventeenth-century altar of some dark wood. Agatha took a pew at the back, unhitched the hassock from its hook, knelt in pretended prayer and then studied the congregation. But all she saw was backs of heads. There seemed to be quite a number of women present. One turned her head. Mrs. Huntingdon! And then Agatha recognized the solid bulk of Mrs. Mason, the chairwoman of the Carsely Ladies Society, two pews in front of her. She changed her seat and went to sit next to her.

Mrs. Mason was clutching a damp handkerchief in her

hand. "So sad," she whispered to Agatha. "Such a fine young man."

"Hardly young," said Agatha and received a look of reproach.

The coffin was carried in and placed in the aisle in front of the altar. "That's Mr. Rice, Mr. Bladen's partner," said Mrs. Mason. "The one on the left at the front." Among the men who had carried in the coffin, Agatha saw a burly middle-aged man with curly ginger hair.

"Who is here from the village, apart from us and that Mrs. Cunningham?" asked Agatha.

"Over there to the right, Mrs. Parr and Miss Webster."

Agatha leaned forward. Both women were crying. Mrs. Parr was small and quite pretty and Miss Webster of an indeterminate age, possibly late thirties. She recognized Miss Webster as the woman who ran the dried flower shop.

"I'm surprised you are all so upset," whispered Agatha, "after what he did to Mrs. Josephs's cat."

"What he did was *right*," muttered Mrs. Mason fiercely. "That cat was too old for this world."

"I hope no one thinks that about me," said Agatha.

"Shhh!" said a man in front waspishly.

The service began.

Mr. Peter Rice paid a tribute to his dead partner, the vicar quoted St. Francis of Assisi, hymns were sung, then the coffin was raised up again and the congregation filed out after it to the graveyard.

It was strange, thought Agatha, but one never thought of people being buried in old church graveyards anymore. A short service in a crematorium was more what was expected. She had always wondered about those churchyard graveside scenes in television dramas and had assumed that the television company had paid a nice sum to the church to dig up an appropriate hole for the show. One always assumed that the old churchyards of England had been full to bursting point since the end of the nineteenth century.

Snow fluttered down among the leaning gravestones and a magpie swung on the branch of a cedar and cocked a curious eye at the proceedings.

"That's his ex-wife," said Mrs. Mason. A thin, grey-haired woman with a weak face was looking bleakly straight in front of her. She was wearing a fox coat over a red suit. No mourning weeds for her.

But the graveside service was so moving and so dignified that Agatha thought there was a lot to be said for staking your claim to your six-by-four in a country churchyard. But when the service was over, she muttered a goodbye to Mrs. Mason and set out in pursuit of the vet's ex-wife, catching up with her at the lych gate.

"My name is Agatha Raisin," she said. "I gather you are poor Mr. Bladen's wife."

"I was," said Mrs. Bladen a trifle impatiently. "It is really very cold, Mrs. Raisin, and I am anxious to get home."

"My car is just outside. Can I drop you somewhere?"

"No, I have my own car."

"I wonder if we could have a talk?" said Agatha eagerly.

A look of dislike came into Mrs. Bladen's eyes. "My life seems to have been plagued by women wanting to talk to me after my husband had dumped them. It is just as well he is dead."

She stalked off.

I seem to be getting snubbed all round, thought Agatha. But there's one thing for sure: our vet was a philanderer. If only I could prove it wasn't an accident, that it was murder, then they'd all sit up and take notice!

Carsely had frequent power cuts, some lasting days, some only a few seconds.

James Lacey pressed Agatha's doorbell the following day. He did not know there was one of the brief power cuts because one could not usually hear the bell ringing from outside.

He glanced down at the front lawn. There was a lot of moss on it. He wondered if Agatha knew how to treat it. He bent down for a closer look. Agatha, who thought she had heard someone outside, put her eye to the spyhole, but not seeing anyone, retreated to the kitchen. James Lacey straightened up and pressed the bell again. By this time Agatha had found crumbs on the carpet and had plugged in the vacuum cleaner in the kitchen at the back.

James retreated, feeling baffled. He remembered all the times he had pretended to be out when Agatha had called.

He went into his own cottage, made himself a cup of coffee and sat down at his desk. He switched on his new word processor, slotted in the programme disc and then stared bleakly at the screen, before putting in another disc and flicking his written words up onto the green screen. There it was. "Chapter Two." If only he had written just one sentence. Why had he decided to write military history anyway? Just because he was a retired soldier did not necessarily mean he was confined to military subjects. Besides, why had he chosen the Peninsular Wars? Was there anything to add more than what had been already written? Oh, dear, how long the day seemed. It had been fun going to see Pendlebury. Of course it had been an accident. And yet there was that bump on the back of the head.

It might be more fun to write mystery stories. Say, for example, the vet had been murdered, how would one go about finding out what had really happened? Well, the first step would be to find out *why* he was murdered, for the why would surely lead to the *who*.

If Agatha had answered her door to him and not looked as if she were avoiding him, he might have dropped the subject. Had he really wanted to write military history, he still might have dropped it. He gave an exclamation of disgust, switched off the machine and went out again. There would be no harm in trying Agatha's door again. He had obviously been mistaken when he had thought she was pursuing him. And he had invited *her* for a drink, not Freda Huntingdon. It was not his fault that Agatha had suddenly decided to leave with that farmer.

It was a fine spring day, light and airy, smelling of growing things. This time, Agatha's front door was open. He went in, calling, "Agatha," and nearly fell over her. She was sitting-cross legged on the floor of the hall, playing with her cats.

"Am I seeing things, or have you two of them?" he asked.

"The new one's a stray I picked up in London," said Agatha, scrabbling to her feet. "Like a coffee?"

"Not coffee. I seem to have been drinking it all morning. Tea would be nice."

"Tea it is." Agatha led the way into the kitchen.

"About last night," he said, hovering in the kitchen doorway, "we didn't have much of a chance to talk."

"Well, that's pubs for you," said Agatha with seeming indifference. "You never end up talking to the person you go in with. Milk or lemon?"

"Lemon, please. I've been thinking, this business about the vet. Did you go to the funeral?"

"Yes. Lot of women there. Seems to have been popular with quite a lot of women, so he can't have gone around putting down *their* cats unasked."

"Who was there from this village?"

"Apart from me, his four remaining fans: your friend, Freda Huntingdon; Mrs. Mason; Mrs. Harriet Parr; and Miss Josephine Webster. Oh, and his ex-wife. Hey, that's odd."

"What is?"

"When I was supposed to be having dinner in Evesham that night I crashed and I phoned Paul's house and this woman answered the phone saying she was his wife . . ." Agatha broke off.

"Well?"

"Well, Paul Bladen told me afterwards that the woman who answered the phone was his sister, being silly or something. But no one else has mentioned his sister. I forgot to ask for her at the funeral."

"We could drive into Mircester and find out," he volunteered.

Agatha turned away quickly and fiddled with the kettle to hide the sudden look of rapture in her eyes. "Do you think it's murder then?" she asked.

He sighed. "No, I don't. But it might be fun to go through the motions. I mean, ask people, just as if it were."

"I'll get my coat." Agatha nipped smartly upstairs, gazing in the glass at her outfit of sweater and trousers. But there was no time to change, for if she did not hurry up, he might decide to call the whole thing off.

"Just going to get some money," he called up the stairs.

Agatha cursed under her breath. What if he were waylaid in the short distance between her house and his? She went down the stairs and out of the door.

Freda Huntingdon was talking to him, laughing and holding that wretched yapping dog under her arm. Agatha clenched her hands into fists as they both disappeared into James's cottage. She stood there in her own front garden, irresolute. What if he forgot about her? But he emerged with Freda after only a few moments. Freda was tucking a paperback into her pocket.

She waved goodbye to him and he walked towards Agatha. "Shall we take my car?" he asked. "No need to take two."

"Mine will be fine," said Agatha. He climbed into the passenger seat. As Agatha drove past Freda, she turned and stared at them in surprise. Agatha gave a cheerful fanfare on the horn and drove fast round the corner out of the lane.

"What did the merry widow want?" she asked.

"Freda? She had lent me a paperback and had come to collect it."

Agatha would have chatted on merrily all the way to Mircester and probably would have driven James away again, but just at that moment she sensed there was a pimple growing on the end of her nose. She squinted down and the car veered wildly to the side of the road before she corrected the steering.

"Are you all right?" asked James. "Do you want me to drive?"

"I'm fine." But Agatha sank into a worried silence. She

could feel that pimple growing and growing, an itchy soreness on the end of her nose. Why should such a thing happen to her on this day of all days? This was what came of eating "healthy" food, as recommended by Mrs. Bloxby. Years of fast food had not produced one blemish. The only solution, Agatha decided, was when they reached Mircester, she would say she needed to buy something from the chemist's—no gentleman would ask what—and then say she was dying for a drink.

She parked in the last space in the town's main square. A woman who had been in the act of carefully reversing into it before Agatha beat her to it by driving straight in nose first, stared in hurt anger. When they got out of the car, Agatha, keeping her face averted, said, "Got to go to the chemist's over there. Meet you in that pub, the George, in a few moments." And then, like jesting Pilate, did not stay for an answer, but scuttled across the square.

In the chemist's, she bought a stick of Blemish Remover, astringent lotion, and, for good measure, a new lipstick, Hot Pink.

James looked up and waved as Agatha came into the pub, but she scuttled past him to the Ladies', her face still averted.

Agatha cleaned her face, applied the astringent lotion and then wiped it off with a tissue. She peered at her nose. There was a bright little red spot at the end of it. She carefully applied the stick of Blemish Remover, which resulted in a beige blotch on the end of her nose. She covered it with powder. The light in the Ladies' was not working, so she could only guess at the effect. She stared upwards. There was a light socket up on the ceiling, but she noticed the light bulb was missing and what light there was in the room

66

filtered through the grimy panes of a window high up over the hand basin. Then she remembered she had bought a packet of 100-watt light bulbs the day before and had left them in her car. She scuttled out again. Again James waved and again she ran past him, her face averted, and out the door. He drank his beer thoughtfully. He had once thought Agatha Raisin deranged. Perhaps he had been right. There she came again, running sideways, and back into the Ladies'.

Agatha looked up at the ceiling. In order to reach the light socket, she would need to stand on the hand basin. She hitched up her skirt and climbed into the large Victorian hand basin and gingerly stood up. She reached up to the light socket.

With a great rending sound, the hand basin came away from the wall. Agatha swayed wildly and then grabbed hold of a dusty windowsill as the hand basin slowly continued to detach itself and fell with an almighty crash on the floor, taking the brass taps with it. A ferocious jet of cold water from a now broken and exposed pipe shot straight up Agatha's skirt.

With a whimper she let go of the windowsill, jumped to the flooding floor and skirting the debris and shot back into the pub, after firmly closing the door behind her.

"Let's go," she said to James. He stared at her in surprise. "I've just bought you a gin and tonic."

"Oh, thanks," said Agatha desperately. "Cheers!" She threw the drink down her throat in one gulp. "Come on!" Out of the corner of her eye, she could see a flood of water appearing from under the door of the Ladies'.

James followed her out. He noticed to his dismay that the back of her skirt had a dark stain on it and he wondered whether to tell her. She was not *that* old, but perhaps she had bladder trouble.

"Now, *this* pub looks much nicer," said Agatha, pushing open the door of the Potters Arms and diving in. Once more, she went to the Ladies'. To her relief it was a modern place with a hot-air hand drier. She took off her skirt and held it under the drier until the water stain began to fade. Then she lay down on the floor and held her wet feet up under it. Time passed. When she emerged, a worried James was on his second pint of beer. "I was just about to send someone to look for you," he said. "Are you all right?"

"Yes," said Agatha, radiant again, for she had discovered that the new make-up had done the job effectively and she was once more warm and dry.

"I bought you another gin," he said, indicating the glass on the table.

Agatha smiled at him. "Here's to detection," she said, raising her glass. And then she slowly lowered it, a look of ludicrous dismay on her face. For into the pub had just marched Bill Wong and a tall policewoman. "Dropped my handbag," said Agatha and dived under the table.

It was to no avail. "Come out, Agatha," said Bill.

Agatha miserably crawled out from under the table, her face red with shame.

"Now, Agatha," said Bill, "what have you been up to? P.W.C. Wood here called me into the George. A woman answering your description went in and vandalized the ladies' room, tearing a hand basin out of the wall and flooding the place. People in the square saw you running in here. What have you to say for yourself?"

"I had a spot on my nose," mumbled Agatha.

"Speak up. I can't hear you."

"I HAD A SPOT ON MY NOSE," roared Agatha. Everyone looked at her and James Lacey desperately wished himself elsewhere.

"And how did that make you tear the hand basin out of the wall?" asked Bill.

"I bought make-up at the chemist's." Agatha's voice was now reduced to a flat even tone. "I wanted to cover up the spot, but the light in the Ladies' wasn't working and I thought it probably needed a new bulb. I remembered I had a packet of light bulbs in the car and went to get one. But the only way I could get to the light was by standing on the basin. It came away from the wall. I was so shocked I decided to say nothing about it."

"I am afraid you are going to have to come with me," said Bill severely.

The fact that James Lacey did not offer to accompany her, that he muttered something awkwardly about staying put and reading the newspapers, plunged him low in Agatha's estimation despite her distress. So much for the knight errant of her dreams. He was going to sit safely while she dealt with a no doubt enraged landlord.

James went out a few moments after they had left. He bought two newspapers and then returned to the pub. But he could not concentrate on the stories. Damn Agatha. What a woman. What a stupid thing to do! And then the ridiculous side of it all struck him and he began to laugh and, once started, couldn't seem to stop, although people edged away from his table nervously. He finally mopped his eyes and, tucking the unread papers under his arm, strode over to the George.

Agatha was holding out a cheque which the landlord of the George was refusing. "Ho, no, you don't get off that

69

easily," he said. He was an unpleasant-looking man with a face like a slab of Cheddar cheese, the skin yellow and slightly sweating with rage. "You charge this woman, officer," he said to Bill, "and I'll see her in court. You charge her with wilful vandalism."

James twitched the cheque out of Agatha's fingers and blinked slightly at the large sum. "You can't afford this," he said to Agatha. "A lady like yourself, existing on a widow's pension, cannot afford a sum like this. Declare yourself bankrupt and then, even if he takes you to court, he won't get a penny. I know a good solicitor just around the corner."

"Good idea," said Bill. "You need a solicitor anyway. He'll want to know why there was no light bulb in the Ladies' in the first place, why the basin fell away from the wall so easily. The wiring in this pub had better be checked, too."

"I'll take the cheque," growled the landlord desperately.

"You'll take another cheque," said James firmly. "Agatha, get your cheque-book and write out one for half this sum."

The Cheddar cheese looked ready to explode again, but a steely look from James silenced him.

Agatha wrote out the new cheque while James tore up the old one.

When they were all outside in the square, Bill said, "If that had been a nice, respectable landlord, I might have charged you, Agatha. Anyway, thanks to Mr. Lacey, it's all sorted out. What about dinner tonight?"

Agatha hesitated. She had originally thought her day with James might end in an intimate dinner. On the other hand, better to continue to play it cool. "Yes, that would be nice. Where do you live? I know your phone number but not your address."

"It's number 24, The Beeches. You go out of town on the Fosse and take the first left along Camden Way until you come to a set of traffic lights, turn right, then take the first left, and that's The Beeches. It's a cul-de-sac." Agatha scribbled the information down on the back of a gas bill. "What time?"

"Six o'clock. We eat early."

"We?"

"My parents. You forget, I live at home. You come, too, Mr. Lacey."

Please, please, *please,* God, prayed Agatha.

James looked surprised but then said, "I'd like that. I'd more or less decided to have the day off. Is it all right if I come dressed like this?"

Bill looked amused. "We're not formal," he said. "See you then."

He moved off, with the tall and still silent policewoman walking beside him.

"I think we need something to eat now," said James. "What about a beer and a sandwich, and then we'll decide who we ask about the sister. We should have asked Bill Wong. Still, we can always do that this evening."

He did not mention the ruined toilet and Agatha was grateful for that. But she felt obliged to say gruffly, "I'm hardly penniless."

"I know," he said amiably, "but the minute that landlord thought you were broke, then he was glad to take any money."

Once they had eaten, he drew out a notebook and pen

71

and said, "Why don't we pretend it's murder and start by writing down all the names of the people we should speak to."

"I think the ex-wife would be a good idea," said Agatha, "although she wasn't very friendly. I know, we can call at the vet's here, his partner, Peter Rice. He'll know whether Bladen had a sister, and that would be a start."

Mr. Peter Rice was a pugnacious man with a large bulbous nose, small eyes and a small mouth. The ugly nose, which dominated his face, was disconcerting, rather like a face pressed too close to a camera lens. His thatch of thick red curly hair looked as if someone had dropped a small wig casually on the top of his rather pointed head. His neck was thick and strong, as were his shoulders. In fact, his body seemed too strong and broad for his small head, as if he had thrust his head through a Strong Man cardboard cutout on a fairground.

He was not pleased to learn that they had queued up in his surgery, not to consult him about some animal, but to ask him questions about his dead partner.

"Sister?" he said in answer to their questions. "No, he didn't have a sister. Got a brother somewhere in London. Fell out a time ago. Brother didn't bother turning up for the funeral." His hands covered in thick red hair like fur moved restlessly over a shelf of small bottles, as if looking for a label that said "Vanish." "Now if that's all . . ."

"Was he a wealthy man?" asked James.

"No."

"Oh. How do you know?"

"I know because he left everything to me."

"How much was that?" asked Agatha eagerly.

72

"Not enough," he said. "Get out of here and leave me to deal with my customers."

"So he inherits and not the brother. Now there's a motive," crowed Agatha when they were outside. "Who would know how much money was involved?"

"The lawyer. But I doubt if he would tell us. Let's try the local newspaper editor," said James. "They pick up all sorts of gossip."

The offices of the *Mircester Journal* came as a disappointment to Agatha, even though the newspaper consisted of little more than three pages. She had naïvely expected something like the newspaper offices she had occasionally seen on news programmes, great enormous rooms with lines of computers and busy reporters. Time and printing changes had passed the *Mircester Journal* by. The offices consisted of several dark rooms at the top of a rickety staircase. A pale young woman with straight lank hair was pounding an old-fashioned typewriter and a young man with his hands in his pockets was standing by a window, whistling tunelessly and looking down into the street.

"May we see the editor?" asked James.

The pale girl stopped typing. "If it's births, deaths, or marriages, I do that," she said.

"None of those."

"Complaints? Wrong name under the photo?"

"No complaint."

"That makes a change." She got to her feet. She was wearing a long patchwork skirt and baseball boots and a T-shirt which said "Naff Off." "Names?"

"Mrs. Raisin and Mr. Lacey."

73

"Right."

She pushed open a scarred door and vanished inside. There was a murmur of voices and then she popped out again. "You're to go in. Mr. Heyford will see you now."

Mr. Heyford rose to meet them. After the vision in the T-shirt and baseball boots he came as a conservative surprise, being a small, neat man with a smooth olive face, black eyes and thin strips of oiled black hair combed straight back from his forehead. He was dressed in a dark suit, collar and tie.

"Sit down," he said. "What can I do for you? I recognize your name, Mrs. Raisin. That was quite a lot of money you raised for charity last year." Agatha preened.

"We both knew the vet, Paul Bladen," said James. "We're having a sort of a bet. Mrs. Raisin here said he was worth a lot of money, but I got the impression he didn't have that much. Do you know how much he left?"

"I can't tell you exactly how much because I can't quite remember," said Mr. Heyford. "About eighty-five thousand, I think. Would have been a fortune once, but that sort of money won't even buy you a decent house now. He left a house, of course, but he had taken a double mortgage out on that, and with house prices being what they are in the slump, Mr. Rice, who inherited, will barely get enough to cover the mortgages. I never thought the day would come in this country when we would consider eighty-five thousand not very much money, so it looks as if you've won the bet, Mr. Lacey."

"So he couldn't have been killed for his money," said Agatha mournfully when they had said goodbye to the editor. "And yet . . ."

"And yet what?"

74

"If he did have eighty-five thousand pounds, why the two mortgages? I mean, the interest must have been crippling. Why not pay off some of the money owing?"

"The trouble," said James, "is that we are making ourselves believe an accident to be murder."

Agatha thought quickly. If he gave up the idea of investigating anything at all, then she would have little excuse to spend any time in his company. "We could try the wife," she suggested. "I mean, as we're here and we've still got time to kill before we go to Bill's."

"Oh, very well. Where do we find her?"

"We'll try the phone book and hope she is still using her married name," said Agatha.

They found a name, G. Bladen, listed. The address was given as Rose Cottage, Little Blomham. "Where's Little Blomham?" asked Agatha.

"I saw a sign to it once. It's off the Stroud Road."

A pale mist was shrouding the landscape, turning the countryside into a Chinese painting, as they drove down into Little Blomham. It was more of a hamlet than a village, a few ancient houses of golden Cotswold stone hunched beside a stream.

No one moved about, no smoke rose from the chimneys, no dog barked.

Agatha switched off the engine and both listened as the eerie silence settled about them.

James suddenly quoted:

"Ay, they heard his foot upon the stirrup,
And the sound of iron on stone,
And how the silence surged softly backward,
When the plunging hoofs were gone."

75

Agatha looked at him crossly. She did not like people who suddenly quoted things at you, leaving you feeling unread and inadequate. In fact, she thought they only did it to show off.

She got out of the car and slammed the door shut with unnecessary force.

James got out of the passenger seat and wandered to a stone wall and looked down at the slowly moving stream. He seemed to have gone into some sort of dream, to have forgotten Agatha's presence. "So very quiet," he said, half to himself. "So very English, the England they fought for in the First World War. So little of it left."

"Would you like to stand here and meditate while I find out which one of these picturesque hovels is Rose Cottage?" asked Agatha.

He gave her a sudden smile. "No, I'll come with you." They walked together down the road by the stream. "Let me see, this one has no name and the next one is called End Cottage, although it's not at the end. Perhaps one of the ones further on."

They nearly missed Rose Cottage. It was set well back from the road at the end of a thin narrow, tangled unkempt garden. It was small and thatched, with the walls covered in thick creeper. "Looks more like an animal's burrow than a house," commented James. "Well, here we go. We can't say we think he was murdered. We'll offer our sympathy and see where that gets us."

He knocked on the door. And waited. They stood wrapped in the silence of the dream countryside. Then, as if a spell had been broken, a bird suddenly flew up from a bush near the door, a dog barked somewhere, high and shrill in the road outside, and Mrs. Bladen opened the door.

Why, I believe she's older than I, thought Agatha, looking again at that grey hair and at the tell-tale lines on the thin neck.

Mrs. Bladen looked past James to Agatha and her face settled in lines of dislike. "Oh, it's you again."

"Mr. Lacey wished to offer you his sympathy," said Agatha quickly.

"Why?" she demanded harshly. "Why should someone come all this way to offer sympathy for the death of a man I've been divorced from?"

"We're very neighbourly people in Carsely," said James, "and wondered if we could do anything to help."

"You can help by going away."

James looked helplessly at Agatha. Agatha decided to take the bull by the horns. "Are you sure your husband died a natural death?" she asked.

Mrs. Bladen looked amused. "Meaning someone killed him? It's more than likely. He was a thoroughly nasty man and I'm glad he's dead. I hope that satisfies you."

She slammed the door in their faces.

"That's that," said James, as they walked down the weedy path.

"We got something," said Agatha eagerly. "She didn't laugh in our faces when I suggested murder to her. Now did she?"

"You know what I think?" he said, holding the gate open for her. "I think we're two retired people with not enough to do with our time."

"Just because you can't get started writing," said Agatha shrewdly, "don't take it out on me."

"This is a lovely little place," he said to change the subject. "So quiet and peaceful. I wonder if there's anything for sale here."

"Oh, you wouldn't want to live here," said Agatha, alarmed. "I mean, Carsely's bad enough, but there's *nothing* here, not even a shop or a pub."

"What's up with that, in this age of the motor car? Oh, look. That sign there. The Manor House. I didn't notice it before. Let's go and have a look."

Agatha followed him silently up a winding drive. She did not want to look at any manor house because manor houses belonged to James Lacey's world and not to hers. The drive, edged with rhododendron bushes, opened up and there stood the manor house. The mist had thinned and pale sunlight washed the golden walls. It was low and rambling and settled and charming, exuding centuries of peace. Even Agatha sensed that wars and conflicts, plague and pestilence had passed this old building by.

A small square woman in a twin set and tweed skirt came out with a black retriever at her heels. "Can I help you?" she called.

"Just admiring your beautiful home," said James, approaching her.

"Yes, it is beautiful," she said. "Come inside and have some tea. I don't often get visitors until the summer, when all my relatives decide they would like a free holiday."

James introduced them. The woman said she was Bunty Vere-Dedsworth. She led the way into a dark hall and then through into a large old kitchen gleaming with copper pans and white-and-blue china on an old dresser which ran the length of one wall.

"Lacey," she said, as she plugged in an electric kettle.
"I used to know some Laceys down in Sussex."

"That's where my family comes from," said James.

"Really!" She had cornflower-blue eyes in a reddish face. "Old Harry Lacey?"

"My father."

"Gosh, small world. Do you ever see the . . ."

Agatha, excluded from that intimidating conversation of the upper classes which consisted of names and exclamations of recognition thrown back and forth, moodily sipped her tea and felt James moving out of her sphere. She could picture him living in a place like this with an elegant wife, not with some retired public-relations woman such as herself who would only be able to swap names with someone from the rather nasty Birmingham slum in which she had grown up.

"What brings you here?" said Bunty at last.

James said, "Our vet in Carsely died and we went to offer Mrs. Bladen our sympathies, but she doesn't seem in need of any."

"No, she wouldn't," said Bunty. "She had a very unhappy marriage."

"Other women?" suggested Agatha.

"I think it was more a question of money, or the lack of it. Greta Bladen was a wealthy woman when she married Paul, and he seemed to spend a great deal of her money. When she left him, that dingy little cottage was all she could afford. She really hated him. I heard how Bladen died. Now if he had been found dead because someone had biffed him with the frying-pan, that someone being Greta, I wouldn't have been at all surprised. But you'd really need to know

79

about veterinary things to shove a syringe full of deadly stuff in him. I mean, think of it. How many of the population would know that stuff was deadly? Maybe his partner wanted the business for himself." And Bunty laughed.

James looked at his watch. "We really must go."

"Must you?" Bunty smiled at Agatha. "Then do come back and see me. I'd like that."

Agatha smiled back, feeling all her social inadequacies fade away, feeling welcome.

"She had a point," said Agatha as she drove out of the village. "I mean about Rice. Surely it would need to be someone with a knowledge of veterinary medicine."

"Not necessarily," he remarked. "That story about the vet who died last year when the horse nudged his breast pocket with the syringe in it and caused his death was in all the local papers. I read it. Anyone could have read it and got the idea."

"But it would need to be someone who knew where he was going and what he was doing on that day."

"Any of his lady friends might know. 'What are you doing tomorrow, Paul?' 'Oh, I'm cutting the vocal cords of one of Pendlebury's horses.' That sort of thing."

"Yes, but say he had said that to me. I wouldn't immediately think of Immobilon."

"No, but a vet might talk about it, saying how deadly it was and talking about the accident of the previous year. I've got a feeling a woman did it."

Agatha was about to exclaim, "So you *do* think it was murder," but decided to remain silent in the hope of more days of investigation together.

* * *

Bill's home came as a surprise to Agatha. She had naïvely expected something, well, more oriental and exotic. The Beeches was one of those closes designed by builders, each house different, with trim suburban lawns, oozing respectability and dullness. Agatha knew that Bill's father was Hong Kong Chinese and his mother from Gloucestershire, but she had not expected him to live somewhere so ordinary. Bill's house was called Clarendon, the name being poker-worked on a wooden sign hung on a post at the gate. They went up a trim path between regimented flower-beds and rang the bell, which played a chorus of "Rule, Britannia."

Bill himself answered the door. "Come in. Come in," he cried. "I'll just put you in the lounge and go and get the drinks. Ma's in the kitchen getting dinner ready."

Agatha and James sat in the lounge, not looking at each other. There was a three-piece suite, shell-backed, in a nasty sort of grey wool material. There were Venetian blinds drawn down over the "picture" windows and ruched curtains. The fitted carpet was in a noisy geometric design of red and black. The wallpaper was white and gold Regency stripe. There were little occasional pie-crust tables on spindly legs. A display cabinet full of Spanish dolls and little bits of china stood against one wall. A gas fire with fake coals and logs burned cheerfully but threw out very little heat.

Agatha longed for a cigarette but could not see an ashtray.

Bill came in with a small tray on which were three tiny glasses of sweet sherry.

"You're honoured," said Bill. "We don't use this room much. Keep it for best."

81

"Very nice," said Agatha, feeling strange and awkward at seeing her Bill, chubby and oriental as usual, in these cold English suburban surroundings.

"May I use your toilet?" she asked.

"Top of the stairs. But don't go standing on the hand basin."

Agatha climbed up thickly carpeted stairs and pushed open the door of a bathroom which contained a suite in Nile green. The toilet had a chenille cover. A flowery notice on the back of the bathroom door stated, "When you have had a tinkle, please wipe the seat."

She tugged at the toilet roll to get a piece of tissue to blot her lipstick and started in alarm as the toilet-roll holder chimed out "The Bluebells of Scotland."

"Dinner's ready," said Bill when she arrived downstairs again.

He led them across the hall and into another small room, the dining-room, where at the head of the table sat his father, a small morose Chinese gentleman with a droopy moustache, a grey baggy cardigan and large checked carpet slippers.

Bill performed the introductions. Mr. Wong grunted by way of reply, picked up his knife and fork and stared at the polished surface of the laminated top of the table. Agatha looked down at a place-mat depicting Tewkesbury Abbey and wished she had not come.

A hatch from the kitchen shot up and a Gloucester accent said shrilly, "Bill! Soup!"

Bill collected plates of soup and passed them round. "Have you got that bottle of Liebfraumilch, Ma?" he called.

"In 'er fridge."

"I'll get it."

Mrs. Wong appeared. She was a massive woman with a discontented, suspicious face and appeared to resent having guests. Bill poured wine.

The soup was canned oxtail. Little triangles of bread were passed around. Even James Lacey seemed stricken into silence.

"Roast beef next," said Bill. "Nobody does roast beef quite like Ma."

"That's for sure," said Mr. Wong suddenly, making Agatha jump.

The roast beef was incredibly tough and the table knives were blunt. It took all their concentration to hack pieces off. The cauliflower was covered in a coat of thick white sauce, the carrots were overcooked and oversalted, the Yorkshire pudding was like salted rubber and the peas were those nasty processed kind out of a can which manage to turn everything on the plate green.

"Days are drawing out," said Mrs. Wong.

"That's for sure," said Mr. Wong.

"Soon be summer," pursued Mrs. Wong, glaring fiercely at Agatha, as if blaming her for the seasons.

"I hope we get another nice summer," said James.

Mrs. Wong rounded on him. "You call last summer nice? Did you hear that, Father? He called last summer nice?"

"Some people," muttered Mr. Wong, taking more cauliflower.

"So hot, it nearly brought on one of my turns," said Mrs. Wong. "Didn't it nearly, Father?"

"That's for sure."

Silence.

"I'll get the pudding," said Bill.

"Sit down," said his mother. "These are your guests. I told you I wanted to watch that quiz on the telly, but you would have them."

Soon bowls of stewed apples and custard were banged in front of them. I want to go home, thought Agatha. Oh, please God, let this evening be over quickly.

"Take them through to the lounge," said Mrs. Wong when the dreadful meal was over. "I'll bring the coffee."

"You really must show me your garden," said James. "I'm very interested in gardens."

"We're not going out in the evening air to catch our deaths," said Mrs. Wong, looking outraged. "Are we, Father?"

"Funny thing to suggest," said Mr. Wong.

To Agatha's and James's relief, they had only Bill for company over coffee. "I'm so glad you could come," said Bill. "I'm really proud of my home. Ma's made quite a little palace out of it."

"Really cosy," lied Agatha. "Bill, are you sure there is nothing odd about Bladen's death?"

"Nothing that anyone could find," he said. He looked amused. "You two have been sleuthing."

"Just asking around," said Agatha. "Bill, do you mind if I have a cigarette?"

"I don't, but Ma would kill you. Come out into the back garden and have one there."

They followed him out into the garden. James let out a gasp. It was beautifully laid out. A cluster of cherry trees at the bottom raised white-and-pink branches to the evening sky. A wisteria just beginning to show its first leaves coiled over the kitchen door. "This is my patch," said Bill. "Makes a change from policing."

James marvelled that Bill, who obviously had such an eye for beauty, could see nothing wrong with his parents' home. Agatha wondered how Bill could have such admiration and affection for such a dreary couple and then decided she admired him for it.

James was becoming happy and animated as he discussed plants and Agatha thought again of her own neglected garden and decided that if this investigation fell through, then gardening might be a subject they would have in common. By the time they returned to the dreadful lounge for more horrible coffee served in doll's cups which Mrs. Wong called her best "demytess," the three were at ease with each other.

"I like to return hospitality," said Bill to James. "I'm always dropping in to Agatha's for a coffee, but she's never been here. Now you know the road, you're welcome to come anytime."

"Have you moved here recently?" asked James.

"Last year," said Bill proudly. "Dad's got this dry-cleaning business in Mircester and he's really built it up. Yes, we're moving up in the world." His good nature seemed to transform his home into the palace he thought it to be and Agatha and James thanked Mrs. Wong very warmly for her hospitality before they finally left.

"It will be a cold day in hell before I go back there again," said Agatha, as they drove off.

"Yes, I'm still hungry. I cut up that beef and pushed it under the vegetables to make it look as if I'd eaten it," said James. "We'll stop somewhere for a drink and a sandwich."

He said this almost absent-mindedly, as if to an old friend, taking her acceptance for granted, and Agatha felt so ridiculously happy, she thought she might cry.

Over beer and sandwiches, they decided to continue their investigations the next day. "What about Miss Mabbs?" asked Agatha suddenly. "Look, we know Bladen was a womanizer. Miss Mabbs was that pallid female who worked as receptionist. What of her? She must have known all about the operation on that horse. I wonder where she is now?"

"We'll find her tomorrow. You can smoke if you like."

"I feel like an endangered species," said Agatha, lighting up. "People are becoming so militant about smokers."

"They're puritans," said James. "Who was it said that the reason the puritans were against bear-baiting was not because it gave pain to the bear but because it gave pleasure to the crowd?"

"I don't know. But I should give it up."

"Bill said an odd thing when we were leaving," said James. "He said, 'Don't go about stirring up muck or you may promote a real murder.' "

"Oh, he was joking. He's a great one for jokes."

FIVE

†

AGATHA would have been most surprised if anyone
had called her a romantic. She considered herself hard-
headed and practical. So she did not realize the folly of wild
dreams and fantasies.

In her mind, since she had said goodbye to him the
evening before, she was married to James Lacey, and most
of her dreams had been of a passionate honeymoon, and the
lovely thing about dreams is that one can write the script,
and James said beautiful and loverlike things.

So Agatha, next morning, forgot all her plans of being
cool and detached. James had said he would call for her
around noon and that they might have a bite to eat in the
pub before trying to find out what had become of Miss
Mabbs.

Agatha decided to make a romantic lunch. So when
James turned up on her doorstep, he shied nervously before
an Agatha in a low-cut blouse, tight skirt and very high

heels, who was glowing at him. He fidgeted nervously in the hall as she waved a hand in the direction of the dining-room and said she'd thought they may as well have lunch at her place.

Through the open door of the dining-room, James saw the table set with fine china and crystal and candles burning in tall holders—candles in the middle of the day!

Panic set in. He backed out of the door. "Actually, I came to apologize," he said. "Something's come up. Can't make it." And he turned and fled.

Agatha could practically hear the ruin of her dreams tumbling about her ears, brick by brick. Red with shame, she blew out the candles, put the china away, went upstairs, scrubbed off her thick make-up and put on a comfortable old dress like a sack, thrust her feet into slippers and shuffled back down to stare at the soaps on television and try not to brood on her gaffe.

She had had a nearly sleepless night and so she dosed off in front of the television set with the cats on her lap, waking an hour later at the sound of the doorbell.

She hoped he had come back—if only he would come back!—but it was Mrs. Bloxby, the vicar's wife, who stood there.

"I was just passing," said Mrs. Bloxby, "and wondered whether you remembered that the Carsely Ladies are having a meeting tonight." For a moment something unlovely darted through Agatha's eyes. She was thinking, Screw the Carsely Ladies.

"I do hope you will come," said Mrs. Bloxby. "Our newcomer, Mrs. Huntingdon, is going to be there, and Miss Webster, who has the shop. We expect quite a crowd. And Miss Simms is bringing along some of her home-made cider, so I thought we would have cheese and biscuits with that."

Agatha realized Mrs. Bloxby was still standing on the doorstep and said, "Do come in."

"No, I'd better get home. My husband is wrestling with a tricky sermon."

So this is what life has come down to, thought Agatha gloomily; another evening with the ladies. Even the knowledge that Mrs. Huntingdon was going to be there could not give Agatha enough energy to change out of her old dress.

But on her road to the vicarage, she remembered that Josephine Webster, she of the dried-flower shop, she who had admired the vet, was to be there. There was no James Lacey, but there was still the interest of amateur detection.

The vicarage sitting-room was full of chattering women. Mrs. Bloxby handed Agatha a tankard of cider. "Where is Miss Webster?" asked Agatha.

"Over there, by the piano."

"Of course." Agatha studied her with interest. She was a neat woman of indeterminate age, neat fair hair crisply permed, neat little features, neat little figure. Talking to her was Freda Huntingdon, who had not bothered to dress up either, Agatha noticed. Agatha did not want to interrupt their conversation. She took another pull at her tankard and blinked. The cider was very strong indeed. She found Miss Simms next to her. "How did you get such powerful stuff?" she asked.

Miss Simms giggled and whispered in Agatha's ear. "Let you into a secret. I thought I would spice it up a bit." She waved her own tankard towards a firkin on a table. "So I poured a bottle of vodka into it."

"You'll get us all drunk," said Agatha.

"Well, some of us need cheering up. Look at Mrs. Josephs. She's looking better already. I thought she was going to go into mourning for that cat of hers forever."

Agatha sat down beside Mrs. Josephs. "Glad to see you looking better," said Agatha politely.

"Oh, much better," said the librarian in a tipsy voice. "Revenge is mine."

"Really?"

"I am to get what is rightfully mine."

Agatha looked at her impatiently. "What do you mean?"

"Silence, ladies," called Mrs. Mason. "Our meeting is about to begin."

"Call on me at ten tomorrow," said Mrs. Josephs loudly, "and I'll tell you all about Paul Bladen."

"Shhh!" admonished Mrs. Bloxby.

Agatha waited restlessly while the proceedings dragged on. But before they were finished, Mrs. Josephs suddenly got up and left. Agatha shrugged and approached Miss Webster. "I saw you at Paul Bladen's funeral," she said.

"I didn't know you were a friend of his," said Miss Webster.

"Not exactly a friend," said Agatha, "but I felt I should pay my respects. You must have been very sorry to lose him."

"On the contrary," said Miss Webster, "I went to make sure he was really dead. Now, if you will excuse me, Miss . . . ?"

"Mrs. Raisin."

"Mrs. Raisin. I find all these chattering women give me a headache."

She got up abruptly and left the room. Curiouser and

90

curiouser, thought Agatha. Damn James. All this was interesting stuff, hints here, hints there. She would call on him before she went to see Mrs. Josephs.

James heard his doorbell at quarter to ten the following morning. Feeling like an old spinster, he twitched the front-room curtain and looked out. There was Agatha Raisin. That old feeling of being hunted came back again. He went through to his kitchen and sat there. The bell went on and on and then there was blessed silence.

Agatha stumped grumpily through the village. A car slid to a stop beside her and Bill Wong's cheerful face looked out. "What's the matter, Agatha? Where's James?"

"Nothing's the matter, and where James Lacey is I neither know nor care."

"Which means you've scared him off again," commented Bill cheerfully.

"I have done nothing of the kind, and for your information I am on my way to see Mrs. Josephs, the librarian. She has something important to tell me about Paul Bladen's death."

Bill gave a little sigh. "Agatha, when there actually has been a murder, a lot of distasteful scandal usually comes to light which has nothing to do with the case. A lot of people get hurt. Now if you're going to dig around an English village trying to make an accident look like murder it will have the same effect, and without any justification. Drop it. Do good works. Go abroad again. Let Paul Bladen rest in peace."

He drove off. Well, I may as well go, thought Agatha stubbornly. She'll be expecting me.

Mrs. Josephs lived at the end of a terrace of what were once workers' cottages. Hers was neat and trim, with a pocket-sized garden where forsythia spilled over the hedge into the road in a burst of golden glory. A blackbird sang on the roof. From a field above the village came the sound of a hunting horn, and as Agatha turned and looked up the hill, she saw the hunt streaming across a meadow, looking oddly out of perpective from her angle of vision.

If Lord Pendlebury was part of the hunt, she hoped he broke his neck. And with that pious thought, she pushed open the small wrought-iron gate and walked up to the door and rang the bell. There was no reply. The sound of the hunt disappeared into the distance. A jet screamed above, tearing the pale spring sky apart with sound.

Agatha tried again, feeling almost weepy, wondering dismally if all the inhabitants of Carsely were going to hide behind their sofas when they saw her on the doorstep.

But Mrs. Josephs had asked her to call. Mrs. Josephs had no right to snub her. Agatha turned the handle of the front door. It opened easily. A small hall with a narrow stair leading straight up from it.

"Mrs. Josephs!" called Agatha.

The little house had thick walls, and silence pressed in on Agatha. She looked in the downstairs rooms, small parlour, small dining-room, and tiny cubicle of a kitchen at the back.

Agatha stood at the bottom of the stairs and shifted from foot to foot.

How sinister that dim staircase looked. Perhaps Mrs. Josephs was ill. Emboldened by that thought, Agatha climbed the stairs. Bedroom on the right at the top, bed made, everything tidy. Box-room full of pathetic pieces of broken china and old furniture and dusty suitcases. No drama here.

May as well use the bathroom while I'm here, thought Agatha. Oh, I know! She probably meant me to go to the library. What a fool I am! But how crazy to go out and leave the house unlocked. This must be the bathroom. She pushed open a door which had a pane of frosted glass.

Mrs. Josephs was lying on the bathroom floor, her eyes staring sightlessly up at the ceiling. Agatha let out a whimper. She forced herself to bend down, pick up an arm and feel the pulse. Nothing.

She turned and ran down the stairs, looking for the phone. She found one in the parlour and dialled police and ambulance.

The first to arrive was P.C. Fred Griggs, the village policeman. He looked like a village policeman in a children's story, large and red-faced.

"She's dead," said Agatha. "Upstairs. Bathroom."

She followed the bulk of the policeman up the stairs. Fred looked sadly down at the body. "You're right," he said. "Can tell by just looking at her. Mrs. Josephs was a diabetic."

"So it wasn't murder," said Agatha.

"Now what put such an idea into your head?" His small eyes were shrewd.

"She said last night in front of everyone at the Carsely Ladies Society that she had something to tell me about Paul Bladen."

"The vet what died! What's that got to do with the poor woman's death?"

"Nothing," muttered Agatha. "I think I'll wait outside."

93

As she went out into the garden again, she could hear the wail of sirens; and then an ambulance, followed by two police cars, came racing up. She recognized Chief Detective Inspector Wilkes and Bill Wong. There were two other detectives she did not know and a policewoman.

Bill said, "Did you find her?" Agatha nodded dumbly. "What time?"

"Ten o'clock," said Agatha. "I told you I was going to see her."

"Go home," said Bill. "We'll be around to take a statement."

James Lacey stood on his doorstep, peering down the lane. He had heard the sirens. Ever since he had failed to answer the door to Agatha's ring, he had been staring at that heading "Chapter Two" on his word processor. Then he saw Agatha trailing along the lane. Her face was very white.

"What's happened?" he called, but she flapped a hand at him and said, "Later."

He felt frustrated. He felt that Agatha held the key to some excuse to take him away from writing for the day. He should not have run away from her lunch like a schoolboy.

He returned to his machine and glared at it. Then he heard the sound of a car turning into the lane and dashed outside again. It was a police car. He watched eagerly as it drove up to Agatha's cottage and stopped. He recognized Bill Wong with another detective and a policewoman. They went inside.

He had brought it on himself, he thought gloomily. The wretched Raisin woman was on to something and he was excluded.

94

Inside her home, Agatha answered all questions put to her. How long had she been in the Mrs. Joseph's cottage? Just a few minutes? Had anyone seen her just before she arrived? Detective Wong. The Chief Inspector nodded, as though Bill had already confirmed that.

"What did she die of?" asked Agatha.

"We'll need to wait for the pathologist's report," said Wilkes. "Now, I gather this arrangement to see her was made at the vicarage last night. What exactly did she say?"

Agatha replied promptly, "She said, 'Call on me at ten tomorrow and I'll tell you all about Paul Bladen.' "

"Anything else?"

"Let me see. I think I remarked she was looking better and she said an odd thing, she said, 'Revenge is mine.' "

"You're sure of that?"

"Absolutely. She added . . ." Agatha screwed up her eyes in an effort of memory. "She added, 'I am to get what is rightfully mine.' "

"Indeed," commented Wilkes. "Very cryptic. Quite like a novel."

"I am not making it up," snapped Agatha. "I have a very good memory."

"Now, Mrs. Josephs said, 'Call me at ten,' yet you went to her house. Wouldn't you think she meant you to phone her?"

"No," said Agatha, "we don't use the phone much in this village to talk to each other. We call in person."

"Mrs. Josephs was due on duty at the library. Why didn't you go there?"

"Because I didn't *think!*" howled Agatha, exasperated.

"What the f——, what the devil is all this about? She just died of natural causes, didn't she?"

"Odd you should think that, when I gather from Detective Sergeant Wong here that you are very ready to believe the death of Paul Bladen was murder."

Agatha threw Bill Wong a reproachful look. "I was interested in Paul Bladen's death and I was just asking a few questions," she said defensively.

"Who all was at the vicarage tea-party last night?"

"It wasn't a tea-party. Cider and cheese. I can give you most of the names, but if you ask Miss Simms, the secretary, she makes a note of everyone who attends each meeting."

Wilkes stood up. "I think that will do for now, Mrs. Raisin. We'll probably be talking to you again. Not thinking of travelling anywhere, are you?"

"What?" Agatha stared at him. "Me? Not travel— You think it's murder."

"Now, now, Mrs. Raisin, at the moment we are simply investigating the death of a diabetic. Good day to you."

Bill gave Agatha a wink behind his superior's back and mouthed silently, "This evening."

After they had left, Agatha decided to try James again. Forget about romance. This was too exciting to keep to herself. But he did not answer his door and she took small comfort in the fact that this time his car was gone.

James had driven into Mircester. To heal the breach with Agatha, he had considered an offer of flowers or chocolates and then had hit upon a better idea. If he found out Miss Mabbs's address, that would be a better excuse than anything to call on her.

Agatha went along to the Red Lion and eagerly discussed the death of Mrs. Josephs with the locals but without really learning anything that she did not know already. She returned home rather tipsy and fell asleep, and did not wake up until five o'clock to hear her doorbell ringing.

Feeling bleary-eyed and hung-over, she went to answer it. Bill Wong stood there.

"Come in! Come in!" cried Agatha. "Tell me all about it, but let me get a cup of strong coffee first. I had too much to drink in the pub."

"How did you scare Lacey off?" asked Bill, ambling into the kitchen after her.

"I didn't . . . Oh, well, I did invite him for lunch yesterday, light the candles on the dining-table and flash the old cleavage. You couldn't see him for dust."

The doorbell rang. "I'll get it," said Bill.

He came back a few moments later followed by James.

"Don't raise your voice," said Bill. "Our Agatha's got a hangover. She's been drowning her sorrows in the pub. She got all dolled up like a dog's dinner expecting an old flame from London for lunch yesterday and he didn't show and she'd forgotten about you calling but you scuttled off anyway."

"Oh," said James. "It's a good thing I'm not a vain man or I might have thought it was all for me."

Bill smiled happily. "Our Agatha's usually got bigger fish to fry, haven't you, Agatha? Why didn't your flame turn up, anyway?"

I can lie as easily as you, thought Agatha. "Threatened with a merger," she said. "But he's going to take me to the Savoy for dinner to make up for his absence."

James felt silly. I really must stop imagining this woman's pursuing me, he thought.

"So," said Agatha, putting down cups of coffee in front of them, "tell us all, Bill. Why have I not to leave the country?"

"What *is* all this?" cried James, exasperated. "It's about that librarian's death, isn't it? It's all the talk at Harveys'."

Agatha told him about the arranged call on Mrs. Josephs and of finding Mrs. Josephs dead. "You, now, Bill," she said. "Is it murder?"

"We're waiting for the pathologist's report," said Bill. "I'll tell you this off the record. There's something funny."

"Like what?" asked Agatha.

"Forensic found scuff marks on the stairs, all the way up from the parlour to the bathroom. Mrs. Josephs was wearing brown leather walking shoes. The stairs aren't carpeted. There were scuff marks which could have come from her shoes, and she was wearing those thick stockings and there are a couple of stocking threads caught in a crack on the stairs.

Agatha's eyes gleamed. "You mean someone could have killed her in her parlour and then dragged her upstairs and dumped her in her bathroom?"

"I don't understand that," said James. "If someone's going to kill her, why bother dragging the body up to the bathroom?"

"I'm speculating," said Bill. "I'm going out on a limb and neither of you must breathe a word of this to anyone."

They both nodded like mandarin dolls.

"Everyone seems to have known she was a diabetic and injected herself with insulin. What if someone gave her a jab of something lethal and then dragged her up to the bathroom where she kept her syringes and left her there hoping we would think she had died as she was giving herself one of her usual injections?"

James shook his head, to Agatha's irritation. "I still don't like it," he said. "Everyone knows about the wonders of forensic science these days."

"Any murderer is usually desperate or deranged," said Bill. "It would amaze you how little they think."

"Did the neighbours see anyone calling at the house?" asked James.

"No, but there's a lane runs along the end of the back gardens. Mrs. Dunstable at the other end of the terrace said she thought she heard a car stopping just at the end of the back lane—you can't get a car along there—about eight in the morning. But she's deaf! She says she felt the *vibrations* of a car, can you believe it?"

"It would be odd if it turned out to be murder," said James slowly. "After what she said to Agatha in front of all those women, it might cast doubts on the death of Paul Bladen."

"She might have committed suicide," Bill pointed out. "Everyone said she was very depressed since the death of her cat. The scuff marks could have been made when she dragged herself upstairs. That's the news so far. I've got to get back to work. Thanks for the coffee, Agatha."

When Bill had left, Agatha returned and sat down at the coffee-table and closed her eyes. "Want me to go?" asked James.

"No, I'm thinking. If I had murdered Mrs. Josephs and injected her with something, I wouldn't leave that lethal something among her bottles and pills in the bathroom. I'm not a very clever murderer. Think of the scuff marks. So I'm driving off with this bottle or ampoule I've used in my

99

pocket. I'm sweating and panicky." She opened her eyes. "I'd chuck it out the car window."

"It's a thought," said James. "And the road from the end of the back lane goes up to Lord Pendlebury's. No harm in just having a look, I suppose. We'll take rubbish sacks so that people will think we're volunteers from the village keeping the countryside tidy. But if you find anything sinister, leave it there and call the police or they might think you planted it."

They took Agatha's car. She drove to the back lane and sat there with the engine idling imagining she had just committed murder. She then drove off up the hill and suddenly stopped.

"Why here?" asked James.

"Because here's where I would chuck it if I were a murderer," said Agatha.

They started searching up and down the road on the right-hand side where anything a driver might have thrown out would have landed. Fortunately people in the Cotswolds are very litter-minded and so there was hardly anything after an hour's careful search to be found but an old broken fountain-pen and one sandal.

"The light's fading and I'm hungry," complained James.

"Let's try further up, nearer the estate," pleaded Agatha. "Just a bit more."

"Damn, I promised Freda Huntingdon a few days ago that I would meet her for a drink at seven in the Red Lion. Besides, it's getting dark."

"I've a flashlight in the car," said Agatha, now determined to keep him out as long as possible.

100

"Oh, well, just a little longer."

They drove farther up the road and got out again, Agatha taking the flashlight and James poking disinterestedly now in the hedgerow.

When Agatha after half an hour of patient walking and searching suddenly cried, "Eureka!" James said crossly, "Look, is it another shoe or something? Freda will be—"

"Come here! Look at this!"

He stumped over. Agatha pointed the flashlight at some tangled shrubbery and nettles in the ditch. Down in the bottom of the ditch was a little brown pharmacist's bottle.

"Well, I'll be damned," he said, giving her a hug.

Glad of the darkness, Agatha blushed with pleasure.

"You wait here and guard it," she said excitedly. "I'm off to phone Bill Wong."

James waited and waited. He glanced at his watch, noticing by the luminous dial that it was nearly eight. Then he thought, I don't really need to stand here. He took a stick which he had cut earlier from the hedgerow to help him in poking around, stabbed it down into the ditch beside the bottle and tied his handkerchief like a flag to the top of it. Now he could go safely off to the pub and the police and Agatha would easily find his marker. He strode off down the road.

Agatha waited on her doorstep, biting her nails. Bill had said, "Wait right where you are," and so she had done just that. But James must be wondering what had happened.

With a sigh of relief, she saw the police car nosing round into the lane and ran out to meet it. Bill and another detective were in the car. "Hop in," he said, "and take us to this clue of yours. We couldn't raise Fred Griggs. It's his night off."

Agatha could not believe it as they drove up the road and found no sign of James. Worse than that, she could not remember exactly where they had found the bottle and so they searched up and down the roadside for quite a long time before Bill finally found the stick with the handkerchief on top.

"At least he's marked the spot," said Bill, squatting down. He shone a powerful flashlight down beside the stick. "There doesn't seem to be anything there, Agatha."

Agatha peered over his shoulder. "But it *was* there," she cried. "Oh, where *is* James? If he just calmly went off to the pub to meet that tart, I'll kill him."

Bill and the other detective searched slowly and carefully, but there was no sign of that bottle.

He finally straightened up with a sigh. "Do you think Lacey's in the pub?"

"Oh, I'm quite sure he is," said Agatha viciously.

It was a busy evening at the Red Lion. The whole village seemed to be crammed into the pub. James was surprised when he received a tap on the shoulder and a voice murmuring, "Police. Would you step outside, Mr. Lacey?"

He followed the man out and started guiltily as he was confronted with an unusually serious Bill Wong and a baleful Agatha.

"I shouldn't have left, I suppose," he said in a rush, "but didn't you find the stick with the handkerchief on it?"

"We found that all right, but no bottle," said Bill. "When did you get to the pub?"

102

"Just after eight. I was meeting Freda . . . Mrs. Huntingdon."

"Did you tell Mrs. Huntingdon or anyone else in the pub what you had found?"

"Well . . ." James shifted awkwardly from foot to foot.

The policeman who had summoned him from the pub had gone back in and now emerged again in time to hear Bill's last question.

"If I might have a word with you, sir." He drew Bill aside. James Lacey stared at the ground.

Bill came back and looked up at James. "So, I gather you said to Mrs. Huntingdon that you and Mrs. Raisin had found a clue to Mrs. Josephs's death, that there was a pharmacist's bottle in the ditch and you had left your handkerchief as a flag to mark the spot. Mrs. Huntingdon had said in a loud voice to a circle of locals, 'We've got a sleuth in our midst. Isn't James clever?' And she told about the bottle."

"Look," said James desperately, "I'm not a policeman. I've looked on it all as a sort of game. But I may have put the stick in the wrong place. Let's go back and look again."

"Come along, then," said Bill. "I'd already thought of that and sent for reinforcements."

Agatha said not a word to James but climbed into the back of Bill's car. "If you please, sir," said a policeman and ushered James to another police car.

There seemed to be policemen all over the place when they returned, searching and searching the hedgerows.

Then there was a shout of triumph. One policeman crouching down a few yards from where James had marked the spot waved them excitedly over. And there, as he pulled some long grass aside, lay a small pharmacist's bottle.

It was tenderly lifted up with tweezers and placed on a clean cloth and shown to Agatha.

"I am sure that's a different shape," said Agatha. "And it hasn't got any label. I'm sure the one I saw had a bit of a label on it."

"You may as well go home, Mrs. Raisin," said Bill. "We'll call on you when we need you."

"I'm awfully sorry . . ." began James miserably.

"You too, Mr. Lacey. We'll be in touch with you."

James faced Agatha. "You must think I'm all sorts of a fool."

Agatha opened her mouth to say that, yes, she did think him a fool, but a sharp memory of how he had helped to extricate her over her own foolishness with the hand basin came into her mind and she said instead, "Let's walk back to my place for some coffee and think about this."

He fell into step beside her. "I can't help thinking," said Agatha, "that the murderer might have been in the pub and heard Freda. So he or she nips out, up the road, and takes that bottle, hides nearby and sees the police arrive, waits till they've gone to the pub to question you and then puts another bottle there which will prove to have contained something innocuous."

"But a clever murderer would not have thrown the bottle there in the first place," protested James.

They walked on in silence, each buried in thought.

Once in Agatha's kitchen and drinking coffee, Agatha, who had been silent for a very long time for her, suddenly burst out, "I've been thinking."

"What?"

"Surely clever murderers belong in fiction. To take a life you must be insane, or temporarily insane. What if some woman knew Paul was going to be up at Lord Pendlebury's on that day? Mad with rage, she biffs him on the head, and then jabs the syringe into him without even knowing the contents of the syringe are lethal. He's dead. She runs off. Now she has committed murder, she really is deranged and terribly frightened. She overhears Mrs. Josephs talking to me at the vicarage and feels she's got to be silenced and she knows she is a diabetic. She injects her with God knows what, panics again, thinks if the body is found in the bathroom, natural death will be assumed. Again, she's in the pub, and hears Freda. More panic. Take the bottle away. More panic. Replace it with another."

They talked for another hour, writing out lists of the women who were at the vicarage and all the women in the pub that James could remember. Then the phone rang. Agatha went to answer it and then came back and sat down wearily at the table.

"That was Bill. Mrs. Josephs was murdered. Someone shot a good dose of Adrenalin into her bloodstream."

"But where would anyone get Adrenalin?"

"At first I thought of Peter Rice because vets have it, but he was nowhere near the village. Bill said farmers usually have a supply, although their drugs cabinets are checked from time to time to make sure they are safely locked."

"Miss Mabbs!" said James suddenly.

"What about her?"

"That's why I called on you in the first place. I found her address. She's living in Leamington Spa."

"But wait a bit. She wasn't at the vicarage, nor was she in the pub this evening, surely."

"No, but she might have been lurking around some-

105

where. In any case, surely she would know more about Paul Bladen than most. She worked with him."

Agatha made up her mind.

"We'll go tomorrow."

SIX

†

AGATHA and James were not able to set out for Royal Leamington Spa until late the next day, for another drama had hit Carsely. The veterinary surgery had been broken into and the drugs cabinet smashed open. It had been neatly and efficiently done. A pane of glass on the back door had been broken, allowing the thief to reach in and unlock the door.

"So that's probably where the Adrenalin came from," said a harassed-looking Bill Wong, "except that P.C. Griggs says he kept checking the premises on his rounds and there was no sign of a break-in before last night."

"He probably didn't even notice the broken pane of glass," commented James.

"Fred Griggs is a conscientious village bobby," said Bill.

"Then do you think someone meant the police to think the Adrenalin came from there?" asked Agatha.

"That could be the case. But how unnecessarily complicated! And this throws suspicion on the death of Paul Bladen. No one we can think of wanted Mrs. Josephs dead."

Then statements were painstakingly taken from Agatha and James about the finding of the bottle.

"They analysed the one we eventually found and it contains traces of a tranquillizer. We have checked with the local doctor and it would amaze you in this enlightened day and age how many women are on tranquillizers," said Bill. "Now I have something to say to both of you. The police at times seem very slow and plodding, but it's a safer way of doing things than having amateurs running around stirring things up. Please do not interfere again."

"If we had not interfered, as you put it," said Agatha hotly, "you would have gone on thinking Paul Bladen's death was an accident."

"And Mrs. Josephs might still be alive. Leave it to us, Agatha."

After the police had gone, James said reluctantly, "It seems we're not exactly popular."

"Yes, I suppose we'd better drop it." Agatha looked reluctant. "Perhaps I should think about some gardening."

"Your lawn at the front could do with treatment," said James. "Come and I'll show you what I mean."

Agatha was first out of her front door. She glanced down the lane and saw Freda Huntingdon standing on James's doorstep and retreated so quickly she bumped into him.

"I've changed my mind," she said, slamming the door and leading the way back to the kitchen. "Have another cup of coffee and I'll tell you about it.

"Now," she began when they were seated, "the way I look at it is this."

Her doorbell rang, sharp and peremptory.

"Aren't you going to answer that?" he asked.

"I suppose so." Agatha got reluctantly to her feet. She peered through the spyhole. Freda was standing on the step. Agatha returned to the kitchen and sat down.

"Double-glazing salesman," she said. "They're so pushy. Not worth answering the door." The bell shrilled again and Agatha winced. "I'll go," said James, rising.

"No, sit down, please. I think we should go to Leamington and question Miss Mabbs. How can that be called interfering? Just a few questions. If we knew more what Paul Bladen was like, then we might know what lies behind his death. After all, what makes someone kill?"

"Passion," said James. "One of his jilted ladies."

"Or money," said Agatha, thinking of her unfortunate experience in London.

But James, secure in the comfort of a private income and an army pension, shook his head. "He hadn't much to leave, not by today's standards."

The doorbell rang again.

"No," said Agatha sharply. "Just wait and whoever it is will go away. Whereabouts in Leamington does Miss Mabbs live?"

He took out a notebook and flipped the pages. "Here we are: Miss Cheryl Mabbs, aged twenty-three, employed for only the short time the surgery lasted in Carsely, lives at 43, Blackbird Street, Royal Leamington Spa."

Agatha's straining ears could not hear anything from outside, but then the cottage was so insulated, she hardly ever did. "I'll just go upstairs and put some make-up on," she said, "and then we'll go. If that doorbell rings again, ignore it."

Upstairs, she peered out of her bedroom window and saw with satisfaction the slim retreating figure of Freda.

She put on a little make-up, not too much or he might be frightened off again, sprayed some Rive Gauche over herself, and went back downstairs. She fed the cats, and as the day was not particularly cold, let them out into the back garden.

"Why don't you get a cat door?" asked James.

"I've had a few scares before," said Agatha, "and when I think of a cat door, I think of a small burglar, writhing his way through it like a snake."

"That doesn't happen. Tell you what," said James, feeling obscurely that he had to make amends for deserting his post the night before, "buy one and I'll fix it for you."

Agatha beamed at him. How domestic they were becoming. A simple wedding in Carsely Church. Too old to wear white. Perhaps a silk suit and a pretty hat. Honeymoon somewhere exotic. "Famous Detective Agatha Raisin Weds," that's what the local headlines would say.

James looked at her uneasily. Her small eyes had an odd glazed look. "Are you feeling all right?" he asked. "You look just the way I feel when I have indigestion."

"I'm all right," said Agatha, returning to earth with a bump. "Let's go."

Leamington, or Royal Leamington Spa, to give it the full title which few people hardly ever use, was a relatively short drive and they arrived there in under an hour.

The day had become grey and overcast, but unusually mild. Although in the centre of the country, Agatha thought Leamington had the air of a seaside town like

110

Eastbourne or Brighton and kept expecting to turn a corner and see the sea.

James, to her irritation, said he wanted to view the public gardens before they started any detective work. Agatha stumped along angrily beside him while he enthused over plants and blossom. She was obscurely aware she was jealous of the scenery and wished some of his raptures could be directed at her. She glanced at him sideways. He was strolling easily along with his hands in his pockets, at peace with the world. She wondered what he thought about her. She wondered what he thought about anything. Why wasn't he married? Was he gay? And yet look at the way he had left that splendid clue to go running after a stupid bitch like Freda Huntingdon.

He was staring up in dazed wonder at the cascading blossoms of a cherry tree when Agatha suddenly snapped, "Are we going to commune with nature all day, or are we going to get on with it?" He gave her a glance, half-rueful, half-amused, and all at once Agatha had a picture of him escorting some woman who would share his enthusiasm for the scenery, who would know all these county names he had talked about at that old manor house, and felt bullying and coarse-grained. "All right," said James amiably, "let's go."

He took out a small street map and consulted it. "We can walk," he said. "It's not far."

They set off. "Where does she work?" asked Agatha. "Oh, and how did you find out about her?"

"I don't know where she works, but I got her address from Peter Rice in Mircester. She isn't a veterinary nurse, simply a sort of receptionist."

Agatha began to wonder if they were ever going to get there, James's idea of "not far" not being her own. But they finally arrived at a long street of shops with flats above them. The shops had probably always been shops. The buildings were Georgian and run down, with cracked stucco and grimy fronts dating from the days before the Clean Air Act, when soot fell on everything.

It was six o'clock. Most of the little shops were closed and the street was quiet. Agatha could remember the days when a street such as this would resound with the cries of children: children playing hopscotch, children playing ball, children playing cowboys and Indians. Now they were probably all indoors watching television, videos, or playing computer games. Sad.

Number 43 turned out to be a staircase between two shops leading to flats above. At the top of the staircase was a battered wooden door and beside it a row of bells with names on cards beside each bell. There was no Mabbs listed.

"Must have the wrong address," said James.

"I didn't walk all this way for nothing," said Agatha impatiently, for her feet were sore. She pressed the nearest bell.

After a few moments the door was opened by a thin, anaemic-looking girl with blonde hair gelled up into spikes. "Wotyerwant?" she asked.

"Miss Cheryl Mabbs," said Agatha.

"She's on bell 4," said the girl, "but you won't find her in. She and Jerry has gone out."

"Where?" asked James.

"How should I know, mate? They usually has fish an' chips and goes to the disco."

"Where is this disco?" James smiled at the girl, who smiled back.

"Not your style," she said. "It's down the road. Rave On Disco. Can't miss it. Wait till later and you'll hear the noise."

"Well, that's that," said James as they emerged out into the street again.

"No, it's not." Agatha looked up at him. "We could have a bite to eat and then go to the disco ourselves."

He shied slightly and looked off into the middle distance. "I really think I would rather go home, Agatha. As the young lady there pointed out, discos are not my style."

Agatha glared at him. "Hardly mine either," she said, feeling her feet throb.

He stood there, looking down at her in polite embarrassment and obviously waiting for her to give in.

"Dinner and think about it?" suggested Agatha.

"I suppose I am hungry. It's a bit early for dinner. We'll find a pub."

Over drinks, followed later by a modest dinner in an Indian restaurant, Agatha reflected that the more time she spent with James, the less she seemed to find out about him. He seemed to have an endless fund of impersonal topics to talk about, from politics to gardening, but what he really felt or thought about anything, he did not say.

But he agreed to try the disco.

Back along Blackbird Street they went. They heard the thud, thud, thud of the disco music as they approached.

The disco was called Rave On and was a club, but they got inside easily after paying a modest entrance fee. "Enjoy yourself, Grandma," said the bouncer to Agatha, who glared at him and said, "Get stuffed," and then realized that James's face had taken on that shuttered look again.

Inside it was full of bodies writhing under strobe lights.

Following closely behind James, Agatha shouldered her way to a black plastic-padded bar in the corner.

James ordered a mineral water for Agatha because she was driving and a whisky and water for himself. "How much is that?" he shouted at the barman, a white-faced youth with a pinched, spotty face.

"On the house, officer," said the barman.

"We are not police officers."

"In that case, pay up, guv. Three pound for every drink. Six quid, squire."

"Do you know Cheryl Mabbs?" asked James. "We're friends of hers."

He pointed. "Over there in that booth, her wiff the orange-and-pink 'air."

Through the stabbing strobe lights and shifting gyrating bodies, they could make out a gleam of orange and pink in a far corner.

"Drink up," said James and tossed his back.

"I'll leave mine," shouted Agatha above the din. "I never did like gnat's piss anyway."

His eyes had that blank look which Agatha had come to interpret as a sign of disapproval. But he said, "We'd better dance our way over. Less conspicuous."

He joined the gyrating figures, cheerfully waving his arms in the air and dancing like a dervish. Agatha tried to follow suit but felt ridiculous. Teenagers were stopping their own dancing to cheer James on.

Inconspicuous, thought Agatha with a groan. The whole damn place is looking at us.

A few more whirls and turns and James came to a stop at Cheryl's booth, wildly applauded by the customers.

It was a different Miss Mabbs from the quiet, pallid girl

in the white coat Agatha had first seen at the vet's. Her hair was sprayed pink and orange and arranged in what Agatha could only think of as tufts. She wore a black leather jacket with studs over a yellow T-shirt with some slogan on it that Agatha could not read in the gloom. Beside her was a leather-jacketed young man with a face like a tipsy fox.

"Miss Mabbs!" cried Agatha. "We've been looking for you."

"Who the hell are you?" said the girl and picked up her drink, which was of as vile a colour as her hair, nudged aside the little paper umbrella on the top with her nose and took a sip of it through a straw.

"I am Agatha Raisin," said Agatha, thrusting out her hand.

"So what?" mumbled Cheryl.

"I met you at the vet's in Carsely. I came along with my pussy."

"Took your pussy along, did you?" demanded Cheryl's escort with a cackle. "Any luck?"

Cheryl sniggered.

"Look here," said James in the authoritative tones of the upper class, "can we go somewhere quiet where we can talk?"

"Sod off," said Cheryl, but the young man put a hand on her arm. His foxy eyes glinted up at James. "What's it worth to us?"

"A tenner and a drink," said James.

"Okay," he said. "Come on, Cher."

They were soon all seated in a quiet dingy pub, perhaps one of the few left in Britain without a slot-machine or juke-box or piped music. A few old men sat around in corners. The bar smelt of must and old beer and old men.

115

"What do you want to know?" asked Cheryl Mabbs.

"About Paul Bladen," said Agatha eagerly. "It now seems he was murdered."

Interest showed in her face for the first time. "And I thought nothing exciting would ever happen in that dump of a village. Me, I prefer the more cosmopolitan life, like," she stated, as if Leamington Spa were Paris. "Who done it?"

"That's what we want to find out," said James. "Any ideas?"

She scowled horribly and took a hearty swig at her glass of brandy and Babycham. "Could be anyone," she said finally.

"There's Mrs. Josephs as well," said Agatha and told of that murder.

"I told him trouble would come when he destroyed her old cat," said Cheryl. "He didn't like cats, and that's a fact. Hated the beasts. But he sweet-talked those old dears in the village a treat. Always taking one or the other of them out for dinner."

"Why?" asked Agatha.

"Why else?" countered Cheryl. "After their money, I suppose. I mean, what other reason could there be?"

"And why would he want their money?" demanded James, flashing a sympathetic look at Agatha, who was now outscowling Cheryl. "I mean, he left a fair bit."

"It was an impression, that's all. He was keen on that Freda Huntingdon. I caught them hard at it."

"Where?" demanded Agatha with a triumphant look at James.

"Right on the examining table. Her skirt was up around her ears and his trousers were down round his ankles. Laugh! I nearly died. But the others? Holding hands and taking them out for dinner was about as far as he got, I reckon. Course he had to soft-soap Mrs. Josephs, didn't he? I mean, she was making things hot for him over that cat. Then there was that funny old creature, Webster. That's it."

Agatha's scowl came back. She estimated that Josephine Webster, she who ran the dried-flower shop, was probably younger than herself.

"None of these ladies is really old," she protested.

Cheryl shrugged. "All look like a hundred and two to me," she said with all the callousness of youth.

"Did he get up to any of this philandering in Mircester?" asked James.

"Didn't know him then," replied Cheryl. "Saw the ad for a vet's receptionist and got the job."

"So what are you doing now?"

"Kennels. Out Warwick way." Cheryl's face suddenly softened. "I like animals. Better'n people any day."

"So all we got out of that unlovely pair," said James as they drove back to Carsely, "was much as we supposed. He was charming the ladies of Carsely . . ."

"And screwing one," said Agatha with a grin.

"I must confess I was very surprised to hear that about Freda," he said stiffly. "Do you think our Miss Mabbs could have been making it up?"

"Not for a moment," said Agatha gleefully.

"Oh, well, I suppose we should now concentrate on Miss Webster. Then there's Mrs. Mason to see. Who was the other one you saw at the funeral?"

"Harriet Parr."

117

"We'll see them all tomorrow," said James. "But better not let Bill Wong know what we're doing."

"And yet," said Agatha, "I can't help feeling that the clue to the whole thing lies with his ex-wife. She must know more about him than anyone. And who was the woman who answered the phone that night I called and said she was his wife? I'll bet that was our Mrs. Skirt-up-to-Her-Eyeballs, Freda Huntingdon."

"Can we please drop the subject of Freda?" he said. Agatha glanced sideways at him as they approached the orange lights of a roundabout. His face looked grim.

Damn Freda, thought Agatha bitterly, pressed her foot harder on the accelerator and sent the car racing homewards through the night.

"Do you think there is a Mr. Parr?" asked James as he and Agatha strolled through the village the next day to renew their investigations.

"I shouldn't think so. There are an awful lot of widows about. Men don't live that long."

"Probably only the married ones," said James.

He put his hands in his pockets and began to whistle something complicated—probably Bach or some old bore like that, thought Agatha.

Mrs. Harriet Parr lived in a modern bungalow on the outskirts of the village. When they reached the gate, Agatha said suddenly, "This is a waste of time."

"Why?"

"I don't remember meeting a Mrs. Parr at the vicarage, and if she wasn't there to overhear what Mrs. Josephs said to me, how can she have anything to do with it?"

"Perhaps Mrs. Josephs was going about saying the same thing earlier."

"Oh, well, let's get on with it."

Mrs. Parr answered the door herself. Agatha began by saying they hadn't met, but she and Mr. Lacey would like to ask her a few questions, and soon they found themselves in a comfortable living-room. Agatha counted six cats. There was something claustrophobic about seeing so many cats in one room. She felt obscurely that at least some of them ought to be outside.

Mrs. Parr was a small woman with curly black hair and an oddly old-fashioned sort of hourglass figure. Agatha decided she was probably wearing a corset. She had hard red cheeks and a small pinched mouth which when she spoke revealed pointed teeth.

It was some time before Agatha could get down to questioning her because she and James had to be introduced to each cat in turn. Then Mrs. Parr fussed over James, asking him if he were comfortable, plumping cushions at his back, before rushing off to fetch tea and "some of my special scones."

"No Mr. Parr," whispered Agatha.

"Might be out at work," said James.

Mrs. Parr came back with a loaded tray. After tea had been poured and the lightness of scones admired, Agatha said, "Actually, we're really interested in finding out about Paul Bladen."

Mrs. Parr's cup rattled against the saucer. "Poor Paul," she said. She put cup and saucer down and dabbed at her eyes with a crumpled tissue. "So young and so brave."

"Brave?"

"He was going to found a veterinary hospital. He had such dreams. He said he could only talk to me. I was the only one with enough imagination to share his vision."

Then they heard the front door open. "My husband," whispered Mrs. Parr. "Don't . . ."

The door of the living-room opened and a tall thin middle-aged man with a grey face and a prominent Adam's apple bobbing over a rigid shirt collar came in.

"People from the village, dear," said Mrs. Parr. "Mrs. Raisin and Mr. Lacey. They both live in Lilac Lane. They've just been admiring my scones."

"What brought you here?" asked Mr. Parr bluntly.

"We've just started asking a few questions about Paul Bladen—you know, the vet that was found dead."

"Get out of here," hissed Mr. Parr. He held the door wide open. "Out!"

"We were only . . ." said Agatha, but that was as far as she got.

"Get out!" he shouted at the stop of his voice this time, his thin tired face working with rage. "Never come here again. Leave us alone."

"I am very sorry we upset you so much," said James politely as he and Agatha edged past the infuriated husband.

"Fuck off, you upper-class twat," yelled Mr. Parr and spat full in James's face.

There was a horrified silence, punctuated only by the sound of Mrs. Parr's weeping. James slowly cleaned his face with a handkerchief. Mr. Parr was now trembling looking appalled at the enormity of his own behaviour.

James put his large hands on Mr. Parr's shoulders and shook him backwards and forwards.

He punctuated each shake by saying, "Don't . . . ever . . . do . . . that . . . to . . . me . . . again."

Then he abruptly released him and strode out, with Agatha at his heels.

"We're really stirring up mud, Agatha," he sighed. He looked back at the neat bungalow. "You know, sometimes when I was coming home on leave, I would look out at little houses like that from the train and imagine secure and cosy lives. What awful emotional dramas lurk behind the facades of all the houses called comfortable names like Mon Repos and Shangri-La, what breeding grounds for murder."

"Oh, it's quite a lively place, the country," said Agatha cheerfully. "I feel we're getting somewhere. Mrs. Parr must have been having a fling with Bladen. Let's try Josephine Webster."

"Perhaps before we get to her, we should call on Freda Huntingdon."

"What? That floozy? How can you bear to look at that slut without blushing?" demanded Agatha.

He stopped and looked down at her, leaning back, hands in his pockets and rocking slightly on his heels. A faint gleam of malice shone in his eyes. "On the contrary, Agatha, I find the idea of a Freda Huntingdon with her skirt around her ears quite delectable."

Agatha walked on. Well, they would call on Freda because Agatha was suddenly sure, had a sudden gut feeling that Freda was the murderer. She, Agatha Raisin, would prove it. Freda would be dragged off by the police. She would be sentenced to life imprisonment. She would be locked away from society and James would never set eyes on her again.

"Why are you racing along?" demanded James plain-

121

tively from somewhere behind her. "I thought you weren't all that keen on seeing the woman."

"I've decided that after all I do want to visit dear Freda," snapped Agatha.

Droon's Cottage, which Freda had bought, was at the back of the village on a rise. It was a Georgian cottage with a splendid wisteria hanging over the Regency doorway, its purple blooms just beginning to show.

"The bell doesn't work," said James and Agatha scowled horribly at this sign of his knowledge of the workings of Freda's house.

The door was opened by Doris Simpson, who cleaned for Agatha.

"What are you doing here?" demanded Agatha, who felt that this excellent cleaning woman was her sole property, although Doris only came one day a week now.

"I does for Mrs. Huntingdon, Agatha," said Doris, and Agatha thought that Doris should at least have addressed her as "Mrs. Raisin" in front of James.

"Is she in?" asked James.

"No, James, her's up at Lord Pendlebury's. Got a horse and he's keeping it in his stables for her. Oh, and Bert thanks you for the loan of the books."

"We'll go up to Pendlebury's and have a word with her there," said James.

"I didn't know you knew Bert and Doris Simpson," said Agatha.

"I sometimes have a drink with them in the Red Lion. Should we walk to Pendlebury's? It's a fine day."

"Oh, all right," said Agatha ungraciously, thinking, trust Freda to ingratiate herself with the aristocracy.

She was cursing her middle-aged feet by the time they

reached Eastwold Park. She was wearing a low-heeled pair of black suede shoes which up until that day had appeared a miracle of comfort. But shoes which had only been worn around the house and for a short walk from the car to the shops had developed hard ridges and bumps on the inside, of which she had previously been unaware.

As they approached the door of the mansion, Agatha felt her working-class soul cringing.

This was intensified by a smell of baked beans coming from the kitchen, which vividly brought back memories of the shabby streets of Birmingham: squalling babies, large belligerent women, and a small Agatha who nursed a dream of one day having a home in the Cotswolds. The food of the poor, remembered Agatha, had always seemed to be tinned baked beans or fish and chips.

Mrs. Arthur opened the door. "He's got company," she said. "He's over at the stables."

"We'll find him there," said James.

Agatha limped after him towards the stables.

Freda and Lord Pendlebury were standing outside, talking. Freda was wearing a tweed hacking jacket, jodhpurs and new riding-boots. She looked as if she had stepped out of a glossy advertisement in *Country Life*.

"James!" she cried when she saw him and she ran forward and kissed him on the cheek. Agatha wished she had not come. Lord Pendlebury sloped over. "What's this, young man? I was just enjoying the company of this pretty lady before you came along," and he gave Freda a doting look. Then he saw Agatha. "Good God!" he exclaimed. "It's that woman back again."

Freda giggled and hung on James's arm, smiling up at him.

123

"We've been asking questions about Paul Bladen's death," said Agatha, harshly and loudly. "We gather you were having it off with him."

"Really!" Freda looked at Agatha with distaste and then her eyes appealed silently to the two gentlemen for help.

"Go away, you horrible woman. Shoo!" said Lord Pendlebury.

"Too blunt, Agatha," murmured James. "Why don't you go home and leave this to me? I'll call in on you later."

Face red, Agatha wheeled round and stalked off. She could feel them all looking at her. Why had she been so blunt? Damn Freda!

James would probably drop the investigation and all because of that floozy.

Her feet hurt and her heart hurt and she was glad to get home to the undemanding affections of her cats.

She felt she should forget about James and go and ask Josephine Webster a few questions. The phone rang.

To her outrage and amazement, she recognized Jack Pomfret's voice. "Look, Agatha," he wheedled. "Okay, I went about things the wrong way. Yes, you guessed it. I went bust in Spain. But I've got a nice little earner lined up and . . ."

Agatha dropped the phone. She found she was trembling with outrage. How *dare* he! She felt almost frightened that he should persist in trying to get money out of her. Think of something else. Think of Josephine Webster. And then there was Mrs. Mason. She had been at the funeral.

But somehow she was too upset to think clearly. She thought about pouring herself a drink and then decided against it. She was not going to end up one of those people who poured themselves a drink the minute anything upset them. So she switched on the television and stared blindly at an American soap, gradually feeling herself relax.

An hour later, when her doorbell went, she jumped nervously, almost frightened that Jack Pomfret had pursued her to the country. But it was James who stood on the doorstep. "Sorry about that," he said. "But you were too blunt. Freda knows you don't like her and so she is not going to take kindly to being questioned by you."

"So did you get anything at all out of her?" asked Agatha.

"When I got rid of the doting Pendlebury, I had a talk with her. She says she had a bit of a fling with Bladen, but that was all. She pointed out, rightly, that she's free and single and can do what she likes. She was quite open about the whole business."

"But why in the surgery?" demanded Agatha. "They've both got the privacy of homes and beds. Doesn't that suggest passion rather than a casual affair to you?"

"Well," he said awkwardly, "Freda's quite a girl."

"Middle-aged woman, rather."

"Let's not quarrel about Freda. I don't think there's anything there to worry about. Let's try Josephine Webster."

Glad of an excuse to be with him again and get away from the phone, Agatha set off with him to Josephine Webster's shop. It was not a proper shop. It was a terraced house on the main street and she used what would normally have been the living-room to display her wares. The shop was dark and heavy with the ginger and cinnamon smells of herbal soaps and perfumes. Bunches of dried flowers hung from the beamed ceiling. Straw hats ornamented with dried flowers hung on the walls.

Neat Miss Webster was sitting at a desk in the corner of this room, doing accounts.

Determined to be more tactful, Agatha bought a cake of sandalwood soap, talked about the Carsely Ladies Society, the weather, and then finally got around to the subject of Paul Bladen.

"A most unfortunate death," said Miss Webster, peering at Agatha over a pair of gold-rimmed spectacles. "Such a sad accident."

James stepped in. "But now, in view of Mrs. Josephs's murder, the police are beginning to think that someone might have murdered Paul Bladen."

"That's ridiculous. I can't believe that."

"There's a mobile police unit being set up outside the village," said James, "and I don't think it's all because of Mrs. Josephs."

Her face had a pinched, closed look. "I am very busy. If you do not wish to buy anything else, please leave."

"But you must have been very close to Paul Bladen," pursued Agatha. "I saw you at his funeral."

"I was there to pay my respects, although I did not like him," she said. "Us village people went to pay our respects. Outsiders like you no doubt went along out of vulgar curiosity, and if you take my advice, leave investigations to the police."

"So that's us, with a flea in both ears," commented James outside. "All we seem to be getting are insults. What about Mrs. Mason?"

"At least we'll get a welcome there," said Agatha. "She lives on the council estate."

"How are your feet?"

"Fine now. I changed my shoes."

Mrs. Mason indeed gave them a warm welcome. More tea and scones. Gossip about the village. But Agatha began to shift nervously. A big murder investigation was taking place in the village. Surely it was odd that Mrs. Mason should not mention that.

"Lot of police around," ventured Agatha.

"Yes, poor Mrs. Josephs. I find it hard to believe. I think she took her own life. She was so upset about her cat."

"That was a wicked thing of Bladen to do," put in James. "Of course, the police now think he was murdered."

There was a long silence while Mrs. Mason stared at him, her matronly figure rigid. "That's ridiculous," she said at last. "No one would kill Mr. Bladen."

"Why?"

"He wasn't the kind of person who gets murdered. He was a man of purpose and vision. A kind man."

"Not very kind to kill Mrs. Josephs's cat."

"That was a *mercy* killing. He told me the old cat was in *agony.*"

Agatha leaned forward. "Just think for a moment, Mrs. Mason, just suppose someone had murdered Paul Bladen. Can't you think of any reason why?"

"No, I really can't. I wouldn't get involved in all this, Mrs. Raisin. I really wouldn't. It's not decent. Perhaps it's the way people go on in the city, but . . ."

"But don't you even want to know who killed Mrs. Josephs?"

"Yes, but that's a job for the police."

They couldn't get anything else out of her and retreated to Agatha's cottage.

"I would like to have a go at that ex-wife, Mrs. Bladen, one more time," said Agatha. "But no doubt she would just slam the door in our faces."

"You know," said James, "we could go back and see Bunty Vere-Dedsworth at the manor house. She might help us in getting Greta Bladen to talk."

"Then let's go," said Agatha eagerly, frightened that if they waited in Carsely any longer, Freda would arrive on the doorstep.

SEVEN

✝

THEY were just about to leave when the phone rang. Agatha started and looked at it as if it were a hissing snake. Was it Freda? Or was it Bill Wong asking them to mind their own business and leave the investigation to the police? He had always had a nasty way of knowing what she was up to.

She picked up the receiver and gave a tentative "Hello."

"Look here, Agatha," said Jack Pomfret's voice sternly. "This is ridiculous. I—"

"Go away and leave me alone!" she screamed and banged down the receiver.

Then she stood and wiped her moist palms on her skirt. "He's mad," she muttered. "I could kill him."

"Who? Are you all right, Agatha?"

She shook her head as if to clear it and gave a sigh. "Someone I used to know. He's trying to con money out of me. He starts a new business. I pay. He knows I found out he was trying to cheat me. But he's insane. He keeps phoning. I feel humiliated. I feel threatened."

The phone rang again and Agatha jumped.

"Allow me," he said. He picked up the receiver and listened. Then he said in glacial tones, "This is Agatha's husband speaking. I handle all her financial affairs. One more call from you and I will suggest to the police that they take a close look at your business transactions." James looked at the receiver before putting it down and smiled.

"What did he say?" demanded Agatha.

"He gave a frightened squawk and rang off. You won't be hearing from him again."

"Why are you so sure of that?"

"Because, my dear Agatha, it's an old-fashioned world, however tough and independent women have become. He now thinks he has an irate husband to deal with. Come along. You look too rattled to drive."

As she climbed into his car, Agatha felt a warm glow permeating her body. He had said he was her husband! Oh, somehow she must tell Freda Huntingdon that!

The day was blustery, with great cloud shadows racing across the fields, where new corn rippled in the fleeting sunlight. Agatha's heart sang. And then her voice sang, "Oh, what a beautiful morning."

"It's afternoon," said James. He switched on the radio, a pointed rebuke, and Agatha sank back into silence.

The manor house looked as it had done before, calm and benign, part of the landscape rather than some building thrust upon it.

"So you're back," said Bunty, looking pleased. "I was just going to have some coffee."

"We need your help," said James when they were all seated in the comfortable kitchen.

He succinctly outlined all that had happened and explained they were sure that Greta Bladen could help them.

Bunty listened carefully, her eyes bright with interest.

"As I told you before, I know Greta," she said. "We all know each other in this little village. I'll phone her and ask her to come up."

She went off and came back shortly to say that Greta was on her way. "You had better let me do the talking," said Bunty. "She can be prickly."

And prickly was what Greta looked as she entered the kitchen and stopped short at the sight of Agatha and James.

"Now you can't run away from people asking questions about Paul's death," said Bunty firmly. "You didn't like the man, but surely you don't want a murderer to be left to roam the Cotswolds in peace. Sit down, Greta, and have coffee. You see, we all feel that if we knew a bit more about Paul Bladen, then we might be able to guess which of the suspects might have done it."

"Including me," said Greta bitterly, but she sat down and shrugged off her short coat.

"Well, it's a dreary story," she said. "As you probably realize, I was ten years older than Paul when I met him. He was working as a vet in Leamington Spa where I lived. I had a dog then I was devoted to, the way only the unloved can become devoted to animals."

Agatha, who had been thinking of her cats, stared down into her coffee cup.

"I took my dog to the vet for some shots. Paul was charming. I could not believe my luck when he asked me out. My parents had died and left me a house and a comfortable amount of money. It was what the romances call a whirlwind courtship. Shortly after we were married, I found my dog dead one morning. The animal had been fit and healthy the day before. Paul was all sympathy and did an autopsy. He said the dog had died of heart failure. Only in later years did I suspect he had poisoned it. Strange in a vet, but he had hatred of dogs and cats. He told me about his dream of a veterinary hospital. He said he would name it after me. I gave him a considerable amount of money to get started.

"During the following year, he regaled me with stories of the plot of land he had bought and how the builders had started work. I was excited and asked to see it, but he said he wanted it to be a surprise. I said, 'At least tell me where it is,' and he said Chimley Road on the outskirts of Mircester. He started to come home very late. He said he was always going over to the building site when he finished work. Then he said we were moving to Mircester to be near the new hospital. He did not ask me for money. He said he had a house all ready but I was to promise not to go near Chimley Road until he was ready to surprise me."

Greta sighed. "I was so much in love with him. That was until I met his partner, Peter Rice, at a party. I had known Peter before, by the way. We were old friends. So I thought it all right to ask him if they would still run the surgery when the new veterinary hospital was opened.

"He asked me, 'What veterinary hospital?' I told him. He gave me a pitying look and said why didn't I go out to Chimley Road and have a look. Alarmed, I set off the next day. It was a long row of terraced houses. No building site.

"I taxed Paul with it. He began to say that things hadn't worked out there, so the building site was in Leam-

132

ington, and when I didn't believe him, he finally came out with the truth. He was a gambler, a dedicated gambler. Not only had he spent all the money I had given him in gambling but he needed more to pay his debts. I refused. He grew ugly. He told me he had only married an old bat like me for my money. Yes, I could have killed him then. But I wanted free of him and so I made him agree to a separation and subsequent divorce. If he did not agree, I said, I would tell Peter Rice all about him."

"So," said James, "one of his ladies could have murdered him because he conned money out of them."

"Surely that's hardly a reason for murder," protested Bunty.

"Oh, yes, it is," said Agatha, thinking of Jack Pomfret.

"So now you've got what you want from me," said Greta in a tired voice, "may I go?"

"Of course, my dear," said Bunty. "But you must realize how essential it is to find out who did this terrible thing."

Greta stood up. "Why? Why is it so important? He died painlessly. He was cruel and useless."

"But there is the murder of Mrs. Josephs," said Agatha quietly. "You must have read about that."

"Yes, but what's that got to do with Paul?"

"She said she was going to tell me all about him," said Agatha, "and the next day she was dead."

Greta shook her head in bewilderment. "I cannot bring myself to believe that Paul's death was anything other than an accident. I don't know this Josephs woman—I mean I didn't know her. Possibly her death is unrelated." Her voice shook. "I've done what I can for you. Please don't trouble me again."

There was a long silence after she had left. Then, "Poor woman," said Bunty.

"Perhaps." Agatha laced her fingers tightly round the coffee mug. "On the other hand, she surely had the most reason to kill Paul. She would know about Immobilon. Perhaps she would have access to Adrenalin, if he had left any of his drugs behind when he left her."

"You're forgetting about the break-in at the surgery," James pointed out.

"The police seem to think that might have been done *after* Mrs. Josephs's death."

"So many women. So many suspects," mourned James. "But we have taken up enough of your time, Bunty."

They thanked her and left.

"We've got one thing," said Agatha, as they drove off. "Money, not passion, seems to be at the bottom of things. Look, Jack Pomfret didn't get any money out of me, right? But the very fact that he tried to trick me, the fact that he has the gall to phone me up makes me want to murder him, gives me a mad hatred and fear of him. Can you understand that?"

"Yes, I think so. If any of these women, I mean any of our suspects, apart from Greta, paid up, there would be a motive. We could go to Mircester and ask Peter Rice what happened to Paul Bladen's deposit book."

Agatha agreed, delighted at an opportunity of more time in his company.

The evening surgery at the vet's in Mircester was just closing. Peter Rice greeted them this time amiably enough but scoffed when they asked if he had any of Paul Bladen's bank-books.

"I cleared all his papers out and made a bonfire of them," he said. "I've put the house up for sale. I could hardly sell it with all his junk around. I asked Greta if she wanted anything but she didn't, so I gave his clothes to charity and the contents of the house are being sold with it."

"Which was his bank?" asked James.

"The Cotswold and Gloucester. But bank managers don't reveal anything about their customers' accounts, even when they're dead, as far as I know."

"You didn't happen to notice if Paul had received any large sums from women recently?" asked Agatha.

He gave a jolly laugh. "He was hardly young enough to be a toy boy. The lawyers will only pass over to me what is left after their bill and the funeral costs have been settled. I'm afraid his banking affairs have gone to the grave with him. But why do you ask? Hadn't been ripping you off, had he?"

"Just curious," said Agatha. "I mean it is odd, now that it's turned out someone murdered Mrs. Josephs. I mean, it definitely makes Paul Bladen's death look like murder."

"Not to me," said Peter. "Pendlebury asked me to do that operation and I said I would never touch Immobilon again."

"Let's get something to eat," suggested James when they had left the surgery.

They chose a nearby pub—but not the one where Agatha had ruined the hand basin—and began to discuss the suspects, or rather, Agatha discussed the suspects while a preoccupied James frowned into his beer.

135

"I don't believe you've been listening to a word I've been saying," said Agatha crossly.

"I've been half-listening. The fact is I've been thinking about committing a crime."

"You?"

"Yes. I've been thinking about breaking into the Cotswold and Gloucester Bank."

"But that's impossible. There'll be sophisticated burglar alarms and laser beams and pressure pads and God knows what else."

"Perhaps not. Let's finish our food and drink and go and take a look at it."

The bank was a converted shop in a side street where old Tudor buildings with overhanging eaves crowded out the night sky above.

"Burglar alarm of course," said James. "We'll take a look round the back if we can get there."

They found a lane which ran along the back of a row of shops and the bank. There were a series of lock-ups, garages, and tall wooden fences, all having a closed, impregnable air.

James counted along. "This is the back of the bank," he said, "what used to be the garden. Surely they wouldn't wire up this wooden door in the wall."

He took a small wallet of credit cards out of his pocket. Agatha bit back the impatient remark she was about to make—that apart from in the movies, she had never seen anyone open a lock with a credit card. He selected one.

Agatha turned away and looked along the lane, which was lit with sodium lamps, making everything look unreal, and, she thought more practically, probably making her lips look purple.

There was a click and she swung round. The door in the wall was standing open. "Amazing," said Agatha.

"Let's get inside before someone sees us," whispered James.

Agatha followed him in. He closed the door behind them and took out a pencil torch. "You've done this before," accused Agatha.

He didn't reply but led the way up a narrow path between two strips of lawn. "Look," he murmured, "there's a kitchen at the back."

"What does a bank want a kitchen for?"

"Make tea for the staff. Left over from when it used to be a shop. Now, let me see . . ."

The thin beam of the torch flicked up and down the building. "I don't see any sign of an alarm here," he said. "I'm going to have a go. Be prepared to make a run for it."

"But we might not hear any alarm," said Agatha in an agony of nerves. "It might just ring inside the police station."

"Where's your sense of adventure?" he mocked.

He took out the card again. Agatha prayed that he would not be able to get the door open. She imagined police cars swooping up the lane, police with loud hailers; the reproachful eyes of Bill Wong. But all she heard was James's voice saying softly, "It's open. Come on."

Now Agatha's heart was hammering so hard, she felt sure it could be heard for miles. The kitchen door closed behind them, the torch beam flickered rapidly to right and left. James opened a door leading out of the kitchen and led the way through.

They found themselves in a square room full of desks and computers. "The office," said James, "which is all we need. Just as well. Look at that door over there. That's the one into the bank proper, where the money is."

Agatha shivered. There was an alarm box over the door and a steady red light glared down on them like an infuriated eye.

"Now," he said, "make yourself comfortable. This might take some time. There are no windows in this room except for that one through to the main bank, which is just as well, for the light from the computer screen could have been spotted from outside."

Agatha sat down in a dark corner and waited, too frightened to watch what he was doing, although she was aware of a computer screen flickering into life and the soft sound of drawers being opened and shut.

It had been a long day and extreme fear had the effect of making Agatha feel sleepy. Her eyes closed.

She awoke with him shaking her shoulder and cried, "We've been caught! The police!"

"Shhh! I've found his account," hissed James.

"Good. Can we get out of here?"

"Yes, I've taken notes. Quietly now."

As Agatha finally followed him down the garden path, she felt sure there must be people living above the adjoining shops, people who were staring down at the two figures in the garden and reaching for their telephones, but when she shot one frightened look back, everything was as dark and silent as before.

Only when they were safely outside did she realize that fear was affecting her physically. "I must find a Ladies' . . . quick," she gasped.

"Are you feeling sick?"

"No, I've got to *pee*," said Agatha. "There's a tide of pee rising up to my eyeballs."

"We'll go back to the pub," he said. "It isn't far."

Agatha cursed her own crudity. But she almost ran back to the pub.

"Now what?" she asked, elated because her fright was over and she had used the services of the pub's toilet.

"Don't you want to know what I found out?"

"Oh, yes."

"Listen to this. In the short time Paul Bladen was in Carsely, he had deposits in his account: one of twenty thousand pounds, one of fifteen thousand, then nine thousand, one of four thousand, four deposits of five thousand, and one for five hundred. That's apart from his pay."

"Who paid him?"

"There's the rub. Didn't say. I've been thinking. I would like to get inside that house of his. We could do it tonight."

"Last orders, please, ladies and gennelmen. If you please," called the barman.

"As late as that!" exclaimed Agatha. "Well, we could start out tomorrow early and—"

"No, tonight." He looked at Agatha's cherry-red coat. "We need some dark clothes."

What monster is this I have unleashed? thought Agatha, looking at his animated face. She could tell him to go on his own. And yet, there would be all the excitement of the adventure, which might lead to . . . They fumbled around in the dark of Paul Bladen's house. "What's that?"

139

he cried, clutching hold of Agatha. "Nothing," he murmured, still holding her. "Your perfume smells divine. Oh, Agatha!" And he bent his lips to hers.

"Agatha! Stop day-dreaming and let's get on," said James sharply and Agatha blinked the rosy vision away, obscurely irritated that he had snapped her out of it before he had kissed her.

Back at her cottage, Agatha changed into a pair of black slacks and a black sweater. She wondered whether he meant her to blacken her face. Better wait and see.

He rang her bell at one in the morning. He too was wearing a black sweater and black trousers. "We'll be causing no end of a scandal," he said cheerfully. "I only hope no one sees me calling on you at this hour of the night," and Agatha thought of Freda and fervently hoped that someone had.

James, who had been drinking mineral water during their last visit to the pub, elected to drive again. Agatha snuggled down in the passenger seat and dreamt they were racing off on their honeymoon.

"Just to be on the safe side," said James, "we'll park a street away and walk."

Paul Bladen's house stood quiet and shuttered in a road of Victorian villas. Agatha remembered her last visit and was glad now she had run away.

James looked up and down the quiet street, which was lined with cherry trees in full bloom. A breeze blew down the street and blossom cascaded about them. "Isn't it sad," mourned James, "that such beauty should be so fleeting?"

"Too true," said Agatha edgily. "But if you stand here for much longer admiring the blossom, then someone's going to see us."

He gave a little sigh and Agatha wondered whether he were wishing he was with someone who could share his love of beauty.

"I think as there is no one around, we should go straight up to the front door," he whispered. "There's a dark porch and once we're there, we'll be pretty much shielded.

"Why bother about dark clothes if we're not going to sneak around the back?" asked Agatha.

"Because it might take me a bit of time to get the door open, and so long as we are dressed in black, there's less chance of us being noticed from the street by any passer-by."

When they were in the shelter of the porch, he flicked the beam of his pencil torch at the door and then switched it off. "Yale lock," he said with satisfaction. "Lovely stained-glass panel on the door. I wonder if Peter Rice knows you can get money these days for Victorian stained glass."

"Get on with it," said Agatha, looking nervously over her shoulder.

And then they heard the sound of slow footsteps coming along the street and stiffened.

"Stand very still in the corner and turn your face away from the street and don't move," hissed James.

They froze.

The footsteps came nearer, stopping every once in a while. "Come on, Spot," said a man's voice irritably. Someone walking the dog.

Agatha could feel sweat trickling down her face.

And then, to her horror, she heard the light patter of paws behind her and then a dog sniffing at her ankles and the sound of the owner walking up the garden path.

141

"Come out of there," cried the owner sharply. Please God, prayed Agatha, get me out of this one and I'll never be bad again.

The dog pattered off. "I'm putting you on the leash now," said the owner's voice. This was followed by a metallic click and then those footsteps slowly retreated out of the garden and off down the street.

"Whew!" said Agatha. "That was close. We should have pretended to be a courting couple," she added hopefully. "Then, if he'd seen us, he would have sheered off."

"On the contrary," said James, "nothing infuriates the suburbanite more than the sight of a couple snogging on someone else's property." He took out a bunch of thin metal implements.

"Where did you get those?" asked Agatha. "You're not a retired burglar, are you?"

"Chap in the regiment. Now, keep quiet while I get to work."

Agatha stood and fidgeted. She hoped the much-advertised deodorant she had put on was working. He tried one implement after the other until there was a soft click.

A moment later, Agatha stood in the hall where she had panicked before Paul Bladen. "Now," said James in a normal voice, "there's a good bit of light coming from the street lamps outside and the curtains aren't closed. So we search around for some sort of study or a desk."

Agatha opened a door in the hall. "I'll try this side," she said. "You try the other."

She could dimly see that the windows of the room she found herself in looked out over the back garden to a railway track. She moved cautiously around in the darkness, feeling with her fingers for a desk. It seemed to be the sitting-room—sofa, coffee-table, easy chairs. Suddenly, with a roar, a late-night passenger train heading for Oxford rumbled along the track at the end of the garden and then crawled to a stop. Agatha crouched down on the floor. The lights from the carriages shone straight into the room. There were a few people sitting reading books or just staring out into space. Then, with a wheeze, the train crawled on, slowly gathered speed, and roared off into the night.

Agatha got up and made her way with trembling legs to the door, fell over something and crashed down, swearing loudly.

James came in and said impatiently, "Try to keep it quiet, Agatha. I've found the study. Follow me. Other side of the hall."

"It's all right. I haven't hurt myself," said Agatha sarcastically. "I knocked something over."

The torch stabbed down. A canterbury lay on its side, papers and magazines spilled across the floor. "You'd think Rice would have thrown these away," complained James, picking them up and putting them back after he had righted the canterbury. "Hardly add to the value of the house."

They crept across the hall and into the study. James approached a desk by the window and gently slid open the drawers. "Nothing here," he mumbled. "Maybe lower down." He slid out a bottom drawer and then his searching fingers found something at the back of it. He drew out a file. "Come out to the hall so I can flash the torch on this."

In the hall, the thin beam of light showed bank-books and a desposit book and bank statements tucked into the cardboard file. "May as well get out of here and take this home," said James.

"Won't it be missed?" asked Agatha.

"No. Rice said he had burnt all the papers. This was jammed at the back of the bottom drawer. He must have missed it."

Agatha, delighted to be outside again and once more in the fresh air, tripped gaily forward down the garden path and fell headlong over something. There was a curse from Agatha, a yelp of canine pain, and then that dratted voice calling, "Spot!"

The dog pattered off to its master. James helped Agatha to her feet.

"What's going on there?" came the dog owner's voice.

They walked to the garden gate. A man stood under the street light, holding a small white dog, his face pinched with suspicion. "Did you kick my dog?" he demanded wrathfully.

"My wife tripped over your dog in the dark," said James coldly.

"Is that so? And what are you doing in there at this time of night?" asked the dog owner.

"I do not see it is any business of yours, but my wife and I were looking at our new home. We have just put in an offer for this house and so I would like to take this opportunity of telling you that you ought to keep that animal of yours on a leash and stop it straying over private property. Come, Agatha."

Agatha, all too conscious of how odd they must look in their black clothes, edged past the dog owner with a weak smile.

She could feel his suspicious eyes boring into their backs at they walked to the car.

"Let's get home," said James. "I'm dying to have a

144

look at those bank statements. What a horrible man. What sort of man goes wandering around the streets with his dog at this time of night? Probably a sex maniac."

Agatha giggled. "He's probably just a respectable suburban insomniac, or his dog's incontinent and he is now wondering what kind of people decided to view a house in the dead of night."

"It's all your fault," said James. "You should look where you're going."

"How was I to know the damn dog would be there?" retorted Agatha.

"I don't know. You never seem to have anything sensible on your feet, always limping about and falling over things."

"Are we having our first quarrel?" asked Agatha sweetly.

There was a long silence. Then he said, "I am sorry. I was a bit strung up. Shouldn't take it out on you. The fact is, I'm not used to burglary."

"You're forgiven."

"It was not an apology," he said, "simply an explanation."

"Then why did you say you were sorry?"

They bickered the whole way home but neither of them could bring themselves to stalk off to their respective residences until that file was examined.

They went into James's house. He lit the fire, which was already set. He sat down in an armchair on one side of the fire and Agatha took the armchair opposite.

"Ah, here's the deposit book," he said. "Good heavens!"

"What? What have you found?"

"A cheque from Freda was paid in—twenty thousand pounds."

"Women's Lib," chortled Agatha maliciously. "Not often the woman pays the man."

"The others are, let me see: fifteen thousand pounds from Mrs. Josephs, nine thousand from Miss Webster, five thousand from Mrs. Parr, four more deposits of five thousand, all from Freda, and five hundred from Miss Simms. Oh, and four thousand from Mrs. Mason."

"Freda!" Agatha looked triumphant. "Do you realize the payments to Bladen come to forty thousand pounds? Now any woman cheated out of that amount of money would feel like murder."

He looked uncomfortable. "I know Freda pretty well. She seems to be awfully rich . . ."

"No one's that rich," put in Agatha.

He stretched and yawned. "I'm tired. Better leave it for tonight. Should we turn this lot over to the police tomorrow?"

Agatha looked horrified. "And have to explain how we came by it?"

"We could say we were viewing the house."

"And the estate agents would point out that we never approached them. All right, we'll tackle these women tomorrow. You had best leave Freda to me."

Agatha thought furiously about how she might be able to dissuade him from seeing Freda alone, but decided to sleep on it.

But as it turned out, she was the one to tackle Freda after all.

She struggled from a deep sleep the following morning with the sound of her own doorbell ringing in her ears.

She pulled on a dressing-gown and thrust her feet into slippers and went to answer the door. Freda stood there, her noisy dog cradled in her arm. "James here?" she asked brightly. "I can't get any reply at his house."

"No," said Agatha, "but come in and keep that dog of yours away from my cats."

"Yes, I think I want a word with you." Freda followed Agatha through to the kitchen. Agatha caught a glimpse of herself in the hall mirror: tousled hair, unmade-up face. Freda was as cool and fragile as a figure in a Fragonard painting. She sat down at the kitchen table, put her dog on the floor, and crossed her long legs. Agatha opened the back door and let her cats out into the garden.

"You've been running all over the place with James," said Freda. "He's a bit of a softy. You shouldn't take advantage of his good nature."

"And just what's that supposed to mean?"

"He has been plagued by every old bat in the village, has he not? I warned him that these frightening menopausal women often get the wrong idea. Give him a break."

"Listen, you murderess," hissed Agatha, "just because you let Paul Bladen screw you on the surgery table doesn't make you Cleopatra. Besides, you had to pay for that, did you not? Forty thousand pounds, to be exact."

The doorbell rang and Freda was up like a shot and running to answer it, her dog yapping at her heels. Agatha followed in time to see Freda throw herself weeping into

James's arms, sobbing, "This dreadful woman. She's accusing me of murder."

"Now, then," he said, "no one's accusing you of anything." He detached himself from her grasp. He looked at Agatha. "Did you ask her about the money?"

Freda let out a gasp. "You have no right to poke about my private affairs. I shall tell the police." She ran out of the door and down the lane, with her dog scurrying at her heels.

"What did you say, Agatha?" demanded James.

"She started by insulting me. She said . . ." Agatha bit her lip. She did not want to put the idea into James's head that she was one of those menopausal women with fantasies. "Anyway, she was vile. So I taxed her about the money. Then you rang the bell and she went to answer it."

"Damn. You'd better get dressed, Agatha, and we'd best go and look at that house of Bladen's officially and then take the file along to Bill Wong, as if we've just found it."

As they drove to Mircester, Agatha said suddenly, "Was Bladen blackmailing them? I mean, all payments are relative. Five hundred pounds from Miss Simms, well, that's a fortune for her."

"Yes, but she's single and so is Miss Webster, and Freda is a widow. Freda seemed quite unfazed by the fact we found out she had been having an affair with Bladen, so how could he blackmail her?"

At the estate agent's, instead of giving them the keys, a young girl called Wendy said she would accompany them. She was a cheerful Sloane Ranger type and talked non-stop to Agatha and James as they walked around the rooms of the house wondering how to get rid of her so that they could pretend to find the file. At last James said, "We would like

148

to be alone to have a private discussion," and to Agatha's relief, Wendy said, "Right ho, drop the keys back at the office when you're finished," and shot off.

They decided to have a thorough search of the house in the hope of finding letters or documents, but there was nothing. Out in the back garden there was an old oil drum with holes banged in its sides which had obviously been used for burning garden rubbish. James poked moodily at the contents with a stick. "This is where Rice burnt the papers," he said, "but we're out of luck. He did a thorough job. Not even an edge of paper left uncharred and legible. Oh, well, let's go and see Bill Wong."

At police headquarters, Bill Wong studied the bank papers and deposit book and then looked up at them, his eyes shrewd. "A man phoned in a report in the middle of the night that two people dressed in black were in Paul Bladen's house and told him they had bought it. That wouldn't have been you pair, now would it?"

"Us?" exclaimed James. "Had it been us and had we found this file, then we would have brought it straight along."

"I wonder. You must stop interfering. Yes, I know. I'm grateful for this and these women will all be inter-viewed—by the police. If I find you have been continuing with your amateur investigations, then I will really have to inquire more closely into the identities of that couple who were seen at Bladen's last night. Do I make myself clear?"

"Yes, very," said Agatha huffily.

"So that's all the thanks we get," she complained as James drove them back to Carsely.

"I'm relieved in a way," said James. "Oh, well, back to that writing."

There was a long silence. Then Agatha said, "I have to pay my subscription to the Carsely Ladies Society and that means calling on Miss Simms. Like to come along? I mean, Bill can't stop us asking a few questions in a neighbourly way. Dammit, he can't stop us talking to the villagers at all!"

"And how's he to know?" said James. "I mean, everyone calls on everyone else in Carsely."

"Miss Simms will be at work until this evening," said Agatha. "Let's try Mrs. Mason first."

EIGHT

†

IT was one of those typically English days. Steady rain drummed down and fallen cherry blossom bobbed along in the rivulets running between the old cobbles in Lilac Lane. They had fortified themselves with coffee and sandwiches, and with a lack of enthusiasm that the one would not admit to the other, Agatha and James set out to speak to Mrs. Mason again.

Mrs. Mason was so welcoming, so obviously thought they had come on a social call, that it was hard to get down to brass tacks. "And you must have some more of my famous scones, Mr. Lacey," said Mrs. Mason. "And that's *real* strawberry jam, not shop-bought. Soon be strawberry season again. I do hope this nasty weather clears up, don't you?" She looked at James archly. "You and Mrs. Raisin are quite the talk of the village. I was saying to the vicar the other day that we would soon be hearing the banns read."

James looked at her in blank horror and nearly forgot

why they had come. "Mrs. Mason," began Agatha, "we really don't want to distress you further, but we would like to know why you gave Mr. Bladen such a large sum of money."

Mrs. Mason blinked rapidly. "That is really none of your business." Agatha glanced around the living-room. Four thousand pounds was an awful lot of money for such as Mrs. Mason to part with.

"We came to warn you that the police are about to make it their business," said James.

"Then I shall speak to the police when they arrive. But how did you find out?"

"Agatha and I were looking around Paul Bladen's house, which is up for sale, and we happened to come across his old bank statements and deposit book. We did give them to the police."

Mrs. Mason studied James, her eyes suddenly sharp. "So you and Mrs. Raisin were looking at a house together. Well, well, romance does seem to be in the air. Quite cheering, really. It shows one is never too old."

And that, as she had planned, had the desired effect of driving James to his feet and towards the door.

Agatha gloomily followed him out. James climbed into the car without holding the door open for her and stared moodily at the rain trickling down the windscreen. Agatha got into the passenger seat.

"Damn all gossiping women," said James, striking the steering wheel. "You, me, it's bloody ridiculous."

"Yes, a laugh a minute," said Agatha dryly, although her heart was sore. "She only said that to get rid of you, and get rid of you it did."

His face lightened. "Oh, that was the reason. How naïve of me."

"You are really over-sensitive on the subject," said Agatha. "It's my belief that you think every woman you come across is pursuing you."

He gave an awkward laugh. "Let's try the Webster female."

Josephine Webster was arguing with a couple of rain-washed American tourists who were trying to haggle over the price of a dried-flower arrangement. "The price is marked on it," said Miss Webster, exasperated. "This is not a bazaar."

"You can haggle over the price of things in antique shops," said James to the Americans in a kindly voice, "but most other places you're expected to pay the price marked."

"Is that a fact?"

The American man and woman fell into amiable conversation with James about their visit, Miss Webster returned to her desk, and Agatha stared out of the window at the main street. She had no desire to tackle Miss Webster while these tourists were in the shop.

"I've no time for Americans," said Miss Webster waspishly when the couple had left. "Always complaining."

"It's not their fault," said James. "They feel they have to protect themselves. A lot of people think American tourists are made of money. Now that couple saved all their lives for this one trip. They have to budget very carefully, and they've probably been told back home that all foreigners are out to cheat them."

"But we're not foreigners," said Miss Webster. "We're British."

James smiled. "Talking about money, we wondered why you had paid such a large sum of money to Paul Bladen."

Miss Webster's face went white and then red. "Get out of here," she called shrilly. "Get out!" She picked up a bunch of assorted dried flowers and waved it at them like a housewife shooing cats out with her broom.

"We're not getting anywhere," said James gloomily after he and Agatha had retreated out of the shop. "Do you want to see Mrs. Parr again?"

"So long as that husband of hers is not around," said Agatha.

But Mrs. Parr did not open the door to them. The curtain twitched and they saw the quick blur of a face behind the glass, but the front door stayed resolutely shut.

"We're running out of people," said James. "Perhaps I should try Freda. If I went on my own . . ."

"No," said Agatha quickly. "Why don't we try Miss Mabbs again? Say we know these women were paying him. Ask her some more questions."

"Oh, all right. But I don't want to have to wait until that disco opens up."

"We can find her where she works. She said it was a kennels 'out Warwick way.' I'll look up the Yellow Pages before we go."

At last, armed with the name of a kennels situated between Leamington Spa and Warwick, they set off.

The rain was slowly easing off, to be replaced with pale-yellow sunlight.

They found the kennels easily enough. Dogs were barking, dogs were howling piteously, and the wet air smelled of damp dog.

154

They went into the office, which was housed in a timber hut, and asked for Cheryl Mabbs.

The man behind the desk looked up sharply. "Friends of hers?"

"Yes," said James.

He stood up. He was a small, thickset man with grey hair and rimless spectacles. "Then you know exactly where to find her," he said. "Get out."

"If we knew where to find her," said James, "we wouldn't be here asking for her. Does she work here, or doesn't she?"

Agatha had a sudden flash of inspiration. She edged in front of James and said mildly, "I am afraid we have misled you, but we do not like to go around announcing who we are. We are social workers."

"Oh." He sat down suddenly. "Why didn't you say so? Although you still make me feel angry. I had a recommendation from you lot that she was on the straight."

Agatha affected an air of weariness, although her heart was beating hard. "What has she done this time?"

"Not told you yet, have they? Pah! That's bureaucracy for you. The whole of England is top-heavy with idiotic pen-pushers. She broke into the drugs cabinet, that's what she did."

"Did you have Adrenalin in there?" asked James eagerly.

"Yes, of course, but the fact is she would have been better off raiding a doctor's or chemist's unless she wants to prevent hard pad and distemper. I called the police right away and they went to her digs and found the stuff. Or what was left of it. She had been flogging pills around some disco in Leamington, claiming they were a new sort of happy pill.

155

I think the youth of Leamington can consider themselves well and truly wormed by now."

James and Agatha were both dying to know what Cheryl Mabbs's record had been, but then, as supposed social workers, they were supposed to know.

"She's a silly girl," said the man. "I'm Bob Picks, by the way. She was a wizard with animals. Why did she want to go and smash up her career? Young people these days, I ask you."

They left him, still shaking his head over the iniquities of youth.

"So," said Agatha outside, "that's where the Adrenalin could have come from. Damn! We can't ask the police, or word might get to Bill Wong that we're still asking questions."

"So many suspects," mourned James. "Tell you what, let's try her digs. She might be out on bail, or that unlovely boyfriend of hers might be there."

Agatha nodded, although she felt suddenly depressed. She could not help remembering how horrified and shocked he had been at any suggestion of a romance between herself and him. The sun struck down, lighting up the grey patches in his black hair and showing the strong lines down the side of his nose. In that moment, he did not look nearly so handsome as he usually did and Agatha took small comfort from that.

They drove to Blackbird Street and parked outside the door to the flats where Miss Mabbs lived.

They walked up the stairs and pressed the right bell this time. They waited a long time and then heard the sound of someone approaching the door. It opened an inch. "Oh, it's you," said Jerry, Miss Mabbs's boyfriend. "Wot you want?"

"Where's Miss Mabbs?"

"In the slammer."

"Can we come in? We'd like to ask you a few questions."

The door opened wider and his foxy face stared at them. "Cost you."

James sighed. "A tenner, like last time."

"Done. Not here. Meet you down the pub. The Fevvers."

"The what?" asked James as they walked down and out into the street. "He meant the Feathers," said Agatha.

"The old men's pub. That's where we went last time. I'm fed up with mineral water. I'll try tomato juice this time."

The pub looked the same, tired and dusty. Dust motes swam in shafts of sunlight striking through the windows. An old man slumbered over his beer in a corner.

James ordered a tomato juice for himself and a gin and tonic for Agatha.

Time passed while they discussed the suspects in the case in a desultory way. Agatha would have liked to debate the possibility that Freda was the murderess. After all, she had paid out the biggest amount of money. But James's face went rigid at the very mention of Freda's name.

James ordered another round of drinks and carried them back to the table. "I don't think our young friend is coming," he said. "Maybe we'd better go back and try again."

At that moment the pub door opened and six youths

came in. Black leather and jeans, flat-top haircuts, mean pinched faces. The leader saw them and jerked his head at the others.

"Trouble," said James.

"I don' like your face," said the leader. A bicycle chain hung from one tattooed hand. "And I'm going to rearrange it." Agatha looked round wildly for help. The barman had disappeared, the old man slept on.

James threw back his head and shouted, "HELP! HELP! MURDER!" It was a terrible shout, deafening and shocking, a bellow. It was as if he had thrown a hand grenade into the group. They darted for the door and crashed out, colliding with one another, while James's terrible shouts went on and on. The old man woke up and stared at him in amazement.

"It's all right," said Agatha, white-faced. "They've gone."

James smiled at her. "Nothing like a good scream for help, I always say. Let's go and sort out young Jerry."

"What's it got to do with him? Oh, you think he knows Cheryl Mabbs did the murders and he's sent along his friends to silence us."

"Romantic idea. But I think young Jerry phoned his friends and told him that there was some rich berk in the pub with a fistful of tenners for the taking. I just can't wait to see him again."

Once more they stood outside the shabby door and once more James pressed the bell. "Who is it?" came Jerry's cautious voice.

"Got the money outer that twat," said James in a gruff voice.

The door opened wide. Jerry saw them and tried to slam the door, but James shouldered his way in. He slapped Jerry hard on one side of his head and then on the other. Then, holding him by the scruff of the neck, he said, "Your flat. Time we had a talk."

"Don't hurt me," squeaked Jerry. "I ain't done nothink."

"Where is it? Which door is yours?" demanded James.

Jerry pointed to an open door. James pushed him inside. "Now, before I really get to work on you, why did you send your friends to beat us up?"

"I dinnet."

There was a one bar heater burning in front of an empty fireplace. James twisted Jerry's arm behind his back and then thrust his face down towards the bar of the heater. "Speak up while you've still got a face left."

"Okay, I'll tell you."

James pushed Jerry down into a chair and stood over him. "I phoned up Syd and said to tell the boys there was good pickings off a couple in the Fevvers, that's all. See, I don't know nuffink about Cheryl. No, don't," he shouted as James loomed over him. "I'm telling you the truff, s'welp me God. It was her idear to steal the drugs from the kennels. Get a bit of cash. She says them hopheads at the disco would buy anythink. Honest."

His voice went on and on, pleading and explaining. It turned out he had not known Cheryl when she was working in Carsely.

James finally turned away in disgust.

Outside, Agatha looked nervously up and down the street. "We should call the cops," she said.

"I wouldn't do that." James unlocked the car door. "It

might all come out. In fact, we'd better get out of here in case that chap at the kennels has found out we're impostors."

When they got back to Carsely, James said, "I'll make us a snack and then we'll tackle Miss Simms."

Agatha brightened. "I'll go to my place, feed the cats and then let them out. They've been locked up most of the day."

The cats gave her a rapturous welcome. Agatha sat down suddenly and watched them while they fed. She felt weak and shaky and on the point of crying. She had had a bad fright in the pub. Bill Wong was right. She should leave this sort of business to the police. But if she dropped the investigations, then James would drop *her* and go back to his writing.

She let the cats out into the garden and stood for a moment watching them frolicking about and then went along to James's cottage.

"I've set our meal in the kitchen," he said when he answered the door. "Come through."

Agatha looked eagerly around the kitchen. It was cheerful and warm. A large bowl of daffodils stood on the window. There was a square scrubbed table in the middle and some elegant ladder-backed chairs. Supper consisted of cold ham and an excellent salad with a cold bottle of white Mâcon.

Agatha studied him covertly as he ate with the absorbed attention he gave to everything and everyone except herself. "It's time," he said finally, pushing away his plate, "for us to separately write down everything we know about everyone. Whoever killed Paul Bladen and Mrs. Josephs did both killings in panic or rage and on the spur of the

160

moment. But first, let's see what we can get out of Miss Simms."

Miss Simms lived on the council estate near Mrs. Parr. She answered the door to them and said cheerfully, "Just finished bathing the kids. I'll be with you in a minute."

"I didn't know she had children," whispered Agatha when they were alone.

"Must be a single parent," said James. "Quite common these days."

The living-room was a mess of discarded toys and picture books. An old television set flickered in one corner. The furniture was of the kind bought on the pay-up plan, which grew old and shabby before the final payment was made.

Miss Simms came tittuping back in on the ridiculously high heels she always wore.

"Drink?" she offered.

James and Agatha both shook their heads. Agatha looked at James and James looked at Agatha and it was Agatha who said, "We happen to know you paid Paul Bladen five hundred pounds. Why?"

"I don't think that's very nice. I don't reelly," complained Miss Simms. "What's it got to do with you, anyway?"

Agatha sighed. "We just want to know who killed Paul Bladen and Mrs. Josephs. We feel if we knew why you gave him the money, it might help. The others gave him thousands and thousands, but they won't talk."

Her gaze sharpened. "There were others?"

Agatha nodded.

Miss Simms sighed and sat back on the low sofa and crossed her legs, her skirt rucked up to show an edge of

161

scarlet lace knicker. How little I really know about the people in this village, thought Agatha. I didn't even know Miss Simms had children. It's the car, that's what. People in villages have become mobile and so they're less curious about their fellows. And television. And yet it's funny how people go on and on about the good old days when they had to make their own entertainment. If it was so great, why did they all rush out to buy television sets as soon as they could?

Miss Simms's voice broke into her thoughts. "I may as well tell you, only it makes me so mad; like when I think of the way that bastard tricked me. He took me out to a posh restaurant in Broadway. He told me all about this veterinary hospital he hoped to start. He said if I gave him some money, he would call it after me. He said he would get Princess Di to open it. I drank too much and well, things got a bit passionate that night and before I knew what was what, I'd written him out a cheque for everything I'd got in the post-office savings. After a bit when he didn't come round again, I got worried. Not nice to be dropped like that. I asked him about the hospital and he said he was too busy to talk about it. I asked for my money back and he got nasty and said I had given it to him of my own free will. I felt such a fool. I work over at a computer place in Evesham. I pay a chunk out of my wages to pay for child care for the kids. I told Mrs. Bloxby. She said I should pray to God for guidance and so I did and do you know what?"

"No, what?" asked James.

"The very next day God sent me a new gentleman friend with a nice job in soft furnishings and he pays me an allowance, like."

"You'll be getting married soon," said James.

162

She laughed. "He's married, which suits me. Don't like having a man underfoot all the time."

"Does Mrs. Bloxby know the outcome of your prayers?" asked Agatha curiously.

"Ooh, yes. She said as how God moves in mysterious ways."

The vicar's wife, reflected Agatha, was always the soul of tact.

"I was so mad with that Paul Bladen, I could've killed him," said Miss Simms. "But I didn't, and so good luck to whoever did."

"But there's Mrs. Josephs."

Miss Simms looked sad. "Forgot about her. Old duck she was. What about a drink now?"

Both cheerfully accepted now that there was no danger of their being thrown out and Miss Simms produced an excellent bottle of malt whisky supplied by her gentleman friend. Agatha paid her membership fee for the Carsely Ladies Society and Miss Simms entered it carefully in a ledger.

"So are you pair going to get spliced?" she said cheerfully.

James put down his glass. "No danger of that," he said evenly. "I am a confirmed bachelor."

Miss Simms laughed. "Wouldn't be too sure about that. When our Mrs. Raisin sets her mind to something, there's no stopping her. Mrs. Harvey in the shop was only saying the other day that we would be hearing wedding bells soon."

"She must have been talking about someone else," said Agatha, pink with embarrassment.

When they had said goodbye to Miss Simms and walked outside, there was a constraint between them. Agatha felt quite tired and weepy.

"I think I'd better go home to bed," she said in a small voice quite unlike her usual robust tones.

"Don't look so upset," he said in a kind voice. "They'll go on talking about us, and when nothing happens, the gossip will die away."

But I want something to happen, wailed Agatha's heart, and to her horror a large tear slipped out of one eye and ran down her nose.

"You've had a rotten day," said James. "Tell you what, we'll walk to the Red Lion and I'll get you a stiff nightcap."

Agatha gave him a watery smile.

The pub was blessedly quiet, only a few of the regulars standing at the bar. They carried their drinks over to a table by the fire.

And then Freda walked into the pub with a man. She was wearing a pale-green tailored suit and a white silk blouse and looked as cool and fresh as a salad. Her companion was a florid-faced middle-aged man with silver hair, dressed in a blazer and flannels. They ordered drinks. Freda half-turned her head and saw James and Agatha. She whispered something to her escort, who let out a great braying haw-haw-haw of a laugh and stared at them insolently.

Agatha noticed James's face was wearing a blank look and that his body was tense. Please God, let him not be jealous, she prayed, at the same time wondering why she kept praying to a God in whom she did not quite believe.

"I think I am tired," said James abruptly.

They left together and walked silently home. Agatha

gave him a sad good night and went to her own cottage. At least the cats would be glad to see her.

She unlocked the door and stepped inside, switching on the hall light as she did so.

There was a square white envelope lying on the doormat. She opened it up. It contained one sheet of paper with a simple typed message.

"Stop poking your nose into things that don't concern you or you will never see your cats again."

Agatha let out a whimper of fear. She ran through to the kitchen and opened the back door. "Hodge, Boswell," she called, but all was darkness and silence. She switched on the back outside lights. The square of garden lay before her. No cats.

She went inside and picked up the telephone and phoned the police.

The windows of James's bedroom overlooked the front of his cottage. He undressed and climbed into bed and switched out the light. Just as he was about to close his eyes, a blue light flickered up and over his ceiling and he could hear the sound of a car sweeping past in the lane outside.

He switched on the light again and scrambled back into his clothes. As he stepped out of his own front door, another police car arrived.

He ran to Agatha's cottage, hoping she was all right, worried that by encouraging her to go on this murder hunt, he might have endangered her.

P.C. Griggs was standing on duty on the doorstep. "You can step inside, Mr. Lacey," he said. "She'll need some help."

"What happened?"

"Someone stole her cats."

James was so relieved that Agatha was not hurt that he nearly said, "Is that all?" but bit the remark back in time.

Agatha's sitting-room seemed full of policemen, plain-clothes and uniformed.

Bill Wong looked up as James came in. He had an arm around Agatha's shoulders, an Agatha who was sobbing quietly. Agatha had never thought of herself as a cat lover. In fact, she sometimes regretted the responsibility of looking after the pair. But now all she could think of was that they had either been slaughtered or that they were locked up somewhere, being mistreated and frightened.

"You'd best sit down and tell us everything you did today," said Bill. "Agatha's in no state to give us a coherent account. Begin at the beginning and go on to the end and don't leave anything out."

The only thing that James left out was that they had both pretended to be social workers. In a flat voice, he described the interviews they had conducted, the trip to Leamington, the finding out about Cheryl Mabbs's theft of the drugs including Adrenalin, and the attack in the pub.

He then fell silent, waiting for a lecture, but Bill said, "We'll have this all typed up and get you to sign it tomorrow. We'll need to interview everyone in Lilac Lane and see if they saw anyone or heard a car while you were both in the pub."

He turned to Agatha and gently questioned her again, taking notes of his own while she confirmed James's story.

James ambled off to the kitchen and made some coffee. Men were dusting Agatha's front door for fingerprints, examining the road outside for tyre tracks, picking over the front garden. He sat down at the kitchen table, listening to the murmur of voices in the other room and reflected that he had initially retired to the country for peace and quiet.

At last he rose and went back to his own house and dug out a sleeping-bag, put his pyjamas, toothbrush and shaving-kit in a bag and returned to Agatha's cottage.

Bill and the others were just leaving. "I'll sleep downstairs here tonight," said James, and Bill nodded.

Mrs. Bloxby, the vicar's wife, was sitting with Agatha when he went into the sitting-room. "That nice Mr. Wong phoned me," said Mrs. Bloxby. "What a terrible business. Agatha should not be left alone."

"She won't be," said James. "I'm sleeping down here. Don't cry, Agatha. Cats are great survivors."

"If they're still alive," sobbed Agatha.

"I'm glad you are staying, Mr. Lacey," said Mrs. Bloxby. "But phone me if you need any help."

James saw her out and then returned to Agatha. "Off to bed with you," he said gently, "and I'll bring you something to make you sleep."

Agatha scrubbed her eyes and trailed up the stairs. Part of her mind told her that such a short time ago she would have believed any sacrifice was worth getting James to stay under her roof and look after her, but the rest of her mind cried out for her lost pets.

After she was in bed, the door opened and James came in carrying a tray. "Whisky and hot water and a couple of aspirin," he said. "I'll be downstairs. Drink up." He sat on the edge of the bed and held the glass to her lips and waited until she had swallowed the aspirin.

After he had left, Agatha lay awake, tears trickling out of the corners of her eyes. Everyone seemed sinister to her now, even James. What did she know of him? A man arrived in a village and claimed to be a retired colonel and everyone took him at face value. And yet, Bunty knew his family, and she, Agatha, had met his sister a year ago. But how formidable, how terrifying he had been when he had been slapping the miserable Jerry around. Ruthless, that was the word for it.

Slowly she drifted off to sleep, plagued with nightmares. Freda was torturing the cats and laughing while James looked on; Bill Wong invited her to dinner and served up the cats, roasted on a tray; and Miss Webster was sitting efficiently at her desk, with Agatha's two cats, stuffed and mounted, in front of her.

Agatha awoke in the morning. Sunlight was streaming into the room, there was a smell of coffee and the hum of voices from downstairs. She looked at the clock beside the bed. Ten in the morning!

She washed and dressed and went downstairs. Her kitchen was full of women: most of them members of the Carsely Ladies Society, Mrs. Harvey from the general store, and Mrs. Dunbridge, the butcher's wife, all being served coffee by James.

They surrounded her as she came in, murmuring sympathy. Her kitchen counter was loaded with gifts of cake and jam and flowers. Even Miss Simms was there. "Took the day off from work," she said.

"That's very kind of you," said Agatha, "but I don't know what you can do."

"Mr. Lacey has had a very good idea," said Mrs. Bloxby. "We're organizing a search. Your cats may have been dumped off somewhere in the village, so we are all going out on a house-to-house hunt. You sit quietly here with Mr. Lacey and we'll report if we find anything."

Agatha abruptly left the room and went up to the bathroom and cried her eyes out. All her life she had forged on, pushy and determined to get to the top of the public-relations profession, all her life she had been alone. All this friendship and help made her feel weak.

When she went back downstairs, red-eyed but composed, only James and Mrs. Parr were left.

"Mrs. Parr has just been telling me much the same story as Miss Simms," said James. "Bladen told her about the veterinary hospital and said he would name it after her. Her husband found out about the missing money and hit the roof."

"I suppose I might have done the same thing," said Agatha slowly, remembering that dinner at the Greek restaurant. "He told me about his plans and I said I would contribute something, but I was thinking of a cheque for twenty pounds. And he was all ready to go to bed with me but I panicked and ran away. Did you have an affair with him, Mrs. Parr?"

She shook her head. "I wouldn't have done. That wasn't how he tricked me. I was so flattered by him because he said I was the only woman who understood him. I am not very happy in my marriage and he made me feel attractive. I should have told you before, but I felt such a fool. I was still a bit in love with him when he died, but after the funeral my mind cleared up and I could see what he had done."

"Mrs. Mason was telling me the same thing while you were upstairs, Agatha," said James. "He was a compulsive

169

gambler, Mrs. Parr, and that's why he needed the money."

"That's odd," said Agatha. "He didn't spend any of it. I mean, what he got out of the ladies of Carsely was still in his account."

"I'll go off and join the search," said Mrs. Parr. "The least I can do."

"Thanks for all this, James," said Agatha, when they were alone. Her eyes filled with tears again.

"Now, now, the time for crying is over. Let's sit down and discuss what we know. Instead of thinking that, say, Freda must have done it because she paid out the most money, what we should be looking for is someone with the *character* to do such a thing."

"Who can say what anyone will do when they're goaded?"

"You wouldn't kill anyone, Agatha, now would you?"

Except Freda, thought Agatha.

"What we should do," he went on, "is make a list of suspects and then divide it up and follow each one and see what she does during the day and who she sees and if there is anything suspicious about her behaviour. Now, the women who gave money to Bladen were Mrs. Parr, Mrs. Mason, Freda, Miss Webster, Mrs. Josephs and Miss Simms. Then we have to take into account Paul's ex-wife, Greta. Also, there is one side of the case we have not been looking at. Bladen was killed up at Lord Pendlebury's stables. Bob Arthur found the body and came running out, saying, 'Looks like someone's done fer him.' Why should he say that? Why not think it a heart attack or something? There's another interesting thing I noticed about Bladen's bank statements. There were no major withdrawals, so he must have had cash to pay for all his food and entertaining. How did he pay the bill at the Greek restaurant?"

"Cash."

"Right. So what about Mrs. Arthur? There's a thought."

"It gets worse and worse," said Agatha. "Where do we begin?"

"I'll begin with Freda. No, don't scowl. My motives are pure detection. You start by watching Mrs. Parr."

"Oh, come on! That woman couldn't hurt a fly."

"She's terrified of that husband of hers. Bladen might have known that. She may yet not be telling us all. He could have been blackmailing her. Give you something to do. You want your cats back, don't you?"

Agatha winced.

"Anyway, I'll get moving on my side and we'll meet up here, say, at six o'clock this evening. Nothing like action to beat the blues, Agatha."

Agatha went numbly about the kitchen after he had left, stacking away the various gifts in cupboards. Apart from cakes and pots of jam, there was a large bunch of dried flowers, but they could hardly be from Miss Webster. Agatha shoved them in a vase and went upstairs to put on the make-up she had wept off.

She was on her way out when she stopped in the hall. The back of the front door was still covered in fingerprint dust. A gleam of sunlight lit up a tiny coloured object sticking among the coarse coconut matting of the doormat. She bent down and looked at it and then picked it out. Puzzled, she turned it this way and that. Then her face cleared. It was a tiny dried petal. It must have fallen off that bouquet of flowers that someone had brought. She flicked it from her fingers and then opened the door.

Then she froze.

Suddenly it was the night before and she was lifting the envelope from the doormat and opening it, taking out the letter, smoothing it out. Surely a flicker of something small and bright had drifted down.

NINE

†

AGATHA felt weird and strange as she walked numbly out into the bright sunlight. Two policemen were asking questions at the other cottages in Lilac Lane. People waved and called to her as she went past but she did not hear them.

Agatha Raisin was no longer thinking about who had murdered the vet or Mrs. Josephs, all she wanted was her cats back.

As she approached Josephine Webster's shop, she saw a white hand twisting the card on the door round from "Open" to "Closed." Of course, half-day in the village. With such a search going on, if Miss Webster had the cats, then she wouldn't have them in the shop or in her flat above it.

Agatha returned home and got into her car. She parked a little way away from the shop and waited, not noticing people passing up and down the main street, intent only on Josephine Webster.

And then Miss Webster came out, neat and trim as ever, and got into her car, which was parked outside the shop. She drove off. Grimly, Agatha followed. Miss Webster drove down into Moreton-in-Marsh and turned along the Fosse. Agatha let a car get between her and her quarry and followed. Miss Webster headed for Mircester, her little red car sailing up and over the Cotswold hills on the old Roman road which ran straight as an arrow.

Agatha followed her into a multi-storey car-park, parked a little bit away and waited until Miss Webster got out and locked her car, then got out of her own.

Josephine Webster went first to Boots, the chemist's, tried various perfume samples, and then bought a bottle. From there, she went to a dress boutique. The day was unseasonably chilly and Agatha shivered as she waited outside. At last, she risked a peek through the shop window. Miss Webster was turning this way and that before a mirror, wearing a low-cut red dress. She said something to the assistant and disappeared back into a changing room. After ten minutes, she came out of the shop, carrying a carrier-bag. From there, she went to a lingerie shop and Agatha again froze and fidgeted outside until Miss Webster appeared carrying a carrier-bag with the lingerie shop's name on it.

When she walked on, followed by Agatha, and turned in at the tall Georgian portico of the public library, Agatha was beginning to despair. It was all so innocent. Fear for her cats had tricked her memory. That little petal had probably fallen off the bouquet that morning. But the doggedness, the single-mindedness, and the tenacity that had made

174

her successful in business took over. She waited outside for half an hour and then cautiously walked inside. No sign of Miss Webster.

Had she seen her and escaped out of a back door? In her frantic search to find a way out of the back of the library, Agatha nearly ran into Josephine Webster, who was sitting in a leather chair in one of the bays, calmly reading, her shopping bags beside her.

Agatha picked the next bay, took a book at random from the shelves and pretended to read. Her stomach rumbled. She should eat something, but she dare not risk leaving the library.

After two hours, a rustle of bags in the next bay warned her that her quarry was about to depart.

She waited a few moments and then cautiously got up and poked her head round the bay. Josephine Webster was disappearing in the direction of the exit. Agatha followed, heart beating hard again now that the pursuit was back on.

Miss Webster tripped gaily along, as if she hadn't a care in the world. She turned in at the door of Mircester's Palace Hotel.

Agatha, hovering at the entrance, saw her head up a passage at the side of the reception under a sign which said "Rest Rooms."

She bought a newspaper from a kiosk in the foyer, sat down in an armchair and barricaded herself behind it, lowering it from time to time to make sure Miss Webster had not escaped.

After a full hour, Agatha saw Miss Webster emerge. She was wearing the new dress and was heavily made up. She had obviously left her bags and coat in the cloakroom. Agatha jerked up the newspaper as Miss Webster crossed

175

the foyer in a cloud of scent and lowered it again in time to see her going into the bar.

Feeling stiff and hungry, Agatha threw aside the newspaper and looked cautiously round the door of the bar and then jerked her head back.

Miss Webster was sitting talking to Peter Rice, ugly red-haired Peter Rice, Bladen's partner. He must have entered the hotel and gone into the bar when Agatha's whole attention was focused on watching for Josephine Webster.

She sat down again in the foyer, her mind working furiously. It could be an innocent meeting. Yes, wait a bit. Miss Webster had a cat. She could have taken the cat for treatment to Mircester and struck up a friendship with Peter Rice. No harm in that. But . . . Greta Bladen had said something about Peter Rice being an old friend.

She looked about her. There was a sign pointing to the hotel restaurant. She walked along to it. The staff were just setting up the tables for the evening meal, but the maître d'hôtel was there. Agatha asked him if a Mr. Rice had made a booking for dinner. He checked. Yes, Mr. Rice had booked a table for two. For eight o'clock. Agatha glanced at her watch. Only six-thirty. They wouldn't leave the hotel. Somehow, she had to see Greta Bladen before returning to the hotel to keep a watch on them.

She stopped at a phone-box on the road to the car-park and phoned James, but there was no reply. She drove off, praying that Greta would be at home.

Greta answered the door and frowned when she saw her visitor was Agatha.

"I must speak to you," pleaded Agatha. "You see, I've been threatened. Someone stole my cats to stop me investigating and I think I might know who that someone might be."

Greta sighed but held open the door. "Come in. I don't quite grasp what you are saying. Do you mean someone is trying to stop you investigating Paul's death?"

"Yes."

"Well, I haven't got your cats."

"Could you tell me what you know about Peter Rice?"

"Peter? Oh, he can't have anything to do with it. I've known Peter for ages."

"Tell me about him anyway."

"I don't know very much. He lived a couple of doors away from me in Leamington in the old days. We were friends, played tennis together, but never anything romantic. I mean, I never thought any man would look at me that way, and so I was glad of Peter's company. Then Paul came along.

"I thought Peter would be delighted that I had found happiness at last, but he threw a very ugly scene. He said he had been going to ask me to marry *him*. I was so much in love with Paul that somehow that made me callous. It was only old Peter behaving in a most odd way. The next time I saw him he apologized for his behaviour and said he was moving to Mircester."

"And you never saw him again?" prompted Agatha.

"Well, I did, of course. I met him when Paul went into partnership with him and, as I told you, it was Peter who suggested I check out the site of this supposed veterinary hospital. I told him long afterwards how I had been cheated. After my divorce, we went out for dinner a couple of times, but there was nothing there and I really don't think there ever was anything there."

"Then how do you explain the scene when you told him you were going to marry Paul?"

"Oh, that. I think Peter is the kind who would have been jealous if any close friend, male or female, got married. He was a very solitary man. Come to think of it, I suppose I was the only friend he had in Leamington.

"Why did he decide to open the surgery in Carsely?" asked Agatha. "I mean, there are lots of villages closer to Mircester, and larger ones, too."

"Let me think. He said something about that when I met him one day in the square. He said, 'I'm finding that ex of yours something useful to do. I think it's better we work apart. I've told him to start up a surgery in Carsely. Keep him out of my hair. I said, 'Why Carsely?' and he said that some friend of his who had a shop there said it was a good place for business."

"Josephine Webster," said Agatha. "So that's the connection. And I think I know where my cats are."

She got up to leave. She looked wild-eyed and her face was working.

"If you suspect anyone of anything," said Greta, "go to the police."

Agatha merely snorted and went out to her car.

She thought furiously on the road to Mircester. Josephine Webster could have tipped off Peter Rice about Mrs. Josephs. She could have been in the pub to hear Freda telling everyone about the discovery of that bottle and warned Rice, or she could have removed the bottle herself.

Agatha flicked a glance at the dashboard of her car.

Eight o'clock. Peter Rice would just be sitting down to dinner.

She drove straight to the veterinary surgery and parked outside. She got out and took a tyre-iron out of the car. The surgery was a low building set at the back of a small car-park. A light was burning over the door. Agatha moved to the side of the building, which was in darkness but with enough light for her to make out a glass-paned side door. She had no time or expertise to emulate James Lacey's burglarly techniques. She smashed a pane of glass in the door with the tyre-iron.

A volley of hysterical barks greeted her ears. Grimly ignoring them, she tugged out the remaining glass with her gloved hands, reached in and unlocked the door.

Eyes glittered at her in the darkness and somewhere among the barks and yelps she heard several plaintive miaows.

"In for a penny, in for a pound," muttered Agatha and switched on the light.

"Shhh!" she whispered desperately to the cages of animals. Her eyes ranged along them. And there, together in a cage, were Hodge and Boswell.

With a glad cry, she undid the latch and opened the cage.

The barking and yowling suddenly died abruptly. Agatha, reaching in to get her cats, was aware of a heavy air of menace. She heard a soft footfall and turned around.

Josephine Webster smiled up at the waiter as he pulled out her chair for her in the restaurant. Peter Rice sat down opposite. The maître d' bowed over them and presented menus and made suggestions.

When their order had been taken by one of his minions, he gathered up the huge leather-bound menus and then suddenly said, "Will the other lady be joining you?"

"What other lady?" demanded Peter Rice, and Miss Webster giggled and said, "One of your harem, Peter?"

"A lady came in earlier and asked if you had booked a table for this evening."

"What did she look like?" asked the vet.

"Middle-aged, straight brown hair, expensively cut, quite smart clothes."

"No, she won't be joining us," said Peter. "Hold my order. I've got to do something in the surgery. Give Miss Webster a drink and look after her until I get back."

James Lacey was worried. He had called at Agatha's cottage several times without getting a reply. He had not been able to get much more out of Freda. Her friend with the silver hair stayed with her all the time, and James could not manage to get a word with her in private.

He decided to pass the time until Agatha's return trying to write his book, but instead he found himself writing about the case. He wrote on and then gave an exclamation, took out one character and tried to fit the evidence he had to it.

He was roused from his efforts by the phone bell. Bill Wong stood there with Inspector Wilkes. "Where's Agatha?" asked Bill.

"Isn't she back? We were supposed to meet at six. Isn't her car there?"

"No, I'm getting worried. We'll need to ask around and see if anyone saw her leaving the village."

"I'll go out and try to find her myself," said James. "Here, take a look at my notes, Bill, and see if you come to the same conclusion."

James went straight to Josephine Webster's shop. It was in darkness, as was the flat above, and he got no reply to his banging and knocking. A head popped out of a window next to the flat above the shop and a man's voice said, "Ain't no use you ringing and banging, fit to wake the dead. Her goes to Mircester on half-day."

James went back and got his car and told Bill he thought Agatha might be in Mircester. He suddenly knew where Agatha had gone and prayed he would not be too late.

Agatha slowly straightened up.

Peter Rice stood in the doorway, looking at her. She was aware again of the strength of that body which supported the disproportionately small head. She had left the tyre-iron lying beside the shattered door. Her eyes flew this way and that, seeking a weapon.

"Don't even think of it," he said. He produced a small automatic pistol from his pocket. "Through to the examining room, Mrs. Raisin," he said. "We won't be disturbed there."

Even though she felt weak with fear, even though she felt her bladder was about to give, Agatha gave the door of the cage with her cats in it a kick as she passed and tried to send them telepathic messages to escape. Rice switched off the lights in the room with Agatha's cats and the other

181

animals and switched on the lights in the small examining room.

Keeping the pistol trained on Agatha, he asked, "How did you know it was me?"

"I didn't really," said Agatha. "But I guessed Josephine Webster had been the one to take the cats and leave that note. I followed her and saw her with you. You can't shoot me. The police will find my body and they'll know it was you."

"Mrs. Raisin, you broke into my surgery. I saw the light and a figure inside who rose, I thought, as if to attack me. I shot you. I was defending my life and property."

"I left a note, saying where I would be," said Agatha.

He studied her for a few moments and then smiled. "No, you didn't, or that Lacey fellow would be here. Anyway . . ." He raised the pistol an inch.

"It was because of Greta, wasn't it?" said Agatha.

"In a way. But I didn't think of killing him then. I didn't even think of it when she told me how he had been cheating her. No, it was when he started cheating me, ah, then I began to get really angry. That famous veterinary hospital of his. So good for conning gullible women. We had a receptionist here, a nice girl. Paul got his claws into her. She was to persuade the customers to pay cash as much as possible and pass the money to him. Did she get a cut of it? Of course not. All was to go to that hospital which, of course, was to be named after the receptionist. I had taken a long fishing holiday. This is a wealthy practice. I had hired a young vet to stand in for me when I was away and to work with Paul because Paul mostly handled all the cases of horses and farm animals. When I came back, I remarked that trade had dropped by a considerable amount. I suspected the temporary vet, but that was when I was talking to one of the customers in the square and we were complaining about taxes and business taxes in general. 'I suppose,' says she, 'that's why you want so much money in cash. To avoid tax. The girl always asks for it.' Of course I got hold of the girl and she broke down and said she had only been stealing for the greater good, namely the founding of that fictitious hospital. I sacked the girl but not Paul. Oh, no. He was going to have to pay me back. But I wanted him out of my hair. Josephine said Carsely was a good place, and so I told him to set up a business there and trick the ladies with his stories if he liked, but every penny was to come to me, and just in case anything happened to him, I got him to make out his will in my favour. I said unless he paid me back in full, I would go to the police."

Agatha stayed rigid, seeing out of the corner of her eye that her cats had slid into the room beside her.

"I still wouldn't have killed him. But one of the women he tricked was Miss Josephine Webster, whom I had come to love. She came to me, crying and sobbing, and told me the whole story. I knew he was up at Pendlebury's. I was going to curse him, sack him, punch him on the nose, that was all. The stables were empty apart from Paul. I saw him with the syringe, I knew what was in it, what the operation was and something took over and the next thing I knew he was dead. I slipped off without anyone seeing me. I thought I was safe. I was furious when I realized he had taken a double mortgage out on that house, so instead of gaining by his death, I lost. House prices are rock bottom at the moment. Josephine and I were going to announce our engagement after the fuss had died down. She knew what I had done. Then that Josephs women came here. She said Paul had tricked her and she was going to tell the police the truth. She said Paul had told her that I had encouraged him to dupe the women out of money. I promised to pay her back. Then I panicked when Josephine phoned me and told me that you, you Nosy-Parking bitch, were about to hear all from Mrs. Josephs. Josephine told me she suffered from diabetes. But still I didn't mean to do it if she saw sense. I tried to give her the money back, but the silly old bat wouldn't take it. She said she was going to the police after talking to you. I jabbed the Adrenalin into her. The minute she was dead, I went into a blind panic. I dragged her upstairs in the hope that when she was found dead in the bathroom, they would think it suicide or accident. I chucked the empty bottle out of the car window, as if by getting rid of it, I had got rid of the stain of murder. But you had to interfere again, you and that Lacey. 'Take her cats,' said Josephine. 'That'll shut her up.' What a mess. What a bloody mess. But I'm going to marry Josephine, and nothing's going to stop me."

Hodge jumped up on the examining table and sat looking from one to the other.

Agatha could suddenly smell her own fear, rank and bitter, and so could the cat. Its tail puffed up like a squirrel's.

"So, Mrs. Raisin, I need to get this over with. I advise you to stand still and take what's coming to you."

His finger began to squeeze the trigger. Agatha dived under the table as a shot rang harmlessly above her head.

One beefy hand dragged her out from under the table. Panting, he threw her against the wall. Hodge flew straight into his face, clawing and spitting. In his panic, the vet tried to shoot the cat off his face but the shot went wild, smashing into a cabinet of bottles.

Agatha tried to drive the examining table into his stomach as he tore the cat from his face and flung it across the room. She had seen people in films doing that, but it was bolted to the floor. She dived to the side as he fired again, wrenched her ankle and fell on the floor.

She shut her eyes. This was it. Death at last. And suddenly Bill Wong's voice like a voice from heaven said, "Give me the gun, Mr. Rice."

There was another shot and a cry from Bill. Agatha screamed, "Oh, no!" and then felt strong hands tugging at her and James Lacey's voice in her ear, saying, "It's all right, Agatha. Don't look. Rice has shot himself. Don't look. Come with me. Keep your head turned away."

Agatha rose, clinging to him, and buried her face in the rough tweed of his jacket.

Three hours later Agatha, bathed and wrapped in her dressing-gown, sat in her sitting-room with the cats on her lap, being fussed over by James.

"Bill Wong will be calling on us," he said. "Is he grateful to us for having solved two murders for him? Not a bit of it."

"Us?" demanded Agatha. "I was the one who found out about Rice."

"I had more or less come to the same conclusion," said James, "although it took me some time to guess Josephine Webster was involved. What put you on to her?"

Agatha told him about finding that shred of dried petal on the doormat.

"But you should have come to me," exclaimed James, "or told Bill Wong."

"I only thought of the cats," said Agatha. "Funny, isn't it? I thought my heart would break when they were taken, but here they are, purring away, two animals to be cared for and fed, and now they just seem like an everyday nuisance."

"Though from what you say, Hodge saved your life," James pointed out. "I wonder if they got Josephine Webster. I wonder if she was still sitting there in the hotel restaurant waiting. Bill and his boss went right there while we had to go to the police station and make endless statements."

"So you had worked it all out yourself?" said Agatha.

He threw another log on the fire and sat down. "Once I had written down what everyone had done and said, Peter Rice seemed the obvious suspect. He was strong enough to have dragged Mrs. Josephs up the stairs, he knew where Bladen would be on the day he was murdered, he knew about the operation on that horse. One always thinks of murderers as planning everything scientifically, but in Rice's case it was all panic and then luck. All he had to do was sit tight and let Mrs. Josephs make her accusations to the police. The police wouldn't have thought the philandering and conning tactics of Paul Bladen had anything to do with Peter Rice. I think it was our nosing around that rattled him so badly."

"Don't say that," pleaded Agatha. "That means we are both directly responsible for Mrs. Josephs's death."

"Well, he would probably have panicked anyway."

The doorbell rang. "That'll be Bill," said James, "come to read us the riot act."

Bill was on his own. "An off-duty call," he said, sinking down wearily on the sofa beside Agatha. "Yes, we got

Webster. It must have seemed a lifetime to you, Agatha, when he was trying to kill you, but there she was, drinking martinis, just where he had left her.

"She denied the whole thing, but when we took her to the station and then told her that Rice had confessed everything to you, she broke down. Cruel thing to say, but we hadn't yet told her he was dead.

"She had been having an affair with Rice for a few months, up until Paul Bladen arrived in Carsely. Before her affair with Rice, she had been a virgin. Think of that, in this day and age. I think her affair with Rice made her feel like a femme fatale, and so, when it seemed that Bladen was courting her as well, it went right to her silly head. That snowy evening you were supposed to meet him in Evesham, that was the evening she went to his house and gave him the cheque. So the grateful Bladen took her to bed. Even if it hadn't been snowing, he probably wouldn't have turned up to meet you, Agatha. She was the one who answered the phone to you.

"But Bladen was up to his old tricks. He asked her for more money and she grew alarmed and said she could not afford any more. So he lost interest in her, and the repentant Miss Webster went back to the arms of Peter Rice and told him all about Bladen. So, to Rice, history was repeating itself. He had, I gather from what you said in your statement, Agatha, been deeply in love with Greta. Paul had taken her away. Now Paul was doing the same thing with Josephine. But what put you on to them?"

"I found a dried-up flower petal on the doormat," said Agatha proudly, "and realized it had probably fallen out of the note about the cats, and so I knew dried flowers meant Josephine Webster."

Bill looked puzzled. "We wouldn't have missed anything like that."

"That's what I thought," said James. "Someone brought you a bouquet of dried flowers, Agatha, the morning after, so it probably fell from that."

"Why should you be looking closely at the doormat?" exclaimed Agatha, exasperated. "Your men were searching *outside,* where whoever delivered the letter had stood, as well as all over the back garden, because whoever took the cats must have got into the garden by the lane which runs between mine and James's garden. They wouldn't bother about the doormat."

"I think you'll find it came from the bouquet after all, Agatha. You made a lucky guess, and a near-fatal one for you. I'm not going to lecture you tonight on the folly of amateurs interfering. Goodness," he laughed, "I suppose it's a case of rank amateurs setting out to catch a rank amateur."

Agatha glared.

"Anyway, I'm glad it's all over. I'm off on a special training course, so I won't see you for a few weeks." Bill stood up. "Has the doctor seen you, Agatha?"

She shook her head.

"You'd best see him tomorrow. You're going to be a wreck when reaction sets in."

"I'll be all right," said Agatha. She gave James an adoring look, which he returned with a startled one and then stood up and said, "Do you want me to get Mrs. Bloxby to stay with you, Agatha?"

"No," she said, disappointed that he was not volunteering to fetch his sleeping-bag. "I'll be all right after a good night's sleep."

After they had left, Agatha rose and went up to bed, the two cats trotting after her. She smiled before she drifted off to sleep. It was all over. She had survived. She felt great. No need to see any doctor. It would take more than one murderer to get Agatha Raisin down!

TEN

†

THE next few days were glorious for Agatha, despite the fact that James had sent her a note saying he was shutting himself up to write for a few weeks.

So many people came to call to hear about how Agatha had solved the murders of Paul Bladen and Mrs. Josephs, and Agatha stitched away at her story, embroidering the details, so that by the time she gave a talk to the Carsely Ladies Society, it had become a real blood-and-thunder adventure.

"How exciting you make it all seem," said Mrs. Bloxby after Agatha's talk. "But do be careful. It can take a little time for reality to set in, and then you might suffer badly."

"I was not lying," said Agatha hotly.

"No, of course you weren't," said Mrs. Bloxby. "I particularly liked that bit when you said to Peter Rice, 'Shoot me if you dare, you evil fiend.' "

"Oh, well," muttered Agatha, shuffling her feet and

avoiding the steady gaze of the vicar's wife, "a bit of poetic licence is allowed, I think."

Mrs. Bloxby smiled and held out a plate. "Have a slice of seed cake."

From that moment, Agatha began to feel extremely uncomfortable. Her version of events, which had become a highly coloured adventure story, had indeed come to seem like reality. As she walked back from the vicarage, she noticed how *dark* the village seemed and how the light near the bus shelter had gone out again.

The lilac trees were all out in Lilac Lane, whispering in the night wind, nodding their plumed heads as if gossiping about Agatha as she scurried homewards underneath, thinking that the smell of their flowers reminded her of funerals.

She went inside. The cats did not come to meet her and she let out a whimper of fear and ran to the kitchen. They were curled up together in their basket in front of the stove, happy in each other's company, fast asleep and not caring about one frightened mistress who wanted them to wake up and keep her company.

She reached out a hand to switch on the electric kettle and all the lights went out.

In blind terror, she stumbled round the kitchen, searching for a torch, until some sane voice in her mind told her it was only another of the village's frequent power cuts. Forcing herself to be calm, she remembered she had candles in the kitchen drawer, found one and lit it with her cigarette lighter. She held it up and found a candlestick. May as well go to bed, she thought.

This was how they had gone to bed in the old days when the cottage was built, people walking up this very staircase with the shadows leaping before them in the wavering candle-flame. So many generations. So many dead. Just think how many had gasped out their last breath in this very bedroom. Her dressing-gown at the back of the door looked like a hanged man. Faces stared at her out of the pretty flowered wallpaper. She was in a cold sweat.

She forced herself to make her way downstairs to the phone in the hall. She put the candle on the floor, sat down on the floor herself, cradled the phone in her lap and dialled James Lacey's number.

His voice when he answered sounded brisk and efficient. "James," said Agatha, "can you come along?"

"I'm writing hard. Is it important?"

"James, I'm frightened."

"What's happened?"

"Nothing. It's just that that reaction everyone's been warning me about has set in."

"Don't worry," he said. "Help is on its way."

Agatha stayed where she was. Her fear had gone now that he was coming, but she decided she had better remain looking as frightened as she had been. Perhaps she might throw herself into his arms. Perhaps he would hold her close, and say, "Agatha, let's give all those gossips a treat and get married." Perhaps he would kiss her. What would that be like?

This rosy fantasy went on until she realized that a considerable amount of time had passed. Of course, he was probably packing his pyjamas and shaving-kit, but still . . .

The doorbell rang, making her jump. Yes, she would throw herself into his arms.

Mrs. Bloxby said gently, "Now, now, Mrs. Raisin. I knew this would happen."

Agatha opened her eyes and backed off in confusion. She had seen a dark figure on the step and had taken it to be James.

The vicar's wife was carrying an overnight bag. "Mr. Lacey phoned me and I came as quick as I could. The doctor's on his way."

Feeling almost ill with disappointment, Agatha allowed Mrs. Bloxby to lead her to the kitchen. The lights came on again. Everything was normal.

By the time a sedated Agatha was in bed, the doctor had left, and Mrs. Bloxby was sleeping in the spare room, she could only reflect woozily that James was a beast and a bastard.

Agatha spent a long and miserable time of panics and nightmares, glad of callers during the day, glad of the members of the Carsely Ladies Society, who took it in turns to sleep in her spare room during the night. Not one woman mentioned James Lacey and Agatha's heart was sore with rejection.

And then her fears ebbed away and her mood was improved with long sunny days.

In such a small village it was inevitable that she should meet James again. He smiled at her in a kindly way and asked after her health, he said writing was coming easily and he was working hard. He said they must have lunch sometime, that very English remark which usually means absolutely nothing. Agatha looked at him with bitter hurt in her bearlike eyes but replied politely and coolly, thinking they were almost like a couple who had once had an affair, regretted now on one side.

And then one morning, as lunchtime was approaching, Agatha's doorbell rang. She no longer rushed to it expecting to see James. Bill Wong stood on the step.

"Oh, it's you," said Agatha. "You must have been back from that course ages ago."

"I was," said Bill, "but another case came up which involved liaising with the Yorkshire police, so I've been travelling a bit. Aren't you going to ask me in?"

"Of course. We can have coffee in the garden."

"Lacey around?" he asked as he followed her through the house.

"No," said Agatha bleakly. "In fact, apart from little talks like 'How are you' and 'Isn't the weather great' over the grocery counter, I haven't really seen him."

"Odd, that. I thought the pair of you were as thick as thieves."

"Well, we're not," snapped Agatha. She had bought a new garden table and chairs. "Sit down, Bill. I was just going to get a bite to eat. Cold chicken and salad suit you?"

"Anything. Your garden could do with some flowers. Give you an interest."

"I suppose. I'll get the food."

Over lunch, Bill told her about the case he was working on and then they finally got around to discussing the case of Peter Rice.

"It's odd," said Bill, "when you think of the pair of them, Rice and Webster. Hardly Romeo and Juliet to look at, but there was passion there, real passion. Take one man who feels he's too ugly to get a woman and one virgin and that's an explosive mixture. When Rice found out she'd been sleeping with Bladen, it must have nearly broken his heart. History repeating itself. First Greta, then Josephine. But Josephine is back in his arms again. She's not shocked he's killed Bladen. Now they are bound even more closely by the crime and still more after the death of poor Mrs. Josephs."

He looked about him. "You wouldn't think when you drive through one of these pretty Cotswold villages how much terror and passion and anger can lurk beneath the beams of these old cottages. You know, Agatha, Lacey's an odd bird. Some of these army chaps are. He's only in his fifties, not dead old for these days."

"Thank you," said Agatha drily.

"If he'd been married, he might be an easier mark, but these army bachelors, well, it's as if they've come out of the monastery. Play it cool and he'll come around."

"I have no interest in him," said Agatha evenly.

"I think you have too much interest in him and that's what frightened him off," said Bill.

"Oh, really, so young and so wise. What's *your* love life like?"

"Pretty good. You know the Safeways supermarket in Mircester?"

"Yes."

"There's a pretty girl called Sandra works at the check-out. We've been dating."

"That's nice," said Agatha, who felt obscurely jealous.

"So I'd better go. Keep away from murders, Agatha!"

After he had left, Agatha drove down to the Batsford Garden Centre at the bottom of Bourton-on-the-Hill and looked at flowers and plants. They also had full-grown trees. Instant garden, that was the answer. But just a little

196

to start. Something for the borders round the grass at the back and a hanging basket of flowers for the front of the cottage. She bought some Busy Lizzies and pansies and decided she would get started by planting them.

The work was relaxing and the cats played about her in the sunlight and she was so absorbed in her work that it took her some time to realize her doorbell was ringing.

If only it would be . . .

But Agatha recoiled a step when she opened the door. Freda Huntingdon stood there.

"What do you want?" asked Agatha crossly.

"To bury the hatchet," said Freda. "Come along to the pub. I feel like getting plastered. I'm sick of men."

Curiosity warred with distaste in Agatha's mind and curiosity won.

"What's happened?"

"Come to the pub and I'll tell you."

Only the idea that it might have something to do with James drove Agatha into accompanying Freda.

Freda bought them both large gins and they sat down.

"I'm thinking of selling up," said Freda. "Nothing's gone right since I came here."

"You mean Bladen?"

"That and other things. You see, George, my husband, was much older than me, but oodles of money. We used to travel a lot, go exotic places. But George kept a strict eye on me and I used to think of all the freedom I'd have if he dropped dead and left me the money.

"Well, he did. I had a couple of unfortunate affairs, and so I thought to hell with it; I'll move to the Cotswolds, get myself a dinky cottage and look around for another husband. I got my eye on Lacey. Sorry I was such a bitch, but I really fancied him, but not a hope there. That business with Bladen threw me. I really believed he was head over heels in love with me. I really believed all that rubbish about that hospital. When George was alive, I thought I was the clever, worldly, shrewd one, but it was George who had the brains. Then Tony came along. That chap you saw me with in the pub. No Adonis, but good business, Gloucester way. His wife called on me yesterday. His wife! And he swore he was a widower." Freda snivelled dismally. "I'm just a stupid old tart."

"You need another big gin," said Agatha, ever practical.

James Lacey read over again what he had written and groaned. Thanks to his experiences in the Bladen case, he had thought he would write a mystery story. How easily the words had come. How rapidly the thousands of little green words had built up on the screen of his word processor. But it was as if a mist had cleared. He was looking down at pages of total rubbish.

The windows of his cottage were all open because it was a hot day. From next door, he could hear the sound of voices and the clink of glasses and china. He went out into his garden and peered over the hedge. Bill Wong and Agatha were sitting having lunch and absorbed in conversation. He wished he could go and join them, but he had been cool to Agatha, had snubbed her, and now he had cut himself off.

He returned to the house and pottered about miserably. Later he heard Bill leave and shortly after that, he saw Agatha driving off.

198

He went back out into his garden in the afternoon and began to weed the flower-beds. He heard movement from Agatha's garden and once more looked over. She was planting a row of pansies. He was sure she didn't know anything about gardening. If he hadn't been so stupid, he could have strolled over for a chat. But really! All those women expecting him to propose! And Agatha herself, the way she had looked at him.

But on the other hand, she had nearly been killed. He had misread her looks before. It was all the fault of that bloody captain's wife in Cyprus. He should never have had an affair with her. What a scandal that had been. She had pursued him, flirted with *him,* but when the scandal had broken, he was the guilty party, the beast that had seduced her and tried to take her away from her noble and gallant husband.

He settled down to read a detective story by Reginald Hill and found it depressingly good.

In the evening, he heard the sound of noisy singing coming along the lane.

Puzzled, he went out and stood in the evening air on his doorstep.

Lurching along the lane, arms about each other, singing, "I Did It My Way," came Agatha and Freda Huntingdon.

When they came abreast of him, they stopped singing. Freda hiccuped and said, "Men!" and Agatha Raisin grinned and gave James Lacey the victory sign, but the wrong way round.

James retreated inside and banged the door as, laughing and shouting, the unlikely pair went on their way.

A delicious new case...

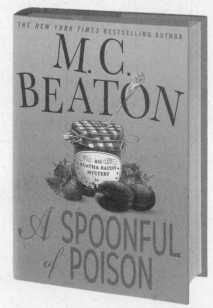

"Few things in life are more satisfying than to discover a brand-new Agatha Raisin mystery."
—*The Tampa Tribune*

Cranky but loveable Agatha Raisin ran a successful public relations firm in London before setting up shop as a private detective in the Cotswolds. So it's hard to refuse when the vicar of a nearby village begs her to help publicize the church fete—especially since the fair's organizer is a disarmingly handsome man.

Agatha brings out the crowds for the fete, all right, but there's more going on than innocent village fun. Several of the offerings in the jam-tasting booth turn out to be poisoned, and a festive family event becomes the scene of two murders....

www.minotaurbooks.com   www.stmartins.com

AVAILABLE WHEREVER BOOKS ARE SOLD

St. Martin's
MINOTAUR